A PROMISE IN DEFIANCE

ROMANCE IN THE ROCKIES BOOK 3

HEATHER BLANTON

A Promise in Defiance

Book Three

By Heather Blanton

Published by Rivulet Publishing

Copyright 2016 Heather Blanton

All rights reserved under International and Pan-American Copyright Conventions. By payment of the required fees, you have been granted the non-exclusive, non-transferable right to access and read the text of this e-book on-screen. No part of this text may be reproduced, transmitted, down-loaded, decompiled, reverse engineered, or stored in or introduced into any information storage and retrieval system, in any form or by any means, whether electronic or mechanical, now known or hereinafter invented, without the express written permission of Rivulet Publishing or the author.

This novel is a work of fiction. Names, characters, places, incidents, and dialogues are either the product of the author's imagination or are used fictitiously. Any resemblance to actual events, locales, organizations, or persons, living or dead, is entirely coincidental and beyond the intent of the author.

Cover DESIGN by http://www.ravven.com/

Scripture taken from the HOLY BIBLE

KING JAMES VERSION - Public Domain

A huge *thank you* to my editors and beta readers: David Webb, Kim Huther, Vicki Prather, Vicki Goodwin, Heather Baker, Becky Hrivnak, Connie White, Lisa Coffield, Linda Hames Carter, Kaye Starr Ferguson, Sandy Chase, and Jody Zilske for formatting!

And a huge shout-out to the awesome Becky Hrivnak and Diane Estrella! Your generosity and selflessness to help a starving writer will earn you both many crowns in Heaven, if no money here on earth. Thank you!

Heather Blanton

Please subscribe to my newsletter
by visiting my website
authorheatherblanton.com
to receive updates on my new releases and other fun news. You'll
also receive a FREE e-book—
A Lady in Defiance, The Lost Chapters
just for subscribing!

FOREWORD

Dear Reader,

Jesus was the greatest storyteller of all time. As a writer, I pray my words will be a fraction as powerful as His. His ability to change hearts and minds with a simple story is fascinating to me. Hence, the model for my Defiance tales.

Readers who have been with me for a while now know that the town of Defiance is analogous to our culture. My characters, like you and I, do not live in bubbles. They face challenges to their faith every day. Sometimes they make the Lord proud. Sometimes they don't. Sound familiar?

The theme of *A Promise in Defiance* is that our choices have consequences . . . but there is always grace. We are poor, flawed vessels for delivering His truth to a dark world. He never expected us to be diamonds. Lumps of coal are fine with Him. Who we are doesn't change one iota Who HE is, though. He is the very Creator of the universe. The God Who loves us so much, He sent His Son to die for us . . . even while knowing that sacrifice would not make us perfect, but would make us something better: redeemed!

My readers know I love to research, and there is a ton of actual historical information in my stories. My character Delilah Good-night is based on the real Mary Hastings, a Barbary Coast madam. Such a debauched person, I actually held back a little in creating Delilah. In other words, she isn't as bad as she could have been!

A big hat-tip to the Wyoming newspaper archives (http://news papers.wyo.gov/). I could have stayed lost in all those articles covering the Indian problem, Red Light Abatement Laws, and so much more! A real step back in time.

Finally, I would like to specifically thank Barbara Barton for her wonderful book *Pistol Packin' Preachers: Circuit Riders of Texas* (http://amzn.to/1t8Bksn). These frontier preachers faced Indians and outlaws to deliver the Gospel over hundreds of miles of wild terrain. The insight I gleaned from them was invaluable to developing my character of Logan Tillane.

Thank you for journeying along with me as Charles and Naomi and all the family once more try to tame Defiance!

God bless, y'all!

Heather

When the unclean spirit is gone out of a man, he walketh through dry places, seeking rest, and findeth none. Then he saith, I will return into my house from whence I came out; and when he is come, he findeth *it* empty, swept, and garnished.

Then goeth he, and taketh with himself seven other spirits more wicked than himself,

and they enter in and dwell there:

and the last *state* of that man is worse than the first.

Matthew 12:43-45

PROLOGUE

"*I* don't know, Matthew." Delilah rose from her desk and carefully swished her large, enticing bustle over to the bar. She felt the man staring, no doubt with lust. His eyes glittered with the hunger men never seem to conquer. "Defiance is done, I suspect. Once Diamond Lil left and McIntyre closed the Iron Horse," she turned two shot glasses up and uncapped a bottle of whiskey, "that sealed it for me."

Matthew leaned the chair back on two legs. He was a big man, about the biggest she'd ever been acquainted with, and the wood protested under his weight. She handed him his drink, ignoring that handsome, square jaw and broad chest, and strolled to the window to look out over the streets of Salt Lake City.

"You know, you are a fine figure of a woman," Matthew observed. "That curly auburn hair of yours shimmers like honey. You could pass for a respectable woman—if you'd dress right."

Annoyed by the assumption that she *wanted* to be respectable, she turned sideways so he could get a better view of at least half her curves, and the low neckline on the verge of overflowing. Slowly, she swept a sultry glance over him. Such were her weapons. And she was well-trained in the art of war. "Save the flattery. Defiance is dead and I'm comfortable here."

Salt Lake City was going to keep her well-heeled for quite some time, but she didn't smile at the traffic below. This town turned her stomach. She couldn't run this brothel like she wanted. It had to be quiet, almost respectable. No shows. Nothing raunchy, nothing that might draw attention to the house. A bunch of pious hypocrites, these Mormons couldn't hand over their money fast enough, but it all had to be hush-hush. Which proved the old adage: no matter how many wives a man had, he still wanted a little forbidden fruit.

She did smile at that—a dark, bitter reflection of her revulsion. *Saints, my eye . . .*

But at least a simple brothel might not get her run out of town. Her last place had pushed the boundaries . . . and a moral citizenry had risen up against her.

Prudes.

Behind her, Matthew gulped down the shot and sighed with satisfaction. "Delilah, any woman who can run a cathouse in the middle of Salt Lake City ought to be able to restore a two-bit mining town to its former glory."

She snickered softly at the joke and shook her head. "It hasn't exactly been hard. Give a man a poke or a bribe in this town and you can get by with a lot."

"And that's my point. Nobody stops you. Once upon a time, McIntyre owned the finest brothel west of the Mississippi. Men will talk about the Iron Horse for generations." He raised an eyebrow at her. "Unless you give 'em somethin' else to talk about. Come on, I know you want to open another Fox Den. And you can. Bigger. More . . . entertaining."

That brought her head up slightly. She swallowed her own drink, tapped pretty painted nails on the rim. "Oh no, I don't doubt I could rival him. But fancy furniture, pretty gals," she looked over her shoulder at Matthew, "girls with no *boundaries*. It all takes money."

"You sell this place. I'll fund the rest."

Delilah narrowed her eyes at him. "That is suspiciously generous." She wandered back to her desk, settling in the chair, all but burying it beneath her huge bustle, and rested her elbows on the blotter. "What do you want out of this? And don't lie to me. Men are worse gossips than women. I know McIntyre ran you out of Defiance."

His face puckered up like she'd shoved a lemon in his mouth. "True—he did. Because I wasn't prepared to stay." He laced hands the size of bear paws over a flat stomach and shook wavy blond hair off his forehead. "Now I'm ready to settle down in Defiance." Suddenly, he leaned forward and pressed a hand down on her desk. "And I want it wilder and woolier than it was before. 'Cause that's the kind of town that suits me . . . and he'll hate it."

———

CHAPTER 1

"*P*reacher! Preacher! Wake up!"

The pounding passed from Logan's dream to the fuzzy edges of wakefulness, fading into the sound of thunder. Rain beat on his tin roof, steady and peaceful—

"Preacher!" the voice screamed again. "The church is burnin'!"

Logan's eyes flew open. The orange glow reflecting on his bedroom walls pulsed with the pounding on his front door. He tossed back the covers, shimmied crazily into his breeches, and raced outside, still buttoning his fly. He nearly knocked down Deacon Taylor, the man who had been hammering on his door. Waving an apology, Logan raced past the man toward the burning building. He skidded to a stop though, halted by the hellish heat. Several men had formed a line leading from the water trough to the church, but the heat held them at bay as well, their buckets still full.

"Where's that fire engine?" someone yelled over the roaring flames.

Logan pushed a hand through his dark, soaking-wet blond hair. *God, no, not my church . . . my church.*

Only then did he notice the rain. Hard and cold, huge drops

drenched the futile firefighters, ran down his back, into his eyes. Yet his church burned at an astonishing speed, the ravenous beast of fire gulping it down from pew to steeple.

Deacon Taylor stepped up beside him and shook his head. "I'm sorry, Preacher. If this rain isn't stopping it, then we might as well be spittin' on the flames for all the good those buckets are gonna do. Shoot, they can't get close enough to toss the water anyhow."

Logan bit down the bitterness. If he'd only listened. And obeyed.

He'd clamped his hands over his ears, turned away from scriptures he knew he should study, avoided quiet time before the Lord, anything to drown out the still, small voice. Therefore, God had taken the final step to get this new preacher's obedience.

Content shepherding a flock of good, God-fearing folk, Logan would not entertain the possibility the Lord had something else, *someplace* else, in mind. He couldn't mean to send him *there*. Not back to real sinners.

Taylor slapped a hand on Logan's back. "Don't take it so hard, Preacher. You can do services in my barn until we get the church rebuilt."

"I reckon you'll be rebuilding it without me, Deacon."

Taylor cocked his head as if he hadn't heard quite right what with the flames and the rain. "What's that you say?"

"He's been telling me to move on. If I'd listened, you'd still have a church."

Taylor's mouth worked futilely for a moment. Finally, he managed, "Well, where you going?"

Logan watched the flames claw at Heaven and heard the scripture as clear as if God were standing beside him.

Arise, go to Nineveh, that great city, and cry out against it; for their wickedness has come up before me.

Dread pooling in his heart, he answered Taylor with one word: "Defiance."

*B*oth Logan and his horse, Flint, warily eyed the busy street of Defiance. It hadn't changed much. Filthy miners flowed like a river in spring, mud flaking off their clothes as they rode along on their horses and mules. The constant din of shovels banging on the gold pans hanging from the saddles reminded him of bells on Christmas morning. Above the noise, men shouted and cursed as they sought to maneuver wagons pulled by antsy horses into the current of traffic. Freight shifted and creaked. Leather squeaked.

Then Logan became aware of faint whistling accompanied by strange rumbling thunder, building in volume. To his surprise, a small but unstoppable herd of Black Angus rushed down the thoroughfare. The traffic parted like the Red Sea. Logan kneed Flint off to the side to give the animals room. The roiling river of beef was controlled by a handful of cowboys yipping and slapping ropes to keep things flowing.

They passed Logan by and he resumed his trek. Ranching had moved into the valley. That was new.

He drew his horse up in front of the Iron Horse Saloon, puzzled by the silence from within. It sure didn't *sound* like the West's most wide-open saloon and brothel any more. The red, white, and blue sign over the door explained everything and nothing. It proudly proclaimed "Town Hall".

Town Hall, huh? Though, to Logan's way of thinking, there wasn't much difference between the kind of man who frequented a public house, a cathouse, or a courthouse.

He scratched his head, resettled his dusty Stetson. Maybe Defiance had changed some. Two minutes in town and he hadn't seen a fight or a prostitute yet.

He caught a heavily bearded miner passing by on a mule. "Excuse me, friend, I'm looking for the Broken Spoke."

The man pulled up on the reins. "Broken Spoke ain't there no more, son. It closed. You could try—"

"I'm actually looking for the building itself."

The man's bushy eyebrows scrunched together and he rubbed his chin. "Well, it's still there, such as it is." He chucked a thumb over his shoulder. "Turn left at the assayer's office. Follow the street straight into Tent Town. You can't miss it. It's in pretty rough shape. Say," he grinned with the possibility of an idea, "you gonna open another saloon in its place?"

Logan grinned back. "Not exactly." He tapped the brim of his hat. "Much obliged for the information."

"Well, hold on," the man urged his mule closer. "Seein' as you're new in town, I reckon I'd be doing you a favor to warn you about Delilah."

"Delilah?"

"She bought all five saloons in town. Closed four of 'em. She's openin' a new Iron Horse of sorts. You know it?"

The good mood Logan had thought to entertain faded some. "Yes, I know the Iron Horse."

"But bigger and bawdier than that place she had down in Austin. And she don't want no competition. She's made that more than clear, especially to the saloon owners who didn't want to sell."

"I see." Logan was not surprised by the woman's goal, only at the timing of her arrival . . . and his. "Well, I thank you, friend, for the information." He nudged Flint and headed for Tent Town. Logan already missed his flock of amateur sinners. He surveyed the street and its mud-encrusted citizens. He'd vowed never to come back to this place.

And in a way, maybe he hadn't. Certainly, the old Logan had not returned. The old Logan was dead and buried.

Only problem was, he feared this town was capable of resurrecting him.

8

CHAPTER 2

*L*ogan jerked the warped, dilapidated door nearly off its hinges to get inside the Broken Spoke. The door's resistance was a harbinger. The inside sucked the wind out of his soul.

No part of the saloon had gone untouched by the elements. The canvas walls, anchored to waist-high pine knee walls, were ripped in a dozen places and flapped lazily in the late summer breeze. The roof, all but gone, hung in mildewed tatters. The back wall of warped, graying pine still stood, but leaned inward at a sharp angle. If it fell, it would crash onto the sagging, rough-sawed plank bar. Broken chairs, dead leaves, and shards of glass littered the floor. He wandered in and brushed his hand over a rusty heap of a buck stove crumbling in the center of the room.

Disheartened, Logan exhaled and rubbed his neck. "Lord, I'll need an army to fix up this place."

"So why bother?" The sultry feminine voice from behind him made Logan whirl.

A woman stood in the doorway, beautiful, curvaceous . . . dangerous. She had her lovely auburn hair swept up and back in a bun while jaunty little curls ran down her neck. The unusual olive tint to her skin fascinated him. Her red silk dress clung to her tightly, almost like a second skin, and ample breasts fought their restraint. Her eyes, the color of polished amber, glittered like a cat eying easy prey.

Logan removed his hat. He could appreciate her beauty. He could also appreciate the way she wielded it like a sword. "Can I help you?"

She strolled in slowly, smoothly, each movement of her body calculated to entice and mesmerize her prey. "I'm Delilah. You the owner of this place?"

"Yes, ma'am." Her method of hunting to him was, however, an old, worn-out strategy.

"I've been waiting for you."

In more ways than one, Logan supposed. He sensed his first battle in Defiance had walked right through his door. He scratched the thick stubble on his jaw. "I suppose you want to buy me out?"

Her eyebrows rose almost imperceptibly.

"I've heard you're trying to shut out the competition."

"Hmmm." She pondered that a moment before sauntering over to the bar. "Doesn't that make me a smart businesswoman?"

"I suppose so."

She turned to him and leaned back on the bar, striking a seductive pose. "I'd rather be friends than enemies, mister. This place is a wreck. It'll cost you more to fix it up than you'll make in a year. I'll give you what you paid for it."

"Long as I leave?"

"Or at least don't open another saloon."

"Well," he rubbed his eyebrow and meandered over to the bar to stand beside her. "You don't have to worry about that. I'm not opening a saloon." He fought to hold back a smile. "But I can honestly say I hope my business will be in direct competition with yours."

She scowled and stood up to him, her pink lips forming a tight, unhappy line. "What is your business?"

"I'm going to open a church."

It took a moment, but when his meaning registered Delilah's mouth fell open. "A church?"

"A church."

"So, that means you're a . . . ?"

"Preacher. I'm here to share the Gospel with all the sinners in Defiance—professional and otherwise. I hope to win souls for the Lord . . . help make this town a place for decent folk to live."

"Oh," she chuckled, backing away from him, "oh, if this don't beat all." Delilah shook her head as if she either couldn't believe her luck or his foolishness. "Preacher, have you got your work cut out for you."

"So my Boss tells me."

She rested her hands on her hips and looked up at him through long, dark lashes.

She sure has pretty skin. My, if I was a weaker man . . .

"I've come here to put Defiance back on the map, Preacher. I'm gonna turn this town back into one hell-raising, hard-drinking boomtown." Her eyes flickered with heat. Licking her lips, she dragged dainty, manicured hands slowly across the tops of her breasts. "If I were you, I wouldn't stand in my way."

"Two Spears?" Naomi strode to the edge of the yard and peered into the forest of pines. "Two Spears, come back to the house this instant!"

A stubborn silence greeted her command. "Two Spears?" she called again, her frustration growing. She hated sounding annoyed. Charles's son from a previous relationship, somehow he wound up spending more time with Naomi than his father. Time that was tense and unpleasant.

Two Spears watched everything she did with dark eyes full of

11

hate. She couldn't blame him. His Indian mother had been murdered by white soldiers, his renegade stepfather had been shot dead by Charles. Not a recipe for raising a happy child.

Lord, reaching this boy is going to take love and compassion I'm not sure I have. Fill me up with Yours. Shaking her bangs out of her eyes, she yelled again but tried to sound more concerned than angry. "Two Spears, where are you?"

Hoofbeats, muffled by the forest, reached her ears and she turned toward the road. A moment later, Charles emerged from the trees, coming in at an easy lope. In spite of her stress, she took a moment to enjoy the sight of her handsome husband, dark hair blowing beneath his Stetson, body moving as one with the horse, riding as effortlessly as she breathed. He'd gone out to survey timber. She was relieved he hadn't taken all day to do it.

He saw her and waved, but something of her turmoil must have showed. His light expression faded as he rode up, his narrow beard and mustache framing a mouth tense with concern. He dismounted quickly and wrapped the reins around the hitching post in front of their cabin.

"What's the matter?" Striding to her, he surveyed the yard. "Where's Two Spears?"

"I don't know."

"What do you mean you don't know?"

She raised her hands to her hips and tried to let that be her only expression of annoyance. "Exactly that. I asked him to catch some fish for supper while I pulled weeds in the garden. When I went to check on him, he was nowhere in sight."

Charles lifted his hat and ran a hand through dark wavy hair as he searched the yard again. Dropping the hat back in place, he fluttered his lips in exasperation.

Naomi and Charles had *inherited* Two Spears the day after their wedding, not even two weeks ago. His grandfather, the great Ute chief, had dumped him on their doorstep. The struggle to adapt to marriage *and* a child was wearing on them both.

"You think he's run off again?" he asked, staring into the trees.

She sighed. "I should have been watching him more closely, but it's been over a week since the last time. I thought he was finally settled."

"More likely, he's just patient. Like his grandfather." Charles turned, unwound the reins, and swung up into his saddle. His Southern drawl, which normally poured off his tongue like Tupelo honey, couldn't mask his regret. "I'm sorry, Naomi." Leather squeaked as he sighed deeply. "It seems my past—"

"May never stop haunting us." She shook her head and laid her hand on his knee. "I said I was in this for the long haul. I won't back away, but *you* can't keep avoiding that boy. Try to find it in your heart to treat him like a son."

"Can *you*? He's an Indian."

The statement shocked her. "He's a child."

"Naomi, out here, he's the enemy. Trying to raise an Indian boy as a son in Colorado will be harder than raising a Negro as a son in Alabama."

Offended, and a little surprised at Charles, she stepped back. "Are you worried what people will think?"

He snorted in disgust. "The naiveté of that question, princess, shows you don't understand what we—*I*—have gotten us into."

"Then explain it."

He reached into his saddle bag and withdrew a newspaper. "This will." He handed it to her. "Read it. Emilio's working on the bunkhouse. I'll have him find the boy. I have a meeting in town." Naomi shot him a scowl and he raised his hand to ward it off. "It'll only take a few minutes and then I'll join the search."

She unfolded the newspaper as he galloped away. The front page of *The Chieftain* was crammed with stories, many of them about the Utes and the trouble the renegades were stirring up. Two Spears's stepfather, One-Who-Cries, had truly been a blood-thirsty savage who attacked without mercy, but in typical fashion, the newspaper was littered with hateful references to all the Utes —lumping good and bad together.

"No peace commission until the Utes are well-whipped," she whispered, scanning the lengthy article. "Ten dollars a head would be a fair price to offer for the *ears* of every dead Ute . . ." Repulsed, she flinched over the sentiment. " . . .prompt and vigorous action against the savages . . .what these savages want is plunder and scalps . . . the first and essential thing is to punish these redskins promptly and so terribly as to make them feel that they can no longer . . .ravish white women with impunity."

Disgusted, she folded the newspaper closed with a snap and glared at the cloudless blue sky. *They call that journalism?* It sickened her, the slanted, narrow-minded rants. The vast majority of Indians were peaceful. Most of the tribes had surrendered and moved to reservations. Granted, they were starving and at the mercy of the federal government there, but they were peaceful. Their leaders often spoke out against the renegades, well aware violence only earned more of the white man's contempt.

Two Spears—when he wasn't scowling—had a sweet, handsome face. Long dark lashes, shoulder-length black hair that shimmered like a raven's feathers, and skin the color of coffee touched with cream. But life on the reservation had made the ten-year-old hard and suspicious, and that broke her heart.

As far as she was concerned, the hard times were behind him now. He was in a good home, with people who cared about him, who would come to love him. Here he could learn about Jesus, find forgiveness, discover a life of peace. He had a future and it was bright with hope and opportunity.

God had brought the boy into their lives, and Naomi resolved to show him compassion, his father an abundance of grace, and both of them patience.

If it killed her.

She could do all things through Christ, after all, including love two stubborn men from different worlds.

CHAPTER 3

*M*cIntyre crushed his cigar out in Davis Ferrell's ash tray and squinted at the lawyer. "What do you mean, you don't know?" He frowned, aggravated the question had leapt from his mouth for a second time that day.

A skinny man, dapper to a fault and as brave as a mouse, Davis shook his head. He leaned forward, nervously tapping short, clean fingernails on the desk. "I'm sorry. I'll have to dig deeper, Mr. McIntyre. Whoever is buying up the saloons is using a company to hide his name. But I do know where to look. The company is based in San Francisco."

McIntyre thought what he'd asked of Davis was a simple request. *Apparently not.* "Well, in the meantime, I'll find out who's pushing these deals through here in town."

"That, at least, I can help you with."

McIntyre tilted his head, pleased. "I'm listening."

"Each time the saloon owners have come here this week to sign the paperwork, a woman has accompanied them, signing for MLM Company. She goes by the name of Delilah Goodnight."

The blood in McIntyre's veins ran cold and he mentally kicked himself. He should've known closing the Iron Horse would create an opportunity. Like nature, Delilah abhorred a vacuum.

He'd seen the woman convert small, grimy, hardscrabble mining towns into shameless, godless meccas that would make Lucifer blush. Men rode for miles to experience her unique forms of entertainment. The worst kind of men.

So she was here to capitalize on the Iron Horse's demise, as well as the ready supply of lonely miners. Then today's business was of the utmost importance. He pulled his pocket watch out and checked the time. Five after two. Where was this buyer for the Broken Spoke?

As if in answer to the question, a man slowly pushed open Davis's office door. He dragged his hat from his head as McIntyre acknowledged him with a nod.

The stranger stepped into the room, moving confidently like a tiger in command of his environment, although this animal wore a Colt .45. The room shrank under the gentleman's impressive height and a build so solid it could make a big man feel small. McIntyre was not intimidated, but neither did he like being towered over.

He rose to meet the man nearly at eye-level. Shoulder-length ash-blond hair, stubbly, dimpled chin, and intense blue eyes struck a jarringly familiar chord. "I know you," McIntyre whispered.

The stranger nodded. "Yes, we've met."

When McIntyre heard the slightly raspy voice, the memories rushed back.

The stranger seemed to know it and crushed his hat to his chest. "I wondered if you'd remember me." He hooked a thumb into his cartridge belt. "You took everything I had a few years back. My money, my stake, everything . . ."

Tension thick as cigar smoke filled the room.

"Yes. I recall." McIntyre had the urge to apologize, but quelled it, and tried to read the man's face, which was as forthcoming as granite.

"That card game was the best thing that ever happened to me."

McIntyre tilted his head in surprise. "That is . . .magnanimous of you. We had harsh words . . .to say the least."

"You were fair. You warned me. You told me to either quit playing or quit drinking."

"You did neither, and when the cards turned, you lost your temper."

A glaring understatement. The man had started a brawl in the Iron Horse still talked about today. He had at first refrained from using the well-worn gun on his hip. Instead, he'd thrown punches like a sledgehammer, sending men tumbling and furniture flying. When McIntyre finally intervened, the young firecracker had drawn his revolver with uncanny speed.

But McIntyre had been faster.

Barely.

A draw.

McIntyre hadn't had a closer match before or since. The slightest drag on his holster and this stranger could have put a bullet in him. Instead, even though the other man had cleared leather, something had stopped them both from firing. Fingers on their triggers, revolvers at identical heights, they'd merely stared for a moment, then nodded and holstered their weapons. Both would live to fight another day.

The truce had not been born of fear . . .but of respect.

"Well, I don't act like that no more." The man extended his hand. McIntyre didn't hesitate. They shook, burying the hatchet. "Logan Tillane, in case you forgot."

McIntyre smiled ruefully. "I did not." He sat as Logan and Davis exchanged pleasantries.

"So, I've looked the building over," Logan said to both men as he took the only other seat in the small office. "It's rough, all right." He shifted to McIntyre. "I don't reckon you have a nicer one for the same money?"

"Unfortunately, no." McIntyre sucked on his teeth, noting the differences in Tillane versus the last time he'd seen the man. A mere boy then, but lean and mean, he'd crawled out of Defiance, bloody, bruised, and penniless. He'd gone on to harness the rage, becoming a gunhand the toughest men feared, and wealthy men hired.

McIntyre couldn't reconcile that boy with the man before him. Logan exuded quiet confidence instead of barely-controlled rage. He was dressed modestly, and dirty from traveling, yet his clothes were not threadbare. He had packed on several more pounds of muscle, evidence the man was living well. His hair had been trimmed sometime in recent memory by a real barber, although it needed a healthy trim now. Not to mention a shave.

He could pass for an ordinary man . . . unless one looked at his marred knuckles and noted the scar hiding on his stubbly chin. Hints that belied darker days. "What interests you about the Broken Spoke?"

"Well, Mr. McIntyre," Logan fanned himself with his worn, tan Stetson, "I need a house of worship."

---

*M*cIntyre tugged the brim of his hat lower to block the late afternoon sun and strolled down the busy boardwalk on Main Street. Beside him, Logan sidestepped a miner and continued with his story. "After years of cowboyin' and workin' as a hired gun—whichever paid more—I hit Denver between jobs. Not a penny to my name. Hungry and hungover. Nursing a busted hand. A young girl gave me a hand-bill inviting *sinners* to a tent meeting."

McIntyre nodded a greeting to several passers-by, slapping Bob Jamison on the shoulder as they worked their way toward the livery. Not really distracted by the pleasantries, he quickly returned his attention to Logan.

"I went because they were serving stew." The preacher gave him a quick, crooked smile. "But I left with a whole lot more than a full stomach." He shrugged sheepishly. "Anyway, Preacher Beals took me in, fed me, clothed me, taught me. He and his family were a Godsend. I started helping him in church then I started preachin'—"

"Preaching?" McIntyre repeated, incredulous over this change in the young man who could have been more notorious than Billy the Kid or Jesse James if he'd continued on that path.

"Yes—me—preaching. When a church opened up in Kansas I took it. Only thing was, I *knew* I was supposed to come back here. I just didn't want to."

As they strolled, McIntyre laced his hands behind his back and tried to comprehend the momentous changes in his own life, much less Logan's. Would wonders never cease? And how many times had they prayed for a preacher over the last several months? But Logan? He was the last man on earth McIntyre would have expected here.

Of course, as of late, God had been busy twisting expectations. "Well, I have as startling a revelation for you as you have had for me. I too am a Believer."

Logan's head snapped around. Gawking, he nearly walked into a post, but caught himself at the last second. McIntyre grinned, stepped off the boardwalk, and crossed over to the construction site that was his wife's hotel. Rising from the ashes, the second story was nearly framed in. He was pleased with the process.

He pulled a cheroot from his pocket and pointed at the work in progress. "That was our hotel, or more precisely, my wife and her sisters', but it burned. It won't be ready for another month or so. I do have room for you, however, at the Iron Horse," he grinned at Logan, "which is really more of a boarding house now.

And the town hall. And a newspaper office. You are more than welcome to stay there as long as you need."

Logan stuck a finger in his ear and twisted it. "I'm not sure I heard you back there."

"You did." A smile twitched on McIntyre's lips as he lit the cheroot and tossed away the match. "You are not anymore shocked than I still am."

"Well, I'll be . . ." Logan faded off, shook his head in apparent amazement. "The Lord certainly does work in mysterious ways."

"And sometimes, He spells it out." Not willing to elaborate on the myriad ways God had changed a sinner into something closer to a saint, McIntyre squeezed Logan's shoulder. "Get your belongings. Come back to the town hall. I'll leave word for my sister-in-law to show you to a room."

"You're *married*?" Logan's voice rose to a falsetto.

McIntyre had to laugh. "Happily so." He wondered how many more surprises Logan could take in a day. "You can meet her at dinner tonight. In the meantime, I am supposed to be looking for my son." Logan opened his mouth and McIntyre raised a hand, cutting him off. "Don't ask. Get settled. I'll see you this evening."

He strode past Logan, but the man followed. "Wait. I think there's something you need to know."

McIntyre drew up.

"A woman named Delilah stopped by the Broken Spoke while I was there. She wants to buy it."

"Yes, she has bought several properties in town this week."

"I don't reckon I need to ask if you know her."

McIntyre felt the tension in his brow. "Everyone knows Delilah."

"She said she's here to put Defiance back on the map."

McIntyre puffed on the cigar and thought back to his past. The days before Naomi and Christ had come to Defiance. The days when bedding a prostitute, drinking whiskey, and killing men to maintain his power had been his lifeblood. He wouldn't go back to that. *Ever.* He lived in the Light now, and the thought of falling into that darkness again was truly terrifying. He didn't want to test the limits of God's grace.

"Back on the map?" he repeated. That was possible for the town. There were still so many men here living in *defiance* of the Light. Plenty of fodder for Delilah's ravenous appetite. Could he stand by and do nothing to stop the woman? Was it even any of his business? He was certainly no one's nanny. Besides, Defiance had a preacher now. Wouldn't this be his bailiwick? "It is interesting to me that, while Satan has seen fit to send his mistress here," he narrowed his gaze at Logan, "God has sent you."

Logan's brow creased at the observation. "I noticed that too. You know, when I first started preachin' in Denver, I wasn't afraid to wrangle an unruly drunk right on out to the sidewalk. But how do you handle a woman . . .?"

"Knowing Delilah? Like an unchained demon."

*L*ogan pulled his saddle bags off his big bay mare and slung them over the corral's rail. Unstrapping the saddle, he called to an old codger brushing down a sorrel. "Hey, young fella, you got room to keep my saddle here?"

The elderly gentleman chuckled as he pulled a curry comb down the animal. "Tack room is at the end of the barn. There's one pole open." He tossed up a hand. "But I ain't responsible for stolen property."

"I'll risk it." *At least until I have room to store it someplace else.* "Thank you."

Logan lugged the saddle back into the barn, found the tack room, and hoisted the saddle up on the rack, beneath two others. He was admiring a Mexican-style saddle bedecked with silver conchos when he heard a sort of strangled cry or growl.

Concerned, he spun towards the sound. He heard it again from outside the barn, clearer this time. A child's cry? Followed by the unmistakable deep, throaty laughter of men. He launched from the tack room, raced through the barn's back doors, and skidded to a stop near the corral. He scanned the barnyard but saw only milling horses and the old man. "Did you hear something?"

"Hear what?"

The sound again, louder and clearer. A child raging, screaming against something . . .or someone. "That." Logan ran toward a row of sage and cedars. He burst out unexpectedly on the shore of the Animas River. Two men were holding a child between them, and they froze as if they'd been caught taking the whole cookie jar.

"What are you two doing to that boy?" Logan asked, marching toward them. "Let him go."

The two men exchanged mulish glances. One raised a big Bowie knife. The other tightened his grip on the boy and said, "This is none of your affair, mister."

Logan knew this man was the dangerous one. He had dark eyes, one that wandered off hard to the right, a mess of greasy, curly hair, and a sneer that openly promised trouble.

"Get on outta of here before Shelby decides to carve you up next."

The child, a young Indian boy, squirmed like an angry rattlesnake. Fury radiated from him. No fear. Just hate. He speared Logan with a searing gaze that said he didn't expect help, only more torture.

Lord, what can I do here? "You'd best let him go."

"The little savage tried to steal my horse." The man with the knife nicked the boy's cheek, drawing blood.

"Hey now," Logan stepped forward, fearful things were about to turn sour. "That's not gonna happen again."

"He's just a filthy redskin," the man with the crazy eye said, flinging a dirty strand of hair out of his face. "*And* he's a thief."

"Then you should get the marshal," Logan said to him, but then switched back to the man with the knife, "but you're not going to hurt him again."

The man grinned, revealing a row of yellowed, misshapen teeth. "We'll deal with you afterward." He lowered the knife to the boy's face.

"This is no way to build a flock," Logan muttered, resigned to the trouble coming down the pike.

Both men gawked. "Flock?" the one with the knife repeated. "You a preacher?"

"I am. And I want to be a man of peace. Let the boy go."

Laughter started in the two troublemakers, low and slow, and bubbled its way up to full-throated hee-hawing. Logan sighed. It would be too easy to slide the .45 from its holster . . . especially since the man without the knife was as big as an oak. Why bother with a fight. It would be no trouble at all to just drop him. But he couldn't, of course. Not like that.

Slay the giant, David.

The thought puzzled him at first then the idea lifted the corner of his mouth.

CHAPTER 4

*L*ogan reached down, snatched up a river rock the size of his fist, and lobbed it at the man's head. The stone beaned him right between the eyes. His face went blank, the knife slid from his fingers, and he folded to the ground.

Instantly, the boy grabbed the weapon and swiped with the blade, cutting the other man's forearm. Logan lunged as the bully howled. He snatched the knife away, and at the same moment used his leg to sweep the boy's feet out from under him. He landed on his back with a gravel-crunching thud.

"Stay down." Logan placed a foot on the boy's chest and pointed the knife at the bleeding man who instantly raised his hands high. Blood ran down his arm, dripping from his elbow. It evoked no sympathy from Logan. "You, get your friend and get outta here."

The man lowered his hands a little, an uncertain expression on his face . . . but suddenly he snapped his fingers with recognition. "I know you. You're Logan Tillane." Loathing tinged with fear crept into his expression. "I thought you was dead."

And it would be better if most folks thought that. "Logan Tillane is dead."

The man shook his head, disagreeing. "I was standing right there when you drew on that marshal in Wichita. I ain't never *seen* a hand that fast. I—"

"Listen to me," Logan took a step toward him, gritting his teeth. "Logan Tillane *is* dead." He hated to do this but he lowered his hand, let it hover over his gun. A clear warning. "Do you understand me?"

"Yeah," he sounded thoughtful. "Sure. I won't breathe a word."

Logan ran the hand with the knife over his mouth, wondering how God expected him to build a church here when his old reputation still hung on him like the stink from a polecat. "Get your friend outta here."

The man hesitated. "Are you really a pre—?" He shook his head, as if he couldn't believe the impossible. "Nah, it ain't so." He grinned and backed away. "But I won't say a thing."

Logan knew he was lying. The news was too big for a little brain like that. By nightfall, word would be all over Defiance that a gunslinger had come to town calling himself a preacher. Eventually, he would have to prove it. Gunslinger or Man of God.

"Two Spears," a thick, Hispanic voice called. "What have you done now?"

Convinced the trouble with the two rowdies was finished, Logan dropped the knife and acknowledged a tall, dark-skinned boy hurrying toward them. "You know this young 'un, son?"

"*Si.*" The kid pushed some strands of black shoulder-length hair behind his ear and reached for Two Spears.

Gaining his feet, the boy squirmed and tried to kick his captor. "Let me go, Emilio!"

"I will not. Mr. McIntyre told me to find you . . .*again.*"

Logan didn't miss the resigned tone draped under the heavy accent. And this little troublemaker was McIntyre's son. "Not his first rodeo, huh?"

"First ro—?" Emilio frowned, then nodded when understanding dawned. "Oh. *Si*, and I do not think it will be his last. He hates it here among the white men."

Logan glanced over at the two troublemakers half-staggering, half-marching toward Main Street, one rubbing an impressive goose-egg on his forehead, the other leaving a trail of red droplets. "Reckon I can understand that, if all the neighbors are as friendly as those two."

Logan then sized up the two boys. Two Spears was wearing dungarees, new boots, and a plaid shirt, but his hair—straight, and black as crow's wings—touched his collar. He wore pure hate in his eyes, so palpable Logan could feel the burn of it.

Emilio was similarly dressed. A strapping young man, verging on twenty or so and probably Mexican. Temperance and wisdom lived in his dark, steady gaze. Thankfully.

Eager to snuff the tension, Logan offered his hand first to Two Spears. The boy only glared. Shrugging, Logan moved to Emilio. "Folks call me Preacher."

The Mexican kid's eyes widened like full moons. "Well, I hope you're tough, *señor*. That man," he chucked a thumb at the two blowhards, "The one who is bleeding, his name is Smith. He spends more time in jail than out. He likes to fight."

"He's gonna be disappointed. The only fightin' I do now is on my knees."

Emilio's face hardened, as if he didn't appreciate the bravado. "Don't say I didn't warn you."

* * *

*E*milio pulled an uncooperative Two Spears up on the saddle in front of him and backed Matilda away from the hitching rail. "I am tired of having to find you every other day."

The boy crossed his arms and huffed. Stoic silence met Emilio's comment. He wondered half-seriously if Señora Naomi would be angry if he spanked the boy. "That's what you need," he muttered, steering the horse into the flow of traffic. "My sister used to beat me and I would not wish that on you. But a *spanking* —I think much can be learned from a good spanking."

Emilio caught a glimpse of Smith and his friend, Shelby, staggering through the crowd on the boardwalk. Headed for Doc's. Again. He would worry about Hannah, except he knew Doc was there. Doc was a tough old rooster.

He looked down at the top of Two Spears's head. "You are fortunate that preacher came along when he did. Those two white men are very dangerous. They would kill you just as soon as look at you. Stay away from them."

"I am not afraid of any white man."

Two Spears didn't speak often, but when he did it was more of this nonsense. Emilio rolled his eyes. "You are foolish. Those two hung me from a lamppost one night, with my head in a trough. I nearly drowned. They will kill you for sport."

Two Spears seemed to find that interesting and loosened his arms a little. "Why didn't you?"

"What? Drown?" Emilio shifted in the saddle, uncomfortable with the answer. "Your father . . .he made them stop."

Ordered to cut the rope, Shelby had unceremoniously dropped Emilio on his head. As he rose up out of the water, sputtering and coughing, he heard the gunshot, saw Shelby scrambling away into the shadows, dragging a game leg . . .and Mr. McIntyre pressing a .44 to Smith's head. Scared stupid, Emilio tumbled out of the trough and ran like a scalded dog. The second gunshot echoed down the alley after him.

He was surprised to learn the next day that Smith was *not* dead. Like Shelby, though, he had a limp.

Both men had been shot in the leg as a warning. Emilio remembered being certain these men had lived simply because Mr. McIntyre had been in a good mood.

Since then, God had done a lot of work in his *patrón*, and Emilio often marveled over the changes. As violent, as brutal as

Mr. McIntyre had been, he was a good man now, striving to be even more so.

And Emilio wanted to be just like him. "Give Mr. McIntyre a chance, Two Spears. He is brave, and would die for the ones he loves. I know. I've seen it."

"He does not love me. He does not even want me here."

"If you would stay put, perhaps he would change his mind."

CHAPTER 5

*H*annah Frink poured a dab of peppermint oil into a metal spoon and held it out for Doc. The older man was lying on the bed, eyes closed, cheeks flushed, which made his shock of unruly blond hair seem brighter, more the color of dry hay. The spider veins around his nose had spread and his abdomen seemed to protrude. Yet, he kept resting his hand on his chest.

"Here, Doc, take this."

The grizzled physician's eyes flew open. He cleared his throat and sat up. Swinging his legs off the bed, he paused to adjust his spectacles. "Oh . . . I, uh," he cleared his throat again, "reckon I dozed off."

Hannah raised the spoon. "I saw you touching your chest. More indigestion?"

Doc took the spoon and downed the medicine. "Just a touch." He tapped the utensil on his leg and stared at the floor. Hannah had the feeling he wanted to say something, but couldn't find the words.

She tried to help. "Doc, is everything Okay? Do you feel all right?"

He slapped his thighs and stood. "Right as rain. Just slowin' down a little, is all. I'm entitled, I reckon, at sixty-four."

He strode out of the room with a stiff limp. Hannah grabbed the bottle of oil off the night stand. As she followed him, the front door flew open and two rough-looking characters stumbled in. Shirts half-tucked, torn breeches, holey boots, Hannah assumed they were homeless beggars. The goose egg in the middle of one man's forehead and the rivulets of blood running down the other's arm told a familiar story.

"Doc," the man with the goose egg said, "My pard Smith here's been cut. Need to get him fixed up."

Hannah grabbed a towel from a stack on the counter and raced to Smith. "Gracious, get that arm up before you bleed out all over our floor."

He gazed at her with suspicion, amplified by the wandering eye, but grunted and gave her his arm. She wrapped it quickly and she and Doc led him over to a metal table. She resisted the desire to wipe her hands on her skirt after they'd helped him settle on the table. The man's shirt was filthy and he smelled like moldy cabbage. His dark brown hair was tangled and greasy, making her wonder why a bath was so hard to come by for some people. His friend, watching her from the window, hadn't put much stock in personal hygiene, either.

Hannah grabbed another towel and commenced wiping the floor. The second man tucked strands of dirty blond hair behind his ear and watched her, a lecherous grin spreading on his stubbly, pockmarked face.

"Hmmm, somebody got you good," Doc muttered, examining Smith. "Missed the tendon, thank God." Doc strode over to the counter to gather up supplies.

"Yeah, a little half-breed tried to steal Shelby's horse." Smith punctuated the accusation with a curse.

Doc's rummaging for bandages and alcohol slowed a hair. Hannah carried the bloodstained towel to the sink and they exchanged a quick, but knowing glance. She poured alcohol over her forearms and hands, faster than washing, and used a towel to pull open a drawer. From inside, she grabbed a roll of surgical thread and a box of needles.

"Here." Doc laid a thick patch of gauze on the man's wound. "Press down firmly."

The man obliged as she and Doc placed needles, a bottle of alcohol, scissors, gauze strips and squares, and thread on a metal tray.

Beside them, the patient grumbled on. "I was gonna skin him good, when some fella intervened. Distracted me, and the redskin cut me. But I'll settle up . . .with both of 'em."

Praying the man was not talking about Two Spears, Hannah set the tray on the examination table as Doc slowly peeled back the gauze. Fresh blood sparkled on the cloth, but the wound had mostly stopped flowing.

With the confidence of years of practice, Doc wiped away the blood and cleaned the wound. Smith hissed out a breath as the alcohol touched the tender flesh. Hannah pursed her lips, knowing full well Doc could be more gentle if he so desired. She gauged the length of the wound, four or so inches, cut the necessary amount of string, and threaded it through a needle.

Doc probed the wound, eliciting twitches and more hisses from Smith. "You don't exactly wear out the idea of gentle, do ya?"

"You want gentle, go to a hospital with nuns. There's one in San Francisco." Doc straightened and stepped back. "All right. Finish cleaning the wound, Hannah, and stitch him up."

"Wait, what?" Smith protested. "I don't want no tow-headed little girl sewing on me."

Doc dropped his hands on his hips and stared blandly at the man. "She needs the practice and you're not hurt that bad."

"Quit your crying, you big baby." Shelby walked over from the window, still leering at Hannah. "This pretty gal probably has good hands." His eyes roved over Hannah and her skin crawled into gooseflesh. "I sure would like her to work on me."

From nowhere a scalpel appeared in Doc's hands and he pressed the tip into the man's throat. "Now, none of that, son. You'll behave in here."

The fella backed up a step, hands raised.

"You disrespect my nurse and I'm not likely to forget that. Could be a problem the next time you need my services. You're liable to lose all kinds of valuable parts."

Smith waved his friend away. "Shelby, hush your mouth and let her be." Scowling, he slid his arm forward to Hannah. "Go ahead."

Hannah went to work, remembering the stitches she'd put in Billy out on Redemption Pass. Nothing but whiskey and a saddle repair kit to work with, but she'd saved her man's life. God had blessed them. And she'd never felt so good, so fulfilled, as she did when she was nursing. Besides being a mother, it was her calling.

"So," Doc began, peering over Hannah's shoulder, "This Indian boy who cut you, was he about, oh, fifteen or sixteen?"

Smith winced at a prick. "Not exactly."

Shelby laughed and settled into a chair by the cold stove. "Nah, it was a little kid. Not more than ten or twelve."

Hannah gritted her teeth, determined to concentrate but she knew they were talking about Two Spears. Her heart sank. *Will that boy never learn to stay out of trouble?*

"Mean as a snake," Smith argued back, "and fast as a rabbit, but I'll break him of stealing horses and stabbing white folks—ouch!"

"Sorry," Hannah rolled her tense shoulders and tried to care. "It would help if you wouldn't talk."

Doc leaned a hair closer. "But patients do, Hannah. And often-times they'll say things you don't want to hear. You have to learn to separate yourself from anything but the medicine."

"I understand."

Shelby raised his feet and rested them atop the stove. "Nah, the boy ain't no trouble. It's the man you ought a worry about, Smith. You try to get back at Logan, you'd better do it in the dark from behind."

"Will you shut up!" Smith yelled, jerking away from Hannah. The needle pricked his skin and he yowled at her like a scalded dog. "Woman, I'm gonna backhand you—" Doc's scalpel appeared at Smith's throat this time and the patient gulped.

"You boys need to calm down now and let Hannah finish her work." Doc placed the blade against Smith's jugular. "Understand?"

Smith nodded at Doc, more out of anger than fear, judging by his clamped jaw. Hands shaking, Hannah dabbed at her patient's arm, a fresh trickle of blood coming from where she'd nicked him, and continued her work.

"This fella Logan," Doc said, pressing the blade deeper, "That wouldn't be Logan Tillane, would it?"

Smith peered down at Doc's hand. "Yep."

"Two things you should do, Smith, if you want a long life. Pay your doctor's bill . . . and leave Logan Tillane alone."

"*H*e's gone again?"

Naomi's sister, Rebecca, spoke in an accusatory tone, and it pricked McIntyre a little. She flung her thick brunette braid over her shoulder and went back to inking with a roller the blocks of type that composed her front page.

The opposite of her petite, fair-haired sisters, Rebecca was tall with thick dark hair and regal features. Significantly older than Naomi and Hannah, about forty he guessed, she was also a thunderstorm of wisdom and elegance. McIntyre respected that spark, that passion.

And she was now turning said passion toward a newspaper.

33

Every prosperous, civilized town needed a newspaper. Working on a Washington Printing Press, she and her husband, Ian, had paid dearly for the thing, an iron monster the size of an ice box. And they had it positioned right in the front window of McIntyre's old saloon, sending the message that Defiance was, indeed, up-and-coming, civilized . . . safe.

McIntyre could guess the first headline: *Charles McIntyre Unfit Father.* He'd never said he was fit. He had a great number of fears over what kind of father he would be, due to the scallywag his own father had been. But claiming an illegitimate half-breed involved far more than mere paternity. The clash of cultures he could see coming might well be epic. It worried him. Specifically for the boy's safety.

"Naomi tells me you don't spend any time with him." The acrid smell of India ink permeated the former saloon. Rebecca set the roller back on the ink table and carefully transferred the page form to the press's bed. "Perhaps if you would show the child some compassion, he might settle down."

McIntyre controlled the urge to let a petulant tone creep into his own voice. "Neither you nor your sister seem to grasp the gravity of what I have been asked to do." He grabbed the Devil's Tail, the press's handle, and waited for Rebecca to slide the page forward.

Satisfied things were in place, she cranked a spindle, rolling the page beneath the press's weight, called a tampen, then reached up and took hold of the handle. "I'd rather do this myself. I'm still learning."

McIntyre acquiesced with a nod and stepped back. "You've read the newspapers from around the country, Rebecca. You know how most people regard Indians."

She grasped the handle, positioned herself to pull, but paused. "What I know is nearly all of the newspapers out West print the most blatantly outrageous falsehoods and bigoted comments I've ever read in my life. It's as if they are determined to cause the annihilation of the Indian."

"Slaughter and lies always sell newspapers."

"Well, our paper isn't going to be like that. We'll print the truth —and only the truth—on all stories. No opinions. We will refer to the Indians by their tribal names. They deserve respect. They're human beings—not *Injuns* or *redskins.*"

Tired of talking to her back, McIntyre strode to the other side of the press. "I'm not sure Defiance is ready for the unvarnished truth about anything, much less about the Indian problem." None of this, however, was the reason for his visit. "I did not come by to discuss that or Two Spears. I wanted to let you know you'll have an extra guest for dinner tonight. A preacher has come to town and he will be staying here until his church is ready."

Rebecca straightened up. "A preacher? A real one?"

"Well, if by real you mean a Godly man, then yes, I think he is. His conversion may be even more unbelievable than mine."

Frantic, moving like her hands were on fire, Rebecca released the handle and rolled the bed back from the press. "I have to redo the front page. I have to write a new story. Where is our preacher?" She removed the chase containing the page and took it back to her desk. "I need to see him right away." She scanned the news stories, painstakingly laid out backward with blocks of type. "Here, I'll pull the story of Wilhelm Fassbender's gold nugget."

McIntyre watched as Rebecca removed the story, one word, sometimes one letter, at a time. "Rebecca," he softened his voice and stepped over to her. "Our preacher has a past."

Her hands slowed.

"He would be most fortunate if it did not follow him to Defiance. If he does not want to answer all your questions, don't push him . . .please."

*L*ogan paused at the front window of what was once the Iron Horse. He noted for an instant his rough appearance: dirty saddlebags tossed over one shoulder; worn clothes in need of washing, shaggy hair. The gun on his hip felt showy. Back in Willow he had quit wearing it. He knew he couldn't be so trusting in Defiance.

The traffic streamed past him in the glass and he took a deep breath. *I'm not sure I'm ready for this, Lord. Am I solid enough?*

A woman's face appeared on the other side of the window. Logan tipped his hat and strode to the door. He let himself in and the acrid scent of India ink assailed him.

The woman wiped her hands on her apron and approached him. "You're not by any chance our new preacher, are you?"

He removed his hat and ducked his chin. "Yes, ma'am; that's the plan leastways."

"I'm Rebecca Donoghue." The two shook hands. "Charles told me to expect you. Get you settled." She motioned to the printing press behind her. "You can see the Iron Horse serves several different purposes now. It's a town hall and a newspaper office. There are bedrooms upstairs. He said you can stay as long as you need."

"That's generous of him, but," he let the saddle bags slide off his shoulder, "as soon as the church is livable, I'll be staying there."

"I understand." Rebecca shifted uncomfortably and her brow creased. "I was wondering if I might interview you for the paper. The town needs to know you're here."

Logan rubbed his chin with the back of his hand. She was right, of course. Folks had to be made aware they had a place to come and hear God's Word. "I guess that would be all right."

The crease didn't leave her brow. "You don't have to answer any questions you're uncomfortable with. I understand you, uhm . . .have a past."

A past. A gun for hire by anyone with the gold, no questions asked. A reputation for a lightning draw and a long trail of nameless corpses. A hard-fought battle to defeat his taste for whiskey. "Ma'am, a gunslinger-turned-preacher doesn't just have a past. He has a target painted on his forehead."

Her mouth fell open into a little 'o.'

"And the truth is," he went on, "I've been hiding out with a small church in Kansas, avoiding what I've been called to do—preach the Gospel in Defiance."

Her hand slowly slid into a pocket on her apron and emerged with a pencil and note pad. "May I quote you? Or some form of that?"

Logan couldn't say why, but he trusted Rebecca in spite of not knowing her from Adam's house cat. He'd met a few reporters, and even a dime novelist, in his time. She didn't strike him as that shallow . . .or hungry. She was not a sensationalist, and he was rarely wrong about people. His lips slid into a sideways grin. "How 'bout *some form?*"

---

*N*aomi stepped out in the summer sunshine, leading her horse, Buttermilk, out of the small, temporary lean-to. She paused to drink in the view of her cabin, its new cedar roof in place. The home she adored, framed by the soaring San Juan Mountains and a cloudless, sapphire sky. The gurgling Animas River rolled past the home site, winding its way through sixteen thousand acres of McIntyre land. The water sounded joyous, almost like children giggling.

Contentment swelled in Naomi. Charles's land. Her land.

Lush, green, rolling pastures waited for the two thousand head of cattle on their way up from Texas. Starting tomorrow, the crew that had put a roof on her home and finished the bunk house would start on the barn, and a few days later, their ranch would be teeming with cattle and men.

She wouldn't lament the loss of peace and quiet. After spending almost a year in the hotel seating customers, serving food, and scrubbing pans, she was tickled to have something to do outside again. She never thought she'd be anything but a farmer's wife, her toes wiggling in warm Southern soil.

But now she was a rancher's wife.

And a mother.

Hoof beats drew her away from the woolgathering to the path coming out of the forest. Emilio burst from the shadows, cantering toward her on his little roan, Matilda, Two Spears scowling like an ill-tempered old woman from the front of the saddle. She pulled Buttermilk forward and met the boys in the front yard.

"I see you found our yearling." She raised her hand and touched Matilda's nose as the horse came to a stop.

Emilio lifted the boy from the saddle and set him on the ground. "*Si.* And I gave him a good talking to about staying put." He shot Two Spears a stink eye. "You and Mr. McIntyre are good people. He has a good home here. His people, like mine," he paused ever so slightly, "will disappear. Some things you cannot stop."

Naomi's heart went out to Emilio. He didn't remember the village he'd been born in, his parents had been murdered when he was very young, and that awful sister of his, Rose, who had raised him, was now in prison. Until this moment, Naomi hadn't really considered just how lonely Emilio must be. Yet he never let it show. Smiling often, always working, he seemed more focused on moving forward. With that handsome grin, hair as black as Two Spears's, and a strong but gentle disposition, she doubted he'd be a single man long either . . .if he could just get over Hannah. But she couldn't fix that situation today.

"Well, boys," she rested a hand on her hip, "sometimes family isn't who brought you into the world." She dared a look at Two

Spears and gentled her voice. "Sometimes, it's the people who are here to help you survive it."

Had she seen the tiniest softening in Two Spears's tight, dark scowl? She hoped so.

"*Si*," Emilio whispered.

Praying she'd said at least one thing right to help these boys, she changed subjects. "I guess Charles is still out looking for *Trouble* here." She wagged her thumb at the boy. "He was supposed to give me a ride into town. You didn't see him anywhere, did you?"

"Only when he told me to find Two Spears."

"All right, well . . ." she faded off. She could hitch the wagon for her and Two Spears, let him ride Buttercup with her, or saddle another horse. Was that the height of stupidity? "Two Spears, if I let you ride your own horse into town, will you give me your good word, *as a man*, that you will not run off?"

The boy dug his thumbs into his front pockets and shifted his weight from one foot to the other.

Naomi extended a hand. "If you give me your good word, I will trust you."

She knew the value Indians placed on truth and doubted he would lie. Most likely he wouldn't answer at all. Instead, after pondering a moment, the boy grabbed her wrist, the way Indians shook hands. "I give you my good word."

Both she and Emilio grinned. "All right then."

"Would you like me to saddle one?" Emilio started to dismount, but Naomi waved him down.

"No, if you wouldn't mind, find Mr. McIntyre and let him know Two Spears and I will be there directly."

"*M*r. McIntyre!" Emilio spurred Matilda and raced past the hovel of a miners' camp on the edge of town to catch his friend. "I found him!"

Men, suspicious of his presence too near their cabin watched him race by, hands on their guns.

Mr. McIntyre spun his sorrel and trotted back, cutting the distance between them. "Where was he?"

Emilio knew he should approach this gently. Smith and Shelby each had one bad leg. Mr. McIntyre was liable to make it two. "He was at the livery."

The men fell in beside each other, horses going at an easy walk. "Fine. Now, what aren't you telling me?"

Emilio would never play cards with Mr. McIntyre. He'd never been able to lie to him or hide information. "Smith and Shelby had hold of him. Supposedly he'd tried to steal Shelby's horse."

Mr. McIntyre's face darkened. "Those two. I should have run them out of town when they tried to drown you. My mistake."

"*Si*, but a preacher saved him. Beaned Shelby right between the eyes with a rock."

McIntyre laughed. "I see our new preacher is winning converts." He shook his head, as if at a loss, but his amusement quickly faded. "Is Two Spears all right?"

"Yes sir." The two men rode in silence for a moment, the wide valley surrounding them, warm summer sun shining down. The grass was as green as Emilio had ever seen it, thanks to a snowy winter. "Your cattle will arrive soon, *si*?"

"Yes. Within the week." Mr. McIntyre tilted his hat back and looked over at Emilio. "Regarding my cattle, I have been meaning to speak with you. How would you feel about moving out to the ranch and assisting my foreman? I can rely on you, Emilio, and I know that. You've proven yourself."

Emilio puffed up at the praise. He appreciated the words, the trust.

"I would like you involved in this new venture. It seems that Rose told me once you worked with cattle."

"*Si*, I did." Stolen cattle. A huge herd that was hidden in a wide, green, *secret* maze of canyons in Arizona. Emilio had been thirteen or fourteen at the time, he didn't know for sure. "I drove them, fed them, slept with them for a year."

"You would be interested, then?"

Emilio couldn't stop the grin he was sure outshined the noonday sun. "Yes sir."

"You won't be in town as much." Mr. McIntyre's voice picked up a hesitant edge. "You won't see certain people as often."

Emilio wasn't sure if he meant Hannah, specifically, but not seeing her would be a good thing. Now that Billy had come back into her life, she didn't have room for any other man. She was still his friend, but somewhere along the way he'd realized he'd wanted more. About that time, Billy had shown up. The winner was clear. Besides, he was the father of her baby. Emilio had to get over her. Not seeing her every day would help. "I will be glad to be out on the ranch."

Mr. McIntyre nodded approvingly, as if understanding the choice. A man couldn't live his life in love with a woman who couldn't return the affection. A man would move on and forget her.

Emilio intended to do just that.

CHAPTER 6

*E*milio sat on the cot and stared at the shelf of personal items on the wall opposite him.

After the hotel had burned, he had moved back into the little room behind the Iron Horse's bar. Instead of falling asleep to the sounds of drunken laughter and a poorly-played piano, he heard the noises of a family. Little Billy's muffled crying, or Hannah and Mollie giggling like silly girls, or the soft muttering of Ian and Rebecca working late on the newspaper. Occasionally, Billy picked up his guitar and strummed a few songs. Good, peaceful sounds.

He pondered the shelf again. Everything he owned would fit into one saddle bag. Two shirts, one pair of pants, a few sets of unmatched socks. A small Bible. An arrowhead he had found down by the river.

Nothing else. And he would never have anything else if he didn't get his head out of the mud. Hannah was taken. Rightly so. Still, his heart hurt.

A soft rap on his doorframe mercifully interrupted his useless thoughts.

"My, you look lost in deep contemplation."

"Hey." Emilio stood and nodded at Mollie. So similar to Hannah in looks, down to the shimmering blue of her eyes, he was both happy and disappointed every time he saw her. "*Si*, I was thinking I don't have so much to take to the McIntyres' bunkhouse." She was a year or two older than Hannah, and carried herself differently. Working in the Iron Horse, she had seen and done things Emilio hoped Hannah would never do . . . things Mollie would never do again.

She ambled in, twirling her finger in a long, golden lock of hair. "Mmm. Packing will be easy then. I came to see if you needed any help. "She glanced around the dim walk-in storage room that gave up precious inches to his cot. "I'd sure enjoy a ride out to the ranch, if you don't mind bringing me back."

Mollie bit her lip and batted long, thick eyelashes at him. She sure had a way of looking at him sometimes . . . a way that, if he would look back, might open new doors.

"Funny how girls can do that. Do you practice it?" He wrenched his lips into a frown, but had to fight to keep it.

Mollie huffed and dropped her hands on her hips. "What do you mean? I just wanted to go for a ride. The weather is so nice today."

"You can quit begging." He gave up and let the frown give way to a full grin. Shaking his head, he turned and grabbed his saddle bag from a hook on the wall. "You can come."

"Well, don't do me any favors."

He paused. *Girls. So sensitive.* Would he ever learn when to joke with them and when not to? Or were they offended at random? He ducked his head in apology, at least suspecting how to make amends. He straightened to his full height and faced her. "*Señorita*, would you like to accompany me to the McIntyres'? I would be most honored with the pleasure of your company."

Mollie held on to her mad for a moment, but then burst out laughing. "*Si*. Yes."

*N*aomi and Two Spears slowed their mounts to a trot through town. As usual, the street swarmed with miners and reeked with the stench of unwashed bodies and horse manure baking in the sun. The air clanged and chimed as pans swayed back and forth on pack saddles.

Men still stared at her when she rambled around town, but now they knew better than to say anything unless, one, the comment was excessively polite, or two, they were personal friends. Touching her was absolutely out of the question. No one had been that stupid since Tom Hawthorn had just about choked the life out of her.

Today, however, they weren't staring at her. Or, more accurately, they weren't staring at her *only*. Suspicion, anger, disgust filled strangers' eyes as they studied the boy, and *then* her.

How can they look at a child with such hate?

Two Spears was not oblivious to the atmosphere. He straightened in the saddle, pulled his shoulders back, puffed up his little chest. He might be afraid of these white men, but he wouldn't show it. Her heart swelled with pride at his courage.

"Where were you exactly when Emilio found you in town?" She thought perhaps to get his mind off the crowds with the question, and she had neglected to ask for details earlier. She'd merely assumed he'd been wandering about.

"At the livery, stealing a horse."

He said it so matter-of-factly she wasn't sure he'd heard him correctly. "You were stealing a horse?" They rode up to the hitching post in front of the town hall, but didn't dismount. "Well," she said, flustered by the detail. "Ahem . . . where is the horse then?"

Two Spears stared straight ahead. "The men who owned it caught me and were about to cut me."

"What?" Naomi asked breathlessly. She turned in the saddle to look directly at him. "What happened?" She scanned him head to toe, feeling like a fool for not getting this information earlier. "Are you all right?" And why didn't Emilio say anything?

"A . . . *preacher* came along and threw a rock at one man. The other man I stabbed."

Naomi's heart felt as if it might drop right into her stomach. Her mouth wouldn't function for a moment. Finally, she whispered, "Stabbed?"

Charles burst through the batwing doors and stomped out on to the boardwalk. Judging by his scowl, he knew some of this story, but Naomi was shocked when he turned the glare on her. "And just what is he doing on a horse? Were you trying to give him an opportunity to steal another? And cause more trouble?"

Naomi should have taken a breath, but Charles's tone instantly struck her like a match on sandpaper. "I was trying to get to town so I could help with dinner, seeing as I didn't know where *you* were." The second the words left her mouth, she regretted them.

She and Charles both sagged a little.

"I'm sorry. I only just discovered," she cut her eyes at Two Spears, "he did more than wander into town."

"If Logan had not come along," Charles spoke more gently as he stepped forward and pulled the reins from Two Spears's hands, "those men would have killed you."

"Charles!" Naomi snapped. The boy did not need that information. "Are you trying to scare him?"

He whipped his glare back to Naomi. "Yes. *And* keep him out of trouble and in *one piece.*"

Charles's face flushed, and his brow creased hard in the middle with a baleful look. She'd rarely seen him this angry, but felt sure she could match him. About to dismount and go toe-to-toe with her loving husband, a calmer voice spoke from the doorway of the saloon.

"No harm done. And the boy is all right." A man stepped up beside Charles—tall, solid, a bit weathered, shaggy blond hair

45

curling at his collar. Icy blues eyes warmed when he looked at Two Spears, then Naomi. He inclined his head, as if she amused him. "You must be Mrs. McIntyre."

"I am. And you, sir?"

"You can call me Preacher."

"Preacher? You're a *real* preacher?"

Charles inched forward, clearly still irate. "We can cover introductions later. You and Two Spears need to understand something." He pinned the boy with a hard stare. "Those two who accosted you today are dangerous. You cannot go around antagonizing men like that."

The boy's scowl melted off his face, fear and confusion replacing it.

"*Charles.*" Fuming, Naomi dismounted and stomped up to her husband. "You can't tell him things like this. He's just a boy."

"Excuse me," the preacher said softly. He purposely stepped between the warring parties, forcing some breathing room, and rested a hand on Two Spears's horse. He grinned sideways at the boy. "Have you ever seen a printing press, son? A real one in action?"

Two Spears shook his head. "I would rather see you throw another rock."

"Well, uh . . ." Looking a little chagrined, the preacher glanced at Naomi and Charles, and rubbed his neck. "Uh, maybe we could go outback and toss a few into the water."

Two Spears leaped from the saddle like an excited squirrel and stared up at the preacher with a hint of adoration. The man towered over him. Yet the boy didn't look intimidated in the least.

The preacher dropped a hand on Two Spears's shoulder. "Let's let these two finish their talk."

He started to usher Two Spears inside when the boy stopped and looked up at Naomi. "I saw a grizzly once defend her cubs from a hunter." He shifted to Charles, his face scrunching in disapproval. "The hunter lost an eye."

Stunned looks ricocheted amongst the adults. Biting down a grin, the preacher ushered the child inside. Naomi tried to hold on to her anger with Charles, but the image of the grizzly and the matter-of-fact way Two Spears viewed their feud melted it. Simultaneously, she and Charles chuckled.

He hung his head and rested a hand on his gun. "That boy is wise beyond his years."

"Yes, he is." Naomi hooked her hand inside Charles's vest. "You can't treat him like he's a huge inconvenience, and you can't scare him into behaving with stories like that. You'll just push him away."

"I cannot emphasize enough to you the prevailing opinion out here of Indians, Naomi. Since settlers have been coming West, there have been merciless clashes over land." He clutched her shoulders. "But the only thing the papers ever report is the massacres of whites. Indians aren't even seen as human. They're more reviled than Negroes."

Naomi realized that Charles's anger was actually an expression of fear, and it sobered her. "Is he in that much danger?"

"Absolutely. And if he'd taken that horse and run off, he may have gotten himself into a situation where there was no help."

"All right. I understand." She started to walk past him, but as his hands slipped away she stopped and clutched his fingers. "But if you want to stop his running off, you need to show him that you care. You could start by apologizing to him."

She didn't wait for an answer.

CHAPTER 7

*T*he big man—filthy, scruffy, stinking to high heaven—
snatched his bowler from his head and stepped hesitantly into Delilah's office, such as it was. She wasn't happy about
conducting business in a tent, she wasn't happy construction had
not yet started on her saloon, and she was not happy about a
preacher coming to town. Most of all, she was not happy about a
nasty, unkempt vagrant with a wandering eye daring to waste her
time.

She stared at him across her desk. "Otis said you have something important to tell me. I hope for your sake, you do." She
picked up a letter opener and waved it menacingly. "I am in a foul
mood, Mr. . . . .?"

"Smith. Randall Smith." The man rubbed his chin, licked his
lips. "I think you'll want to know what I know. I heard you was
buyin' up the saloons in town. But one of 'em is owned now by a
preacher."

Delilah did not react to the news and let an awkward silence
express her boredom. The man licked his lips again. "He ain't just
any preacher. I don't reckon you'll be able to buffalo him, if he
don't want to sell."

"And why not, pray tell?" She tilted her chin slightly, not interested in telling the man she had no need of buying out a *church*.

"He's Logan Tillane."

Ice coursed through Delilah's veins. She felt her face go slack and quickly masked her surprise. How could she have not recognized him? Had it been that long? "I thought he was dead."

"Nope. He just got religion."

Delilah leaned back in her chair and tapped the palm of her hand with the letter opener. "So Logan Tillane is the preacher in Defiance." In a way, it seemed fitting. He'd rolled right through some of the meanest, orneriest towns in the West, untouched, unscathed. Men were terrified of him and his gun. They called his uncanny skill The Devil's Hand. The gals he'd beaten attached a different meaning to the moniker.

When had she seen him last?

The question hadn't fully formed when the memory slapped her in the face.

Thirteen years ago. That saloon in Dallas. She touched her cheek, reliving the sting.

Staggering drunk, Logan had literally stumbled into the Brass Lantern, trailed by two other cowboys. He had commenced banging on the bar, hollering about either getting a poke or starting a fight, whichever came first. Delilah knew his voice instantly and her heart beat wildly with joy for the first time in over two years. She abandoned the cowboy's lap she was warming and raced over to her old flame.

"Logan, it's me, Victoria." She looked eagerly into his blue eyes, the innocent, dreamy girl bubbling to the surface once more. "Victoria from Dodge City."

He shoved his hat back on his head and returned her gaze with a rubbery, lecherous grin. "Well, Fictoria from Dodge Thity," he slurred thickly, dropping a clumsy hand to her shoulder, "lez you and me find a room upstairs. I'll bring the bottle."

He'd made her such beautiful promises. He'd sworn his eternal love, vowed he'd never have another. Yet, after only two short years apart, he didn't even remember her? Dumbstruck, she backed away from him. "Go away." A foolish thing to say, but it was all that came to her.

Logan's face clouded over. It seemed he had found his fight. He exploded on her like a rabid animal. Growling, shoving, punching, he got in several good swipes before anybody had the courage to pull him off.

The memory disturbed Delilah and she pushed past it, back to the sleazy man in front of her. "So, he's Logan Tillane. Why are you telling me this? What do you want?"

"An Injun boy started to steal my friend's horse today. I was about to *correct* the savage when Logan saved his hide." The man's lip curled. "If there's anything I hate more than an Injun-lover . . . I don't know it."

Men and their prejudices. Delilah despised their pettiness, but never failed to exploit it. She laid the letter opener on the desk, signaling the talk had become more cordial. "I take it, then, you want to run Tillane out and help me get that saloon?"

"For a price."

His arrogance annoyed her and she picked up the letter opener again. "You think I need you? You think men like you aren't a dime a dozen?"

"Miss Delilah," he took a step forward, "I can tear a man apart with my bare hands. I can convince Tillane to leave Defiance. And anybody else you want gone."

She huffed a petulant breath and studied the man's hands. Scarred, a bit gnarled. A brawler's hands. "I have Otis. He handles my trouble."

"Nobody in Defiance knows Otis. They all know me. They know I'll fight before I talk."

"Then why didn't you take care of Tillane when you had the chance?"

Keeping his gaze on Delilah, Smith slowly hiked up the sleeve of his dirty jacket to reveal a bloody bandage. "I was in need of a doctor. The little Injun got in a lucky strike, but I'll settle that score too." He pulled his sleeve down. "Besides, I'm white."

Yes, there was that. On occasion, Otis's black skin had been an unnecessary impediment. For example, none of the carpenters she'd hired would even consider discussing their work on the saloon with him.

"And I'll tell you something else, Miss Delilah. I don't drink. Not a drop. I'm a good man to put to work in a saloon. Won't drink up your profits and I'm always sharp."

She had to consider that. A tough, sober man might be worth his weight in gold. The decision should have been an easy one, but her thoughts were troubled by Logan and why they hadn't recognized each other.

Annoyed her vanity had gotten in the way of business, even for a moment, she forced herself back to the matter at hand. She owed her partner his due. Matthew wanted McIntyre dethroned, and Smith could possibly be helpful there. "Do you have any other skills worth mentioning? How versatile are you?"

"Well, I don't know about versatile, but I'm mighty *willing . . .* " He winked. "And I don't ask a lot of questions. You tell me to do somethin', it'll git done."

Point taken. "You ever worked as a bouncer in a saloon?" Not that it mattered. She was merely curious.

An oily grin answered her question. "Ever heard of a little place called the Long Branch?"

---

*M*cIntyre sat on one leg folded beneath him, his arms wrapped around his knee as he rested in the grass on the banks of the Animas. Chewing a blade of grass, he watched Logan and Two Spears skip rocks over the water.

The setting sun brushed the distant, craggy mountains in

peaceful hues of red and purple. The warm air, a haze of insects glowing in the twilight, and the innocent recreation reminded him for a moment of summers back in Georgia . . . especially the summer he'd felt like the man of the house for the first time.

McIntyre recalled with perfect clarity the feel of his father's wrist as he'd grabbed hold of it, preventing the man from striking his mother a second time—or ever again. The frail bones of a hand that never labored other than to lift a glass or slap a woman.

McIntyre feared nothing more than becoming a man like his father. Distant, selfish, violent. For a while he had been—until Naomi. And Christ.

Though he knew he'd never strike *her*, he'd already made more mistakes with Two Spears than he cared to calculate. Would he ever hurt the boy?

Haven't I already?

McIntyre tossed away the blade of grass and rose to join the pair at the water. He would not become his father. "I used to be pretty good at this." Confident he hadn't lost his touch, he jerked his string tie loose and tugged on his collar.

Logan tossed him a rock. "Put your money where your mouth is then, McIntyre."

He grinned at the wry challenge, but the expression melted off his face when he saw the look of suspicion, even dread, in Two Spears's eyes. He had a lot of ground to make up. Clueless where to start, he stepped up to the water's edge. Maybe something as simple as skipping stones could be a move in the right direction. He leaned a little to the right and chucked the stone, trying to spin it flat and direct.

It hit the water and skipped once, twice, three times, and kept going. At the fifth skip Logan started clapping and counting out loud. On its seventh hop, Two Spears had stepped up beside McIntyre, mouth agape.

"Ten!" Logan whistled in amazement as the stone finished its trek on water. "McIntyre, remind me never to play cards *or* skip stones against you for money."

"The trick is," McIntyre squatted so he could look up at Two Spears, "get as flat a rock as you can and then flick it quick." Two Spears inched back, but his face showed no emotion. McIntyre understood and dropped his gaze to the ground. "Say, there's a good one." He picked up a flat, smooth stone that had been worn down to the size of a half dollar, and turned it over and over. "Yes, nice and smooth. Try this one." He offered it to Two Spears.

Hesitantly, the boy took it from him, pausing only an instant as their fingers met. Not wanting to crowd him, McIntyre rose and backed away a foot. Two Spears turned, then stood as he'd seen McIntyre, feet spread, arm reared back.

"All right, take your hand," McIntyre pulled the boy's arm back another few inches. "Here. Good. Now, keep the rock level with the ground and flick it. But the motion is more in your wrist than your whole arm. Understand?"

McIntyre demonstrated a few times, moving the boy's arm back and forth. Two Spears attentively followed the throws, adjusted his stance, cast a few shadow throws himself then finally chucked his stone.

It skipped once. Twice, then skittered again and again as McIntyre and Logan called out together, "One, two, three, four . . ." All the way to seven before the stone disappeared beneath the surface.

Two Spears almost looked happy, and McIntyre gave the boy an approving nod.

"Well," Logan clapped his hands together, "That was impressive, but if you two will excuse me, I think I'm going to slip inside and wash up for supper. Two Spears, you'll rival your pa there in no time. You have a natural talent for skipping stones."

Pa? McIntyre was caught off guard by the word. Even Two Spears's chin came up a hair. Logan seemed not to notice and strode back inside the town hall.

Left alone with the boy, McIntyre scratched his beard and said a quick prayer for wisdom. "Two Spears, let us sit for a moment and speak some truth."

The boy dropped right there and stared stoically at the flowing, sparkling water. "One-Who-Cries said a white man cannot speak the truth. Only lies."

McIntyre inhaled a long, deep breath, and released it slowly as he sat beside the boy. Knowing so much rested on his words, he plucked another piece of grass and prayed for wisdom. "Not all white men are liars, just as not all Utes are murdering savages. There are some we can trust on each side." He tied the green blade into a knot and shrugged. "Most, I believe, in fact. And I don't recall that I have lied to you."

"One-Who-Cries told me you took my mother against her will. You used her, and did not come for her when she was moved to the White Mountain Reservation."

McIntyre flinched at the accusations. Would his past never stop wreaking havoc on those he cared about? But he knew better than to call the renegade One-Who-Cries a liar. Two Spears had spent more time with the savage than he had with McIntyre. He had to tread lightly on the boy's hero. "Two Spears . . . your grandfather. You love him and trust him, yes?"

The boy nodded. "Yes."

"He brought you to me. He entrusted me—" He bit that off and sought a word the boy would understand. "He *honored* me by bringing you here, for you to join my family. Would he have left you with a white man who told only lies?"

Doubt creased the boy's brow, but he didn't respond.

"The Utes say that all members of the tribe are brothers and sisters. Is this not so?"

"Yes."

"For those of us who follow Jesus Christ, we believe that also. I want you in my family. Naomi and I want to raise you as our son.

I'm sorry I have not made you feel welcome. It's just that I know it will be hard for you—"

"Because I am Ute."

"There are many white men who hate the Indian."

"And to them I will always be Indian," the boy turned his head and looked at McIntyre with staggeringly wise eyes, "no matter how you raise me."

McIntyre couldn't argue with that. Most people, in fact, would never see past the color of Two Spears's skin. He ripped the blade of grass in two. "I will raise you to be a man, Two Spears. Then, which world you live in will be your choice."

---

*L*ike a well-oiled machine, Hannah and her sisters bustled around the little kitchen in the former saloon, getting their Saturday night meal on the table. The crowded conditions and smell of a pork roast rubbed in rosemary brought back fond memories of the hotel: all the hard work they'd shared —cooking, cleaning, and running their own business together.

The pleasant musings dispelled Hannah's concern over Smith's threats for only a moment. His vitriol for Two Spears, a mere child, was so harsh. Something about the man and his anger haunted her. He struck her as dangerous. But perhaps not as dangerous as this Logan Tillane Doc had told her about: a gunfighter with a deadly aim, a punch like a sledgehammer, and a thirst for whiskey that only made him meaner. Defiance still had a tendency to attract the dregs of society, much to her dismay.

Shaking off the dark thoughts, Hannah sat down at the table with a bowl full of boiled eggs and started peeling. "Rebecca, how's the newspaper coming?"

Her older sister poured a steaming pot of cooked potatoes through a strainer, pulling back from the steam. "It couldn't be better. We've got nearly one whole issue typeset and ready. We shouldn't have any problem getting one hundred or so copies out Monday."

"We're getting there, girls." Naomi shoved a tray of biscuits into the oven, seemed to ponder something for a moment, then shut the door. "We've got a newspaper, a preacher, and a town hall." She turned to her sisters. "We need a school and a dress shop, and I'll call us civilized."

"Speaking of preachers," Hannah rolled an egg on the table, breaking the shell, "I guess you've met him? Who is he? Where does he come from? Is he young, old, handsome, ugly?"

"Oh, he's young and quite handsome." Smiling, Naomi whisked a pie from the stove top to the table.

Hannah was a bit surprised at her sister. "You're married. You have no business noticing such things."

"I'm married—not dead."

Rebecca chuckled, and brought the bowl of steaming potatoes to the table. Tossing her dark braid out of her way, she sat and put the masher in her hand to work, smashing the spuds with determination. "She's right, Hannah. No harm in admiring *from a distance*. But speaking of marriage, my next question should be obvious."

"When will Billy and I set our date?" Hannah started on another egg. "He won't be back for a few more days. We'll see."

She was so torn about things. Not about her love for Billy, but would marrying him mean she would have to make a choice between nursing and working in the family business again?

"I think you should let Preacher do it," Rebecca said. "That way you can pick any date, instead of waiting for the circuit preacher to come back around."

"We'll see," Hannah said again. She wasn't sure she had a preference. Though, if there was a preacher in town, it seemed like the weddings *should* be in his bailiwick now.

"Charles offered Emilio a job on the ranch," Naomi said casually.

This was news to Hannah, and the idea pleased her . . . but something about it bothered her as well. And why did Naomi feel the need to interject that information right then?

"I think he needs to be in town less," Naomi explained, as if reading Hannah's mind.

A strange hesitation in her sister's voice brought Hannah's head up. She discovered her sisters watching her. The contrast between the two women was stark: blonde, petite Naomi, as headstrong and stubborn as she was pretty; tall, dark-haired Rebecca with her regal features and quiet, wise disposition, she was an anchor for them. The differences kept them balanced and united. "What? Something I said?"

Naomi folded her arms across her chest. "He's in love with you, Hannah, and you act like nothing has changed between you two."

"Nothing has changed. He's still my friend."

"You cause him pain," Rebecca said, speaking more gently than Naomi. "Especially when he sees you with Billy."

Hannah was flabbergasted. Yes, she'd pulled back from Emilio because Billy had shown up. But couldn't they still be friends? "Well, I don't know what I'm supposed to do about it. I'm treating him just the same as before."

"And therein lies the problem." Rebecca started mashing again. "You're too . . . *familiar* with him. You need to treat him less like a brother and more like a man with a broken heart. He needs a little distance."

Hannah gruffly smacked an egg down, busting too much of the white. Her brow scrunched in annoyance. She didn't want to put any distance between her and Emilio. She liked him. Enjoyed his friendship. "Where is Emilio anyway?"

Naomi shrugged a shoulder. "With Mollie, I think. They were taking his things out to the bunkhouse, I believe."

News of his new job hadn't bothered Hannah until now, and

the impact of the change struck her. She wouldn't see him near as much.

He'd also been spending a lot of time with Mollie lately.

Was the ranch a good move? Would he heal his broken heart with Mollie's help? Hannah had no right to be worried or jealous . . . but she was, a little. Surprisingly.

Irritated by the turn of this conversation, she tried to toss it back on Naomi. "So, how are things with you and Charles, Naomi? Is the honeymoon over yet?"

Hannah regretted the spiteful question when her sister's expression fell.

"I think the honeymoon ended when Two Spears showed up on our doorstep. Oh," she waved away the negative tone, "I don't mean that we don't want him. It's just been a little . . . restrictive, let's say."

Rebecca scooped a finger of potatoes and tasted them. "That might be why Charles is grumpy. Or, perhaps, *frustrated* might be a better word."

Naomi blushed and turned back to the stove. "The addition of our room is almost complete. We'll get our privacy back."

"What about when you have twenty ranch hands hanging about?" Rebecca sprinkled some salt into the potatoes. "How much privacy will you have then?"

"Oh, I know it will be different, busy, but I have no doubts Charles will make us comfortable. I just pray we can get Two Spears to settle in." She poured a little bacon grease into a frying pan and swirled it around. "I'm tired of scouring the territory for him, and today was the closest he's come to getting in real trouble. Charles was truly concerned for him."

Smith invaded Hannah's thoughts again. "Sounds to me like that dust-up scared Two Spears pretty good." She dipped an egg in a cup of water to wash it. "Maybe he'll settle down now. Give you two a chance to raise him."

Apparently tired of the introspection, Naomi moved the

conversation away from her family. "About this trip Billy's on . . ." She reached for a bowl of corn fritter batter. "He's gone to hire a manager for the hotel?"

"He said when he was in Dodge City, a kindly woman took him in after he was beaten, gave him breakfast, and paid him a dollar for a chore. That one dollar helped him get out of town." She picked up the last egg. "Eleanor was an unwed mother too. Only, Billy said, the father of the baby never went back for her. He hopes to, maybe, balance the scales I think."

Naomi shook her head in disbelief. "I would have never believed that philandering boy would turn out to be such a good man." She dropped a dollop of batter into the grease. "And I've never in my life been so glad to be wrong about someone."

"And what a businessman, too," Rebecca interjected. "Running a mercantile *and* the hotel. His father would be proud."

Hannah frowned as the change in topic reminded her of the one thing she wanted and that getting it might be in jeopardy.

Naomi apparently noticed the sullen expression. "What's the matter, darlin'?"

Hannah leaned back in her chair. *Time to confess.* "Oh, it's just that Rebecca and Ian have the newspaper. You and Charles have a ranch. Billy has two businesses to run and, well, I'm a little worried I'll get sucked back into the hotel again. Or the mercantile. I want to keep helping Doc. I want to be a nurse, not a clerk."

An awkward silence spoke volumes. Rebecca smiled, a little sadly, Hannah thought, and sighed. "Marriage is about compromise. It's never easy, and it's always a challenge finding the happy medium. But you two will work it out. Have a little faith. Billy loves you and wants you to be happy."

The back door opened and a tall, handsome stranger trudged into the kitchen, dragging his hat off.

"Oh, Hannah," Naomi motioned with her spoon at the stranger, "you haven't met our preacher."

Hannah rose to shake the man's hand as his friendly yet penetrating blue eyes struck her. She noted his impressive height, broad shoulders, and shaggy blond hair. No wonder Naomi commented on his looks; the scars, one across his chin, another smaller one along his jaw, only added to his rugged handsomeness. "I'm Hannah Frink."

"Hannah," he took her hand. "I'm Logan Tillane. Or you can call me Preacher."

CHAPTER 8

*L*ogan immediately thought Hannah was a pretty little thing, like her sisters, but different—more wide-eyed, and bubbly maybe. Those clear blue eyes and that fetching smile put him in mind of a girl he'd known back in his teenage days. A girl he had not allowed himself to think of in years, or how much he still missed her.

He shook Hannah's hand and the pleasant greeting on her face changed inexplicably to fear. She jerked her hand away as if he'd burnt it. "Logan Tillane," she squeaked. "Doc said you're a bad man."

The blunt statement caught everyone off guard, as evidenced by their sudden, awkward silence and uncomfortable glances. Logan lowered his hand. "Doc?"

"Our town doctor. I work with him some. I sewed up a man's arm today—a man who's pretty unhappy with you . . . but Doc said *he* should be afraid of you."

Logan licked his lips and raised his hat to his chest, a contrite move, he hoped. "Well, a while back, that man would have had great reason to fear me." He fanned the hat nervously. "I ain't like that no more. Christ changed me. *Everything* about me."

Hannah smiled, and then her shoulders lowered a little. "God does have a way of pulling us out of the muck of our mistakes."

Logan relaxed too. "Yes ma'am. He sure does. I hope my background will allow me to reach folks without them feeling too judged. After all, if God can save a sinner like me, nobody is beyond His reach."

Rebecca waggled a wooden spoon at him. "Can I quote you on that, Preacher?"

"Yes ma'am, you may."

The group chuckled, but Hannah's expression soured. "I hope you haven't changed so much you can't defend yourself. I don't think that fella I tended to today is through with you. His name is Smith, and he's in trouble all the time."

Logan took a deep breath. He had not been tested much, not by out-and-out violence until today, and it had grieved him to settle things that way. Either Smith would crawl back under his rock or find excuses to make more trouble. Sounded like he would be back for more. "I reckon I'll do what I have to."

***

$\mathcal{B}$illy Page stood quietly at the door of the empty saloon. Empty except for a plump woman, her graying, drab brown hair pulled back in a tight knot, fluidly dragging a mop across the stained floor. She almost seemed to dance with it as she swayed left and then right, working her way back behind the bar. The scent of the pine cleaner almost covered the stench of stale beer and vomit . . . almost.

He had come to Dodge City to take her away from all of this, if she would go. He hoped she would. Billy wanted to repay Eleanor for her kindness to him a few months back. The woman had bailed him, a complete stranger, out of jail and even pushed Wyatt Earp around on his behalf. But it was her last words that haunted him.

I was a Hannah, only no one ever came back for me.

Billy couldn't make that right, but maybe he could improve the woman's lot in life. He cleared his throat and pushed through the batwing doors. "Eleanor?"

The woman turned, still holding the mop. In the few months since Billy had seen her, she'd aged a fair amount. Her hair was nearly all gray now. Only a few streaks of brown remained, and she'd lost some weight. Enough to add to the wrinkles around her eyes and mouth. Dodge City was weighing on her.

She stared at him for an instant with only suspicion in her brow, then her eyes lit up and she grinned. "Billy. Why, I'll be . . ." She rested the mop against the bar and came out to greet him. "It's good to see you. Oh . . ." her face sagged, "unless you're headed home 'cause things didn't work out with your gal."

Billy pulled his bowler off and pressed it to his chest. "No ma'am. Things worked out well. Hannah's agreed to marry me, and we have a beautiful little boy."

Even as a touch of sadness shadowed the lines in her face, Eleanor clasped her hands over her heart and sighed. "I'm happy for you. I truly am." She slapped him on the arm. "This place stinks. Let's go back and have a little breakfast."

———

*A*s Billy took a sip of coffee, he thought back to the morning Eleanor had found him out back, beaten to a bloody pulp and robbed blind. *If it hadn't been for her . . .*

She slid a plate of bacon and eggs in front of him and he smiled up at her. "I remember how good our last breakfast was."

She chuckled and went back to the stove to finish. "So, after you saved Hannah from the Indians, and she plucked a bullet out of ya, she agreed to marry ya, huh?"

A thought struck him. "You know, if all that hadn't happened, I don't know if she would have found it in her heart to forgive me. And I might have lost her to another fella."

"Nah." Sounding very sure, Eleanor sat down with her own plate and a cup of coffee. "She was just being stubborn and prideful, and maybe wanted you to suffer a little. The Indians and the bullet shortened your sentence."

"I guess." He didn't know. Didn't want to know. He had Hannah and Little Billy, and that was all that mattered to him now. That and getting some decent help.

"Now, back to what you said about the hotel. You come here to hire a manager?"

He felt the wry smile twist his lips. "If she's not too tied down to Dodge City."

Eleanor's fork stopped at her mouth and she stared at it for a moment. Slowly, she slid her gaze to Billy. "You mean me?"

"I do indeed. The Trinity Inn is a nice place, with a fine restaurant. I need reliable help to run it. You'll get room and board and $50 a month."

"*Fifty—?*" she bit that off and set her fork down on her plate. "I don't make half that here," she whispered. However, concern for something overtook her expression, chasing away the shock.

"So, Eleanor, are you tied to Dodge for family reasons? You mentioned you had a child."

"Oh, I lost track of her so long ago."

"Her?"

Eleanor heaved a great sigh and shoved her plate away. She drummed her fingers on the edges of it. "I reckon you're no one to judge."

She said it with resignation. Billy sensed a confession coming and shook his head. "Not by a long shot."

"I had a special man for a time many years ago. He ran off and left with me a baby girl."

Her eyes shone with the memories and Billy shifted, lost as to how to comfort the woman. Other than listen.

"A woman alone in that situation doesn't have a lot of prospects. Your Hannah was lucky. She had her sisters. I was by myself and sometimes I made bad choices. Kept bad company."

The regret played out in her eyes, glistened there. "When my daughter . . . *blossomed*, you could say . . . well, men started noticing. There was a boy too. Oh, I could see the trouble coming from a mile away. He drank and he had a terrible temper. His future was an early grave; I didn't need to be a genius to see that. I got her a job at a hotel in Stillwater and sent her off. Told him she ran away and I didn't know where."

Eleanor rose and went to the stove, but she didn't grab the coffee pot on top, just stared at it. "I've not seen her or heard from her since she left. I don't know if she's alive or dead. I wrote her, but she never answered. I've stayed in Dodge—" her voice broke. She sniffed and tried again. "I've stayed, hoping she might come home one day."

A sad silence fell, and Billy let it play out. This was not a time for words. Staring at Eleanor's broad, pudgy shoulders, he knew the woman was deciding.

"Maybe . . ." She wrung her hands in her apron. "Maybe lying to the boy was a terrible thing. Maybe lying to them both was cruel, but I wanted my daughter to have a clean start." She rounded on him slowly, biting her lips as if holding back a sob. "No." She shook her head. "I thank you for your offer, but I ain't ready to leave. I can't just yet."

Disappointment stabbed deep in Billy. He had been so sure she would say yes. He liked Eleanor and could imagine how the sisters would take her in. He had wanted so badly to make a difference in the woman's life.

"Maybe I'll come later," she offered, more out of politeness he thought.

Billy rested his elbows on the tabled and dropped his chin onto his hands. He hadn't meant to cause the woman such distress. How terrible to not know what happened to her daughter. Notions popped into his head. Notions of Pinkertons. Specifically, one named Pender Beckwith. It seemed he couldn't let go of the idea of helping Eleanor. "What was your daughter's name?"

"Victoria. Victoria Patterson."

"Pretty name. What of the boy? What happened to him, do you know?"

"Oh, Lord," she raised a hand to Heaven, "maybe that's one thing I did right. That boy turned out to be a cold-blooded killer. A gunslinger. Even beat one man to death with his bare hands, so they say." She hunched her shoulders as if shaking off a chill. "Tillane. Logan Tillane. Beast of a man."

---

*D*elilah smiled and shrugged her shoulder seductively at the men of Defiance as she made her way down Main Street toward Western Union. They nodded appreciatively, knowing full well they would be visiting her establishment. A few feet behind her, Otis, a Haitian the size of a volcano, followed. Big and bald, grayish scars from a plantation owner's whip marred the ebony skin on his neck and arms. He had one job and he did it well. If a man dared look too lecherously at Delilah or attempt to touch her, his glare withered most men. The smart ones didn't take it any further.

Otis was a man simmering with rage, and it boiled to the surface easily, willingly. She doubted it would take the rubes in Defiance long to figure out annoying her protector was like playing with a stick of dynamite. Black dynamite that disliked white men intensely.

Pleased with her bodyguard, whatever his scars, Delilah sashayed down the boardwalk, but stopped abruptly. She heard the weeping before the crowd parted, revealing a young lady sitting on the stage office's bench, sobbing into her hands as if her whole world was coming apart.

Only virgins cry like that.

Confident in her assessment, Delilah subtly signaled Otis to stay back. Pasting on an expression of concern, she approached the young lady. "Honey . . . honey, is everything all right?"

The girl looked up, revealing striking green eyes rimmed with misery, nose red from the sniffling, and shook her head. "He's dead. My—my fiancé is dead."

Her sobs erupted again and Delilah quickly dropped down beside the girl, taking her hand. "Oh, honey, I'm so sorry. Tell me what happened."

The girl shook her head, fighting for control, and finally managed to gain her voice. "I answered his letter. He said he had a profitable claim. He needed a wife and—and could pay my fare. He—" She sort of hiccuped and sniffled noisily. "They said he was shot. Only a few days ago." She hugged herself and shook her head. "I just got off the stage. I don't have anything. Nothing. No place to stay. The marshal said Jay's claim has already been claimed by somebody else." Panic crept into the girl's voice. "What am I going to do?"

As she buried her head in her hands, Delilah tamped down her delight at meeting this little lost lamb. "Shhh," Delilah hugged the girl. "There, there. Don't you have family, an ex-husband, anyone?"

"No one," the girl sobbed. "I've never been married. I came here against my parents' wishes. They were furious with me—called me foolish and incorrigible."

Two of Delilah's favorite words. "Well, now, you listen to me." She lifted the girl's chin to assess her looks. About twenty, with mysterious catlike eyes, delicate features. Pretty, but they'd need to do something about her flat, drab blond hair. "Everything is going to be all right. I've got a tent you can use—uhm, stay in . . . and I'll get you some dinner." She pulled the astonished girl to her feet. "We'll just take this one day at a time."

"Why—why are you helping me?"

"Why?" Delilah feigned complete astonishment. "Because it's the right thing to do. I can't leave you alone, here on the street. I couldn't call myself human if I didn't help you, especially when I have the resources."

The two women started walking back toward Tent Town, and Otis drifted into the shadows of a doorway as they passed by him. "What's your name, dear?" Delilah asked, nearly choking on the sugar in her voice.

"Mary Jean."

"Ah, such a pretty name." Delilah pulled a hair, still wet with tears, from the girl's cheek and tucked it behind her ear. "Innocent and pure, just like you, I bet."

CHAPTER 9

*L*ogan leaned on the bar and scanned Rebecca's article announcing the arrival of a pastor, while Emilio loitered at the door of the dilapidated church. Almost amused, Logan read aloud phrases that struck him as carefully *crafted*. " . . . a new era dawns in Defiance . . . the preacher brings with him myriad experiences and insights . . . and he seems unafraid of our town's rough-and-rowdy ways."

Translation: The Kingdom of Heaven is at hand. A man of God who has enough sin in his background to embarrass even the residents of Defiance has come to share the Good News.

But Rebecca's final sentence, "All are welcome at the Crooked Creek Chapel," swelled Logan's heart with . . . peace.

She had written a fine article, all without using his name.

He suspected that wouldn't hold water for long. He rubbed his smooth chin, hoping the shave, haircut, and bath might go a ways in making him less easily recognizable. He would introduce himself simply as Preacher, and see where that got him.

"Emilio, thank you for bringing me this. And to your questions, please tell Rebecca I think the article is fine, and Mr. McIntyre that his crew can start whenever they're available." He glanced up at the torn, mildewed canvas. "Let's build a church."

The young man straightened and snugged down his worn, tan cowboy hat on his head. "He said he could have men here this afternoon."

Accepting help graciously had been one of the hardest lessons Logan had had to learn about being a pastor. Giving folks a way to serve the Lord was not the same thing as accepting charity. Charles McIntyre had the means to renovate this building. The sooner a church was up and running, the better. Besides, Delilah's place was going up at a breakneck pace. "This afternoon is fine."

Emilio nodded and slipped out the door to deliver the messages.

Logan folded the paper and laid it on the bar. Searching for his enthusiasm, he surveyed his ramshackle church. While he'd swept it clean of leaves and broken glass, and turned up the few remaining chairs, he knew God hadn't sent him here to play house.

Other men would build this church. His job was to fill it with people.

He dragged his hat off the bar and headed out to round up a flock. He hadn't yet stepped into the mud of Bonanza Street when he noticed Delilah making her way toward him down a warped boardwalk, a brawny, wide-chested Negro following close behind her.

Logan waited on the bottom step, refrained from putting on his hat, and watched her. She sauntered up in a red silk dress, as smooth as a house cat headed for its favorite spot in the sun.

"Preacher." She flipped a fan open like a switchblade and waved it back and forth at her throat.

"Miss Delilah. What can I do for you on this fine day the Lord has made?"

Her delicate features tightened, golden brown eyes narrowed, seeming to glitter. "You shaved and cut your hair."

Logan scratched the back of his neck, now bare. "Yes ma'am. Cleanliness is next to Godliness, I've been told."

Myriad emotions raced across her face, but he couldn't make heads or tails of them. Recognition, possibly? But he could read suspicion and disdain without a doubt, especially as her lip curled into a sneer.

Such a dark expression clouded an otherwise stunning beauty. She had a face men should sketch or paint, not buy. Defined lips, high cheek bones, flawless olive skin touched with a hint of peach, surrounded by wisps of honey-colored hair. Surprised by his distraction, he cleared his throat. "Is there something in particular I can do for ya?"

His question seemed to interrupt her thoughts, but not her intense perusal of him. "Seen the paper? There's a nice article on you. A little light on the facts, I thought." Her eyes roamed over him, as if she was searching every scar, every shadow on his face. "Looks to me like life's been hard on you. I see a lot of miles."

He shrugged one shoulder. "Rough miles on a road that was leading me straight to hell. I've found a better way to live, Delilah. Peace and joy like I never had." He softened his voice, offering sincere humility. "I wish you'd let me tell you about it sometime."

Her cheeks flushed a deep red, but not with embarrassment. Anger. "You pious piece of—" Delilah bit that off. She fought for self-control and Logan could see the victory didn't come easy. The battle left him perplexed.

"What I mean is," she raked a curl off her forehead and tucked it up, "don't *you, especially* you, ever talk to *me* about the Gospel."

Her antagonism toward him and the Gospel mystified Logan. Not that it mattered. It wouldn't stop him. He dropped his hat on his head. "I can't promise it won't come up sometime, Delilah."

He stepped down into the mud. As he passed by her, she whispered over her shoulder, "True, you're not much for keeping promises."

ot much for keeping promises? Delilah's mysterious observation followed Logan down the rutted narrow path that served as a road here in Tent Town, but he determined he wouldn't look back at her. She was playing some kind of game and until he knew the point, or at least the rules, he wouldn't deal himself in. Besides, she was a little too easy to look at.

The hum of men's voices, grumbling horses, and the jingle of tack surrounded him as his boots squished in the mud near the bath tents. Apparently, the proprietor had no qualms about flooding the lower part of Tent Town with used water.

Inside the tent he heard water slosh and splash, and a man cursed about the unsatisfactory temperature. Logan stepped over a large puddle as he and another man coming from the opposite direction made for the same dry spot. The man started at first to hold the patch of earth, but then recognition dawned in his eyes. They widened, and he took a step back. Rather than challenge Logan, he waded through the ankle-deep puddle and carried on.

Logan hung his head. Rounding up a congregation wasn't going to be easy if these folks still thought he was a kill-happy gunslinger.

The faint smell of urine and fresh-cut pine laced the air as he ambled forward. A hundred or so yards up, hammers whacked and lumber thudded as men crawled like ants in and out of the skeletal structure of an up-and-coming building, the second floor on the rise. The bones of Delilah's new saloon?

Across from the construction site, men gathered at a bar. The remnants, he guessed, of a former saloon. No walls, no chairs, just a plank floor. A long, polished, ridiculously ornate mahogany bar drew in the customers like flies. Even at this early hour.

The bartender, a young girl with pert features and drab blond hair piled messily atop her head, poured beer from mammoth kegs resting on sawhorses behind the bar. Men, holding their shots of liquor or mugs of beer, milled about on the empty floor. Trying to ignore the smell of the demon rum, Logan wandered into the midst of the patrons and glanced around.

"Might breezy on a cold day, isn't it?" he asked of no one in particular.

One man looked over, looked again, and moved away. The bartender heard Logan's question and lifted emerald green eyes his way. With a hesitant jerk of her chin, she invited him over. "What can I get for you?"

"You mean besides a roof and four walls?"

"Whether I've got walls or not shouldn't bother you. Liquor and beer taste the same. What'll you have?"

Logan licked his lips pondering the young lady instead of his desire to order a round. She sounded something less than enthusiastic, even rehearsed.

"Nothin'." At the girl's scowl, he quickly added, "Thanks, though. I was just curious."

"Well, if you must know," she pulled the towel off her shoulder and commenced to wiping down the bar, "this hunk of wood is going in Delilah's new place. We just opened for business a little early."

"I see." Logan shoved his hands in his pockets, both impressed and repulsed by Delilah's entrepreneurial spirit.

"Now, across the street there, we've got a tent with a live show." The girl's voice quivered, as if she was nervous. "The girls don't keep a shred of clothing on. The midnight show is especially rowdy, if you take my meaning."

The girl's discomfort rolled off her like heat from a blacksmith's fire. Working diligently on the mahogany, she cleared her throat and added, "Delilah's girls are the next street over. See Smith. He'll show you to the right one." She paused. "He's taking bids for the virgin, as well." She dove back into wiping the bar with a frenzy.

Logan froze. *Virgin?* Slowly, he reached out and stilled the girl's hand. He opened his mouth to ask about that, but the shame in her countenance abruptly changed his course. "What are you doing here?"

She wouldn't look at him. Or couldn't. "I found myself in a tough situation, mister. Delilah gave me a job. I just serve drinks and . . . and tell folks about her attractions."

"Attractions?" Logan released her, dropped his hand on his hip. "I can see you don't want to be a part of this. I can help you."

"I agreed to stay. I'm workin' off some food and rent." When she met his gaze, Logan saw the hint of anger in her tight lips and strained jaw. "Besides, why would you help me? *Because it's the right thing to do?*"

"Because Christ loves me, and He asked me to love my neighbor."

Tears suddenly sprang to her eyes. "Where were you a week ago?" Without another word, she moved to the other end of the bar and started combining low whiskey bottles.

And just like that, the door slammed shut. Logan knew he couldn't push too hard, but how his heart ached for this girl. She'd gotten herself into a deal with the devil. He only knew Delilah by reputation, but she was one mean wench. A degenerate. She'd put on some pretty debauched shows in her Abilene saloon, at least as best he could recall. He'd never walked in the door sober.

And in a few weeks, she would be—what—*auctioning off* a virgin . . . to the highest bidder?

God help us . . .

CHAPTER 10

*D*isturbed deep in his soul, Logan ambled out of the saloon and stood once more in the muck. Looking at his boots, he didn't miss the symbolism. Men trudged past him, lunch pails in their hands, suspicion and fear in their eyes. Some headed to the mine, some to their claims. He drummed his fingers on his thigh and wondered what made Delilah want to take a filthy, hardscrabble town like Defiance and turn it into a Barbary Coast. Why make something bad *worse*? Selling virgins? What kind of a person wanted to live like that?

A lost one.

The still, small Voice reverberated in his soul like a thunderclap. Regardless of what Logan thought about Delilah, if she died without knowing Christ, her choices would send her to hell.

He looked over his shoulder at Mary Jean, pouring a miner a glass of whiskey.

And who knows how many with her.

The urgency to fight washed over him, but so did the fear that he was outmatched and outgunned in this town. Was he still vulnerable to an old weakness? *God, why do You think I can go from settling livestock disputes between neighbors to fighting this kind of debauchery? I'm not ready for this.*

I can do all things through Christ Who strengthens me.

The scripture didn't comfort him—only because he was being ornery. He wanted to whine. He walked on, repeating the scripture slowly, savoring the words. "I can do all things through Christ Who strengthens me."

A man stumbled out of a tent and tumbled into Logan. He caught the big fella before he landed in the mud. "Whoa there, partner."

Sweaty, bleary-eyed, rich with the sweet, spicy scent of opium, the stranger swayed but nodded. Logan ground his teeth at the ceaseless depravity going on around him. He had the irrational urge to run and leave it all. Run back to his nice neighbors and amateur sinners back in Willow.

The man's eyes narrowed, as if he couldn't see clearly. Logan clutched his shoulders and wrestled him to a steady, standing position, aware he was balancing the man on one good leg. He recognized the stiffness in the other leg as an artificial limb. After a moment, Logan carefully released him. "You all right?"

The man wobbled precariously. Resigning himself, Logan grabbed the man's beefy shoulder. "Here, friend, let me help you get home."

The confusion left the drunk's face and he straightened up. He peered at Logan through wild, dark hair, then slapped his hand away. "I don't need your help."

Logan dipped his head and backed off. Reminding himself he was definitely not in Willow anymore, he extended his hand. "Good enough. But if you ever do, my friends call me Preacher."

The man's graying brows shot up. "A *preacher*? Or is that just some sort of nickname?"

"Well, it's both I reckon." Logan did not withdraw his hand until the man brusquely staggered past him. Undaunted that the friendly gesture had been rejected, Logan turned around. "What about you, friend? What do you go by?"

The man, big and wide like a redwood, paused, hiked his pants a little higher, and pivoted back around to Logan. It seemed he had regained some balance. "Wanted. In two states and one territory."

Logan bit back the fact that he could double those numbers. He had to try, though, to get past the ridiculously misplaced pride. "I'm sure you are. And you're certainly wanted at my church. I'll be preachin' this Sunday. Just come by the Broken Spoke. From now on it's the Cripple Creek Church."

The man guffawed, long and loud, a booming sound that even drowned out the thunder of hammers from Delilah's saloon and frightened a nearby mule. It brought a young Oriental girl out from the tent the man had just exited. A group of men passing by slowed to a stop, staring at the big man having a knee-slapping laugh. One of them wore a bandage on his arm. Logan recognized him from the ruckus over Two Spears. *Smith*.

Distracted, he didn't see the punch coming from his possible new congregant until it was in his face. He pulled back at the last second, but the hammer blow still sent him sprawling into the side of the tent. For a moment he was sure the man had pierced his jaw with a railroad spike, the pain was so intense.

His opponent's laughter died. "Preacher, they call me Big Jim Walker." He flexed his big, meaty fingers. "And the only way I'll come to church is if you knock me clean unconscious and set me in your front pew."

Logan rotated his sore jaw and straightened up, impressed with Big Jim's right cross. Amputees could be ornery, as so many felt they had to keep proving their manliness. Big Jim packed a wallop, but it was nothing to brag about. "Unconscious, huh? I can do that. But I believe you might enjoy the sermon more if you was to come voluntarily."

Big Jim's jaw went slack but a slight smile quickly curved his thick lips. "You knock me out, Preacher, I'll come to church. I'll sit in your front pew. I might even wear a tie."

The swelling crowd of men chuckled. The little Oriental girl held her breath. Smith leaned forward a hair. Why was he so interested?

Logan knew much was riding on this situation. Would it be worth it? Would these people understand and respect strength over simple words? By scrapping, could he convince them he was a changed man? He didn't see how. "I don't think a preacher should fight. Don't seem . . . befitting."

"You talk like a man who has a choice."

"Don't I?"

"No."

Logan rubbed his pounding jaw. He wasn't getting out of this. "A tie, huh? Well, I don't give much thought to how a man dresses, but I like your idea. Will you give me your word?"

"What?"

"Give me your word that if I land one punch, you'll come to church in a tie."

The crowd chuckled again, louder this time. Big Jim suddenly looked unsure. His glance darted around at the onlookers. Sanity came back quickly. With it, his swagger, and he shook hair out of his eyes. "No, that ain't exactly what I said."

"Ah, if I knock you out with one punch, you'll sit in my front pew, and you'll wear a tie?"

"With a fancy knot." Big Jim raised his fists.

Behind him, the man from the livery shook his head, as if he knew this would be a fast fight, although Logan couldn't tell who he was bettin' on. "You're not a welcher, are you?"

"Preacher, I ain't never welched on a bet in my life."

"They say there's a first time for everything."

"This ain't it."

The crowd had grown to a sufficient size to advertise the

outcome well. Logan took a breath, said a prayer, and raised his own fists. "You're sure I have to knock you out?"

In answer, Big Jim swung, his arm coming round like an unstoppable sledgehammer. Logan leaned back, let the fist whiz by, stepped in, and put everything he had into the uppercut. He clocked Big Jim Walker in the precise center of his chin.

Big Jim's expression never even changed, but he tumbled backward just like a California redwood: slow, forceful, stunning in the sheer magnificence of the fall. He hit the ground with a corpse-like thud.

The crowd stared at Big Jim lying in the dirt. Logan rubbed his knuckles. "I expect to see you all Sunday morning. Ten o'clock sharp. Drunk. Sober. Doesn't matter to me or the Lord. Just come."

He let that sink in. After all, he had been tighter than Dick's hatband when the Lord had found him at that tent revival in Denver. God was no respecter of whiskey, wine, or water. And Logan knew firsthand that the Lord's grip was stronger than the temptation of even the finest whiskey.

He marched off, the crowd's thunderstruck gaze burning into his back.

---

*R*ebecca didn't even have to look up from her notepad. She heard the door and almost instantly smelled the cloying perfume. In Defiance, only one kind of person smelled like that. She took a breath and turned to the woman striding toward her.

A tight, red satin dress, the wrong shade to go with her auburn hair, proved Rebecca's suspicions. Even if the low neckline hadn't spelled it out, the heavy rouge and red lips would have. What a shame. The woman was pretty. She didn't need the face paint.

"Good afternoon." The woman stuck out a red-gloved hand.

Rebecca rose and the two women shook. "Good afternoon. May I help you?"

"I'd like to take out an ad in your newspaper."

The thrill of running a business clashed with Rebecca's dread over just what this woman might want to advertise. "Um, all right." Rebecca retrieved the notepad and pencil from her desk. "The rate is one cent per word."

The woman's eyes glittered. "That seems more than fair." She turned and strode to the window. Watching the traffic, she adjusted her dress, actually tugging her shirtwaist lower. "Opening in two weeks . . . the newest saloon . . . stage . . ." she spoke slowly, "and sporting house . . . from Delilah Goodnight." She tossed a dismissive glance at Rebecca. "My name should be in all capitals." She paused for a moment then continued. "The Crystal Chandelier . . . live performances of audacious acts . . . girls of the highest quality . . . willing to fulfill . . . any desire."

Rebecca's hand moved slower and slower.

"Fresh Flowers . . . coming . . . Saturday nights only."

Rebecca slapped the pencil down, livid. "You expect me to advertise your . . . your . . ."

"Bawdy house?" Delilah turned around slowly. "Brothel?" She dropped a hand on her hip and sauntered over to Rebecca. "Honey, the place I'll be running . . . those words don't even. Come. Close. I'm going to make the Iron Horse look like a monastery."

Rebecca clenched her jaw, buying a moment to think before speaking. "It's closed. The other saloons—brothels—*were* on their way out. Defiance is becoming civilized. You can't open another place . . ."

"*Can* and *will*. You can take my money to advertise it, or I'll just do it the old-fashioned way. Parade it."

Rebecca shuddered to think what that meant, but she couldn't run an ad for this Crystal Chandelier. Her paper had standards. As did she. "I won't take your money."

"Fine." Delilah spun in a swirl of crimson silk and headed to the door. She reached for the doorknob, but spared Rebecca one last comment. "You newspaper people. Always so self-righteous when it suits you. I noticed you veiled your preacher's background. Well, I'll be sure to give you something to write about and you can tell the whole story."

Speechless, Rebecca merely stared as the woman let herself out and strolled down the street like a bored panther.

"Now there's a bonny lass. Who was that?"

Ian's Scottish burr sounded strange, dreamy almost, as he walked in carrying a ream of paper. He leaned his head to the left, watching Delilah. Rebecca scowled at him. "Another madam has moved into town."

Ian snapped his mouth shut. Yes, he'd been gawking and Rebecca wanted to throttle him. The gray in his thinning hair and thick beard belied her husband's wisdom, as had his leering. He quickly stepped over to her and took her hand. Grinning, he pulled it to his chest, hazel eyes stealing her heart all over again.

"Women like that, my lovely wife, are not worth the rouge they're painted with. Forgive me for staring? She was rather . . ." he cleared his throat, "uhh, shapely. A man of my age can appreciate beauty. And may I emphasize that *appreciation* is quite a different thing from lust."

Rebecca had to giggle, eager to let some of her anger drain away. "Appreciate away. Just don't touch."

"Tell me, what was she doin' here? Another dove looking for Charles?"

"Worse. She wanted to buy an ad. To advertise her new . . . brothel."

"I see." He rubbed his chin. "I was hoping the brothels would be closing, all of them."

Rebecca picked up her pencil again. "She knows our preacher. She accused me of lying about his . . . background."

Ian lifted a brow. "And this bothers ye because . . .?"

"Because she's right. When we started this paper we said we'd print the truth. No agendas, and, yet, in our first issue I tell a story in such a way as to hide certain facts."

He squeezed her hand. "I doubt it will be the last time, Rebecca, that we've to make such decisions. Can ye truly print the unvarnished truth? I don't think it's in a mon's nature."

"I thought it was in mine."

cIntyre peeled off his coat and folded it over his arm. The noonday sun was welcome if a little too warm. He stepped into the shade of the assayer's building and continued studying the progress on the hotel's construction.

A crew installed cedar shingles on the roof and one man stood on the balcony, painting the windows. The rhythm of hammers from the roofers and saws from carpenters inside barely rose above the clatter of street traffic. Sounds of progress. Another few weeks and the Trinity Inn would be ready for business once again.

Hopefully this time they could keep it safe. The image of the hotel in smoking ruins hit him hard, reminding him of the moment Ian had implied Naomi was dead, lost in the fire. A chill crept over him and he thought to chase it away by smoking a cheroot. He lit the cigar and stared at the match's flame for a moment, amazed at the changes in his life. In his town.

"McIntyre."

He tossed the match and greeted Logan with a nod. "Preacher. What can I do for you?"

A deep crease in the man's brow and taut expression said plenty. "What's the law like in this town?"

McIntyre exhaled a puff of smoke. "Pender Beckwith is a fine, brave marshal. I feel we are fortunate to have him. He has done quite a bit to rein in the town. Does that answer your question?"

"I'm not sure. How much policing does he do in Tent Town?"

"What are you after?"

"Of all the things that went on in the Iron Horse, did you have limits?"

Naked limbs entwined like snakes writhed in McIntyre's brain, and he pushed the image away. "Not many, to be honest." No sense sugarcoating it. Logan most likely remembered anyhow. "Where is this line of questioning going?"

"You know Delilah has a reputation for . . ."

"Debauchery even I wouldn't sink to."

"Yep. She's gonna be selling virgins."

"Aye, that's not all." Both men turned at Ian's voice. "Delilah came by the paper wanting to place an ad. Rebecca turned her away. The place this woman is opening is nothin' short of Nero's circus." He handed McIntyre a piece of paper. "Read that."

McIntyre scanned the note in Rebecca's handwriting. His disgust grew with each word. "Crystal Chandelier . . . live performances . . . audacious acts . . . fulfill any desire." The final sentence hit him hardest of all. "Fresh, sweet Flowers available Saturday nights only." He'd been tempted many times, but in the end had stayed away from inexperienced girls. He'd held on to at least a morsel of honor. Delilah's depravity sliced him to the core. He felt too much of a kinship with the woman, like inbred cousins.

Logan inched closer and lowered his voice. "She's taking bids now. It's a silent auction." He removed his hat and ran a hand through his sweaty, ash-blond hair. "We have to stop this."

McIntyre handed the note back to Ian and took a thoughtful puff on the cheroot. He lamented the loss of information that used to stream regularly into the Iron Horse. He had not known about this circus and had to learn of it from Rebecca and Ian, of all people.

What kind of live acts? He shuddered to think. Delilah had a reputation for purposely shocking patrons and appealing to their most base, most degenerate lusts. Her saloons had been called Gates to Hell.

And men had stormed them eagerly.

Auctioning virgins was a new low, however, even for her. She could go lower, he knew. Given the chance, she would, and gladly take Defiance with her. Those live shows were her calling card and they had no boundaries.

The old McIntyre wouldn't have had any qualms about strong-arming Delilah right out of town, or taking The Crystal Chandelier in a crooked poker game. This new McIntyre had to find a different path.

"Preacher, let's you and me go see Beckwith. Ian, do you think you could find Corky? Ask him to wait for me at the town hall."

---

*M*cIntyre leaned against the doorway of the marshal's office, dreading the inevitable explanation. He could see the doom-and-gloom in the man's taut, bony face.

"The problem we have, Preacher, is there are no books to begin with. Much less laws on them."

Marshal Pender Beckwith settled his aged frame into his office chair and raised his feet to his desk. A tough-as-rawhide lawman, he had the face and disposition to complement the reputation. His chiseled, lean cheeks sucked in on a stogie. He exhaled, blandly studying McIntyre and Logan through the smoky haze, as if waiting for them to come up with a solution.

Logan scratched his head. "You mean there are no decency laws?"

"I mean until Defiance is officially incorporated and at least an interim town council seated, there are no laws. McIntyre pays my salary and I keep the peace. Penalties are based on what I've had firsthand experience with, or what McIntyre deems appropriate." He sent McIntyre a sideways glance. "And neither McIntyre nor I have much in the way of experience with enforcing decency laws."

Logan wilted and took a seat in front of the marshal's desk. McIntyre rubbed his neck, attempting to loosen some tension, and shame. "Ian and I are working on the incorporation paper-work and bylaws. We have to file those before we can have any kind of an election."

"I'm sure there are some *state* decency laws," Beckwith motioned with his cigar. "I can wire to Denver and inquire of the attorney general. But, generally speaking, what goes on in Tent Town is on my back burner, unless violence is involved."

"In the meantime, she's going to auction off a young girl like she's a prime steer." Agitated, Logan rose again and slapped his hat against his leg, raising a small dust cloud. "I can't let that happen." He pleaded silently with Beckwith, who simply stared back, his face expressionless. Logan shifted to McIntyre. "I can't let that happen."

CHAPTER 11

M cIntyre waved at Corky through the window. The short, pudgy man chatting inside with Rebecca nodded curtly at her and hurried out to the street.

"Yes sir. Mr. Donoghue said you wanted to see me."

"Let's take a walk." He and Corky ambled down the busy way, boards squeaking beneath them, their heels thumping on the wood. "You spend much time in Tent Town, Corky?"

"Well, since you closed the Iron Horse, I'm there more than I used to be. Only now . . ." he trailed off, as if he might be speaking out of turn.

"Go on. What?"

"Well, that woman Delilah, she's closed the other saloons, I guess you know that." He shoved his hands into his pockets and obligingly turned sideways between a couple of miners carrying pickaxes. "I used to get my drinks for free from the Vaticelli brothers 'cause I chopped wood for 'em. No deals like that now." Agitated, he waved his finger in McIntyre's face, "And the girls are charging more." Chagrined, Corky ducked his head in apology, and backed off. "Sorry."

McIntyre scratched his beard and contemplated just what questions he had. "Let's talk about Delilah. What is she getting into over there? I have heard rumors . . ."

Corky wrinkled his nose as if the stench of a dead animal had filled his nostrils. "She's a bad one, Mr. McIntyre. I mean, I ain't no saint or anything. That's obvious, but there were things your girls wouldn't do. Delilah's gals," he shook his head, "they're puttin' on shows." The man tugged at the buttons at his collar, as if uncomfortable with this explanation. "If men don't have the money for a poke, the girls will . . . well, gather up an audience, and, ummm, *perform*, you could say," his voice hit a higher pitch, as if he couldn't believe what he was saying, "with each other, and I don't mean dancing or singing."

"I see." McIntyre's stomach turned over. *No boundaries.*

"I'm just a simple man, Mr. McIntyre. To my way of thinkin', a visit to a whore should mean *me* visiting *them* in *private*. Delilah's got crazy stuff goin' on."

"And I imagine it will only be worse once her saloon with that theater is open." Now McIntyre felt a twinge of concern for Corky. He had no business asking the man to inject himself in the filth over there. On the other hand, an innocent woman was in danger. Or was it *women*? "Do you know about the auction?"

Corky took a long moment before answering. "Yes sir. Pretty darn despicable, in my opinion."

"Agreed, and I'll stop it if I can figure a way. Do you know who the girl is?"

"Girls. Once it gets started, a different one every Saturday. And no sir—" The loud jangle of a wagon almost drowned out Corky's words. "That's bein' kept secret."

Men, gathered near their horses, whooped and hollered as the wagon passed. McIntyre followed their gazes and saw it was transporting several young Oriental girls. Their downturned mouths and lowered heads filled him with guilt as they snuck fearful glances at the rowdy men. McIntyre knew where these girls, these victims, were headed. Could they be items for the auction as well?

Watching the traffic fill in behind them, he said, "If you hear anything about that, or anything else that could be of interest to me, will you let me know?" When Corky didn't answer right away, McIntyre added, "I'll make sure it is worth your time."

Corky looked up at him with a mixture of confusion and caution. "I—I heard you got religion. And I know you got married."

His concern was clear, and it wouldn't be the last time someone expressed it. Did Charles McIntyre have enough darkness left in him to control Defiance? Was he in any position to crack the whip over this town?

Was that his job anymore?

"You make it sound as if I am dead and buried, Corky. I would remind you that some of the most dangerous men in the world have been men of faith . . . with wives."

The answer seemed to satisfy the man. He nodded. "I'll keep my ears open."

McIntyre, however, discovered the answer left a bad taste in his mouth, as if it had smacked too much of denial. Of who he was, and what kind of man he wanted to be.

---

*L*ight from the lamp overhead flickered on the new wood walls of Cripple Creek Church. Grinning like a giddy fool, Logan grasped the sides of the freshly sanded pulpit, built just for him, and inhaled the scent of pine, pitch, and . . . beer and urine. Even in here he could smell Tent Town and its sewer.

His gaze wandered to the windows and out into the dark.

Lanterns, points of light, flowed, bobbed, and weaved in the inky blackness. He could hear the men marching by, laughing as they passed the church.

A soft thud drew his eyes to the door. He wondered if someone was approaching and paused. No one knocked, and after a moment he heard another thud, followed by fading laughter. The hee-hawing of men mocking God.

He used to be one of those scoffers. In fact, he had a vague memory of violently disrupting a tent revival some years back. *In Texas, maybe?*

He recalled stumbling drunkenly over several pews, the terrified screams of outraged women piercing his skull. A tough, hard-bitten circuit preacher had promptly tossed Logan out on his ear.

He wondered what that man would do about Delilah and her auction.

Drag her by the hair to the edge of town and toss her into the dirt? An appealing picture, but Logan knew that was the wrong approach. Yet he had no idea what the right approach was.

He counted the sixteen empty pews in front of him, eight on each side, with a mix of exhilaration and terror. Could he reach this town? Delilah?

He'd been out and about. Shook hands. Slapped men on their backs. Gone down to the cribs and introduced himself to the ladies, to convince them he was a friend.

More often than not he saw confusion, disdain, but mostly fear in their faces. They knew who he was . . . and they didn't believe he had changed. Most likely, they believed he would fail them. How many preachers had they seen wallowing in the gutters, Bibles and bottles in hand, mumbling scriptures? Or worse, drinking, swearing, *and* consorting with wicked women while condemning such behavior from the pulpit.

He had known such men.

He feared becoming one of them.

"Oh, Lord," he whispered, "What am I doing here?"

Riddled with insecurity, he walked over to the front pew and picked up his Bible. A large, black leather-bound book, it had belonged to the first pastor of the church back in Willow. He opened it, praying God had a Word for him. He needed to know he was not alone in Defiance.

The verse his eyes fell on offered no comfort.

For unto you it is given on the behalf of Christ, not only to believe on Him, but also to suffer for His sake . . .

———

"*I* am not sure Logan thought this out well," Charles said, sliding a chair out.

Part of Naomi wanted to agree. As he and Two Spears settled at their small kitchen table, she set the fried deer steaks in front of her two men. "Yes, I can certainly see the problems with the location." She returned to the stove for the gravy and biscuits. "I'd just as soon never walk through that end of town ever again." She set the items on the table and pushed a fork closer to Two Spears, who was reaching for a steak as he still preferred eating with his hands. "Especially with a child in tow."

"Exactly." Charles unbuttoned his twill vest and draped it over the chair. "He should have thought of this."

"Maybe he did." Naomi sat down, the three bowed their heads, and she said grace softly and with much gratitude. Food started passing and she took a steak for her plate. "Jesus said it was the sick who needed a physician. Tent Town is sure in need of a spiritual doctor. And if he'd put his church on or near Main Street, would anyone from Tent Town come?"

Charles squirmed a little. "Are you saying you think we should go to church there?"

She was passing the mashed potatoes to him and stopped. Their eyes locked. "Are you saying we shouldn't?"

"No." He took the bowl and plopped some potatoes onto his plate. "I'm not quite sure what I think."

"We can't *not* go, Charles." Naomi was well aware Two Spears was hanging on their every word and she tried to keep any frustration from her voice. "Logan needs our support." She put food on the boy's plate as she reasoned aloud. "If no one comes tomorrow, he'll be sitting there alone."

"Ian and Rebecca are going."

Naomi sighed. It felt wrong to miss services, there or anywhere. Sometimes appearances did matter. "If we don't go tomorrow, folks in Tent Town will figure we think we're too good for that church. That we don't want to go church with . . . them."

"I *don't* want to go to church with them."

His bluntness surprised her, but not his sentiment.

"Naomi, I do not ever want to step foot in Tent Town again. How do you reconcile loving your neighbor while staying away from corrupting influences?"

"You think they'd corrupt you?" Fear wiggled in her gut. The image of Charles kissing Amaryllis would haunt her until the day she died. She believed him when he said nothing like that would ever happen again. So . . . "What exactly are you afraid of?"

He stared at his steak, fork in one hand, knife in the other. "I think we should talk about this later."

Naomi smiled weakly and looked at Two Spears. He had stabbed the steak, but couldn't quite seem to figure out how to use the knife to cut it. She waited a moment, but Charles, who was closer, was oblivious to the boy. She laid her napkin on the table and moved to Two Spears's side.

"You're doing much better. But remember," she took his hands and repositioned them, pressing the blade of the knife into the meat and up against the fork, "press the blade here and *saw*." She pulled the knife back and forth a few times, her hands covering the boy's. A moment later she released him, and he cut his own piece of meat.

He raised the utensil with the impaled bite and studied it suspiciously. "I do not understand why you use a spoon, a fork, or a knife for everything when hands work better."

Naomi chuckled and sat down again. "Well, hands do work better, but utensils keep our hands cleaner, and we can eat hotter food."

The boy scrunched up his lips and frowned in contemplation. "Yes, that might be good."

After dinner, Naomi and Two Spears sat in the glow of the fire, playing marbles. At first he was stiff, withdrawn even, but the more he played the more he liked the game. Having a natural aptitude helped. After a particularly successful shot that sent marbles scattering, Naomi was surprised to see the boy look up at Charles. His father had his head down at his desk, writing furiously and flipping through papers.

Oblivious. He might as well be alone.

Two Spears did not look up again.

Something was on her husband's mind and Naomi determined to find out what it was. She helped Two Spears to bed and then went in search of her brooding Heathcliff.

She followed the smell of a spicy cigarillo and found him on the back porch, leaning on a post, staring out at their valley. Bathed in silvery moonlight, a wide, rolling expanse of grass unfolded before them, two miles long. The Animas River meandered through the heart of it, a stone's throw from where they were standing. Jagged snowcapped peaks hemmed them in on all four sides.

Naomi loved it. She felt safe and secure here, as if the mountains were guardians. He had put his waistcoat back on and she slid an arm inside it, around his waist, seeking his warmth. Obligingly, he pulled her into a firm embrace.

"I don't know why we call this the back porch," she said. Her head on his shoulder, arms around his steely waist, she scanned the star-studded sky and sublime, silver valley. "*This* is where the view is. I must stop ten times a day to stare at it."

"And I will appreciate it even more when our cattle are milling about down there, getting fat on that fine grass."

Naomi closed her eyes and laid a hand on his chest. Through the white cotton, she could feel his heartbeat. Steady and strong.

He kissed the top of her head, let his lips linger then rested his cheek against her hair. "Your Ladyship, have I told you lately . . .?"

When he didn't finish, she looked up, puzzled. He was staring at her with the kind of passion and tenderness that glowed in the dark. She trailed a finger along his jaw, loving the feel of his beard. "Have you told me what?"

"Something romantic and foolish?"

"Not yet. Perhaps if you weren't so preoccupied, you could think of something."

His expression changed, hardened a little, and he went back to his valley.

"What's wrong?" A long silence passed. The longer it went on, the more Naomi wondered if Charles was hiding something. "What don't you want to tell me?"

"It's not *what* I don't want to tell you. I don't know *how* to express it."

She pulled back a little. "Try. You've been brooding so much lately; you're hesitant to go to church tomorrow; you're afraid of what's happening to the town. None of this sounds like you."

He raised his chin and took a deep breath. "I am . . . uneasy."

Naomi frowned. Somehow that was supposed to make perfect sense, but it didn't, not to her. "I'm sorry . . . I don't . . ."

"Defiance. The pendulum had begun swinging to the town being more civilized. I fear it is about to swing back, worse than before."

"And while that is not good, you're afraid of . . . what specifically?"

"Things are different now, Naomi. I have a wife. I have a son."

He looked at her then, eyes intense and grave. "When Tom Hawthorn had you in his grip, I have never come so close to killing a man without completing the task. *You* saved his life. I made a choice for you I wouldn't have even considered before."

Naomi touched her throat, recalling the drunken bully's attempt to strangle her. And the terrifying, soulless man Charles became in that instant.

She shifted in front of him and clutched his shoulders. "You didn't kill that no-good wretch. You shamed him publicly. And you didn't murder One-Who-Cries, even after everything he put us through. You *gave* him a chance not to fight. I don't understand what's got you so worried now."

He drummed his fingers on her ribs. "I feel like the town is slipping away. If I can't control it, I can't protect you and Two Spears."

That explained a lot, and she actually felt some relief. "I was afraid you were withdrawing from us. That you . . . regretted Two Spears being here so much you were looking for ways to avoid him . . . and me."

He hugged her close again. "No, and I am sorry I gave you that impression. It's quite the opposite."

She finally understood the conflict raging within him. "Charles, you have a battle on your hands, and it's one I've fought before. At some point we have to come to terms with the fact that we're not in control of anything, no matter how much we like to pretend we are. This town, my safety, our future—it's all in God's hands."

"Then what am I good for? As a husband, as a father? As a businessman in this community?"

"Do you remember when we first met you asked me if I was familiar with Dante?"

He chuckled. "Yes. I said I would prefer to rule in hell rather than serve in heaven."

"You wanted to rule. You still want to rule. You want to do

things your way. It's time to figure out how to be a servant and do things God's way."

She could see the unhappy crease in his forehead, and planted her index finger in the middle of it. "Yes, I'm talking to you, Charles McIntyre." She slid her hand to his cheek. "Serving God doesn't mean you turn into a doormat. Serving God will make you a better, wiser leader."

A smile twitched on his lips. He hesitated a moment, then kissed her, kissed her again. The third time she grabbed his cheeks and held him. The deeper kiss ignited a spark of passion between them that flooded Naomi's body with heat. "I love you," she whispered.

"More than life itself," he whispered back, dragging his lips down her throat. "I awake every morning amazed at how fortunate I am . . . and I'm sorry my poor choices keep haunting you."

She knew he was referring to Two Spears, and tilted his chin up. "Would you prefer that he still be living on that reservation? Hungry? In poverty? At least as your son, yes, even as a half-breed, God has given him a better chance in life."

"If I don't foul him up."

"You won't."

"My father was not a good role model, as I have said before."

"You have something your father never did."

"And what is that?"

"Jesus."

He conceded the point with a slight nod.

"That boy is your son for a reason. There are no accidents, Charles. No coincidences."

"Only the Hand of God?"

She smiled, remembering the time she'd said those words to *him*, during a poker game. They had played for ownership of the hotel, and Naomi had won. "Yes. Only the Hand of God."

"Can you love him, Naomi? Like your own?"

She had wanted children all her life and hadn't conceived with

John. What if she couldn't have children? What if she could? She pictured Two Spears's dark eyes, and the way they filled with joy over a horse race. Or the age-old wisdom he spouted more readily than a preacher's sermons. Oh, the answer was so easy. She smiled up at her husband. "I think I loved him the moment I saw him. How could I not?"

CHAPTER 12

*H*annah quietly closed the door on the sleeping patient, careful not to spill the bloody bandages in the bowl on her hip. The usual procedure was to burn such items, but Doc hadn't started a fire today. A lovely July afternoon, she could hardly believe summer was upon them. The last year had gone by in a blur.

She quickly washed her hands with alcohol then peeked into the second examination room to check on Little Billy. She gasped when she saw him not napping on the pallet on the floor, but standing at the end of the bed. He had pulled himself up using the footboard, and beamed at his mother, quite proud of the accomplishment.

Gurgling and bouncing, he waved at Hannah, a little tuft of downy blond hair dancing as he moved. Her heart exploded with love. "Oh, my goodness, look at you, little man! You're standing up!"

She rushed to him and swung her little peach into her arms. She hugged him tight and kissed the top of his head. "Oh, Momma is so proud of you." She made silly noises as she kissed him all over his face. He giggled and kicked and whipped her braid around.

"Well, I can see you two haven't missed me."

Hannah spun. Billy leaned against the doorjamb, bowler in hand, rakish smile on his face and silver-blond hair combed neatly to the side.

"Dada!" Little Billy kicked and reached for his father. Hannah and Billy both gasped.

"I told you he wouldn't forget you." Elation surged through Hannah. She rushed Little Billy over to his father and blinked back tears.

Billy's eyes glistened and he took his son in his arms. "Yeah, he didn't."

"It'd take longer than two weeks." Fighting a lump in her throat, Hannah stepped back to give the two a moment. Watching them together, she wondered how she could ever have second thoughts about her future with the father of her child. Well, 'second thoughts' wasn't even the right phrase, really. Just . . . a longing to have her cake and eat it too. Her family *and* nursing.

Billy closed his eyes and hugged his son. "I hate myself for having missed any time with him and you." He took a breath, seemed to sniff away some overwhelming emotion, and commenced to dancing with his son. "My boy, my boy." He rocked and dipped joyously with Little Billy in his arms, working his way over to Hannah. He smacked a quick kiss on her cheek and winked. "I've missed my family."

"And we missed you."

He stopped. "Then when are we going to make it official?"

She ran a hand through his neatly combed silvery blond hair, purposely tousling it, and then let her fingers linger on his cheek. "It just so happens, in your absence Defiance gained a full-time preacher."

Billy backed up, brows raised. "Really? Where did he come from?"

"Oh, boy, can I tell you some stories about him."

Billy slipped an arm around her and drew her next to their son. "Save 'em for dinner tonight." He kissed her again and Little Billy, watching intently, giggled. Billy kissed him too. "Can I take him with me? I assume the store is closed."

Though he'd held no reprimand in his voice, Hannah frowned and stepped back. "Doc had an emergency, and Roy Jenkins came to the store, all cut up and bleeding everywhere. What was I supposed—"

"It's all right, Hannah." Billy tapped her on the chin. "It's all right. I'll see you later. Either at the store or back at the Iron Horse."

"We're trying not to call it that anymore."

"Then what should I call it?"

"How about home?"

---

*L*ogan set the Bible on the pulpit, hesitated, then removed his cartridge belt and holster and set them on the table behind him. He wouldn't wear it while preaching, but it wouldn't be far away. He wasn't worried about protecting himself as much as he was the folks who might come today to hear his sermon. In more than a few places in the West, preachers got shot at pretty regularly. He didn't figure Defiance would be any kinder.

Licking his lips, he touched his black string tie, hoping it was straight, and marched to the front door. Reaching for the knob, he stopped short. A whiff of something putrid assailed his nostrils and he drew back. The front of his church smelled like an outhouse. Pressing the back of his hand to his nose, he slowly pushed the door open.

The early morning sun beat down on the stoop, but he didn't see anything amiss. Oh, but the stench was overwhelming out here. Fighting a gag reflex, he stepped out and took in the full view of the church entrance.

Brown clumps covered the door. Someone had peppered it, top to bottom, with feces. Human or otherwise, he couldn't tell. Oh, but it smelled worse than any dog scat he'd ever stepped in.

Exhaling slowly, he noticed the tittering and chuckling going on behind him. Humiliation and fury washed over him like bad whiskey. Cheeks flaming, he wheeled on the small crowd, a mix of miners and prostitutes, even a few children. They watched him expectantly, their faces masks of mockery, but the fear was there and they would run if things changed.

Logan's fury grew, unfurling in his heart like a writhing, angry dragon. He ground his teeth and tried to think, pray. He found himself instead wishing for a lightning bolt from Heaven. Reflexively, his hand went to rest on the butt of his gun, but touched only air. An audible gasp passed through the meager crowd, their expressions betraying their concern. They expected violence from him, gun or no gun. The children gasped and ran. Adults started backing away.

Their distress loosened something in Logan. Behind the terror in their eyes, he saw the pain, the emptiness . . . and his anger drained away. He had a chance to show them he had changed. How Christ had changed him.

"Church is gonna start a little late today." Astonished he could sound so calm, he slipped back inside and marched to the pulpit. He grabbed it with one hand, but it couldn't stop him from going to his knees.

Anger and humiliation slammed into him and his knees buckled. His throat tightened with the emotion of it all and he hammered his fist on the floor.

How, God, how am I supposed to get through to these people? They're just lookin' for a fight.

Then don't give them one.

I don't have the control. I don't have the patience. I don't have the love to do this.

But I do.

Logan fell back on his calves and looked up at the ceiling. At a loss, he covered his face with his hands and sagged, so tired he felt like he could melt right into the cracks between the boards.

My grace is sufficient for thee.

Logan wanted to argue but a sound at the front door twisted him around. He had distinctly heard water, a huge splash of it. And another. Shadows moved, evidenced by the flashing light around the doorframe. Another splash and this time water leaked beneath door, creeping into the sanctuary.

Slowly, the door opened and Mary Jean peered in, tilting her head away from the feces. She blinked against the dim light as Logan rose to greet her. She ducked her head and spoke to the floor, perhaps embarrassed she had caught him on his knees. "We brought some water and scrub brushes, Preacher. We'll help you clean your door."

Logan had no words. He could barely believe anyone had come to help. Much less her. "We?" he finally managed.

The door opened all the way to reveal Big Jim Walker, his barrel-chest covered in a sheepskin vest that added to his impressive girth. And he wore a black silk tie.

Frowning, he rattled the empty bucket in his hand. "Sorry I didn't see who did it, but I'll find out."

Logan climbed to his feet. "No." The old Logan sure wanted to find the man responsible. He wanted to throw him on the ground and kick him until the scoundrel's ribs shattered. Every. Last. One.

The new Logan, who stood in this church with two unbelievers, wanted to show them how a real man of God handled adversity. It wouldn't be easy. The anger didn't want to let go.

He rolled a shoulder and shook his head. "Let's just clean it up." He trudged over and took the bucket from the big man's hand. "Thank you."

"I ain't a church-going man, Preacher. I'm here because I don't welch on a bet. I'm cleanin' up because I hate a coward." He wagged a thumb at the door. "This was cowardly. I find out who done it, I'll drag him here for a sermon. Then beat him with this." He knocked on his thigh, and the wooden sound dispelled any doubts Logan might have had about Big Jim being an amputee.

Still, he could appreciate the humor the image dredged up and let a smile slip. "Well, uh, I appreciate . . . your desire for justice." He tugged on his ear, pondering the possibilities. "Let's hope you don't have to lose a limb to get it."

Big Jim chuckled, snorted, and then erupted into booming laughter. He slapped Logan in the ribs. "That's a good one, Preacher."

CHAPTER 13

Sunday morning a chill hung in the air. Mornings in the Rockies. Naomi pulled her wrap tighter as she climbed up into the wagon, her spirit light and breezy today. She smiled broadly at Two Spears and Charles as they settled in. Her grin caught Charles off guard.

He raised a suspicious brow. "You look like the cat that ate the canary."

"I'm just happy." She lightly ruffled Two Spears's hair, earning a frown. "My family is going to church with me."

Charles didn't respond. His wary expression melted into concern as he popped the reins.

"We had a church on the reservation."

Intrigued, Naomi inclined her head to the boy. "You did? Did you ever go?

Two Spears studied a broken fingernail with great interest. "He wanted to cut my hair, so I did not go back. Is your preacher going to want to cut my hair?"

Naomi didn't know if she was horrified or amused. She shifted to Charles, hoping for an explanation.

"Indoctrination." He practically spat the word. "I met an army officer last year. He was headed to the White River Reservation to discuss sending the Indian children off to boarding schools back East." He didn't seem to care if his disdain was evident. "He had a theory he called 'Kill the Indian and Save the Man.' Remove them from their culture and they would naturally assimilate into White culture."

Naomi put her arm around Two Spears, surprised at the fierce sense of protection that roared to life in her. "You will not have to cut your hair, Two Spears. Not for a preacher. Not for anyone."

*T*he ride to church was mostly uneventful. When their buggy rolled into Tent Town, men stared, especially at Two Spears, but hard looks from Charles had them backing down in quick order. A woman in nothing but a camisole and bloomers hung on a man in a lewd way. Naomi quickly distracted Two Spears with questions about life on the reservation, his mother, and his grandfather, and even an intense examination of that broken fingernail.

Finally, they pulled up in front of the church. Naomi was relieved to see Ian and Rebecca, as well as Emilio, Mollie, Hannah, Billy, and Little Billy, but their grim expressions squashed her spirits. She noticed a young lady sweeping water off the stoop. The whole front entrance was wet, as was the door. A man the size of a grizzly bear, wearing a sheepskin vest, tossed a brush into a wooden bucket and wiped his hands on his pants. Logan emptied a bucket of water on the steps, carefully washing off some grime.

"What's happened?" Charles asked, locking the brake.

"Why dunna we send the ladies inside," Ian suggested from the stoop, motioning to the door. "And the lad. We gents need to talk for a moment."

Naomi and Two Spears stepped down and joined her sisters at the bottom of the steps.

"I'll be right in, ladies," Logan took the broom from the young woman, a pretty girl of about twenty or so, and motioned to the entrance.

The girl moved slowly up the steps. Naomi sent questioning glances at her sisters and Mollie as they followed, but they shrugged or shook their heads. Seeing as how this was church, and strangers were certainly welcome, Naomi approached the young lady inside the doorway. "I don't think we've met. I'm Naomi Mil—sorry, McIntyre now. I haven't been married long."

The young girl smiled, weariness evident in her vivid green eyes. "I'm Mary Jean."

"It's nice to meet you. This is my son, Two Spears."

To her credit, the young lady did not look surprised or offended. Instead, she smiled sweetly and shook his hand. The rest of the girls introduced themselves as well. Naomi tried to pay attention to the pleasantries being exchanged amongst the ladies, but outside the men were talking in hushed whispers. She discreetly pulled away from the group and tried to catch some of the conversation. The words *coward*, *scat*, and *covered* didn't enlighten her at all.

The grim look on Charles's face didn't make her feel any better, either.

The men filtered in and escorted the ladies to their seats. Naomi waited a moment for Charles to look at her, to say something, but his attention was riveted on Logan walking to his pulpit.

The big man in the sheepskin vest sat in the back row, with Mary Jean, but several inches away. Both outsiders, but not together. Or at least Naomi sensed they didn't make a habit of coming to church. Suddenly the big man rose, snatched off his ragged black hat, and limped forward to the empty front pew.

"Told you I don't welch on my bets."

The preacher grinned and nodded at the man. "I see that." Logan then turned his gaze on his little congregation. "I had a sermon in mind, something a little more introductory, you could say, but I see now that's too simple." He huffed a breath and laid the Bible down again. He stepped out from behind the pulpit and laced his fingers together like a contrite child. "I'd like to start this morning, instead, by asking forgiveness, from you and from God." Stillness fell over the room. "I didn't want to come to Defiance. I was pastoring a church back in Willow, Kansas. A little church full of folks with big hearts. And, honestly, what I'd consider little sins. Biggest problem I fought there was gossip."

The congregation chuckled softly.

"Since I've been in Defiance, I've been in a fistfight," he cut his eyes at the man in the front pew, "I've stopped a beating, possibly worse," his eyes landed on Two Spears. "I've seen sin and debauchery and heard of horrific activities going on here that would make the residents of Sodom blush. And just this morning, the church was vandalized."

The women in the room gasped and their mouths fell open. Mary Jean, Naomi noted, did not look in the least surprised.

"Anger and disgust have filled my heart more than once since coming back to Defiance," Logan continued. "Especially today. I wanted to curse this town. I wanted to leave and never look back. I thought after what I found outside my door this morning, there was not one decent soul on this side of Main Street. I beg your forgiveness. The fact that I was wrong allows me to stand before you today . . . humbled . . . and encouraged."

Naomi understood well. Her first several months in Defiance, she had wanted to scream at God every day for stranding her in this vile place. She looked around the room now, at this tiny congregation, and her throat tightened. What a miracle He had wrought. A husband, a son, family, and friends.

Things had even worked out for Hannah.

The strange expression on Billy's face abruptly changed the

direction of Naomi's musings. Staring intently at Logan, brow deeply grooved, Billy squinted as if he was trying to identify what species the new preacher was. He cocked his head to one side, then slowly to the other, then shook his head and seemed to go back to merely listening to the sermon.

"I reckon, then, I'll talk about something none of us probably want to hear," Logan went on. "Suffering for Christ."

That snatched Naomi's attention back to the sermon. She wondered if the suffering was over . . .

Or just beginning.

"Two Spears, it's all right if you'd like to get a couple of peppermint sticks." Naomi winked at Hannah across the mercantile counter as the boy approached the jars of candy. "I think *I'll* take a couple of pieces of licorice myself."

Hannah finished tying on her apron then took the lid off the peppermints. "Take an extra piece as a present from me."

Two Spears stared longingly at the candy and Naomi held her breath, waiting. Slowly, he reached inside the jar and withdrew three red-and-white sticks of the sweet treat. He then gave Hannah a tiny smile. To Naomi, it felt as though the sun had suddenly emerged after a month of cloudy days.

A little progress. Thank You, Lord.

Hannah came back to her end of the counter, beating down a smile. "He's settling in."

"Yes. I think so."

"We got a letter from little Terri. She's settling in fine with her aunt."

"Oh, I'm so relieved to hear that."

The young girl had been captured by One-Who-Cries after he brutally murdered her family. Though Naomi or Rebecca or even Hannah would have adopted her, she had wanted to go to her aunt in Nebraska. Naomi prayed she would be able to put the terrible episode behind her and live life to its fullest.

Hannah eyed the list in Naomi's hand and reached for it. "Want me to get those?"

"No, it's just a few things. Really more of an excuse to come into town. It's like a bee-hive out at the house."

"Don't you mean ranch?"

"I don't know if it's officially a ranch till the cattle show up, but the barn is nearly done. Everything's coming together. How about you? How is Doc doing? Is he ready to retire and turn over his practice to you?"

Hannah snorted. "Hardly. I have so much to learn it's daunting. And while Billy is busy with the hotel, I'm stuck running the store."

Raised voices outside on the boardwalk drew their attention to the window. A beautiful woman in a striking azure dress stopped to address a group of men. Flaunting bare shoulders and playing at being coquettish, she gave them each a paper. They read it and their faces lit up like torches, evidently pleased with some delightful news. Grinning like bears in salmon season, they tipped their hats and left the woman, one gawking man being snatched away by the others.

The woman peered inside the mercantile, saw Hannah and Naomi staring, and made a beeline for the door. Naomi didn't miss the smirk on her face.

Hannah gasped softly. "Shoot, that's gotta be Delilah." She sounded utterly scandalized. "Rebecca was telling me about her. She's going to open—"

She bit off her explanation as Delilah pushed open the door. The woman surveyed the empty store with the bored expression of a well-fed mountain lion. She ended her search with Naomi. Holding her gaze, she breezed over to the counter. Pretty through the window, the woman was stunning up close. High cheekbones, pouty lips, an hourglass figure, and luxuriously thick auburn hair piled high made Naomi feel as bland as an old tintype.

Delilah immediately reminded Naomi of a similar meeting with several of Charles's *Flowers* here in this very store.

The meeting hadn't gone well.

But things had changed in the last year. People had changed. Naomi determined to remember who she was in Christ and be a better reflection of Him. Swallowing her pride, she extended her hand to the woman. "Good afternoon." She heard Hannah gasp. "I'm Naomi McIntyre, and this is my sister, Hannah Frink."

Delilah's eyes widened, then that smirk returned. She glanced at the hand. "Are you mocking me?"

"No." Naomi raised her chin. "Just trying to be friendly."

"Adorable." Delilah shook Naomi's hand, but her grip was slight and perfunctory. "Here." She passed a hand-written flyer to Naomi. "This is my new business. Why don't you help me spread the word?"

Naomi scanned the advertisement. Twice. The first time she thought she must be mistaken. But with the second reading, her stomach twisted into an angry knot. "I don't even know what to say to this."

"You don't have to say anything. Pass the flyer to someone who might enjoy my parlor. Or visit us yourself. I'm sure we could entertain you."

Slowly, so Delilah didn't miss the point, Naomi carefully wadded up the flyer and squeezed it into a little ball. Fighting to keep from shoving the paper right between the woman's painted lips, she pushed the flyer into her sternum instead. "I don't know anyone that deranged."

Delilah's face picked up some ugly edges. She plucked the wrinkled flyer from Naomi's hand. "That's doubtful. Still, I won't waste this on you." She turned on her heel, her huge bustle swishing like a live animal. She took a few steps, but stopped short when she spotted Two Spears. "My, look at the handsome little half-breed." She bent down to him. "I could use a boy like you to empty our chamber pots. That's all you nasty little savages are good for."

Growling, Naomi lunged for Delilah, imagining her hands around the woman's throat, but Hannah stretched across the counter and held her back. "No, Naomi!"

Naomi strained against Hannah, nearly dragging her over the counter. Delilah turned and grinned with wicked amusement. "Oh, is he yours?"

"Yes, he's my son."

"Too good to advertise my place, but you'll sleep with a filthy redskin?" The grin melted away. "Don't preach to me."

Naomi broke Hannah's grip from her shoulder. Charging up to Delilah, she poked her hard in the breastbone. "Don't ever call my son that again."

Even as she tried to stare down Delilah, Naomi felt the pangs of conviction. She'd let that temper run away with her again. Delilah ran her tongue over her teeth, kissed the air between them, and sashayed out of the store.

When the door closed behind Delilah, Naomi squeezed her eyes shut and tried to tamp down an explosion of fury warring in her chest. She squeezed her hands into tight fists and ground her teeth together to keep from raging like a wounded bull.

Oh, Lord, forgive my temper, but she cannot talk that way about Two Spears.

She heard a soft shuffle beside her and a small warm hand slipped around her forearm. She gazed down into the boy's dark eyes, eyes filled for the first time with something other than fear, suspicion, or anger.

Naomi would have called it hope.

CHAPTER 14

"Well, Johnny Reb, it's been a long time."

The gravelly voice of a ghost from his past brought McIntyre's head up from the mine report. Lane Chandler stood in the doorway, gangly body leaning on the doorpost, worn cowboy hat tilted back at a hard angle, unkempt blond hair resting on his shoulders. A sideways grin spread and lit the man's tanned face like the sun coming out from a cloud.

"Lane." Darned glad to see his old army buddy, McIntyre rose and skirted his desk, hand extended.

Lane pulled off a glove and the two shook. "Good to see you, friend." They gripped forearms, as close to a hug as they would come. "Reckon you thought I was never gonna git here with those Longhorns of yorn, eh?" Lane said, weathered lines gathering at the corners of his hazel eyes.

"Lane, if anyone could get me those cattle, I knew it would be you." McIntyre motioned to a chair in front of his desk. "Please, have a seat."

"Obliged." The man sat down and worked his other glove off as McIntyre poured him a drink.

"Here." He handed his friend a shot glass. "That should settle some trail dust."

Lane slapped his gloves across his worn chaps, raising a dust cloud. "It'll help, but soon as I update you I'm gonna find me a saloon and do some real drinkin'."

Troubled, McIntyre sat down. He'd wait to tell Lane about his entertainment choices until after he knew where his cattle were. "How far behind you are they?"

"Should roll in tomorrow around midday." He set the empty glass down with a clink. "You're ready, I reckon?"

"Yes. All the fences are up, the bunkhouse is ready. Just finished the barn and corral. I understand the cook coming with you is staying. I hope that is still the case."

"Yeah, Dub's a young man, but he's lookin' for a cooler climate. Says Texas is too hot for him."

"Can he cook?"

"Like my momma." As their laughter faded, Lane shifted forward, getting down to business. "So, we lost a few along the way—accidents, wolves." He laced his fingers together and rested his elbows on the chair arms. "I think some Utes skinned us for a couple down near the border. Even so, I'm comfortable tellin' ya you've got a solid herd of two thousand head rollin' in, including the seventy-five Hereford bulls."

"And you are still confident the Herefords are the way to go?"

"I know cattle like you know poker. This English breed is putting weight on the hoof and turning the Longhorns into a beefy, hardy breed with high yields." He grinned sideways. "Besides, it's too late to change your mind now."

"Yes, I suppose it is."

Lane slapped his chaps and stood. "I need a drink and a pretty gal. Point me to the Iron Horse."

"Lane . . ." McIntyre trailed off and Lane picked up the cue. He sat down again, slowly, and waited.

"I did not mention it in any of my telegrams, but I have closed my saloon."

"Oh."

"And I am married."

"*Oh*," Lane said with raised eyebrows.

"And I am a church-going man now."

Lane's eyebrows dove down. "Oh. Are you sayin' there's no liquor or girls in town?"

"No, I am not saying that."

Lane exhaled and swiped a relieved hand over his mouth. "Whew. You had me worried. It's one thing if *I* can't find some distractions, but you've got a whole crew comin' in tomorrow. I tell them this is a dry town and they'll use it for kindlin'."

McIntyre didn't like hearing that. What kind of men had Lane hired for him? "Lane . . ." He didn't quite know how to express his concerns. "Can you keep a tight rein on your boys? Let me rephrase that. You will keep a tight rein on them. I have a wife and child your boys will respect. Any drinking or carousing they do best not interfere with them or ranch work."

Lane looked puzzled, even a touch annoyed. "You didn't tell me I needed to hire choirboys."

McIntyre picked up a pencil and rolled it around his fingers. "There is one saloon in town. She bought out all the competition. Right now, she's serving liquor and offering various forms of . . . mischief, and she's going to be opening a theater. Eventually, I hear, an opium den as well."

"Wait," Lane waved his hand. "I don't understand. Who's *she?*"

"Delilah."

Lane exhaled a curse and sat back. "Well, no wonder you're worried. How far is your ranch from town?"

"About an hour."

"That'll be some help. They won't be ridin' in every night, but Fridays and Saturdays I reckon your marshal is liable to have his hands full."

*L*eaning on the bar, Delilah listened for a moment to the sounds that had played in the background of most of her life: men muttering, laughing, cursing; the slap of cards and the triumphant cry over a winning hand; the jangle of chips being dragged across the felt; a tinny piano belting out a lively tune. Beneath it all, the sultry voices of her girls issuing their siren's call.

Only the saloon of The Crystal Chandelier was open. The theater was still a week away from its first show. The men didn't mind too much. From the moment she had flung open her doors, the crowd had been steady and strong. The girls in their cribs were producing well. She flipped through the papers in front of her, covered in names and numbers, tallies at the bottom. Yes, they were turning a nice profit.

The upstairs girls here in the saloon would begin receiving callers Saturday night. The Celestial Flowers, however, were destined for her auction. In the meantime, all these little ladies were working the floor, advertising their potential, but serving drinks only. The tease never failed to have the men queuing up for opening night.

"What's the matter, Big Jim? You look a little down."

Delilah didn't look over at Mary Jean addressing a customer, but the softness in the girl's voice intrigued her, and she continued listening.

"Ah, I ain't down."

From the corner of her eye, Delilah saw the big man in a sheepskin vest drop his two bits on the counter.

"I was thinkin' about that Preacher."

Mary Jean poured Big Jim a shot and took his money. "Thinkin' 'bout what?"

"I'm still rankled about that mess on his door. Whoever did that'll try somethin' new. Tomorrow is Sunday. I was pondering staying sober and seein' if I might catch me a scat-smearin' coward sometime tonight."

"Coward?" Smith's voice. He had slipped up on the other side of Big Jim.

"Smith." Big Jim's tone turned hard. "I don't reckon you had anything to do with the "paint" left on the Preacher's door? Sounds like somethin' you'd do."

"You callin' me a coward?"

The two men faced each other.

"That's enough, boys." Delilah did not deign to look up. "No fightin' in my place. You know the rules. All fights go to the ring out back."

Silence stretched out for a moment. Delilah did wonder between these two, who was the toughest. By all accounts, Smith was the meanest and sometimes that was more than enough to win a fight.

"You'd best be careful, Smith." Big Jim tossed back his drink, set the glass down, and stomped away. Mary Jean took his glass and hurried away to the dry sink behind the bar, as if to avoid Smith.

"Did you do that?" Delilah asked still without looking up. "Have you no better morals than to desecrate a house of God?"

"It was just a little warning of what's coming his way."

"Leave the Preacher alone for a bit. Make a little trouble for McIntyre. I don't care how you get to him, just make him suffer."

"That's his foreman sittin' over there in the corner. I heard him say McIntyre's got a herd of two thousand head comin' in tomorrow. Guess he wants to be a big cattle baron."

This could be useful information. "How many men in the crew?"

"Didn't ask. Probably at least twenty."

"Free drinks for all of them when they come in the first night." Delilah turned and scanned the crowd, looking for the foreman. "Where's McIntyre's man?"

Smith chucked a thumb over his shoulder. "Dusty fella, sitting under the lantern."

"Mary Jean," Delilah called without looking at the girl, "bring me a bottle and two glasses." She handed her receipts to Smith. "Put these on my desk upstairs. Mr. Foreman over there looks like he could use a bath . . . and a friend."

*I*t felt good to be back in the saddle again. Naomi didn't get to ride nearly as much as she'd like, and a day on horseback was heaven. Surveying the green valley in front of her, teeming with Charles's herd and watched over by the sentinel San Juan Mountains, sublime contentment filled her soul. A hundred yards off, cowboys shouted and whistled as they drove the animals the final mile to the river. She was officially a rancher. Or at least a rancher's wife.

Overhead, the sun peeked in and out of lacy clouds; the mountains stared down with calm indifference. She caught the scent of sage and leather on the summer breeze. Full of herself, she cut her eyes at Two Spears. The boy had a gift for riding. Horses took to him. And even at his young age, he had raced ponies at the White River Reservation with respectable success. He sat now atop a good-natured little sorrel, sure-footed and fast.

Her palomino, Buttercup, was faster. "Race you to the river."

In a blink, they were off, slapping leather, charging through the waist-high grass. Naomi hunkered down, loosened her pull on the reins, and grabbed a handful of mane. Two Spears laughed and yipped like a coyote beside her, his horse Mandan keeping even with Buttercup.

The wind rushed past her ears, hooves pounded, and her heart galloped with the simple joy of rocketing along the plains on the back of a fast steed. Sleek and muscular, the horses stretched out, eager to move, enjoying the contest as well.

Naomi and Two Spears stayed some distance out from the herd, but they lunged past one long-legged, dust-covered cowboy who had pulled away from the cattle. Taking a moment to enjoy a smoke, he watched them streak by, disapproval evident in his scowl.

She figured the man was not happy at seeing Two Spears. The boy didn't seem to notice, and today, neither would Naomi. Two Spears was nudging ahead! "Come on, girl, gid up!" She slapped the quirt across her horse's rump.

Two Spears, howling, barking and waving his arm in the air, kicked Mandan, getting a little more speed from the gelding. The little horse edged another foot in front of Naomi.

Shoot! He's going to beat me.

Thundering over a small hill they galloped on, until skidding to a stop at the river's edge. Both she and Two Spears collapsed into laughter, circling their horses around each other.

"You ride well," the boy said between panting breaths. "For a woman."

"OH!" Naomi swatted the boy's thigh, feigning anger.

Downstream, two thousand head of cattle mooed and sloshed lazily in a long stretch of the water, and milled about on both sides. At least two dozen cowboys hollered and waved lariats, keeping the beeves under control.

"Not too many white folks can compete with an Injun on a horse."

Naomi gasped at the insult and spun her horse around to face the dusty cowboy with a stub of a cigarette hanging from his mouth. Two Spears's face clouded over and his mouth flattened into a thin, angry line. Oh, how she wished he hadn't heard that.

Naomi rode her horse over to the man. He tipped his hat back, revealing the stark contrast between his dirty face and clean forehead. "You must be the missus."

"Yes I am," she half-whispered, half-growled. "And he's my son. I don't appreciate the use of the word *Injun*."

"Oh, my apologies, ma'am." He dipped his hat in a contrite gesture. "My apologies, son," he said to Two Spears. "It was poorly-worded praise. I only meant to compliment you on your riding skills. You sit the saddle like you was born to it."

"Yes, he's a natural." Naomi extended her hand, eager to start anew. "I'm Naomi McIntyre. This is my son, Two Spears."

The man removed a worn glove and took Naomi's hand. "Lane Chandler. Your foreman."

Pounding hooves interrupted the introductions as Charles rode into the meeting, his tailored suit as dusty as Lane's mail order clothes. "Is everything all right?"

Naomi saw concern, perhaps suspicion in her husband's eyes. She reached out and touched his arm. "Fine. We were just getting introduced to Mr. Chandler."

"Reckon I owe you an apology too. I believe Mrs. McIntyre and your boy there know I meant no harm, but I'll watch my language in the future."

Naomi leaned into Charles and whispered, "He used the word *Injun*."

"And it won't happen again," Lane promised.

Charles looked more puzzled by the apology than appreciative of it. "See that it doesn't."

"Yes sir." Lane lowered his hat. "I'll take half the men and get 'em settled in the bunkhouse, then bring in the rest about dark, minus those riding night herd."

Charles waited a moment before answering, creating an awkward pause. "As the opportunity arises, instruct these men on their language, as well."

A look of understanding passed between the two. Lane nodded and trotted off to see the hands. Charles didn't look at Naomi but steered his horse over to Two Spears. "I saw your race. You beat Naomi. *I* have never beaten Naomi." He started to touch the boy's hair, seemed to re-think it, instead merely nodding as he passed by him. "Keep that up and she will put a frog in your bed."

As Charles trotted after Lane, a plethora of expressions played out on the boy's face—confusion, uncertainty, but finally, the faintest hint of pride.

"You do ride well." Naomi nudged Buttercup to pull up beside Mandan. "And you're the first man in the house to beat me."

Two Spears frowned and slapped his reins back and forth across the saddle horn. "Why would you put a frog in my bed?"

"Would you prefer a snake?"

"Yes."

Naomi found the deadpan answer so endearing, she couldn't help herself. Laughing, she leaned over and hugged Two Spears. At first he was stiff, surprised, but softened a little after a moment. Naomi tapped him lightly on the nose. "You are adorable, Two Spears."

Mandan tossed his head and nickered, as if he agreed.

---

*M*cIntyre thought better of Lane explaining things to the men. Especially since he felt as though he'd missed an important moment back there between the foreman and Naomi. He trotted up beside Lane. "I decided I'll address the men. Makes more sense coming from me what I expect . . . of all of you."

Lane raised his hat, dropped it again. "You didn't tell me your son was a half—I mean—Indian," he corrected.

But McIntyre had heard the intended word. *Half-breed.* "I didn't know that would disturb you." He did not try to hide his annoyance.

"Well, we've had a fair amount of trouble with 'em in Texas. Bloodthirsty, merciless savages."

"I would not necessarily disagree, but that makes it all the more important to raise Two Spears without hate and bigotry." He slid his gaze over to his foreman. "Wouldn't you agree?"

"I know he's just a boy. Took me by surprise is all. You know," Lane shifted in the saddle to face McIntyre, "generally speaking, these hands will be good as gold around you and your wife. They know their place. The boy, though," he sucked his teeth. "I'll do my best, but some of these riders have lost family to the Comanche. One Indian is the same as another to them."

McIntyre pulled up his horse and Lane stopped too.

"Then we need to make it abundantly clear that my son is to be treated with the same respect as me."

Lane seemed to think about it for a second before nodding. "Yes sir."

McIntyre had the distinct impression his foreman acquiesced merely to end the discussion rather than solve a problem.

That would do . . . for now.

---

*M*cIntyre leaned back on the corral fence, waiting for the men to finish picking bunks and unloading bed rolls. Thick clouds rolling in from the east cut the evening sky in half, and thunder echoed off the distant mountains.

Gradually, the men filtered out to the bunkhouse porch and either draped themselves over porch rails or settled on benches and chairs.

"That's the last of them," Lane said, pulling paper and tobacco from his pocket to roll a smoke.

McIntyre didn't move. Instead, he studied the men. Mostly young, in their twenties and thirties, dusty, haggard, and unkempt. Shaggy hair. One veteran with no hair. Lean, weather-beaten faces in need of shaves. Curious eyes. He didn't see any animosity in their stares. Good. Now he would watch for the change.

He pushed off the fence and approached them. "Lane here has

assured me that you are fine, experienced cowboys. He has also assured me that you are not choirboys."

Chuckles rippled through the group.

"And that's fine." McIntyre pushed his hat back an inch. "What you do on your own time is your own business . . . as long as it does not affect your work here at the King M Ranch." He shoved his hands into his pockets. "Now, there is only one saloon in Defiance—"

"What?" A young man, who had been leaning his chair back, dropped it with a thud. "You still got the Iron Horse, right?" He seemed to think better of his bold tone, and changed it to something more contrite. "I mean, I thought you owned that too. I was eager for a look-see."

"I did own it. I closed it. Now Delilah Goodnight has come here and opened a new place."

The boys muttered amongst themselves. A few hooted, and a couple whistled with delight.

"I see most of you know her. So let me be perfectly clear. If you go to Delilah's for a night of entertainment and do not show up here for work the next morning, don't bother showing up at all."

They did not react vernally to the pronouncement, but understanding dawned in their expressions. A few nodded. McIntyre wanted to say more, warn them about her place, urge them to avoid it, but he knew that would be stunningly hypocritical at this point. These boys knew him by his old reputation.

"One last thing. This is my home. Treat it with respect. My wife and son live here. Treat them with the respect you would show me. Watch your language and behave like gentlemen in front of them. *Both* of them."

Lane stepped up beside him. "You boys will be interested to know that there's a rugby ball in the bunkhouse if you're inclined to play. And Mr. McIntyre has also been gracious enough to supply us with a few bottles of whiskey a week, cards, and poker chips."

The bald gent, a weather-beaten cowpuncher several years past retirement, swung his head up. "You're providing whiskey? What about women?"

The men chuckled. McIntyre did not. "The whiskey is to be used in moderation. If there are any drunkards among you, you will not be here long."

Faces clouded. Stares hardened. Lane jumped in. "Delilah has promised us all free drinks Saturday night, so that's where you can tie your knot in the devil's tail. Behave yourselves out here."

McIntyre looked at Lane, unhappy about the news. Delilah didn't give anything away, especially liquor. "When did she make that offer?"

"Yesterday. Strutted up and introduced herself. Bought me a drink." That sideways grin tipped his mouth. "Don't worry, Johnny Reb. I know she's tryin' to buy friends. And I'm not for sale."

"What about them?"

"I'm their foreman, not their momma. Oh," Lane snapped his fingers and addressed the men again. "There's a church in Defiance now too, boys. You won't believe who's pastorin' it." He paused for effect. "Logan Tillane."

A man at the end of the porch—lean, lanky like a grasshopper, and a little older than most of the others—cursed and rose so fast he knocked his chair back. "Tillane?"

"Relax, Cloer. The way Delilah tells it, he's gone all religious and such." Cloer's wide eyes didn't relax. Lane elbowed McIntyre lightly. "Last time Cloer ran into Logan, the man threatened to kill him. But he was so drunk, and Cloer was so fast, Logan missed the shot."

More chuckles circulated, but McIntyre heard the fear, the uncertainty. He waved his hand. "Logan is a good man. Whatever was between you, I'd put money down that he is willing to let it go. And he is a good preacher. Who better to talk of the love of God than a man who has been in some dark places?"

"You sure he ain't still there?"

McIntyre didn't see who asked the question. He shrugged a shoulder in answer. "I'm as sure as I can be of any man. For what that may be worth."

CHAPTER 15

"Quit botherin' me, Preacher. I ain't comin' to your stupid church." Amanda, a once-pretty black girl, tried to shove past him on the street, her pale lips pinched in annoyance. Her gaunt face reflected hints of innocence, especially in her still-alluring amber eyes. Her complexion, however, looked washed-out; her eyes were dilated, and red-rimmed. The smell of opium and the stagger in her walk revealed the addiction she'd fallen into. "Tell Mollie and Emilio to leave me alone too. I've had it with you people."

Logan bit his tongue and stepped aside. The girl marched on, disappearing in a throng of miners. A raindrop hit him on the shoulder. Above the murmuring traffic thunder rolled ominously in an angry sky.

A young Oriental girl, not more than fourteen, shoved a flyer in his hand. Bowing respectfully, she drifted away, disappearing into the crowd like a ghost. It took Logan a moment to realize she'd even handed him anything. The headline on the paper roared at him.

Dip your wick at Delilah's new Crystal Chandelier. Come bid on a virgin!

He closed his eyes against the drawing of a naked woman and wadded up the paper, dropping it to the ground as if it were on fire.

Several tents up, a woman screamed and Logan heard the familiar sound of fists landing on flesh. Two men tumbled into the street, punches flying. The woman appeared at the tent flap, half-dressed, hands clasped in front of her face, almost as if in prayer. Logan waited a moment to see if anyone would intervene. Men and women on their way to the sluices, to the Sunnyside Mine, to wash clothes, or to anywhere but there, merely walked around the scuffle. Fights in Tent Town rarely drew a crowd.

The combatants didn't waste energy on words. Grunting like animals, they punched, kicked, gouged, and clawed. Logan had to give it to them. He'd rarely seen men try as hard as these two to wear each other out. At least neither one of them had a gun or a knife. About to intervene, Logan gladly pulled back when a group of miners surged into the fracas and separated the two. Both groups swore and cursed loudly as they pulled the men apart and dragged them in opposite directions.

Logan sighed, his heart heavy. The overwhelming depravity in Defiance sat on his shoulders today like a leering gargoyle. He hurried through the throngs of men, pushing at the bodies, desperate for a quiet spot to pray.

He could not accept that Pender Beckwith would do nothing to stop Delilah and her sordid auction.

The old Logan cried to be set free. The old Logan wanted to deal with this woman in the worst way. A few drinks in him and he would beat her until she crawled from Defiance on bloodied hands and knees. He grimaced at the thought, sickened by it, sorry for ever raising a hand to any woman.

No matter what, he would not resort to that to stop Delilah. *Then how, God?*

He wondered if McIntyre had this same struggle. The two of them certainly had this in common: their past mistreatment of women. Now, here they both were, trying to serve the Lord in a town as decadent as Sodom or Gomorrah. And Logan, at least, felt like he was failing.

For such a time as this.

The scripture from Esther whispered in his mind . . . again. Ever since McIntyre had pointed out that Logan and Delilah had rolled into town at nearly the same time, the words had been echoing, repeating.

Without knowing how he'd gotten there, he found himself standing beside the Animas River, its rocky shores covered in driftwood. He stumbled across the loose river rock to a dead tree and collapsed. His knees had gone out from under him. It felt like his heart was giving out too.

"God, I can't do this. There's too much here." *Too much evil, too much resistance.* He rested his face in his hands and massaged his forehead. *Help me, Father. I feel so alone. I need someone to talk to, but I'm the pastor. I'm the one who should be strong, have all the determination to carry on . . .*

"Preacher?"

Startled, Logan rose and spun.

Mary Jean had again caught him praying. Wisps of her mousy ash-brown hair dancing around her face, she clasped her hands in front of her and lowered her chin a little.

"Mary Jean. You must think I never get off my knees."

"Isn't that a good thing?" she asked softly.

Logan ducked his head and smiled, properly chastised. He climbed to his feet and sighed. "Yes, yes it is. In this town, in front of all these hard-hearted people, I forget that a man is strongest when he's on his knees."

She ambled forward, slowly, as if making sure of her welcome. "My father used to say that."

"Your father was a Godly man?"

"He was a preacher," she said carefully, as if she wasn't comfortable with Logan's description. "I never would listen. I was a handful at home. I signed up to be a mail-order bride just to get away. I do impulsive things like that. Daddy and Momma warned me to follow the Lord or I'd wind up in a bad place." A bitter chuckle escaped her lips. "They were right, I reckon." She shrugged. "What were you prayin' about? You look mighty troubled."

"Oh," Logan glanced up at the sky. "This auction. I have to stop it."

"That won't be easy. Delilah's planning on making a lot of money off it."

He shook his head and muttered, "Satan goes about like a roaring lion . . ." He studied Mary Jean for a moment, wondering about her future.

An innocent young girl, one who's made some poor choices. We are all guilty of that. But maybe I can help her.

"Mary Jean, contact them. Your parents. Let them know you're all right." Logan stepped over the driftwood to her, desperate to do something right in this town. "I'm sure we can get you stage fare to go home."

Head lowered, brow creased, she traded places and sat down on the tree. "It'd be too hard to go back. They were right—about everything. I'd feel like a dog crawlin' home with its tail between its legs."

"Does that really matter?" Logan sat beside her. "You're living in a vile place, working in a . . . a . . ." He let that pass and moved on. "Filth and debauchery is a way of life here. This ain't no place for a young girl. Swallow your pride and go home." He put his arm around her, surprised at himself, yet the touch of another human strengthened him. "You're the prodigal child, and your father will welcome your return."

"Do you think so?" She looked up, hope glowing in those breath-stealing green eyes. "Do you think he'll let me come home?"

Caught somewhere between plain and pretty, Mary Jean had

undeniably beautiful, flawless skin, and lips the color of a peach. Ashamed he'd noticed, he pulled his arm away, wondering what had come over him. *Loneliness, that's what.* "You're his daughter. He loves you. Of course he will."

---

*L*ogan and Mary Jean exited the Western Union office and stood quietly on the busy boardwalk. The high-noon sun, bright and inviting, brought out her pink parasol and he tugged his well-worn Stetson a little lower. A group of backpack-heavy miners slogging past forced him and the girl off to the side. They waited to speak until the men had passed.

"Well . . ." She tapped a toe and smiled at him. "All I can do now is wait."

"I'm sure your pa will be glad to have heard from you, Mary Jean. He and your ma are probably worried to death over you."

Biting her bottom lip, she twirled the umbrella slowly. "We'll see."

The uncertainty in her voice weighed on Logan. Had he misled her? Mary Jean knew her family situation better than he did. What if her pa rejected her?

No, Lord, surely he won't. "How 'bout some lunch? Martha's Kitchen isn't Delmonico's, but I hear there's a passable chicken pie . . . I'm buyin'."

The twirling parasol sped up. Her green eyes hit him and he realized it had been a long time since he'd been sober enough to really notice a girl. Back in Willow there had been a couple of farmers' daughters who were pretty . . . but not like Mary Jean. She made him think of a flower that closed at night and opened up for the sun in the morning. He wanted to see her petals reach for the light. She mattered to him. The feeling at once scared him and put a spring in his step, though he wasn't sure if this was a pastor's affection for her . . . or something more.

. . .

*M*artha's Kitchen had long plank tables set out in front of it, covered by a rickety tin roof. Customers walked to the window of her small kitchen to place their order. Only a few men were eating lunch yet. Logan paid for the two tin plates filled with the broth-rich chicken pie, then carried them over to Mary Jean. She sat at the end of the table closest to the street, watching the stage roll by.

"Wish you were on it?"

She blinked and took her plate from him as he sat across from her. "I don't know what I wish for. I wasn't happy at home. I just wanted some adventure. Becoming a mail-order bride was foolhardy, I suppose, but it was a way out of Weaverville."

"Was your town really that bad?"

"It wasn't the town." She used her fork to tear a piece of piecrust loose, but then only swirled it around in the broth. "I come from a Quaker family, Preacher. I thought I was gonna suffocate there." She looked up, but stared past him. "I want to sing. That's all I really, really want to do. I'm sorry Jay got killed, but if we'd gotten married I would have only hurt him. I was planning on running off eventually. To San Francisco or someplace." She did look at him then. "Am I a horrible person?"

Her eyes pleaded with him to say no.

"You're young. We all do stupid, cruel things when we're young. Make bad decisions. Fall in with bad people."

She flinched a little.

"Mary Jean, I ain't judging you. If sins have weight, then I truly have been weighed, measured, and found far more wanting than you. I've *killed* men. But I would urge you to go home. Maybe you'll leave again, I don't know, but be smarter about it. And don't burn your bridges."

Surprise rolled across her face, and then, to Logan's surprise, changed to sympathy. "I can see you carry a terrible weight. We

129

had a hand on our farm who'd had some trouble with the law." She regarded him with a strange intensity, as if she were trying to look into his soul. "He had that same look in his eyes. Like . . . like he was running from a deep hurt. Or tryin' to."

Logan took a bite of chicken and then nodded. "It's a scar, I think. Of sadness. Regret. The people I've hurt . . . the knowing— the *understanding*—of the misery I've wrought. That leaves its mark. But at least a scar is evidence of healing."

Logan would like to see Mary Jean leave Defiance unscathed, without any scars of her own. But if she didn't, she needed to know there was a Healer. "I can't erase the things I've done, Mary Jean, but God has forgiven me. I know that. I live for Him now. He has brought me a peace I'll never be able to put words to. Remember that when hard times hit—wherever you are—He'll be there for you."

The moment seemed a bit too weighty, like he was pushing, so Logan leaned back. "Sorry. That's what you get when you have lunch with a preacher."

Mary Jean picked up her cup. "Small price to pay." She lifted the mug to her lips, and Logan was pretty sure she was hiding a smile.

---

*E*milio had enjoyed a private place to sleep for so long that living in the bunkhouse would take some getting used to. If he could.

He washed the day's dirt off in the rain barrel out back, dunking his head and flipping the water off. As he came up, he heard a violent thud from the other side of the wall and stilled. Excited hollering, maybe some scuffling, muffled by the logs, reached him. Curious, he snatched his hat off the bench and hurried in the back door, water dripping down his back.

Willy and Lane had Cloer snugged up between them, and

Lane was holding a bottle of whiskey away from the ranch hand. A deck of cards littered the floor. "I mean it, Cloer, we ain't gonna tolerate it." Lane saw Emilio and tossed him the bottle. "Do somethin' with that while we put him to bed." Emilio caught the liquor.

"Hey," Cloer growled in angry protest. "*I* bought that bottle."

Lane snatched the man's shoulder back to get his attention off the drink. "Sleep it off and maybe we'll let you back in the game."

Cloer eased off and raised his hands in surrender. "Fine."

The two men relaxed their grip. Somehow, Emilio knew, Cloer wasn't one to take good advice so peaceably. Older than all but one of the men, he had a bitter edge to his weathered, tanned face, as if cowboying was a punishment, not a job. Emilio wasn't surprised when the man twisted loose from Lane and Willy and lunged for the bottle.

Emilio struck Cloer's jaw with a fast, hard jab. The ranch hand stopped, his face went blank, but he didn't fall. Emilio clocked him one more time, harder.

A few boxing lessons with Billy had paid off. Cloer went stiff and fell backward like a skinny cedar. Lane whistled in awe as the man went down. "Good punch, kid. Out cold. You shoulda yelled 'Timber.'" He and Willy bent down and dragged their friend over to an unmade bunk on the bottom row. "Say," Lane strode back over to Emilio. "You're not gonna tell McIntyre about this, are you?"

"Any reason I shouldn't?"

"Well, I'm the foreman. I reckon it should be my place to do it." Lane yanked his red bandana loose from his neck and dabbed at the sweat on his forehead. "But Cloer's wife left him a while back. He still ain't over it. I just wanna cut him a little slack. If you're willin'."

Lane hooked a thumb through his belt loop and looked at Emilio with a hopeful expression.

Emilio wasn't sure keeping his mouth shut was the right thing to do, but it also seemed wrong to run to Mr. McIntyre with every little problem. "*Si*. No more trouble, though."

"Ah, he's a good fella, long as he ain't drinkin. Liquor makes him a little crazy. We'll keep him straight." Lane touched his forehead in a mock hat-tip. "You got my word."

CHAPTER 16

*D*elilah's heels clicked curtly as she strode across the wood floor to her bedroom window. In the distance, the towering mountains, jagged dragon's teeth, clawed at the twilight sky. Her gaze traveled slowly down the steep slopes, slid across the rooftops of the golden-lapped buildings of Main Street Defiance, to settle on Tent Town.

The Crystal Chandelier happened to occupy the highest point of land on the valley floor. The vantage point gave her a respectable view of Lime Creek and its rickety sluices, hundreds of dingy tents and small cabins with their smoking stovepipes, and worn laundry hanging forlorn and still.

Men and mules, heads lowered in exhaustion, trudged to and fro beneath her window. To the left, a row of new, bright white tents contrasted with the filth around them . . . on the outside. These were the cribs for the older and less desirable girls.

A grubby little kingdom, but all hers.

She gazed over at the steeple of the Crooked Creek Chapel and her anger flared like a match. Charles McIntyre truly had an enemy in Matthew Miller, and she had an agreement to keep on

Matthew's behalf, but Delilah would make sure she settled the score with Logan as well.

He had forgotten her. All those pretty words and promises whispered with desperate innocence so long ago weren't even memories now. Not to him, anyway. She wondered if he even remembered being seventeen back in Dodge City. That was about the time he'd started drinking. Was that why he'd never come for her? Had he even looked?

If he'd rescued her from that place, how different their lives might have turned out.

Delilah hugged herself and turned from the window . . . and the memories. Her simple room was filled only with an armoire, a huge brass bed, her vanity, and a hairdressing chair. More furniture was on the way. She always enjoyed making her boudoir a sanctuary despite the time it took to get the lace, satin, and furs shipped. But soon . . .

She ran her hand over the cold brass knob on the foot of her bed. Soon she would get Logan up here, remind him of everything he'd let slip away, and then she would tear from his heart any vestige of goodness or faith. If it killed her, she would leave him a wreck of a man no god could save.

A gentle knock on the door pulled her away from the dark thoughts.

"Your hot water." Otis's voice.

Delilah let him in and he set the pitcher over at the salon chair. "Send Mary Jean in."

*D*elilah inhaled the fresh scent of pine in her bedroom as she quickly and skillfully dropped the opium into the wine glass. *Lumber smells like success.* Pleased that The Crystal Chandelier was finally open, and the theater only lacked a few small touches, she turned slowly to Mary Jean.

Now, to get one last piece of inventory stocked . . .

A towel draped around her shoulders, the girl sat in the salon chair, its back pulled up to Delilah's vanity. A basin and the pitcher of warm water waited, but first the wine.

Delilah glided over to Mary Jean and handed her the glass. "You'll love this. It's called sherry."

"Thank you." The girl accepted the wine and took a small sip.

Delilah returned to her vanity and poured her own glass. "That chair you're sitting in came direct from France. It has a lever and I can lean it back. You won't strain your neck so much while I wash your hair."

"Goodness." Suspicion or hesitation laced the girl's voice.

"Why do you sound so . . . unsure?"

"I was . . . I was thinking about . . ." Mary Jean faded off, tried again. "I was just wondering why you're doing all this for me. The dress, the room, this." She motioned with the wine. "I don't wanna keep going in debt to you, Miss Delilah."

"Debt?" Delilah tried to sound positively shocked. "Mary Jean, I bought you the dress because you work for me, and you must look nice now that the Chandelier is open. I want to wash your hair so that I can show you how to style it. Yes, you do owe me some rent, but you're working that off at the bar . . . However . . ." She smiled warmly at the girl. "Well, I will admit, my dear, you certainly have assets that are being wasted."

"I don't want to do that." Mary Jean said firmly. Chin raised, she took another sip of wine.

"Of course. I understand. But that's not what I'm talking about. I want to put you on the stage."

Mary Jean's eyes rounded. "The stage?"

"I've heard you singing behind the bar when you clean up. You have a lovely voice. Anyone who can sing that well surely dreams of the stage."

Clearly entertaining the idea, Mary Jean's eyes filled with

starlight. Delilah kept the smile from her lips and nonchalantly nudged upward the girl's hand holding the wine.

Absently, Mary Jean took another sip. "I sang in our church choir and soloed often."

"I knew it." Delilah lifted her own drink between them, "Here's to a future on the stage."

Delilah could imagine the fantasy playing out in Mary Jean's mind. Another innocent eager for the glare of the house lights and applause of an adoring crowd.

The girl took another sip of her sherry. "What would I sing?"

Delilah moved back a step to observe Mary Jean. The girl's head swayed ever so slightly, and her eyelids drooped a tad. The laudanum was slowly snaking its way through her blood.

"I'm sure our customers will love anything you choose to perform. I'll let you do anything you want on my stage, Mary Jean." She took the drink away, set it on the vanity beside the sink, and lowered the chair. She gathered the girl's hair, a boring mix of dull brown and grayish blond, and dropped it into the basin. Yes, raven hair would suit Mary Jean much better. Men would be killing themselves for this sweet, young thing when Delilah was finished with her. They would bid any price, any stake, any size gold nugget.

Already counting the money, she slowly poured a vase of warm water over the girl's scalp. "Sing like an angel and I will make sure you're as beautiful as one."

---

*E*milio slowed his horse to a trot and hung back from eleven of the new hands from the ranch. Young men around his own age or a little older, they had bathed and shaved, even washed their clothes, and oiled their boots for their first trip into town. Dub, a short redheaded fella whose nervous, jerky way of moving unnerved Emilio, had declared the group would be getting roostered up good tonight. The others had laughed and howled like wolves as they jumped into their saddles.

Emilio did not have a good feeling about this outing.

They made it to town just as the sun slipped behind Red Mountain. The group trotted down Main Street, nodding and tipping hats at the folks who looked their way. And most did. A crew this large got attention. The cowboys liked it. Their voices rang louder, their laughter more boisterous.

Garcia wheeled his horse around and fell in beside Emilio. Mexican like Emilio, Garcia used his dark eyes and straight white teeth to impress people, especially women. He wore a big sombrero, a black bolero jacket, and rode a saddle covered in shiny silver conchos.

The big white grin flashed at Emilio, but he did not want to talk. He found the young man cocky as a prize bull. Yet Garcia was patient too. He continued to stare.

Finally, Emilio sighed. "What?"

"Why are you here, my friend? You act as though we are heading to a funeral, what, with that sour face and hunched shoulders. Do you not like good whiskey and bad women?"

Emilio didn't think it wise to say he was here on Mr. McIntyre's behalf. His *patrón* had asked him to keep these men out of trouble, if possible. That explanation would only invite ridicule. "I wanted to see someone in town."

Garcia's grin spread. "I see, *Niño*. You like the *bad* whiskey and *good* women."

Niño? Emilio chose to ignore the insult. There was probably enough trouble coming tonight without starting it on the street. "If you worked at being a cowboy half as hard as you do at moving your lips, you would be foreman tomorrow."

Garcia's grin disappeared so fast, Emilio wondered if he'd imagine it.

The man's brow dove, forming a deep 'v' in his forehead. "You can call me a lot of things, *Niño*, but not cow*boy*. I am a *vaquero*." Up ahead the group kicked their horses into a lope as they turned the corner at the assayer's. The rutted, weedy way to Tent Town. Men hooted and yipped to vent their excitement. "Aha!" Garcia's good humor returned instantly and he took off after them. "Enjoy the funeral," he taunted over his shoulder.

---

*E*milio grabbed the doorknob to the town hall and newspaper office, but paused. He wanted to see Mollie. He wished he could visit with Billy. They often played cards on Saturday night.

He wanted, most of all, to see Hannah and Little Billy.

He didn't *need* to see either of them.

The decision was yanked from him when the door opened. Mollie smiled up at him, her pretty, petite face glowing with a smile. "I thought I saw you walk by the window." She stepped back and waved him in. "Come on. Billy and Hannah are in the kitchen."

Emilio appreciated the red gingham dress Mollie wore. It showed off her tiny waist. A red ribbon held her long golden hair back and brought out the color of her lips. He caught an invitation in her expression that warmed him. When she grabbed his hand and pulled him toward the kitchen, he concentrated on the softness of her skin and the delicate structure of her fingers. He could get over Hannah if he put his heart into it.

I have to.

Emilio had missed his friend. He and Billy shook hands vigorously, and slapped each other on the back. "Good to see you."

"You too, you too," Billy swept some wayward hair off his forehead and winked at Emilio, sky blue eyes full of relief. "Ready for some cards? I'm feeling lucky tonight."

Emilio would never have thought this citified *gringo* would become a friend. Yet somehow they had gone from fighting each other in the street to being as close as brothers. Not for the first time, Emilio doubted the move to the ranch. It meant giving up more than Hannah. Emilio valued his family. "No cards for me tonight."

Hannah brushed by him, Little Billy on her hip, and danced her fingers down his forearm. "Emilio, good to see you."

"You too."

She handed the baby, now eight months old, to his papa. The two giggled and cooed for a minute, Billy making funny faces at his son. He pressed his lips to the baby's forehead and exhaled loudly, vibrating his lips. Little Billy kicked and laughed with delight at the silly sound.

"Emilio, can I get you some coffee?" Mollie strode over to the stove. "And a piece of pie?"

"No thank you. I am not staying long."

Billy sat down at the small kitchen table. "Tired of losing at poker?" He set Little Billy on top of the table and gave him a spoon to examine.

"Not by a long shot." His eyes roamed the kitchen, looking for a clock. "Maybe tomorrow night. Right now I have to go. I just wanted to stop by and say *ola*."

Billy pulled a pocket watch from his vest. "It's nearly eight. Where are you off to?"

Emilio hadn't expected the question, and the delay in his answer earned him some suspicious looks. "I have to go to The Crystal Chandelier."

Mollie and Hannah gasped. "Emilio," Mollie whispered, as Hannah's mouth formed a perfect little 'o'.

Billy rose and handed Little Billy off to Hannah. "Let's you and me step outside for a second, brother."

Emilio nodded goodnight to the ladies, trying hard to linger longer on Mollie than Hannah. She did look pretty in the lamp-light. He blinked and followed Billy out to the boardwalk.

"I heard about that place soon as I got back." Billy sauntered over to a post, fell against it, and folded his arms. "What's come over you wanting to go in there?"

Emilio wasn't thrilled to reveal the reason to Billy. He felt vaguely like *la chacha*, a nanny, but his friend misread the silence.

"Emilio," Billy straightened up and rested his hands on his hips. Studying his feet, he wagged his head back and forth. "There's no way to say this, but I guess we've got to tackle it now." He looked up at Emilio. "I know you're in love with Hannah."

A mule kick to the gut couldn't have been more jarring. Why were they even talking about this?

"But trying to run away from it by going to places like The Crystal Chandelier . . .that's not a good plan."

Emilio took a deep breath and dragged a sweaty palm over his face. "It's not what you think."

"Then what is it? That's one reason you moved out to the ranch, isn't it?"

"Billy . . ." Emilio splayed his hands out, ready to come clean, get it all in the open. Confess that he would die for Hannah . . . but it struck him that he would die for any one of the members of this hobbled-together family. An unwed mother. The boy who had abandoned her. A former prostitute. "Billy, I don't love Hannah that way." The lie was hard to spit out, but right. "You and her, Little Billy, Mollie. You are my family."

Billy worked his jaw back and forth as if he was pondering the explanation. "Then why are you going to The Crystal Chandelier?"

Emilio rolled his eyes. "Eleven of Mr. McIntyre's new hands are there. He asked me to keep an eye on them. I think they are all going to be in jail before midnight."

Billy exhaled, lines of stress around his mouth and eyes melting away. "You need any help?"

"I do not think so. If anything happens, I will let them go to jail." He ambled down to his horse and plucked his hat off the saddle horn, but paused as an idea struck him. He peered around the animal's head. "You weren't worried, were you? About Hannah and me?"

Billy shoulders jerked back. "You two have some history. I just want to be sure you're done with it."

"Did she give you any reason to think otherwise?"

"Honestly? No."

Emilio settled into the saddle, a little depressed by the forth-right answer. It made him want a beer. "*Sí*. Good." He tipped his hat at Billy and turned the horse toward Tent Town.

---

*B*illy slipped his hand into Hannah's and they meandered down the river's shoreline in perfect peace. The sun had sunk below the towering peaks leaving a beautiful peach glow in the sky, but night would fall fast now. Though this would be a short walk, he loved the sound of the water and being alone with the future Mrs. Page. Mollie was sweet enough to watch Billy for a few minutes so he could do this properly.

Butterflies cavorting in his stomach, Billy touched the ring in his breast pocket.

"Do you miss your parents, Billy?"

The question nearly made him stumble, unexpected as it was. Hannah could do that—throw him off balance—because he never knew where her mind was going. Was he a cad if he told her the truth? Hannah already knew his parents had sent him away rather than let him marry her and raise the baby. She didn't know his father had threatened to disinherit him. His mother . . . his mother was trapped in a loveless marriage, and couldn't have affected things one way or the other. He supposed he had some pity for her, but he felt like he'd made a pretty clean break from his family. They'd forced him into it.

"No, I don't," he said. "I mean, I miss my mother some, but you and Little Billy, and your sisters, you're all my family now. I don't even think about Pa." He stopped and they faced each other. "What made you ask about them?"

"What kind of life can we have together if your family never accepts me?"

He didn't know what to say. He'd accepted things. Frank Page thought he was too good to acknowledge a bastard grandson, so Billy had walked away and wasn't ever going back. Nothing would come between him and Hannah and Little Billy again. Not parents. Not Indians. Not another man. Therefore, he only knew one way to answer Hannah.

Holding on to her hand, he dropped to one knee in the damp sand, pulled a ring of rubies and white gold from his pocket, and held it up for her inspection. Too much of the light was gone to make out her face clearly, but he could see the tears sparkling in her eyes. *"Therefore shall a man leave his father and his mother, and shall cleave unto his wife: and they shall be one flesh.* God will bless our marriage, Hannah. I don't need anybody else's blessing." When she didn't raise her hand to accept the ring he assumed it was because he hadn't asked the actual question. He cleared his throat. "Hannah, I love you. Will you marry me?"

The pause between the question and her answer dragged on a bit too long. Growing concerned, he was about to speak when she placed her hands on his cheeks and pulled him to his feet. Still holding him, she said softly, "I do love you more than anything. Yes, I will marry you."

Relief and joy exploded in his heart. He kissed her deeply, passionately, hungry for every ounce of her. He folded her into his arms, pulled her firmly against him, and wallowed breathlessly in her sweetness. Her soft curves and the way she *fit* with him warmed his thoughts like too much whiskey. Desire, foolish and intoxicating, begged his hands to roam.

He tried not to remember the one time they had been together, but he couldn't block it out. He wanted to loosen her braid and let all that golden hair rain down on him like a waterfall. He dragged his lips to her neck, kissed her jaw, hugged her tighter, and nibbled on her ear. Lightheaded, he backed away and held her at arm's length before he crossed a line. He could hear her breathing hard. He imagined he could even hear her heart pounding.

"Oh my," she whispered so softly he almost didn't catch it. "You make me dizzy."

He squeezed her hand. She felt like his wife already, but the rest of that commitment would have to wait. They wouldn't be together as husband and wife until they were wed. He exhaled, a long, deep breath. Soon. . . "We need to speak to our new preacher and see when—"

"Billy," Hannah interrupted, still sounding a bit breathless. "You haven't put the ring on my finger."

Laughing, he slapped his forehead and slipped it off the tip of his pinky. He didn't even remember putting it there, but at least he hadn't dropped it. "My beloved."

Hannah extended her hand and Billy pushed it down her finger.

"Goodness, it's a perfect fit." She held out her hand, but the light was gone. "Hmmm. Guess we'll have to go inside if I actually want to see my engagement ring." She moved her left hand to his face again. "It doesn't matter. I'm sure it's stunning. All I really want is you."

He refrained from kissing her, well aware his self-control was as fragile as butterfly wings. A lack of self-control had caused too much heartache already. He could wait. But he was going to find the preacher tomorrow. "How about we announce the engagement Wednesday night when everyone comes to the hotel for dinner?"

"Yes, all right."

He wrapped his arm around her and they started back for the town hall. She rested her head on his shoulder as they strolled along the path. He would have felt ten feet tall if it wasn't for one small thing.

Why had she taken so long to answer?

CHAPTER 17

*E*milio sat at a corner table watching the crowd in Delilah's. A darkness he could almost see and most definitely feel crept through the room like the smoke from the cigars. Perhaps it had been so long since he'd been in the Iron Horse that he had forgotten the feel of a saloon . . . but he didn't think so. Across from him, Corky guzzled a golden beer.

A banjo and piano kept the atmosphere jangling. Some gal who thought she could sing joined them and screeched out "Sweet Betsy from Pike." Poker chips rattled. Men muttered, laughed, cursed with abandon as they raked in their winnings. Several young girls, mostly Oriental, circulated in the room, delivering drinks. They moved about stiffly and kept their eyes downcast as if they'd rather be anywhere but here.

Emilio tried not to stare as other women—wearing the sheerest robes he had ever seen—pranced down the stairs, advertising vacancies in their beds. They quickly returned upstairs, a man in tow.

Over and over.

A few tables away a man bellowed a curse, flipped over his table, sending cards, half-full mugs of beer, chips, and bags of gold flying. He was immediately tackled by the three other players at the table, and several inconvenienced customers shoved back, booing and hissing. A chair flew through the air, shattering against the wall right behind Emilio. Otis and Smith came from nowhere and leaped into the fray, great arms swinging like oak trees in a hurricane. In mere moments, the fight was squashed. The two bouncers, looking greatly displeased, each had an ornery patron under each arm. Trapped, flailing and protesting, they were dragged to the door and tossed from the building.

Corky and Emilio exchanged disgusted looks. The Crystal Chandelier had anything but Light in its four walls. Repulsed by the depravity here, Emilio was ready to head back to the ranch. Surely Mr. McIntyre didn't expect him to stay the whole time.

He was rising from his seat when he saw Smith sit down at a table with Cloer and Dub. A moment later, a round of beers and a bottle of whiskey landed on their table.

Curious, Emilio sat back down. He didn't need to hear the conversation to get the gist of it. Smith was buying friends. And judging by the serious looks and grim nods, he had made the purchase. Cloer, the oldest of the hands at about thirty, seemed out of place on the ranch, at least to Emilio. The man trembled when he moved, like he needed a drink. And he skated away from any work he could. Shirker. He should work for Smith because Emilio doubted he was going to work long for Mr. McIntyre.

Abruptly, the music died, and Otis lifted Delilah's petite frame to the bar. Emilio couldn't help but notice her tiny waist, pleasing curves, and generous bosom, all encased in a dress the color of red roses and tighter than fish skin. Her auburn hair was twisted stylishly atop her head and held in place with expensive-looking pearls.

The woman had a beautiful face, once a man made it that far. The shadow of something hard and dangerous hid there, concealed in tiny lines and brushed over with powder. He knew that look. Just like his sister Rose, Delilah was a tough customer. Best never to underestimate her.

"Boys!" She patted the air to quiet them. The banjo and piano stopped. "Boys." Slowly, the chatter died. "I am pleased to announce the opening of our Celestial Virgin Auction."

Men clammed up like she'd slammed a door. The silence was abrupt and . . . *hungry*. Appalled, Emilio surveyed the room full of eager faces. Then, a strange, ghostly, melodic sound reached his ears. Like the gentle plucking of a guitar but different. Music, though. Haunting. Sad.

"Yes, can you hear that gentlemen?" Delilah clasped her hands over her heart. "A song from the Orient. A song of lost loves. Broken hearts."

The notes floated in the air and entranced the room. Delilah eyed the crowd, wearing an evil smile cold as a gold nugget.

"A refined young lady from China," she went on, "sold into slavery because she displeased her father. Isn't her music beautiful? And *she* is quite beautiful. Only sixteen. An unopened blossom." Delilah raised her chin. "If you would like a chance to meet Sai Shang, opening bid to enter the other room is $100 dollars." She motioned to the giant Negro waiting at the entrance to the theater. "Give your money to Otis. If you've already made a silent bid, you may go on in."

Several of the miners raked their winnings and bags of gold from their tables and scurried forward. Emilio noted that the cowboys watched with ill expressions.

Maybe they'll stop this. Someone has to . . .

"Ain't you got somethin' a little less pricey? Cloer called. The other cowboys grumbled and nodded in agreement. "How 'bout some ugly virgins?"

The room rumbled with laughter. A miner called out, "Reckon that's what you get for being a cowboy instead of a miner."

"Yeah, broke."

More laughter and complaining rolled through the saloon like a distant peal of thunder. Harsh words flew between cowboys and miners, but Delilah hushed them. "Boys, that's enough. We're all friends here." The arguments died, but not the hard looks. "As to your question about *ugly* virgins, my advice would be start saving your pennies if you're of the mind to purchase a budding Flower."

Livid, Emilio lunged to his feet. "This is wrong. You cannot do this."

Delilah's eyes narrowed at him. "Son, everything in here is wrong. That's what makes it so much fun."

"Everything is overpriced too." Garcia slammed a beer on his table. "But you miners don't care. You spend your money like the fools you are, playing in the mud all day."

The insult begged for a fight and Emilio flinched, knowing it was coming. Bellowing and cursing erupted instantly around the room. Men jumped to their feet, flipping chairs over behind them. The punches started swirling like debris in a twister.

Delilah, surprisingly agile for a woman in a dress that tight, slid to the floor and ran to Otis. "Stop this fight, but whatever you do, keep this door closed."

She grabbed the cashbox from his large hands and hurried inside the theater, slamming the door shut behind her. Emilio grabbed Corky's shoulder. "Go get the marshal."

Corky didn't have to be told twice to fetch help. Eyes wide as harvest moons, he bolted from the saloon. Emilio shot in the opposite direction. Dodging and ducking flying chairs and fists, he raced to the theater door. Otis and Smith were busy trying to bring the melee under control. Taking advantage of their distraction, he tried the knob. Locked.

He couldn't call himself a man if he let this auction happen, but how to stop it?

God, there must be some way . . .

All he had were his bare hands and . . . Desperate, he looked around for anything that would get him through that door. He spied a miner's backpack tucked in the corner behind the piano. A pickaxe was strapped to it. Not wasting a second, Emilio grabbed the tool, ripping it free from its leather ties, and went to work on the door.

He swung hard, splintering and shattering wood. Otis and Smith both saw him, tossed aside the men they were dragging to the door, and made a beeline for him, knocking men down and throwing punches as they went.

Emilio swung over and over, harder and faster. A larger piece of wood tore free. One more strike and he had a hole. He leaned in for a look—

His collar tightened painfully around his neck and he was snatched violently away from the door.

"No—no, boy." Otis tightened his grip on Emilio's shirt and grabbed his pant leg, hefting him into the air. Suddenly, Emilio was looking down at the wild fracas.

Oh, this isn't good ...

A gunshot rang out from the front door and the fighting halted almost instantly. Otis dropped Emilio like a rotten piece of meat, but on his way to the floor Emilio caught a blessed glimpse of Marshal Beckwith, smoking gun pointing at the ceiling, tan blazer swirling around his knees. Beside him, Deputy Wade Hayes stood with his twin Peacemakers drawn on the crowd.

Emilio pushed to all fours, his shoulder throbbing from the fall.

The girl ...

Beckwith thrashed through the crowd, shoving men aside, searching for the initial troublemakers. "All right, I want to know who started this."

A chorus of voices accused the cowboys as Emilio staggered to his feet and clawed his way within earshot of the lawman. "Marshal, the theater," he yelled over the heads of bleeding miners and cowboys. "They're auctioning off a young girl. You have to stop it."

Beckwith stormed toward Emilio, eyes blazing. "Where?" The grim expression on his bony, chiseled face encouraged Emilio.

"The theater."

"Wade, no one leaves," he ordered as he and Emilio strode toward the theater. Reaching the door, it opened unexpectedly. Delilah surveyed the crowd as she brushed her hands down her slender waist. "What seems to be the problem, Marshal?"

The scowl deepened on Beckwith's face. "This is my third excursion to Tent Town this week. Make no mistake, somebody is going to jail. At the very least for disturbing the peace. If you have a young girl in there against her will, I reckon I can arrest you for kidnapping."

"There's no one in there at all." She pressed herself against the doorframe, purposely showing off her curves. "See for yourself."

Beckwith surged past her, entered the room and looked all around. *Too late.* Emilio knew the theater was empty, and his spirits sank. Where was that little *señorita* now? In a tent somewhere with a filthy, drunken miner?

Beckwith came back and stopped in front of Delilah. "Since you opened up shop, I've made more trips to Tent Town in a month than I ever have in a year. Somebody already took a potshot at my deputy. You make my job harder than it has to be—more *dangerous* than it has to be because of the rabble you attract. Now we're adding cowboys to the recipe. They mix with miners like oil and water." He leaned in. "You don't calm things down over here I'll hold you personally responsible."

"You can't do anything to me and you know it."

Beckwith's icy stare drilled into her, unwavering.

"Marshal," she laid her hand lightly on his lapel and lowered her voice, "we don't have to be on opposite sides of the table."

He pushed her hand away. "Yes, we do."

*L*ogan rolled over and stared into the darkness. Sleep eluded him. A boomtown had a sound to it like no other. The tinny banjo and weak, warbling voice of some gal who should stick to humming floated over to him. She couldn't drown out the drunken voices raised in anger not far from the church. Another fight was brewing, this time over a missing pocket watch instead of a woman. Shortly, the smacks, thuds, and grunts of a brawl peppered the air. Logan could hear the crowd growing, based on the cheers, mocking insults, and shrieks of women wanting a bloodier show.

Nevertheless, these sounds weren't why he couldn't sleep. Big Jim had said the auction was tonight. The auction of a virgin to a filthy, drunken, toothless miner no doubt.

And Logan was lying in bed, bellyaching about it. Angry, he sat up and swung his feet over the bed. He had to do something. Frantic pounding erupted at the back door.

"Preacher! Preacher! It's me. Emilio. Please, let me in."

Logan shot to the door and jerked it open. "What is it?"

"We have to find her. We have to save her."

"Who?" He grabbed Emilio's shoulder and pulled him inside. "What are you talking about?"

"Delilah auctioned off Sai Shang tonight. I tried to stop it. A fight broke out, and then she was gone. Marshal Beckwith said he can't do anything."

"Let me get my boots. We'll find her."

CHAPTER 18

*O*nly, they didn't find Sai Shang. Doors slammed in their faces. The girls in Delilah's cribs turned them away. Miners hurried off into the dark, afraid to tangle with Logan. For the millionth time, he wondered if he was wrong in trying to deny his past. If for one moment he could turn loose the old Logan . . . if he could grab one man by the throat, or put a gun to the side of a miner's head—

"Preacher."

Logan pulled his gaze away from a group of miners making tracks down the muddy road. Thus far, it seemed Sai Shang had swallowed by the darkness, lost in the rows of cabins and tents.

Emilio nodded at a shack to their left. "I saw Big Jim in the window. Maybe he can help."

The two hurried to the door. Logan pounded on it, rattling the hinges.

A gun cocked, the door opened, and the barrel of a .44 greeted them. "Only drunks and troublemakers bang on a man's door at this hour."

"It's me, Big Jim. Preacher."

The door instantly flew open and the man hobbled out, lowering the gun. "You got more trouble at your church?"

"No, we're lookin' for a young girl. Sai Shang. Delilah auctioned her off tonight. We thought you might know where she wound up."

Even in the faint light, Logan could see Big Jim's countenance fall. "I reckon I do know. You gonna kill the fella that bought her, are you?"

The hesitation in Big Jim's tone told Logan plenty. "Not if I can help it. Tell me where she's at."

"Jim Rizzo, I heard. Least, I know he was biddin' and he's a big spender."

"Take us to him."

"Preacher, this ain't none of my business."

"For God's sake, she's just a girl."

Emilio stepped forward. "*Maybe* sixteen, and not a hundred pounds soaking wet."

"How can you call yourself a man?" Logan hooked his thumbs in his gun belt. "How can you call yourself a human being if you don't help me stop this?"

"I can't save the world, Preacher."

"I'm not asking you to."

After a tense moment, Big Jim dropped the gun into his holster. "Fine."

***

*L*ogan watched Big Jim with awe. Once the man made up his mind about something, he was as determined as a bull and as ferocious as a grizzly. He stormed through Tent Town like a raging thunderstorm. As they approached a low, one-room cabin, screams shattered the night. Big Jim never slowed down or hesitated. Balancing on his wooden leg, he kicked the door in, shattering it as if it had been blown by a stick of dynamite. Logan had never seen anything like it, especially by a man with one leg.

Guns drawn, he and Emilio hurried in after him, but Big Jim had already swept a naked man into a bear hug, and Sai Shang, her dress in shreds, was scrambling off the bed into a corner.

The man flailed and cursed, and Jim hugged him tighter. "Stop squirming, Rizzo, or I'll squeeze ya in two."

"Let me go, Big Jim. I paid for that gal and I'm gonna finish what I started!"

"No, you ain't." Big Jim glanced at the girl and Logan saw the birth of real compassion in the man's eyes. "You ain't gonna touch her."

Holstering his gun, Emilio tore off his jacket and raced over to Sai Shang, who screamed and cowered and turned her back to him.

"Shhh," Emilio whispered as he draped the coat over her.

Rizzo exploded with curses and tried swinging his head back into Big Jim. "She's mine, she's mine, she's mine! I paid good money for her!"

Jim's patience evaporated. He growled, and brought a hammer blow down right on top of Rizzo's head with eye-popping force. The man's bellowing stopped as suddenly as if someone had slammed a door in his face. Silent, he fell limp as a rag doll.

Big Jim huffed and tossed Rizzo aside. "I hope his head feels like I split it with an axe when he comes to."

Logan whistled in awe. "One punch."

Big Jim cracked his knuckles and winked. "Learned it from you, Preacher."

CHAPTER 19

$\mathcal{H}$annah's heart went out to Sai Shang as she sat beside the young girl. Lying on the bed in the examination room, the poor thing looked so small and frightened in the baggy, ill-fitting men's clothes. Her long, tousled, dark hair and a swollen, bloody lip testified to the last several terrifying hours. Hannah couldn't imagine being alone in an alien culture, surrounded by strange people, unable to speak the language. And then to be nearly raped. A shudder shot up her spine as she wiped away blood from the girl's mouth.

Sai Shang flinched and pulled back, her almond-shaped eyes rounding. Hannah dropped her hand. "I'm so sorry. For . . . for all of it. But you're safe now."

A moment passed between them, and Sai Shang relaxed a little. Hannah smiled and dabbed at the lip again. At least Logan had remembered to grab the girl some clothes, but they had to find something more suitable.

She heard the door, and an instant later Doc eased into the examination room, shirt untucked, graying blond hair a tousled mess. Cleaning his spectacles, he approached the girls. "Well, hello." He slipped on the glasses and peered at the patient.

To Hannah's amazement he jabbered something to Sai Shang in Chinese, which unleashed a torrent of babbling from the girl.

Apparently desperate to communicate, she latched on to Doc and started spouting sounds and words that Hannah couldn't begin to understand. Owl-eyed at her outburst, Doc patted the girl's shoulders, pushed her back to the bed, all while speaking soothingly but haltingly in her native tongue.

"Doc, I didn't know you spoke Chinese."

"I worked for the railroad for a few years back in the sixties. I picked up a little."

He straightened up and scratched his head. "Near as I can tell, a bad man had her, meant to have his way with her . . . but a bear saved her?" He shook his head. "Musta missed something in the translation."

Hannah laughed. "No, I think you got it just right. Crazy as it sounds. Sai Shang was sold in an auction tonight over at the Chandelier. Big Jim Walker, the Preacher, and Emilio rescued her and brought her here."

"That so?" Doc *tsked* the situation. "That Delilah. Talk about a woman with no shame. Well, what are you plannin' on doing with this little celestial Flower, now that you've saved her from indentured servitude and a life of prostitution?"

"Well," Hannah squirmed under Doc's skeptical what-have-you-gotten-yourself-into look. "Mollie went to find Mrs. Lee. She owns the laundry. We thought maybe she could keep Sai Shang . . . for a while, anyway."

Doc took a step back and sat on the corner of a small table. "That might not be a bad idea. Put her with her own people. 'Least she could understand something."

Hannah dipped a finger in a small jar of menthol and peppermint and dabbed it on the cut on Sai Shang's lip. "I wish she could understand me. I'd like her to know I'm her friend."

"Say *pengyou*."

"*Pengyou*?"

Little Sai Shang's eyes ricocheted back and forth between Doc and Hannah as they talked.

"*Pengyou*," Hannah whispered, testing the word again, then faced her patient. Moving her hand from herself to Sai Shang, she said, "*Pengyou. Pengyou.*"

Doc intervened and said something more, and Hannah heard *pengyou* in there somewhere. Sai Shang nodded and then gave Hannah a tentative smile.

Hannah beamed. "I'm sure we could be great friends if we could understand each other."

Sai Shang babbled away at Doc for a moment. He rubbed his chin, listening attentively, then babbled something back slow and haltingly, motioning a time or two to Hannah.

"What did she say?"

"She wanted to know if you were a doctor too. 'Least that's what I think she asked."

"Oh. Oh, so you told her I'm a nurse."

"I don't know the word for nurse. Far as she's concerned, you're a doctor. And I told her we'll keep the bad man away from her."

The door opened again and Mollie entered, trailed by an unusually tall, slender, middle-aged Oriental woman wearing a traditional Chinese suit of dark blue silk. Mollie touched the woman's elbow. "I found Mrs. Lee. She said she'd help."

Doc stood up to greet them. "Mollie, Mrs. Lee."

"Mornin', Doc."

Mrs. Lee ducked her chin and did a small bow.

"Hannah, it doesn't look like Sai Shang is too much the worse for wear, but with Mrs. Lee here we can be sure. While you three talk, I'm gonna slip home and fry me up some breakfast. I'll be right back."

"Thanks, Doc."

Mrs. Lee sat down on the bed with Sai Shang and the two started jabbering at a frantic pace. At one point, the older lady pulled the girl's shirt up and touched her ribs, then nodded. She then motioned to Mollie and Hannah, as if explaining their presence. After another few minutes, Mrs. Lee sat back and addressed the girls.

"This man who took her tried to rape her, but she was saved. Yes, he hit her a few times, but she will have only minor bruises." She picked up Sai Shang's arm and pulled back a sleeve to show the marks on the girl's wrists. Both Mollie and Hannah flinched.

Sai Shang pulled her arm away and engaged Mrs. Lee in more conversation. Hannah watched the women's faces carefully. They didn't seem to be having a happy conversation, but she saw the acceptance settle on both of them.

"She has never worked, as she comes from a wealthy family. I explain to her the situation. She can be a prostitute or work in my laundry. She say she choose laundry."

The girl added something quickly and Mrs. Lee nodded, looking more pleased. "She says she work hard. I will not need to sell her to a man for his pleasure. Not that I would, of course."

Hannah touched Mrs. Lee's arm. "Could you tell her that we would like to be her friends and help her in any way we can? We could give her dresses if she needs them."

"We could try to teach her some English," Mollie offered.

"That is very generous of you." Mrs. Lee relayed the information to Sai Shang.

Sai Shang studied Hannah for a moment, then Mollie, and slowly allowed a tiny smile. "*Xie xie.*"

"She say 'thank you.'" Sai Shang went off into another frantic conversation with Mrs. Lee, who listened intently for a moment, then shook her head and pulled away a bit, waving her hand. "She ask me if I can take the other girls away from Crystal Chandelier. I run a laundry, not a boarding house."

Hannah leaned forward, grabbed Sai Shang's hand and held her gaze. "Tell her, somehow, we'll get them out. I promise." *Oh,*

Lord, surely there's something we can do . . . "We'll pray. Tell her we'll pray for them and their release."

Mrs. Lee again relayed Hannah's words. Confusion and finally hope surfaced on the girl's face. She clutched Hannah's hand desperately tight and nodded.

Hannah knew Sai Shang was going to hold her to this promise.

Sunday morning. Billy had a good feeling about the day as he finished tying his tie in front of the mirror. He was proud as a rooster to take Hannah and Little Billy to church on a regular basis. Life was good and he whispered a *thank You* as he stepped into the hallway of the former saloon.

He still had a while before church; the hour was early. He thought he might have a cup of coffee then take a walk, do a little praying and a little thinking. The hotel was nearly complete and he'd found three women in town, miners' wives, who were eager to do something other than sift through cold mud for gold nuggets. He, however, did not want to live in the hotel, and was considering reworking the second floor of the mercantile. It could easily be made into an apartment for his new family.

Approaching the stairs, he heard footsteps and came back from his musings, expecting to see Hannah or Mollie. He did not expect their condition. The two girls trudged up the stairs as if they hadn't an ounce of strength left in their bodies. Their braids were loose and frayed, and they had gray smudges under the eyes.

"You two look as if you've been in a saloon all night."

Both girls started at his voice. Hannah clutched her throat. "You scared me. I'm about half asleep."

"You look it too." Billy didn't mean to sound annoyed, but he was, vaguely. Where had she been?

"I'll let you two talk." Mollie nodded at them both as she slipped past Billy. "See you at church."

Billy returned her nod then patted Hannah's hand as she hugged his arm. "Is everything all right?" he asked.

"I'm exhausted. We've been up all night. If I can just get an hour's nap, I'll be ready for church." She yawned and leaned her head on his shoulder.

Hannah still had not answered his question and he fought the urge for more aggressive questioning. Perhaps she sensed it.

"Emilio and Preacher found the girl who was auctioned off at Delilah's place last night. Emilio asked me to come look her over. I brought Mollie in case I needed any help."

Billy held his face still, but inwardly he was churning. *Emilio. Ever the hero.* He shouldn't be jealous, but he couldn't help himself.

"Anyway, we made sure she was all right and then hid her. Even the Preacher doesn't know where's she's at. It's a temporary solution at best."

A dozen questions raced through Billy's mind, but he picked the most obvious one with which to start. "Where's our son? Why didn't you leave him with me?"

Hannah obviously heard the frustrated tone in his voice. She released his arm and stepped back. "I knocked on your door. Twice. I know you're tired from working at the mercantile and trying to get the hotel ready to open. When you didn't wake up, I decided to take Little Billy over to Rebecca and Ian's."

Properly humbled, Billy nodded and grasped his hands behind his back. Emilio was always awake. Always ready to go. Always ready to save damsels in distress. He groaned at the petulant thought and raked his hand through his hair. "I'm sorry. I should have been there for you . . . and Emilio."

Hannah stepped up to him again and laid a hand on his chest. "Don't beat yourself up. If I'd thought it was important, I would have woken you. All that matters is Sai Shang is safe."

"Yeah." That should make Billy feel better. It didn't.

She kissed him on the cheek. "Wake me in an hour?"

"Sure." Hannah smiled and dragged her fingers across his hand as she disappeared into her own room.

Billy tried not to read too much into things, and rolled his shoulders to release some tension. It didn't help. His inadequacies compared to Emilio felt glaring this morning.

The man had lived a pretty adventurous life. He'd tracked Indians and bandits, grown up in a saloon, met the Indian chief Cochise, knew how to ride and rope, and make medicines out of herbs.

Billy could run a dry goods store and hotel.

Yippy-ki-yay.

CHAPTER 20

*M*cIntyre lifted his feet to the porch rail and pushed back in the rocking chair as Garcia finished his story.

"Emilio, uh, he say things, insult the miners, and the fight broke out." The early morning sun peeked over the cabin roof, hitting Garcia in the face. Squinting, he stepped a little closer to the porch, into the shade. "I slipped out when the marshal showed up."

A fascinating tale. McIntyre laced his fingers over his abdomen and pondered the story, at least this version according to the new man. The summer birds singing a morning greeting and the muffled mooing of cows off in the valley intruded on his thoughts. The sounds should have heralded a pleasant Sunday. Instead, the day was off to a rocky start. "And what of the auction?" he finally asked.

"I don't know." Garcia spun his sombrero in front of him. "The *señorita*, Delilah, she went with some men to a different room. That was the last I saw of her."

Gravel crunched and McIntyre looked past Garcia. Emilio

drew up when he saw the ranch hand. His gaze darted between the two men. "I came to tell you some news, Mr. McIntyre."

"The incident at The Crystal Chandelier. Yes, Garcia was just filling me in."

Emilio looked sideways at the young man. "You weren't there when the marshal showed up."

Garcia raised his chin. "I saw no need to get arrested for a fight I didn't start or want."

"Thank you, Garcia," McIntyre interrupted. "I appreciate the update."

It took the lad a moment to understand he was dismissed. He finally nodded at McIntyre and Emilio. "*Si.*"

When he disappeared around the corner, Emilio approached the bottom porch step and removed his hat. "He told you what happened at The Crystal Chandelier last night?"

"His version. He said you started the fight."

Emilio's eyes bulged like balloons. "*Señor* McIntyre, I—"

"Relax, Emilio. Garcia is buckin' for a promotion. I could see that from a mile away. Besides, I know you would not *start* a fight."

A strained, arguably guilty expression flitted across the boy's face. McIntyre leaned forward. "What aren't you telling me?"

Emilio worried his hat for a moment. "I spent the night looking for the young girl that Delilah auctioned off."

"I see." Admiration and guilt struck McIntyre simultaneously. A young Mexican boy was doing more to make a difference in Defiance than its founder was. "So you did start the fight?"

"No sir. I didn't know what to do. I spoke up. I said we should stop the auction. But the cowboys started complaining the opening bid was too high. Garcia called the miners fools. The miners insulted the cowboys—"

"And the fists started flying."

"*Si.* I did try to get into the room where the auction was but the door was locked."

163

"And none of the cowboys tried to stop this auction."

"No sir. Cloer and Dub got arrested along with Willy and Parker. I don't know if Marshal Beckwith arrested any miners."

Unfortunately, none of this surprised McIntyre. Some ranchers expected their boys to get into trouble and would bail them out of jail. The support would engender loyalty to the brand.

McIntyre did not want loyalty that way. He wanted men of decent and honorable character—or at least men who were smart enough not to get arrested in the first place.

Oh, he would get them out of jail. The bail, however, would come out of their pay. He slapped the arms on the rocking chair and stood. "We will leave them in jail for the day. I'll fetch them this evening. Did you find the girl?"

"*Si*. We took her to Doc's. Hannah and Mollie were with her when I left."

"Hannah and Mollie." McIntyre suddenly realized the full impact of what had happened last night. He doubted Delilah was going to be happy about this interference. "What are they planning on doing with her?"

The tense lines on Emilio's face said he hadn't thought that far ahead. "I don't know." His expression hardened. "But I do know selling these girls, it is wrong. I have seen so much of this. They don't come to good endings. Especially the girls from China."

"I know. I know." McIntyre lowered his head, rested his hands on his hips. "We will figure something out."

"*Si* . . . well, I am going to get ready for church."

"All right." McIntyre watched him amble back toward the bunkhouse.

"He's a good man." Naomi slipped up behind McIntyre and wrapped her arms around him. "Hannah wouldn't have gone wrong picking him either."

McIntyre clutched her fingers at his waist, wishing they had more time before church. He wondered that taking a walk at dusk last evening with his beautiful wife was nearly as satisfying as exploring every inch of her. Different ways of loving her, and both filled his soul.

He spun around to her and gathered her up against himself. He had a suspicion he'd be lucky to get either activity today. His displeasure must have shown on his face.

"I heard. This Delilah is a . . . a . . ."

"The word 'cancer' comes to mind."

"I didn't tell you . . . I ran into her in the mercantile. She was positively horrible to Two Spears. If Hannah hadn't been there . . . well, let's just say I've been repenting ever since."

McIntyre knew Naomi was not trying to be funny. "What did she say?"

"She called him a half-breed and a savage. Said he wasn't good for anything but emptying chamber pots."

McIntyre's teeth ground together. A sneer tugged at his lip and fury flexed his fingers.

"And that is exactly why I didn't tell you."

He blinked. "What?"

"If you could see your face. You care about that boy more than you want to admit. Comments like those bother you . . . *test* you."

He tightened his grip on Naomi and rested his cheek on her head, savoring the soft golden hair that smelled of lilacs. "My father was a worthless human being, as I have said before. He was drunk in a brothel in Savannah when the Yankees raided our home." He paused here, never willing to recall the brutal attack on his mother. He had been caught up in the siege of Petersburg with General Lee, but his father should have been there to protect her. "I vowed a long time ago I would love and protect my own family better than he did."

"But don't lose your soul in the process, Charles. I understand that's what you're afraid of. It's that issue of control again. Who's really in charge?"

Unexpectedly, a verse drifted through his mind. *But our God is in the heavens: He hath done whatsoever He hath pleased.* Would it please Him to protect Two Spears?

"He is a *child*...and my *son*. I am...strangely affected by concerns for his safety."

She bit her lip, obviously hiding a smile. "I think the word you're looking for is 'protective.' And love makes you vulnerable, apt to do foolish things, react the wrong way, as I myself have on more than one occasion." She smiled up at him, tenderly, with understanding. "Thankfully, there is grace. Lots of it."

---

*L*ogan knelt beside his cot and leaned on the mattress. A nail poked him in the kneecap and he shifted his position. He gave thought to letting the nail head grind into him. He felt like he needed some punishment, some torture for all the evil in this town that he *wasn't* stopping.

He buried his face in his hands and groaned. Emilio's story last night of what had transpired at The Crystal Chandelier had them both sick to their stomachs. At least for the time being Sai Shang was safe. But what of the other girls there?

"Oh, God, show me how to stop this flesh trade. Sitting idly by while young women are violated . . . I feel useless here. Show me what to do. The old Logan could have done more for You."

The temptation to cast off his service to God and call down the thunder on Delilah—his kind of thunder—was tempting. He was fast with his fists. Faster with a gun. He could take every one of those girls away from Delilah. Neither she nor her hired men would be able to stop him.

He turned and settled on his rear end, resting his arms on his knees, his back against the cot. If he went back to his old ways, he might save the girls, but how many men would he send straight to hell in the process? Besides, he knew he wasn't supposed to settle things that way. God hadn't saved him just so he could start killing again.

Then what, Lord? What?

Delilah.

Logan knew somehow in his soul that success, failure, life, death, victory over the darkness here, it all hinged on Delilah. Yet he didn't even want to pray for the woman.

"Forgive my hard heart, Lord. Your Word *says Woe unto the world because of offenses! For it must needs be that offenses come; but woe to that man by whom the offense cometh!* . . . She has no idea what she's doing. The darkness she's dancing with. I pray, Father, she'll turn from her wicked ways . . . before it's too late." He pondered his feelings for a moment, struggling with his anger and desire to see her get justice.

Though I speak with the tongues of men and of angels, and have not charity, I am become as sounding brass, or a tinkling cymbal.

Paul's words leaped up and slapped him in the face.

"I know. I know. I need Your compassion, God. Give me a heart that cares, Lord. Help me love Delilah. I can't do it on my own."

---

*A*ny Sunday that did not bring vandalism to the church was a day Logan knew he should appreciate despite his heavy heart. These past few Sundays had passed without any trouble. He surveyed the clean front door with satisfaction, but not joy.

"Thank You for this at least, Lord." He was about to step back inside when he heard . . . snoring? He listened and heard it again. He followed the raw, edgy sound down the steps and peered around the corner of the church.

Big Jim Walker sat on the ground, his back against a rain barrel, snoring loud enough to wake the residents of Boot Hill.

"Big Jim?" Logan approached the man, careful to keep an eye on Sleeping Beauty's gun hand, in case he didn't awaken in a trusting mood. "Big Jim Walker." He kicked his foot. The man stirred and grumbled. Logan felt a little like he was disturbing a bear. "You should wake up."

Big Jim snuffled, flapped his lips, opened his eyes, and assessed Logan with confusion, then surprise. Stretching and yawning, he hauled himself to his feet. "Mornin', Preacher."

"Mornin'. What are you doin' here? Did you sleep here?"

"Ahem, yep," he muttered, arranging his hat, then his vest and cartridge belt and holster. "My partner's been watching our claim on Saturdays, so I could watch yours."

Logan was taken aback. "That's kind of you, Big Jim, but I'm pretty capable of dealing with any unwanted visitors."

"Know you are. I just have a pet peeve about what the bootlicker did to your door. Cowardly acts are a burr under my saddle. And last night, well, I wasn't sure what kind of a mood might come over Rizzo."

"I see. Well . . . will you be staying for church?"

"Nah, but I did tell a couple of fellas in our company about you. They'll be here."

"I thank you for that then and for your help last night." The two shook hands. "I'll keep the front pew open for you, just in case."

Big Jim winked at him. "You do that."

---

*L*ogan stood at his pulpit, astounded by the full pews. True to Big Jim's word, three men he had invited showed up for preaching, and three more filtered in that Logan had invited earlier in the week. Two of the new hands from McIntyre's ranch had ridden in with their boss as well. Nice to know some of them weren't in jail.

Ian and Rebecca nodded courteously at him as they sat; Emilio and Mollie trailing them did the same. And Hannah and her son entered last, followed by Billy. One of these days, he was going to ask the young man what was on his mind. Logan had caught Billy staring hard at him several times, as if he was trying to place him. Logan was pretty sure he didn't know Billy. He nodded at him. Billy nodded back. Still puzzled, Logan turned his attention to the whole congregation.

The church felt almost full. He was grateful, and for an instant, he wondered if he *was* making an impact. Then a noticeable absence hit him hard.

He'd thought for sure Mary Jean would be a regular.

---

*L*ack of sleep fought to pull Hannah under. The hard pew, Little Billy's squirming, not even the walk to church made a dent in her grogginess. All she wanted was a nap.

The jingle of a wagon outside snapped her out of the fog and she passed her son to Billy. "I need to speak with Charles before church. I'll hurry."

Billy's face lit up as he took his son in his arms. "We'll be right here . . . won't we, little man?"

Hannah, hurrying past the pews, was struck by how full they were, especially with new faces. She prayed the numbers would climb every Sunday.

Charles pulled the wagon to a halt in front of the church and set the brake.

"Good morning." Hannah walked to the edge of the church's porch and waved at the family. "Good to see y'all this morning."

"And you," Naomi replied, waiting for Charles to come around. Two Spears jumped down like a little gazelle and gazed up at the church with a bored expression.

Charles helped Naomi and as they made their way up the

steps, Hannah took a step down. "Charles, can I talk to you for a moment?"

He and Naomi both looked taken aback by the request.

"It's about the Oriental girls at the saloon."

Charles and Naomi exchanged understanding glances. "Come on, Two Spears." She laid a hand on his shoulders. "Let's you and me go get a seat."

"I will be right along," Charles promised them then stepped back to the wagon.

Hannah followed. "I promised Sai Shang I would do something to get the rest of her sisters out of The Crystal Chandelier."

Charles's brow rose. "Now why would you promise something like that?"

"Because I know you can do it."

"Me?"

Hannah's shoulders sagged. "You're going to do something, aren't you?"

Well aware that her big china-blue eyes could soften some pretty hard hearts, she gazed up at her brother-in-law like a lost puppy.

Confusion, guilt, and amusement flickered across his face. He leaned down and tapped her lightly on the chin. "Those tricks do not work on me, young lady." A wry smile tipped his lips. "Besides, I already know I have to do something."

Hannah breathed a huge sigh of relief. "I knew you would."

"Sai Shang is hiding somewhere with the Chinese?"

"She's with Mrs. Lee."

"I had assumed as much. It will not take Delilah long to figure that out." Charles put his arm around Hannah and gently guided her toward the steps. "Emilio said only you and Mollie know. Is that still the case?"

"As far as I know."

"Make sure it stays that way."

CHAPTER 21

*A*fter services, Logan shook hands, spent a few minutes talking with everyone at the door, and promised to join the McIntyres at their ranch for supper. Apparently, they were having a big Sunday meal to celebrate the arrival of the cattle.

He felt compelled to go check on Mary Jean first. He spent a few minutes in prayer, trying to determine if he was hearing the Lord or . . . his own heart.

No clarity came. He dragged his hand through his hair and rose from his knees. He felt he should go, but dread nagged him. He really didn't want to go anywhere near The Crystal Chandelier, but he didn't know where she lived. "Lord," he dropped his hat on his head and reached for his cartridge belt and holster. "I pray she's all right. And I pray you'll protect me from whatever I might be walkin' into."

*R*ain, steady and almost peaceful, met him at the door. He went back to his small room in the rear of the church for his duster then trudged through the summer shower. Sunday afternoon on a rainy day in Tent Town didn't slow most of the miners. They worked their claims or headed to McIntyre's mine, downpour or sunshine. A few noticed him as he walked by, but most kept their heads down, focused on their tin pans or paths through the mud. He'd be willing to bet they'd all notice him going into The Crystal Chandelier.

His doubts about this trip, the picture it presented, assailed him as he approached the saloon. Just then he heard an angelic voice singing "Amazing Grace." Shockingly, aside from a piano, no other sound emanated from the saloon. He approached the batwings and peered in. The place was full but at this hour, the patrons were not drunk yet. Something, however, had arrested their attention, and they were all staring in the direction of the bar.

No, the *end* of the bar, in the corner. A man with a cigar hanging from his mouth sat hunched over a piano, playing softly, and watching the singer intently. On the other side of his perch, a young lady with raven hair twisted up in a loose bouffant, and wearing a daringly tight green dress stood alone. A sweet, haunting version of the church favorite passed through her ruby red lips.

Even Logan was mesmerized by the girl's voice for a moment. Without thinking, he drifted into the saloon, pulled his hat to his chest, and moved toward the singer. He shuffled like a man in a trance, the clear, strong voice holding him spellbound.

The voice was beautiful. The girl was beau. . .

Mary Jean?

The trance shattered and reality crashed in, swamping him beneath a wave of pain. The kind he couldn't put into words .

Mary Jean's song ended and The Crystal Chandelier customers applauded with cautious enthusiasm.

"That was great, honey," a man sitting halfway back yelled, "but how about something a little more spicy now?"

Others chimed in, agreeing. Mary Jean's eyes widened. Like a trapped animal, she searched the room for . . . a friendly face, someone who appreciated her choice of song. But when her eyes fell on Logan, her expression changed from uncertainty, maybe even fear, to shame.

She hung her head and scurried to a room behind the bar. The piano player stood up and addressed the crowd, plucking a cigar from his mouth. "Give her a break, boys. Like I said, that was an audition. We'll get her right."

The men nodded, mumbled their approval; a smattering of applause went around the room. Logan choked his hat, wondering if he should go see Mary Jean, or just leave. His insides felt all twisted up and he couldn't make his feet move in one direction or the other.

What had she done to herself? Why the hair coloring?

A whiff of whiskey blindsided him with a craving he hadn't had in months. *I have to get out of here . . .*

"Miss Delilah would like to see you." A deep, throaty baritone voice jarred Logan out of his desperate thoughts. He turned to a mountain of flesh and flannel. A black man, the one he'd seen trailing Delilah, towered over him.

Logan took an instant to clear his head. Maybe it was time to see Delilah, confront this woman. Try to talk to her. Then he would talk to Mary Jean. Maybe this change in her wasn't what it looked like.

But it did look an awful lot like grooming.

---

*a*t least Delilah had not requested his presence in her bedroom. He would have had to say no. Her office was bad enough.

She had the shades pulled and one lamp burned on the desk, where a plush leather chair waited for her. Logan sat down in a simple ladder-back across from it. Shadows hid most of her office, but he knew Delilah was in here with him. He could smell her over-sweet perfume, mixed with the aroma of whiskey.

The black man left the room without a word and Logan set his hat on his knee. "I know you're in here."

"I'm not hiding." Glass clinked against glass. A shot glass full of whiskey appeared in front of his face, held by long, elegant fingers. "Here."

He breathed in the woodsy scent of whiskey. The odor clung to his nose—sweet, evil, tempting, and he jerked back. "No thank you."

She set it on the desk in front of him and meandered around to her side, her bustle swamping the chair as she settled. Logan swallowed and looked past her and the alcohol, trying to forget their nearness.

Delilah leaned forward. In the glow of the lamp, she was startlingly beautiful. The flames flickered in her eyes, highlighted her high cheekbones. Plump, moist lips and waves of silky, auburn hair resting on her bare shoulders tempted him to recall the life he'd once lived. A life with no rules—consequences be damned.

He felt a tightening in his chest. Darkness swirled around him, and he didn't mean the shadows. "What do you want?"

Delilah leaned closer still, bringing more light to her face, and a hypnotic gleam to her eyes. "Have I changed that much?"

Logan didn't know how to answer. She seemed almost to be pleading with him.

"You've aged hard," she said, searching his face, "but I still see the boy from Dodge City."

What . . .?

"Oh, I had to look for him. But he's there. Same eyes. Same lips. And then you shaved and I saw the scar." She slowly dragged a long red nail down her jaw. "You got that hoisting yourself up into Bart Tilley's hayloft, and the hook came undone. Dropped you on your head."

The blood in Logan's veins slowed to an icy crawl. Suddenly, the memories exploded on him like a Texas twister. "Victoria?"

The girl he'd been stone-cold crazy about, but whose name he hadn't said in years. He'd allowed the memories of the stolen kisses or romps in the moonlight to play out only in his dreams.

He stared into her face, seeing the girl, remembering the innocence. Picnics by the pond. A cane fishing pole, bare feet hanging off the dock. A Christmas dance with a kiss under the mistletoe.

Then he'd fallen in with a group of boys fast enough to outrun anything but trouble. They'd given Logan his first sip of whiskey.

Victoria couldn't compete with his love of the bottle. Too many times he'd chosen the booze over the girl. Then one day she was simply gone. She'd climbed aboard a stage and headed off for a job far away from Dodge. At least according to her mother. So Logan had soothed his broken heart with more whiskey and fist fights—gun fights when the mood struck or the pay was good.

"I thought I meant something to you." A hint of acid wove its way around her words. "You promised you'd love me forever. Never forget me." She sat back, hiding her face with darkness. "Two years after I left Dodge, you wandered into Madame Rochelle's place in Fort Worth, drunker than a rat drowning in a barrel of rye."

"I don't remember—"

"I know. You didn't remember me then either. Do you at least remember beating the hound out of me because I wouldn't take you upstairs? If you'd only remembered me, I would have . . ."

Remorse swelled in Logan, crushing his heart. He ran a frantic hand through his hair. Faces flashed before him. Bloody noses, black eyes, bruised bodies. He'd abused so many, including the girl he could have loved. "I'm sorry," he whispered, horrified at Delilah's revelations, at what a monster he'd been. *God, forgive me.* Regret descended on him like a death shroud. He'd thought he'd dealt with his sins, but he hadn't. Because of Christ, he saw how truly evil he'd been and now to have a woman—a woman he had cared for—facing him, recounting his sins, was staggering. He had done such vile things. "I drank all the time back then, especially after you left. It made it—*me*—worse."

Delilah snorted in disgust and came back into the light, her expression a mask of hideous, unabashed hate. "That's supposed to excuse it? The lies? The empty promises?" Her lip curled into a blistering sneer. "What I became?"

"Delilah," Logan surged to his feet, "Victoria," he corrected, "you don't know how sorry I am. I ain't that man no more. I've changed—"

"People don't change."

"You did."

For an instant, the comment seemed to give Delilah pause. She pursed her lips. A sneer warred with a softer expression. The sneer won. "Sai Shang was sold for an evening's entertainment. Mr. Rizzo was to return her to me today at noon. Instead, he informed me that she was taken from his cabin last night . . . without the terms of the auction . . . being fulfilled."

Logan scoured Delilah's face for any hint of the girl she used to be. The face he remembered, yet even the tiniest *shred* of inno-cence had been completely erased and replaced by something dark and cold. "I remember you had a laugh . . ." He sat down again, reliving an afternoon spent running through a cornfield, a kiss beneath a giant oak, and tickling her until she couldn't breathe. "A laugh that sounded like birds singing. I used to love to hear it."

Delilah raised her fingers, as if to drum them on the desk, but folded them into a fist instead. A ruby ring on her finger glimmered like a drop of blood. "I returned to Mr. Rizzo his five hundred dollars. Now I want my property returned to me."

Logan understood he had hurt her. Could he ever make amends? For the moment, it didn't matter. Delilah was clearly done with her walk down memory lane. "I don't know where Sai Shang is and that's the truth." He and Emilio had thought it better if they didn't know.

"You'll be sorry you interfered, Preacher." She spat the word like it revolted her. Her eyes riveted on his. "Hell hath no fury."

Like a woman scorned . . .

Her attention flickered to Logan's left and her chin jerked up. Pain ignited in his head like Fourth of July fireworks, only to be swallowed up by inky blackness.

CHAPTER 22

"*I* know a warning when I get one."

Logan heard McIntyre's voice, but the annoyed Southern drawl was far away, and difficult to heed over this painful throbbing in his head. He touched his temple, his fingers landing on a pretty tender goose egg.

"'e's comin' 'round."

Ian Donoghue. Logan tried to open his eyes. They didn't want to cooperate at first. He persisted and finally they fluttered open. Blinking, he brought the room into focus, Ian and McIntyre staring down at him. "Where am I?" He didn't recognize the Spartan room. "What happened?"

"You are at the Sunnyside Mine office." McIntyre crossed his arms and chewed thoughtfully on his cheek. "Someone delivered you here. Unconscious."

"Wha—?" Logan grabbed the back of the bench he was lying on and pulled himself up. Pain stomped around in his head like a troop of elephants. He groaned and lowered his head into his hands. "What did they hit me with? A sledgehammer?"

"The butt of a gun, most likely." Ian lifted the hair at Logan's forehead. "Ye've got a bit of a cut. I dunna think ye need stitches, but ye should let Doc look at it."

"Where were you today, Logan?" McIntyre asked, concern or suspicion in his voice. Maybe both. "After church? You never made it to the ranch, so Ian and I came to get my men out of jail and check on you. Imagine my surprise when I learned you had been seen going into The Crystal Chandelier. Do you think that was wise?"

"I was . . ." Logan straightened up, tried to think past the blinding pain. He'd been at church. A melody played in his head. "Amazing Grace"? Mary Jean on the stage came back to him with jarring clarity . . . as did his meeting with Delilah. "I know her," he whispered in shock. "God forgive me, I knew her when she was a girl."

"Make sense," McIntyre commanded.

Logan shook his head, trying to rid himself of the headache . . . and the agonizing regret. "I knew her." He looked at both men. "Delilah. We were just kids back in Dodge and I said things, promised her things . . . and I didn't even recognize her."

A heavy silence hung over them like the pall of a funeral. McIntyre took a deep breath and shook his head. "Hell hath no fury like a woman scorned."

Hell hath no fury. The phrase reverberated through Logan like a gong. "She blames me for . . . the way she turned out, I guess."

"But why deliver you to me?" McIntyre turned and paced to the window, one hand behind his back, the other rubbing his chin.

"She wants her property back. She wants Sai Shang. I told her I don't know where she's at. Emilio and I told Hannah and Mollie to hide her."

"She must think *I* know. Perhaps your *misfortune* was a warning shot across my bow: Give up Sai Shang or expect more trouble."

"And don't interfere again." Logan flinched at the ringing in his ears. "That made her almost as angry as taking the girl."

"That dusna' bode well for any of us."

"If anyone knows how the Lord can work in someone's heart, it is you and me, Logan." McIntyre turned to them. "But until He decides to move we have to assume we've kicked a hornet's nest. We must figure some way to deal with it."

"The marshal and I are working on town bylaws," Ian tossed a paperweight in the air over and over, "but it will take a bit of time before we can employ fines or legal punishments against her."

"Maybe we can strangle her."

Logan swung his head in McIntyre's direction, instantly regretting the forceful motion. "Not that I haven't thought about that, but I think, as men of God, it ain't an option for us."

"I meant financially. Strategically."

"Well, while you figure the ins and outs," Logan stood, "I'm going back to see her." His head swam and he teetered for a moment, but he waved away Ian and McIntyre's concern. "I'm fine. I'm fine. Maybe I'll see her after I get some rest. But I can't leave this where it's lying. If I can make her believe I'm sorry, that I've changed . . ."

"Logan," McIntyre regarded him with a mix of pity and impatience. "If I have ever met a soulless woman, it is Delilah. Forgiveness will not come easy to her. If at all. And there will still be the matter of the property she wants returned."

Logan stared at the floor. "I know." The look in her eyes would haunt him. He'd never seen such bitterness. Only God could reach into that abyss. *But aren't we His hands and feet?* "I have to try."

"Well, give it day or so. Perhaps she will be more agreeable after she calms down a bit."

"Or less," Ian interjected under his breath.

McIntyre chose to ignore him. "Besides, you need to recover from that wallop on your head."

And his heart, Logan realized.

*S*ure he was scowling, McIntyre folded his collar up against a dismal rain and second-guessed his motivations for coming to Tent Town. His eyes skimmed over the muddy miners in their worn, drenched clothes, and the half-dressed, used-up prostitutes standing in front of their tents. The air reverberated with the sounds of pelting raindrops, flowing sluices, men cursing their pans, and women squabbling like screeching hens.

He did not want to be here, but Emilio and Logan's courage in rescuing Sai Shang had made him realize he had a responsibility to this town. He had founded Defiance. He wanted the best for it. He was *expected* to protect it from people like Delilah.

Additionally, dumping Logan on the steps of the mine was the same as being called out. He could not ignore that.

He was here for the right reasons . . . wasn't he?

The question dogged him.

Men stared at him as he marched on, but no one spoke. He was glad of it. He was not in the mood for idle chatter. Surely his grim mood was evident on his face. Or perhaps they could see it in his determined stride.

God, You've given me a family I would die for. A town I want to see rise to better things. Why then, do I have this doubt? If You want me to loosen my grip . . . show me how. Make it plain.

Shaking away the confusing thoughts, he refocused on the muddy walk before him and was surprised to see Emilio and Mollie hurrying toward him.

The two of them held a piece of canvas over their heads to block the rain. A gun hung from the young man's side and the girl carried a package tucked under her arm. McIntyre stopped and rested his hands on his hips. Water rolled off the brim of his hat and down the back of his coat, one cold rivulet making its way into his collar and torturing his neck. "It's not Sunday. What are you two doing over here?"

The couple stopped short. Guilt skittered across their faces.

"You remember what happened last time?" McIntyre directed the question at Mollie. Tom Hawthorn's fingers clenching on Naomi's throat were as vivid in his mind right now as if it had happened yesterday. All because she and Mollie had thought they could ramble about Tent Town safe as sprites.

Mollie snugged the package closer, blue eyes wide with concern. "Yes sir. I remember. We'll stay out of trouble."

Emilio patted the gun. "She'll be safe with me."

The answer didn't pacify McIntyre. Emilio could handle himself, but what was worth the risk? "Neither one of you said why you're here."

Mollie motioned with the package. "I brought Sai Shang a few dresses. And I thought we'd peek in on Amanda."

McIntyre pursed his lips and nodded. Amanda had wandered into the Iron Horse some months back looking for a job. Instead, McIntyre had tried to give her a vocation and money for college. The siren song of booze, and perhaps fear of change, had drawn her back into this darkness. Mollie had visited her several times now, to no avail.

One could argue darkness was winning on this side of Defiance, if not for the fact that Sai Shang was safe.

He speared Emilio with a somber gaze. "It is getting late. Get Mollie out of here as quick as you can. And for her sake, keep Sai Shang's whereabouts quiet."

"*Si.* I intend to."

The rain now seeping through his coat, McIntyre quickly stepped past them and resumed the trek to see Delilah, his doubts on his heels.

Assuming he was in the right, just how was he supposed to get her to leave Defiance?

He couldn't physically abuse the woman and demand that she get out of town. He certainly couldn't kill her. He supposed he could play a game of cards with her, but his gambling days were behind him as well. Besides, Delilah was a cardsharp. Short of cheating, a win was not guaranteed. He did, however, have the glimmer of an idea. A faint hope.

He could try a bluff.

Lord, I am not used to being in this position. Give me the words, the strategy, to stop this woman.

McIntyre came around the corner of the cobbler's tent and stopped in his tracks. A large, two-story, pine-lapped building stood on the two lots that had once accommodated the Lucky Deuce and Wolf's Head saloons. A sign painted in garish black, red, and gold announced *The Crystal Chandelier.* Beer. Liquor. Girls.

Might as well say Gate to Hell.

The thought sent a chill through him and he pulled his coat tighter.

This new saloon was high, wide, and imposing. Delilah was known for going all-out and she had not disappointed. He glimpsed a woman staring down at him from a second-floor window. The rain made her difficult to see clearly, but certain curves, a deep purple gown, and auburn curls piled high were unmistakable. He dipped his chin in acknowledgment and marched to the door of the Chandelier.

Inside, men and a few bleary-eyed, scantily clad women shuffled tables around, set chairs aright, stocked the bar. One man was installing a lantern on the wall. The shattered remnants of a similar light had been swept into a pile, along with shards of a broken chair. Still repairing the damage.

McIntyre spotted the stairs and headed for them. A black man the size of a small continent stepped in front of him. "Can I help you?"

McIntyre recognized in the deep voice the honey-like flow of a Haitian accent mixed with the bitterness of Southern slavery. He reached into his pocket for a cheroot, letting the bluff begin. "I am

Charles McIntyre. Delilah will want to see me." He looked away, as if bored with the man, and lit the smoke.

The Haitian apparently agreed. "Follow me."

McIntyre trailed the man to the stairs, dragging his hat off as they climbed. At the top, a door on the right opened and the woman in the purple dress stepped out to greet them.

"This is—"

"Charles McIntyre," she interrupted the black man never taking her eyes off McIntyre. "Been a long time. Come on in."

Delilah was a stunning woman, with the face and figure of a goddess, much of that figure on display. McIntyre's thoughts were of Naomi, however, as he followed the swaying bustle and bare, soft shoulders. Delilah could dance naked in front of him for all the effect it would have. He'd fallen once since declaring his love for his wife and the pain it had caused them both assured him he would never be enticed away from her again.

Confident he was impervious to whatever charms Delilah might dangle, McIntyre slapped his hat against his leg as he paused in the center of the Spartan room. The door closed behind him.

"Pardon the simple furnishings." Delilah glided past him and spun around slowly, showing off her wares. "I'm still waiting on deliveries."

"I see." He took a puff on the cheroot, said a quick prayer, and dove in. "Defiance was halfway to being settled, Delilah. I do not look kindly on our preacher being assaulted. Or auctioning off young girls." He shook his head. "Have you no shame?"

She narrowed her eyes at him, an unusual brown flecked with gold. "Straight to business, eh? In answer to your question, no. You know me. Shame is for people who have a conscience. Now I'll tell you like I told your preacher. Sai Shang belongs to me. I will have her back. And I would suggest you men mind your own business."

"Defiance is my business . . . and I can make it impossible for you to prosper here."

"Hmmm. Let me guess." She laid a finger on her cheek. "You must own the mercantile. Well, *I* own my freight wagons. They'll deliver my beer and whiskey, dry goods, vegetables, whatever I need from Glenwood Springs. As you can see," she motioned to the building around them, "I bought Hadley's lumber mill. I've made agreements with everyone from carpenters to ditch diggers. I don't need your permission or your cooperation." She lifted her chin, clearly pleased with herself. "I do hope you might sell me a steer or two, but if I want a steak, I'll get it, if I have to bring it up from Kansas."

McIntyre had not known about the sale of the lumberyard. The news didn't please him, but he didn't show it. "Every agreement you have made in this town, I can undo."

Indignant, she raised her hand on to her hip. "Do you want things to get that ugly?"

Weren't they already?

"You're a cancer, Delilah. I cannot have a town in which churches are vandalized, preachers are beaten, and women are sold off like cattle. Defiance is going to be better than that. Of course, I could buy you out, and make this a peaceable transaction."

McIntyre immediately regretted the offer. She would see it as weakness and be eager to deride it.

Her thoughtful expression and one slightly raised eyebrow to implied her scorn. "I'm not selling. And I'm not going anywhere. And you've got all the warnings you're going to get."

McIntyre crushed his cheroot into the marble top of her dresser, leaving behind a burn scar. "I am sorry to hear that."

She folded her hands demurely in front of her. "If you were smart," she said softly, "you'd return my property and leave me be."

The threat, hidden in such a winsome tone, evoked a sudden

anger in McIntyre. A righteous anger. He wanted to protect his family, his town from this woman. Let Logan worry about saving her soul. "I don't know how smart I am, Delilah, but I am tenacious. I promise I will make it impossible for you to do business here." Only he didn't know how at the moment.

She shrugged a bare shoulder. "All right. But don't say I didn't warn you . . ."

CHAPTER 23

*M*cIntyre left Delilah's with the keen sense his visit had done more harm than good. Where his former Flower, Rose, had simply been dangerous due to her insanity, Delilah was cold, calculating . . . soulless. He had been right: she'd seen his offer to buy her out as weakness. Worse, she had been prepared before coming here, acquiring her own freight wagons, striking deals with business owners and craftsmen. As if she'd expected McIntyre to interfere. And how had he missed the sale of Hadley's mill?

Between managing the mine and the ranch, his grip on Defiance was slipping . . . at a most inopportune time.

At least the rain had stopped.

He strode back to the town hall—he would never get used to calling the Iron Horse that—and unwound Traveller's reins from the hitching post. In the waning light of day, he swung up into the saddle and turned his gray mare toward home.

The amber light from Rebecca's desk lamp caught his eye. His sister-in-law sat hunched over her desk, bouncing a pencil in her hand and scowling at the paper. She looked as dissatisfied with things as he felt.

*E*milio folded his arms on the corral fence and rested his chin on his wrist, shaking his head in disbelief. Jasper, a black gelding, pranced around the corral with Two Spears on his back. A cantankerous animal, Jasper had never taken to anyone . . . much less someone riding bareback. No saddle was the quickest ticket to getting bucked, but the horse acted as if it was *pleased* to have a rider.

Two Spears had crawled into the corral unobserved, and by the time Emilio stumbled upon him, the horse was calm, almost *curious*. The boy had removed his shirt, tied it around his waist, much like a loin cloth, Emilio figured, and drew pictures in the dirt for a bit. Then he had spent some time moseying around the corral, circling closer and closer to the horse. He had taken another hour to slowly, lightly run his hands over Jasper, lift his hooves, scratch his ears, stroke his face.

The boy's patience awed Emilio.

After that, Two Spears walked away . . . and the horse followed. Five minutes later, he was astride the animal and trotting around the ring.

"I've never seen anyone so young spend that much time with a horse," Emilio said more to himself than Two Spears.

The boy stroked Jasper's neck and tugged on his mane, directing him into a series of figure eights before he responded, all the while keeping keenly focused on the task. "On the reservation, there was nothing to do. But we Utes, we are horse warriors."

"*Si.* I've heard of the races up there."

"We had very swift ponies. This boy is not so fast, I think, but he is willing." Two Spears stopped Jasper, clucked his tongue, tapped his knees, and the horse took several steps backward. Emilio had to shake his head again. The boy, young, small in stature, rode the animal with the confidence of a much older man. "I will try him under saddle now."

Emilio raised his hand. "I'll get it." He marched over to the tack room on the side of the barn, the smell of biscuits from the bunkhouse waking his stomach. Ready for supper, he pulled a bit and a bridle down from a peg, tossed a blanket over his shoulder, but paused when he saw a shadow through the cracks in the barn wall. A slow-moving shadow, as if someone was *sneaking*.

Troubled, he slid silently to the door and peered out. Cloer shoved his hat up on his forehead, put his back against the barn, and sidled slowly toward the corral. He had something in his hand but Emilio couldn't make it out. The ranch hand crept to the end of the building and peered intently at Two Spears. After a moment, he hunkered down and made a quick run to the hay wagon the boys sat on when they watched the events in the corral.

Two Spears trotted Jasper around the ring, using only his legs to steer the animal. Oblivious of his audience, he stopped the horse, backed him up, kicked him forward into an easy walk.

Slowly, Cloer raised something to his mouth. Emilio squinted. A—a . . . a flute? No—a *peashooter*!

Cloer grinned, but it was no smile. "Hey, Geronimo!"

Two Spears whipped his head around to the voice. Cloer put the peashooter to his lips and blew.

Emilio heard a huffing sound, like air escaping, followed by a soft *smack* and Jasper exploded. Bucking like a crazed bull, the horse screamed, spun, and kicked. Two Spears scrambled to hang on, but lost his grip. Clawing for mane, he went flying, pounding into the ground face-first. Emilio dropped the tack in his hands and lunged for the corral, crossing the distance in three steps.

Mr. McIntyre came flying out of nowhere, moving like a streak of lightning. He practically leaped the fence, and dropped to the boy's side.

Surprised by the man's speed, Emilio jumped the fence as well and waved the panicked horse away from them. Circling his arms, hat in hand, he commanded, "Whoa, whoa, boy. Calm down."

Neighing, snorting, Jasper trotted to and fro, eyes rolling with terror. Emilio blocked him at each turn, forcing the animal off to one side. Behind him, Emilio heard the wiggle of fear in Mr. McIntyre's voice. "Two Spears . . . Two Spears—"

The boy grunted. "I am all right."

"Shhh, boy." Emilio approached Jasper and calmed him into standing still.

Mr. McIntyre, on one knee, pulled Two Spears to his feet and checked him top to bottom. "Dear God, he could have killed you. Are you sure you're not hurt?" His concern for the boy made Emilio want to smile.

Two Spears wiped dirt from his lips and spit. "I am not hurt."

Mr. McIntyre checked him over once more and nodded. "Go inside to Naomi." He cut his eyes over at Cloer. "I will be along directly."

Two Spears barely nodded and scrambled off, sliding between the fence rails like an oiled snake. Mr. McIntyre waited for him to enter the house then rounded on the ranch hand.

Emilio sucked in a breath. He'd seen that look many times. Mr. McIntyre's friendly brown eyes turned almost black. A sneer curled his lip. He strode toward Cloer like a demon eager to drag someone to hell.

"Mr. McIntyre," the peashooter slipped subtly from Cloer's hand to the ground behind him. "I—I didn't see what happened. Guess that boy's a little young to be on such a touchy horse."

Mr. McIntyre swung and hit Cloer square in the face, so hard the man spun completely around and stumbled back against the wagon. Blood spurted from his nose. He raised his hands to ward off more blows. "Mr. McIntyre, I didn't do—"

Mr. McIntyre hit him again. "Didn't do what? Have a little fun at the expense of the *half-breed?*" Cloer tried side-stepping away, but Mr. McIntyre nailed him with a right cross and then grabbed the man's vest. "He is my son. An attack upon him is the same as an attack upon me."

He hit him again . . . and again. By now, several hands had gathered and watched in uncomfortable silence as blood streamed from Cloer's nose, mouth, and cheek.

Emilio gave thought to stopping Mr. McIntyre, and took a step forward. Then Lane Chandler raced across the yard and grabbed Mr. McIntyre's hand. For a moment, the two struggled.

"Come on, Johnny Reb. Let this go. Your family is watching."

Glaring at Lane, Mr. McIntyre tugged once, twice, and then finally unclenched his hand and let the fight seep out of him. Lane released him, and both men lowered their arms. Cloer slid to the ground, as mangled as if he'd been kicked in the face by a wild horse.

Breathing hard, Mr. McIntyre straightened, started to rake a hand through his hair, but stopped when he saw the condition of his bloody knuckles. Instead, he squatted in front of Cloer who had his hands pressed to his face. Blood seeped between his fingers. "I am endeavoring, Cloer, to be a better man. I routinely fail." The Southern honey in Mr. McIntyre's accent had turned to venom. "My temper . . . can get the better of me. So let me warn you." He leaned in. "If you ever see me again . . . run."

Cloer half-nodded at his boss.

Mr. McIntyre rose and took a deep breath. He surveyed the hands watching the fight. "Anyone else have a problem with Indians?"

Men looked away, stared at their feet, picked lint from their shirts.

"All right, boys," Lane reached for Cloer, "show's over. Y'all get back to work."

Nearly unconscious, the man clawed his way to his feet with Lane's help, and the foreman all but dragged him back to the bunkhouse.

Emilio climbed through the fence and handed Mr. McIntyre a

bandana. Neither of them spoke as the man wiped his knuckles, removing Cloer's blood.

A few minutes later, Lane led a horse around the corral, a beaten, bedraggled Cloer in the saddle. The foreman plucked a roll of cash from his pocket and shoved it into the man's boot. "There's your pay. Now get outta here."

Cloer came-to enough to spur the horse into a slow, bored walk. While everyone was watching the cowboy crawl off the ranch, Emilio glanced over at Mr. McIntyre's front porch. Two Spears hugged a post, watching the drama intently.

Naomi hurried down the steps and marched across her yard to Mr. McIntyre. Eyes blazing, lips tight, she stomped to within inches of him. Glaring at her husband, she searched his face then suddenly, inexplicably, softened. Huffing, she wiped her bangs out of her eyes and let her shoulders fall. Instead of yelling at him, she took his hand. "Come inside and we'll get you cleaned up."

Scratching his shoulder, Emilio wondered what could have possibly gone through the woman's mind. How could simply looking into Mr. McIntyre's face quench her fury like a bucket of water on a campfire?

It can only be love.

He watched them walk into the house, their arms around each other. Two Spears, his round, dark face expressive as a rock, held the door for them.

Emilio liked very much that the three of them were becoming a family. Like Billy and Hannah. He wanted that. He was darn tired of not fitting into this world. Always feeling a little out of place, a little in the way.

Always alone.

Mollie crossed his mind as he slipped back in the corral to put Jasper away. Maybe he would ride into town and eat supper with her one night this week.

Si, maybe.

*M*cIntyre sat quietly as Naomi wiped down his knuckles with witch hazel. The medicine burned and he wanted it to. Perhaps it could burn away some of this guilt. He was ashamed of his behavior, his lack of self-control. He could have killed the man.

Literally, he could have killed him.

Head lowered over her work, Naomi said softly, "We should talk about it."

McIntyre glanced up at Two Spears sitting at the kitchen table with them, a cookie in his hand. However, he had not taken a bite of it. Instead, he watched his father with an inscrutable face.

Nothing could have made McIntyre feel worse. His bent for violence had shown the boy all the wrong things. Certainly, nothing Christ like. He wondered where was the difference between his own father, One-Who-Cries, and the old Charles McIntyre?

"I have a long way to go, Naomi. I am not sure I will ever get there."

Naomi sighed and capped the bottle. She stared at it for a moment then looked at McIntyre. "*For the good that I would, I do not: but the evil which I would not, that I do.'*"

Paul again. McIntyre had so much in common with the apostle, but he wasn't sure of Naomi's point. Perhaps a puzzled brow betrayed his thoughts.

She squeezed his hand. "You're not alone. We all struggle against doing the things we hate, and yet we don't do the good we know we should. But we don't give up. We ask forgiveness. We move on. *'Being confident of this very thing, that He which hath begun a good work in you will perform it until the day of Jesus Christ.'*"

"He needs to teach me how to let go then." He sat back, dragging his hand across the table. "I want to fix everything. Mete out justice. Set the punishment—"

"Give Him time. You're a . . . complicated project."

He almost laughed but couldn't quite find his sense of humor. "Two Spears, I am sorry if I frightened you. I should not have beaten that man. I want to be a man of peace." A man who steps down from the throne and lets God have His seat back. "It is difficult."

"Why? Why must you not fight?"

"Because when we fight, we are trying to settle matters on our own, rather than trusting God to settle them. Vengeance is His, not ours. And too, fighting certainly does not show love for our fellow man."

Two Spears exhaled heavily. "Do you never fight then?"

"No, I believe there are times when we must stand up, but . . ." When? Frustrated, McIntyre pinched the sweat from his upper lip. "We should try to determine God's leading before we act . . . I suppose." He faded off, revealing his own confusion.

"The more time you spend with Him," Naomi said gently, "the easier it will be to hear His voice."

McIntyre rolled his shoulder. "Apparently I went stone deaf today."

Naomi rose and took the bottle of witch hazel. On her way to the counter, she stopped behind McIntyre. "He still loves you . . . and so do I."

———

One of the most profound moments in McIntyre's life had occurred a year earlier when he accidentally discovered Naomi praying down by the river in town. She had spoken, or more correctly, *fumed* at God. Argued with him even. But, finally, she had surrendered.

Now, as he wandered by moonlight along the banks of that same river, he wanted to pray exactly as she had—as if God were standing right in front of him.

"I am lost, Lord." He picked up a stone and cast it at the water. Not surprisingly, it sank instead of skipping. "For so long, Defiance was my kingdom. I ran it . . . I killed for it. For my glory. My purposes. Now when I want to see it move forward so that it can benefit—bless—others. You have given me an obstacle I have no idea how to get around. Me."

He ambled over to a boulder, but didn't sit. Instead, he studied the magnificent San Juan Mountains washed in the mystical silver of the summer moon. The mooing and snorting of the cattle floated like a song on the air, accompanied by the melancholy yipping of a coyote on the prowl.

He folded his arms against the chill and recalled with a smile Two Spears and Naomi's horse race the other day across that far pasture. Their winsome laughter and unfettered joy had brought an unexpected tightening to his throat.

"I do not deserve any of this yet look what You have given me. And I want to protect it. My family. The town." He kicked a rock. "I feel like I'm doing everything wrong." Beating Cloer to within an inch of his life. Trying to handle Delilah on his own. That visit accomplished nothing.

"But don't I have an obligation to . . .?" *Throw my weight around?* "I cannot do the things I used to, not if I call myself . . . Your follower." He stumbled over the word, because he wanted to follow, but the position did not come naturally to him. He admitted he was tired of leading all the time, especially now that he knew *Whom* he should follow.

Oh, but change didn't come easily. He'd held on tight for so long, leaned solely on his own understanding his whole life. "How *do* I let go? How will I know when to lead? When to fight?"

After a long moment, the answer came drifting to him on the breeze, whispering gently into his heart.

To lead, you have to serve. To fight, you have to kneel.

Nodding, he bowed his head and slipped to his knees, desperate for more of God.

*N*aomi grabbed Two Spears by the shoulder and pulled him back. "Shhh. We don't want to disturb him." The sight of her husband with his arms open in submission, eyes searching the heavens, brought tears to her own. Charles sat and listened when she prayed. Paid attention and asked questions after a sermon or when she read a scripture, but this was the first time she'd seen him . . . broken. Surrendered.

"A man on his knees is weak," Two Spears muttered.

Naomi shook her head. "No. That's when he's the strongest."

*G*rinning like a lovestruck fool, Hannah slid her fingers slowly out of Billy's grasp as they parted at the door of the mercantile. "I'll be back at noon to get him."

Billy bounced his son on his arm and winked at her. "Take your time. This young man and I have a lot we can do today. I'm interviewing for help in the store, and I have a meeting at the hotel. Tell Momma no hurry." Little Billy babbled happily. "What's that? She needs to give us a kiss good-bye? I think you're absolutely right."

Billy waited expectantly, that roguish smile of his melting Hannah's heart. How could she refuse? She planted a peck on his mouth, but he followed her, not letting their lips separate. He slipped his hand behind her head and deepened the kiss, sending a hot flush to her cheeks.

Savoring the electricity he loosed in her, she kissed him once more then retreated to the safety of her son. She pressed her lips to the back of his neck. "I'll see you later." He responded with a giggle and hid his face in his father's chest.

"I love you," Billy whispered to her.

She mussed his perfectly combed hair. "I love you more."

Giggling, she cast him a flirtatious glance and bounced off the porch, then crossed the street to Doc's with a spring in her step. She couldn't have felt any lighter if she were skipping on clouds.

Humming a random tune, she let herself into Doc's. "Good mor—" She immediately spied the tray of instruments scattered across the floor and froze. "Doc?"

Hannah listened for an instant then stepped inside and surveyed the room. Along with the instruments, a chair lay on its side. The door to examination room two was cracked. "Doc?" Fear thrumming in her veins, she hurried to the door and slowly pushed it open.

He lay sprawled across the bed, face pale, lips blue, and obvious bruising on his cheeks and throat.

CHAPTER 24

*H*annah stared out the window of Doc's office, all her crying done. She would miss the man terribly, but sobbing like a baby wasn't helping anyone. Now the anger was seeping in.

Billy came up behind her and wrapped her in a huge, warm hug. "Are you all right?"

"Who would do this?" She leaned into him, comforted by his broad chest and strong arms. "Doc was a good man. Everybody liked him—" she bit that off. Not everyone. Smith and Shelby didn't care for him, but did they dislike him enough to kill him?

"What is it, Hannah?"

Was it worth mentioning? "Smith and Shelby were in here a while back. Doc had to pull his scalpel on Shelby. He was misbehaving."

"Really?" Billy sounded interested. "We should tell the marshal."

"Tell me what?" Beckwith stepped out of the examination room and strode up to them, his boots thudding like thunder.

"I sewed Smith up, I don't know, a month or so ago. Shelby

was with him and they got a little out of hand. Doc pulled a scalpel on them to remind 'em of their manners."

Beckwith rubbed his wide, bony jaw. "I don't know. Doc's got bruises. Somebody attacked him, beat on him pretty good, but not enough to kill him, unless I'm missing something. Looks more like he had a heart attack. He could have died during or even after the attack." Absently, he tapped the star on his chest as he thought. "I'm just not sure."

Hannah couldn't offer a guess. Her heart broke. She couldn't imagine Defiance without the kindly old curmudgeon. Suddenly the door flew open and Wade skidded in. "Marshal, we got another one. Somebody shot Big Jim Walker. He's dead too."

---

*D*elilah rolled the stiffness from her shoulders as she watched the sunrise from her window. She had not slept well. The more she ruminated on Logan and McIntyre, the angrier she got.

All her life, her choices, her decisions, had been dictated by men. Telling her where to go, what to do, when to do it. Even now, she couldn't simply enjoy running The Crystal Chandelier. No. She had to pay her debt to Matthew. She wanted her revenge on Logan. She also wanted Sai Shang back, or her reputation was going to suffer. More than anything, she *wanted* to hurt Logan, but she *needed* to stop acting like a scorned woman.

She reminded herself to think rationally, like a business woman; lay emotion aside and look at the situation pragmatically. She needed to deal with the disappearance of Sai Shang first. If one girl got away, others would think they could escape.

A sharp tap on her door ended her reverie, but she didn't turn from the window. "Come in."

The door clicked and boots stomped into her room. "Your breakfast."

Smith's voice startled her and she spun. "Where's Mary Jean? She brings me my breakfast."

Her hired man stood holding her a silver tray covered with a cloth. "I have some news for ya, so I brought it up." He walked the meal over to her unmade bed. "This all right?"

"Yes." Delilah was not pleased to see that Smith had bathed, shaved, and was wearing new clothes—ridiculously loud checkered pants. Three days and he had no idea where Sai Shang was hiding, but he'd had time to go shopping?

On a low boil, she ambled over and sat down, removing the cloth. "What do you want to tell me?" She surveyed her breakfast of coffee, eggs, bacon, grits, and picked up half a slice of toast covered in strawberry jam.

Smith moved as if to sit on the bed and Delilah lifted a brow. He raised his hands and backed away from the bed. "I just thought you'd like to know the, uh, questioning of Big Jim did lead me to Doc's."

"Doc's? Good." She dipped the corner of the toast in her coffee. "And?"

He tugged on his collar. "The information ain't all that clear. So Big Jim was seen with the Preacher and a kid named Emilio. They took the girl to Doc's. We don't know what happened after that."

"Well, what did Doc say?"

Smith shoved his hands into his pockets and sighed. "Bastard died on us before we could beat any information out of him."

Delilah bit through her toast and froze, fighting the rage welling up inside her. "Died? What kind of condition did you leave Big Jim in?"

"Uh, well . . . he's dead too."

Growling, Delilah snatched up her coffee cup and reared back to toss it across the room, splattering the drink on her bed. "We might've needed him!" She stopped short of throwing it. Seeing a little light in the darkness, she slowly set the cup on the tray and stood. "On the other hand, maybe that's not so bad. They know we're not playing patty-cake now." She was no closer, however, to finding Sai Shang. Smith and Shelby had not looked in the most obvious place. "If they took her to Doc's, and she's not there, try the church."

"Yeah, all right."

"And put the word out. Free beer on Sunday mornings." A mere dig, but a fun one.

"All right." Smith frowned, looking confused.

"This isn't the first town that's tried to shut me down, Smith. McIntyre and Logan have asked for the fight. We'll give them one. You and Shelby have things off to a fine start."

"So you ain't stopping with free beer."

"Stopping? Oh, honey," she raked her gaze over to the window and out at the rooftops and tents of Defiance, "I'm just gettin' started."

CHAPTER 25

*L*ogan closed his Bible and set it on the cot beside him. His distracted mind had kept the morning devotion from being peaceful. His guilt over losing touch with Delilah was equaled only by his concern for Mary Jean. He had the impression she was avoiding him. At least he had not been able to catch her at her tent, and he needed to recover some more before he visited The Crystal Chandelier again. He touched the cut on his head and wondered when he *would* be ready.

"Preacher?"

Billy? Surprised to hear the young man's voice, he picked up his Bible and met him in the sanctuary. Maybe today he could get to the bottom of the strange looks Billy kept giving him. If they'd ever met, Logan couldn't recall it. "Good morning."

The downcast expression and hat crushed to his chest told Logan the boy was not here for anything good. The two shook hands. "Wish this was a call to pick a wedding date."

Logan let his grasp linger, then motioned to a pew. "Have a seat and tell me what's happened."

They each sat on the end of a pew on opposite sides of the

aisle, Logan leaning forward attentively. Billy fanned his hat. "Doc's dead."

Logan had not met the man, but clearly Billy was disturbed at the passing. "I'm sorry. Was it natural causes?"

Billy squinted at him. "My personal opinion . . . no. Not completely anyway."

"I don't understand."

"Somebody beat on him. Maybe not enough to kill him. He was older. Hannah said he hadn't been feeling well. He could have had a heart attack or something during or after the attack. How he died doesn't bother me as much as why he was attacked in the first place."

"You have an idea?"

"Maybe." He leaned forward, piercing Logan with troubled, blue eyes. "Big Jim Walker is dead too."

Logan sat back as if he'd been shoved. He'd had hopes for Big Jim. Had prayed much for him.

"They were both killed last night."

Logan rested his head in his hand, wondering how much higher the tide of evil would get in this town. *Two* funerals to perform. Two. Ah, Big Jim . . .

"Emilio said Big Jim led you to Sai Shang. And then y'all took her to Doc's?"

"Yes."

Billy stood up and wandered over to the pulpit. "If Doc told them anything, they'd know Mollie and Hannah were there. But I don't think he would have. They'll have to follow a different trail."

"You're thinking they'll come after me or Emilio."

Rubbing his neck, Billy turned back around. "That's what I was thinking."

"Do we know who killed him? Big Jim, I mean." Logan tried not to entertain the idea of revenge . . .

"No. But Beckwith is looking into it."

"Well, that's somethin', I guess." He drummed his fingers on the

Bible. "We can do the funerals tomorrow, I suppose." He couldn't recall one he had dreaded more.

"Yeah . . . I was supposed to get a time from you and pass it around."

"Three, I would think."

"Also, uh, I've been meaning to ask you something, Preacher." Billy straightened up and tugged on his vest. "About your time back in Dodge City—"

The front door of the church opened slowly, cutting him off. Smith stood there, legs wide, hands curled into fists, black-and-white checkered pants glaring at them. Logan rose. "You come here lookin' for a fight?"

Snickering, Smith sauntered in, followed by Shelby. Neither of the men removed their bowlers. "We're looking for something."

Logan inched in front of Billy. This was not his fight. "Another little boy to beat up?"

"Nah. Lookin' for a little girl this time. Little Oriental princess about yea tall." He raised his hand to the middle of his chest. "I hear you've seen her."

"No." Logan relaxed his hands that had curled into fists. "You're welcome to take a look."

"We will." He gave Billy the once-over. "Who are you?"

"Just a God-fearin' man. Came for counseling."

Smith grunted and raked a greasy curl off his forehead. "Shelby, go check that back room."

Shelby cut through the three men and slipped behind the curtain. Logan had seen the fear hiding in the man's face, but that didn't prevent an unnecessarily rough search. Furniture scraped and banged on the floor, followed by thuds and smacks, and shattering glass.

Logan scowled. His patience was hanging by a weak, fraying thread. He kept seeing Big Jim asleep on the ground, watching over a church he did not attend.

Shelby popped out of the back. "Nobody back there." He

glanced furtively at Logan as he passed him. "Don't look like he's had any company either."

Smith folded his arms across his expansive chest. "Where'd you hide her? We'll find her if we have to tear this church apart board by board."

Logan eyed Smith top to bottom. He'd either been fighting with or against this type of man for nearly twenty years. He sure was not *with* him, which left an ugly possibility. "You killed Doc . . . and Big Jim?"

A shadow of uncertainty flitted across Smith' meaty face and that wandering eye shifted. "I don't know nothin' 'bout that."

Smith might as well have answered yes. Logan knew the look of a killer. God knew he'd faced enough of them. The memory of Big Jim scrubbing scat off the front door rose in his heart . . .

. . . and ignited an explosion of fury.

---

*B*illy gawked in amazement over the speed of Logan's attack.

The preacher charged at Smith. He hit the man in the gut and launched him backward with the impact of a cannonball fired from a howitzer. Entwined like snakes, the two men burst through the front door of the church, hit the porch, and skidded down the steps. They landed in the road in a shower of wood. Passers-by froze stock-still, taken aback by the commotion.

The two men exchanged blows as they fought to regain their feet. Logan's punches had an immediate effect as Smith's nose gushed blood, bathing his teeth and lips crimson. Logan pelted him with two body blows, but Smith managed one good hit to set the preacher off-balance.

Taking advantage of the moment, Smith pushed Logan away and snatched his gun free. Logan reached for his gun, but his hip was empty. Grinning, Smith cocked the hammer. "I got you."

Billy took a step forward. "You pull that trigger, Smith, you'll have to kill me too. Otherwise, I'll get the marshal."

Beside Billy, Shelby sighed. "He's right. Lot of witnesses." He sounded immensely disappointed. "You'd best think about this one."

Smith and Logan didn't move, but a slight change came over Smith's face. Doubt or resignation. His lazy eye narrowed. "Reckon it's your lucky day, Preacher. But there's a reckoning coming. Next time, there won't be any witnesses, and I'll be playing for blood."

Logan flexed his empty fingers still hovering at his hip. "I know you killed Walker. You won't kill me."

"Tell me where Sai Shang is, maybe I won't."

"Nah, but you'll try. I know your kind."

"Then go heeled."

"I don't need a gun to kill a cockroach."

The insult sent a flush of color to Smith's cheeks. For an instant, Billy thought it might push him over the edge, but the man growled and backed away, keeping the revolver pointed at Logan.

Cursing under his breath, Shelby stomped off in the opposite direction. Smith finally lowered the Colt at a good forty feet up the road. "I'm coming for you, Preacher." He pointed the barrel at him one last time, "and anybody else who gets in my way. Doc. Big Jim. Just the start. I'll do what I have to do to find Sai Shang." He spun on his heels and disappeared down a side trail.

Logan rested his hands on his hips and hung his head.

Billy scratched his head, full of sympathy for Logan. *What a place to try to be a man of God.* "You'd best watch your back, Preacher."

"Yeah, and everyone else's."

CHAPTER 26

"What is the matter with you?" Delilah lobbed a champagne glass across the saloon. A few startled customers flinched and hunkered down over their drinks in case of more projectiles.

Kicked back in a chair, Smith lifted the damp rag from his throbbing nose. "I didn't plan for things to turn out like this." His voice was raspy and low, like he'd swallowed sand. "Logan jumped me."

"And you are no closer to knowing where Sai Shang is!" Delilah slapped the bar. "You are worthless, Smith. You can't find one girl in a town this size? And then you try to take on Logan?"

"I said I didn't start it."

She snatched a mug off the bar with every intention of crashing it against the wall—

"*I* started it."

Delilah stilled, holding the mug in a death grip. Smith leaped to his feet, tossed the rag to the floor, and dropped his hand down to his gun. He hadn't even cleared leather before he was staring down the barrel of Logan's 44. Delilah marveled that she never even saw Logan snatch the gun free.

"Move your hand away, Smith, or this will turn out different from that scuffle in the street."

Smith pondered the suggestion, then raised his hands and backed up to the bar.

"I came to see Delilah." Logan slipped the Colt back into its holster.

Delilah raised her chin, ran a hand over her ribs and waist. These meetings were becoming tiresome. "Fine." She set down the mug. "Follow me. But we have nothing left to talk about, unless you want to tell me where Sai Shang is."

"I told you I don't know." He pulled his hat off and waited. With a shave and a good, clean haircut, she sure could see the boy he used to be.

Without another word, Delilah stomped toward the stairs and Logan followed. She sashayed up the steps, well aware he was watching her hips, but she had the sense, as she'd had with McIntyre, he couldn't have cared less.

What had happened to these men? McIntyre had a wife and possibly that explained this strange ability to resist her charms. It might even explain the shocking offer to buy her out. Logan, on the other hand, had no one. He was all alone. Nothing to lose. No one to protect.

She hadn't tried hard enough, was all. She held the door for him at her room, but squeezed into the opening with him, pressing herself up against him. He raised his hands, as if she was pointing a gun at him, and slipped into the room.

"You can put your arms down. I'm not going to shoot you with these."

Logan stopped in the center of the room, turned to her. "No, I guess you'd just rather have someone knock me in the head."

She closed the door behind her and leaned back on it, her arms contritely behind her back. "That was a bit rash, but I was angry. I am angry. I want my property back."

"Delilah." He took two big steps over to her, apparently got too close, and reversed, looking vexed.

He doesn't trust himself.

"Delilah, two people are dead. The town ain't got a doctor. I lost a friend. Smith is fixin' to get himself killed. You have to stop this."

"Then give me back Sai Shang."

"No." He stepped toward her again, eyes blazing. "You can't have her, and you can't have any more auctions."

"I *can't?*" Her head started pounding as if someone had driven a nail into her forehead. "I don't know why we're having this discussion. Either give me back Sai Shang and leave me alone—or things will get worse."

"Delilah," he softened his tone and clutched her bare shoulders. His hands were hot like a buck stove and she nearly gasped. Heat radiated from him and she felt a flush sweep over her. His bottomless blue eyes, almost ghostly, bored into her and she wanted unexpectedly to touch his face, to kiss his lips. To turn back the pages . . . The desire stunned her.

"Delilah, if this is about me, how can I make things right? I'm begging your forgiveness for . . . for all of it. What can I do to make amends? Name it. Please."

Her mouth went dry. Her heart picked up the pace of a galloping horse. Terror streaked through her body. *No, no, no!* Something in her screamed. "Get out." She slipped past him, pushing him away from her. "Just get out. I'll think about your offer. Maybe I can come up with something."

She squeezed her eyes shut, a futile attempt to block him out. Silence settled in the room. After a moment she heard the soft thud of footsteps, and then the door closed.

*R*ebecca stared hard at the first copy of today's issue. Two hundred more to go. Fingers trembling, she lifted it out of the press.

Still time. Still time to pull it and run something else.

Words matter, Lord. Are these the right ones to move hearts? To get this town to consider the filth Delilah is heaping on it? Help me open their eyes . . .

She read the editorial aloud one last time:

"Defiance has had a most sordid past, but with the advent of a few more energetic and peace-loving citizens, the town has been growing in a different direction. Instead of being the wild and lawless town of former days, Defiance has begun assuming the air of a staid and substantial town. There is even talk of a school.

But by no means the least important sign of progress in our town is the growth of church interests. Laying aside the arguments for or against a denomination, it is commonly accepted that a church is a welcome sign to a stranger. A sign that men and women of good repute abide within the town. There is civility. Lawlessness does not hold sway over the citizens.

However, recently a stranger has come among us who would not merely return Defiance to her rough-and-rowdy ways, but sink the town into a quagmire of heretofore unseen, unequaled moral decay.

Since the arrival of one Ms. Delilah Goodnight, the number of calls Marshal Beckwith has had to attend to in Tent Town has increased tenfold. His jail cells brim over with guests nearly every night now. Incidents of brawls, destruction of private property, and malicious physical harm to citizens are commonplace again. Our marshal and many others have reported witnessing unspeakably sordid, vile, and debauched acts perpetrated in broad daylight.

To add insult to injury, the new house of worship has been vandalized in the most horrible and sacrilegious way, having been painted with excrement. To compound the depravity of disrespect, our very own man of God, the good shepherd at the Cripple Creek Chapel, has been physically abused, and dumped unconscious on the steps of the Sunnyside Mine.

And now it is my unhappy duty to announce the **murder** of two of our most beloved citizens. Doctor George Cook was found lifeless in his office yesterday morning. Though the circumstances are unclear, that violence was done him is inarguable. Big Jim Walker, who as of late had been protecting the church from further vandalism, was shot dead Saturday night.

Have we no shame? Have we no fear? Is it unreasonable to expect such abominable behavior may bring down God's wrath upon us? Only recently did this reporter learn of a **syphilis** outbreak among the patrons of a famous brothel in Denver!

Delilah Goodnight brings nothing good to Defiance. She lives only to issue a dark siren's call, a hypnotic song, enticing men to their deaths. She corrupts the innocent and leads young men to the very gates of Hell. Drunkenness, debauchery, and violence are the result of her presence in Defiance.

Will we not stand against the destructive evil threatening the very soul of our town? Search your own souls, men. Choose this day whom you will serve . . . Delilah must go!"

Hannah loved the smell of freshly cut lumber. The scent filled the new hotel. Lately, Defiance seemed full of the scent of it. She turned slowly, surveying the lobby, and hiked her son a little higher on her hip. "Well, whatcha think, handsome? Is the hotel as pretty as before?"

Billy and Charles had used the old blue prints, originally drawn by Ian. A large lobby with a set of L-shaped stairs against the far wall was divided from the dining room by a false wall. The kitchen created a hallway that led to the back door.

She wandered over to the dining room entrance and peered in at the dozen or so empty tables. A large river-rock fireplace dominated the room. The only thing left from the original inn, traces of soot still marred the stones in places.

"This hotel is prettier." Billy pushed himself off the front desk where he'd been leaning and walked up beside her. "But not as pretty as you."

She gave him a quick smile before meandering over to the empty fireplace, trying to find her enthusiasm. Dishes clattered in the kitchen. "Is that your new help?"

"Yep. Diane, Lesley, and Betsy. So far, they seem to be working out well. Betsy has worked in a hotel before. Diane can cook. Lesley was a maid for a family back in Virginia."

"I think I know Betsy." She'd traded the woman a bolt of cloth for a matching set of buttons.

Hannah was happy the hotel was ready to open. She wasn't happy she would have to split her time between here and the mercantile. Oh, how she would miss Doc and nursing for him. He had taught her so much, but she certainly couldn't go on working without him.

"And, of course, Mollie has experience working here," Billy said. "I think we have a fine staff. I think the hotel may almost run itself."

"Yes. Almost." *If only it would . . .*

Billy took his son from her arms and grinned like a fool, wiggling his eyebrows and wagging his tongue. Giggling, Little Billy promptly grabbed his father's bottom lip. "We're gonna haf time, Hannah . . ." All three of them laughed. Billy shook his head and removed his son's fingers from his mouth. "Hold on, pard, let me talk to Momma a minute."

He set his son on the floor and held his hands. Little Billy practiced his standing skills while Billy talked, bent over. "I started to say, Hannah, we're going to have more time together, as a family. I'll convert the second floor of the mercantile into an apartment until we can decide what we're doing."

"What do you mean what we're doing?"

"Well, I mean, I assume you want to stay in Defiance. Or do you want to get a place outside of town, like Charles and Naomi?"

Hannah chewed on her thumbnail as she pondered the unexpected question. She'd been so preoccupied with how to do more nursing and less clerking or cooking, she hadn't thought that far ahead. Now, without Doc, maybe the career simply wasn't in her future.

"First, though," Billy scooped his son up and faced her, "we need to pick a date. We can't give serious consideration to living arrangements until we're married. What about your birthday?"

Two weeks? So soon.

"We can certainly discu—"

The front door flew open and Emilio and Mollie burst in, laughing to the point of breathlessness. Arms loaded with boxes, they each had two dresses draped over their necks, and multiple hats nesting on their heads. The moment they saw Hannah and Billy, they bit off the laughter as suddenly as if they'd been slapped.

"Billy. Hannah." Emilio lowered his box a few inches. "It's good to see you. I am helping Mollie move into her new room."

"But it's my old room, or at least it's in the same place as my old room."

Little Billy reached out to Emilio. "Dada."

Hannah's heart sank over the child's unexpected outburst and she steeled herself against any reaction that showed shock or disappointment for Billy. Nonetheless, an awkward silence hung over them and Emilio's face looked as if it were made of glass.

Billy, too, froze for an instant, and then smiled. It was brittle at best. "Emilio's got his hands full, little man." Hannah could hear the forced good cheer. "Maybe later."

"Uh, *si. Si*, little man. At dinner."

"Which reminds me," Hannah hooked her arm through Billy's, "It's my turn to cook our Saturday night dinner. Naomi's probably waiting on me." She thanked God for the legitimate excuse to run from this tense situation.

Billy untangled himself from her, but put his arm around her. "I guess we'd better go, then."

---

*O*ut on the boardwalk, Hannah again wrapped her arm around Billy's. They ambled along quietly for a few minutes, Little Billy taking in the people and the noise with eagerness and curiosity. She counted her blessings for a moment, literally. Her son was healthy, Billy had come back for her, and he wanted to marry her. She wanted to marry him. If she didn't get to nurse anymore, well, she still had so much to be thankful for. They were blessed. Did Billy feel the same way? "You know I love you very much."

Billy nodded. Then nodded again. "Yes, I do. Emilio gets under my skin sometimes, but it's not his fault. He's like the brother I never had, and I guess feeling a little competitive with him is normal."

"Normal, but unnecessary."

He nodded again and stroked Little Billy's back. "I know that too."

"And I was thinking about the wedding date . . ."

Billy's step slowed but then picked up again. Hannah said a quick prayer and rushed on. "I think we should wait until the hotel is up and running." She flinched at the subtle downturn of his mouth, but she just had to have time to get her heart right with losing Doc and giving up nursing. "Between that and the mercantile, you're going to have your hands full. Don't you think we should be able to focus on one another?" She squeezed his arm. "I just want your undivided attention." She batted her eyelashes at him and Billy burst out laughing.

"I'm being played like a violin." He narrowed his eyes at their son. "Can you believe how weak-kneed I am when you mother flashes those big blue eyes at me? Harden your heart, son, against the wiles of women. Otherwise, they'll be the ruin of you."

Hannah goosed Billy in the ribs. "Or the *best* thing that ever comes your way."

CHAPTER 27

*D*elilah stared at the liquor inventory, but couldn't focus. Frustrated, she laid the ledger on the bar and tried again. She could still feel Logan's hands on her shoulders, still smell the scent of leather and sweat that surrounded him. She could have so easily reached out and touched the scar on his chin, caressed that smooth, wide jaw.

The lack of the usual boisterous noise from the saloon finally intruded on her troubled thoughts. Noticing the volume, or lack thereof, she turned around to survey the room.

Roughly, about half the crowd was missing.

"Where is everyone today?"

Mary Jean set a clean tray of mugs on the bar. "At the funeral. Two men were killed a day or so ago."

"Oh." Bored, Delilah turned back to the bar and noticed *The Defiance Dispatch* folded beside her. She drummed her fingers. She did not want to read it. She didn't want to give the holier-than-thou pious saints one iota of her time.

Still, she had a moment. Feigning disinterest, she picked it up.

"Oh, uh . . ." Mary Jean had her hand out, as if to stop Delilah. "Uh, you might not want . . ."

Delilah raised her how-dare-you brow and Mary Jean moved to the other end of the bar.

Satisfied, Delilah laid the newspaper flat and scanned the first page. A gold strike near Red Mountain. A billiard hall opening on Main Street. *Not if I have anything to do with it . . .* A new cobbler coming to town. McIntyre's cattle arrived.

Blah, blah, blah.

She flipped the page to the editorials. The headline screamed at her. *Delilah Goodnight brings nothing good to Defiance.*

She picked up the paper and paced in front of the bar, reading as she went, her face growing hotter and hotter. Then one sentence stopped her in her tracks. The one word that could strike terror into the hearts of Delilah's patrons. Even whispering it could make a dent in her business:

Syphilis.

Delilah curled her hand into a tight fist, her nails gouging and ripping the paper. She looked up the stairs and bellowed, "Smith!"

Every man in the room jumped. Mary Jean hunkered down and wiped glasses a little faster. Delilah's chest heaved. "How dare she . . . SMIIIITH!"

The man came skipping down the steps, buttoning his breeches as fast as his fingers would fly, suspenders flapping at his hips. "Yeah, right here. Comin'."

Delilah's vision clouded purple with her fury. "What am I paying you for?"

He blinked at her like a deer startled in the woods. "Uh . . ."

She grabbed his collar. "I am not paying you to entertain my girls. I have something for you to do and it needs to get done right now."

"What you got in mind?"

"Forget the shepherd. Attack the sheep."

217

*N*aomi remembered this hill, windswept and snow-covered seven months ago, and the most forlorn funeral she'd ever attended. They'd buried Grady O'Banion here . . . and only seven people had come to say good-bye to the man.

Today was a different story. It seemed most of the town had climbed up to the cemetery to somberly stand under a brilliant blue sky and pay their respects. A yard from Naomi's feet, the pine coffins rested in their graves, side by side. To her right, Charles, Billy, and Emilio waited respectfully, shovels in hand, string ties dancing in the sad summer breeze. Logan, at the head of the graves, his Bible open before him, spoke soft words of encouragement to the mourners. Especially to Hannah, or so Naomi thought.

However, she sensed his final words struck deep into the hearts of everyone present.

After reading the twenty-third psalm, Logan closed his Bible and hugged it to his side. "I have said many good things about these men. They were well-loved. Valued by this community." He took a deep breath. "But my heart is heavy. I failed them. Especially Big Jim. I dallied. I hesitated to share the Truth with him. I acted like I had all the time in the world, and now I fear I will never see my friend again."

He stopped. Tears glistened in his eyes. He started to speak, stopped, tried again.

"I was sent to Defiance to share the life-changing, soul-saving good news that Christ died for us—each and every one of us—so that our sins could be forgiven. Maybe you don't care about that right now. Maybe you don't think it matters. But knowing Christ is about more than redemption from sin. He is a friend who stays closer than a brother. He is a solid founda-tion when the storms of life rage. He brings a peace into your life that surpasses all understanding. And when you take your final breath . . . he is there waiting to receive you home to Glory."

His gaze lowered to Jim's grave. "I failed him. I didn't tell him any of this. Now I don't know if I'll ever see Big Jim Walker again. I wasn't with him in his last moments. I pray he cried out to Jesus." He clenched his jaw, struggled for control then slowly lifted his gaze to the mesmerized crowd. "I would not fail you. If Jesus can take a mean drunk fast with a gun and faster with his fists, and change him into a humble servant of God—not perfect, but a humble servant of God nonetheless—he can change you, my friends. Believe it." He closed his eyes. "Help them in their unbelief, Lord, and help me live every moment as if it is my last. In Jesus' name, I ask it. Amen."

Beside her, Hannah sniffled and dabbed at the tears. In fact, Naomi heard others sniffling in the crowd behind her. She blinked the moisture from her own eyes.

"For dust thou art . . ." Speaking softly, Logan reached down and grabbed a handful of dirt from the diggings, "and unto dust shalt thou return. Amen." He cast a little of the dirt into each hole. After a few moments of silence, the crowd dispersed quietly and Charles, Billy, and Emilio shoveled soil with quiet reverence.

Naomi watched Logan head down the hill, head lowered, Bible tucked under his arm. A few miners nodded, flashing him reserved smiles as they wandered past him. Most, however, hurried on without acknowledging him. They didn't know him yet. They still feared him, or at least didn't know what to think of him. Naomi knew Logan's closing words had touched some hearts. Seeds had been planted. As long as he didn't give up on the town . . .

She clutched Hannah's shoulder. "Tell Charles I'll be back shortly. I'd like to talk to the preacher for a minute."

Hannah sniffed and nodded. Naomi hurried to catch up with the man. She came alongside him and the two walked in an amiable silence to the bottom of the hill.

HEATHER BLANTON

"What did you think of the service?" he finally asked.

"I thought it was beautiful." She kicked a small rock out of her way. "I'm sorry about Jim. I didn't know him, but he seemed . . . jovial."

"That would be a good word for him." After a few more steps, he added, "And I'm sorry about Doc."

"He was a good man. Gave his heart to the Lord a few months back. Just in time, I guess."

"I guess." He stopped abruptly. "I have a confession to make. When I started this funeral, I was angry. Furious, in fact. I kept thinking all I wanted to do was get my hands around Smith's neck. I know he killed Jim. Probably Doc too I'm guessing."

"And now?"

"I don't know what I'm doin' here. So far I haven't done anything right. And I think I've even gotten a man killed."

"Why would you say that?"

"Jim didn't want to get involved. I made him help us find Sai Shang."

"Maybe you should blame Delilah. You wouldn't have needed Jim if she wasn't selling young girls."

He shoved a hand into his pocket and started walking again. "I don't know. I wasn't prepared for this kind of a battle. There is a darkness in this town—"

"And that's exactly why Defiance needs you."

"I'm not so sure. I don't seem to be making much of an impact."

Naomi pulled her braid around and absently tickled her palm with the tail of it. "I felt exactly the same way when I came here. I was angry at God for abandoning us in this place. With these people. I didn't have the faith to love them."

And then miracles happened.

"I would have never thought some the people would become friends. I wouldn't have guessed in a million years I'd get over the loss of my first husband and *marry* Charles McIntyre," she raised her pointer finger for emphasis, "who was an unrepentant sinner so lost in darkness I sure didn't think he'd ever find the Light." She cocked her head to one side. "And look where we are now." She clasped her hands behind her back and gazed off at the mountains. "My point is, you can't see over the hill, Preacher, but God does. What's coming is probably a whole lot better than we can imagine. But even if it's a hard path, it's all part of His plan."

Logan stopped again and stared at the ground. Naomi stared at him, waiting for him to look up. When he did, she was pleased to see some hope in his eyes.

"You're right. I'm just feelin' sorry for myself."

"I know a little bit about that too." She smiled wryly. "It'll pass."

---

*R*ebecca had known there would be consequences to the editorial . . . but this?

Mouth agape, she let her gaze travel over the decimated newspaper office. Beside her, Ian, her sisters, Billy, Emilio, Mollie, even Charles, stared slack-jawed at the level of destruction.

The press lay on its side. That had taken *at least* two men. Everything loose had been torn from it or twisted beyond usability, the wooden legs shattered. Letter blocks, hundreds of them, littered the floor. Ink had been splattered everywhere, her desk chopped into pieces. A thousand sheets of paper—scattered, wrinkled, ripped, and drenched in ink—looked as if they had been strewn about by a tornado.

Fighting tears, Rebecca covered her mouth with her hand. "We'll never get this cleaned up."

Ian slid a gentle arm around her. "Look at me." Rebecca couldn't tear her eyes from the catastrophe. "Look at me, lass," he repeated gently but firmly. She looked up into his wise, steady, hazel eyes. "We will clean this up. We will put everything back to working order, and we will continue to print the news. They canna stop us."

Naomi shook her head in disgust. "How could they do this while we were at a funeral?"

"And here I thought the trouble would be over Indians." McIntyre bent down and picked up the remains of the Devil's Tail. The wooden casing had been shattered leaving behind only the metal core. He held up the iron handle. "We need the blacksmith, and we need a carpenter. Ian's right. They will not stop us."

CHAPTER 28

cIntyre took a deep, rejuvenating breath and gave in to the allure of cowboying. He could lose his troubles out here in the fresh air, in the freedom of the saddle. Forget the newspaper. Forget Delilah.

He and Two Spears rode alongside Lane, flanking the herd as the crew moved it to greener pastures. Horns clanking continuously, the animals bellowed and snorted, and kicked up a miserable amount of dust. The fella riding drag had the least desirable job at the moment and McIntyre wondered what he'd done to annoy Lane.

For the most part, the herd moved steadily and calmly through a narrow valley naturally contained on both sides by hills filled with tall, thick stands of Ponderosa pines. It opened up a half-mile ahead into a much larger area rimmed by high, steep-sided mesas, easy stations from which to keep an eye on the cattle.

"You've got one pretty spread here, Johnny Reb." Lane raised his quirt and waved it at a heifer wandering away. "It's gonna be a fine place to raise cattle," he looked sideways at McIntyre and Two Spears, "and a family."

"I hope to make it one of the finest ranches in the state. We shall see."

Lane shook his head. "I'd a never pegged you for a cattleman. You sure have changed since I saw you last, what, back in seventy —" he stopped suddenly and tilted his head, staring out at the herd.

Puzzled, McIntyre looked and listened for a moment, but didn't notice anything amiss.

Two Spears lifted his chin. "They are nervous."

"Yeah," Lane whispered.

Then McIntyre heard it. A change. The mooing and grunting changed in pitch, higher and shorter. Some animals slowed their pace, some tried to back up or turnaround. He could almost see the fear spreading through the herd. Their horses too, started prancing, and pinned their ears back.

Lane sniffed.

"Fire," Two Spears said.

"Heck." Lane spurred his horse and took off. "You two stay out of the way!"

Before he'd ridden fifty feet the entire herd's mood had changed. He pounded toward the two cowboys up ahead, also riding flank, holding his hat over his head. Not waving it, though, McIntyre noted. A signal. The two men stood in the saddle and surveyed the turbulent flow of beef.

A shot rang out, but not from the cowboys. The sound came from the shadowy pines across the glen. The herd immediately turned into a churning, spinning sea of angry thousand-pound waves. Then smoke wafted out of the woods, but further up than where the shot had come. When it reached the leaders, the animals broke, followed almost instantly by the whole herd. Running in every direction, the deafening thunder of their hooves shook the ground, rolling over the valley like the sound of an advancing army.

McIntyre knew he and Two Spears were too close. They could

be swallowed by this maelstrom in an instant. "Ride, Two Spears. Get up the hill!"

Another shot. Dirt kicked up a few feet from them. He drew his gun, but he didn't have time to scan the woods. "Now! Go!" He needed to get his son out of this melee. The boy kicked Mandan to a gallop and was easily pulling away when the horse went down, tripping, and rolling. McIntyre's heart lurched to his throat as he shot past his son, but Two Spears leaped from the saddle, hit the ground hard, and tumbled a few feet from the horse.

Holstering his Colt, McIntyre jerked Traveller up, spun him around, and charged back for Two Spears. He looked beyond the boy at a massive wave of horns, hooves, and hides thundering toward them. Two Spears glanced at the cattle headed his way too, and bolted for his father, one arm outstretched, reaching for rescue. McIntyre spurred his horse again, desperate for more speed, to move faster, to beat the wall of beef.

McIntyre grabbed Two Spears's hand, snatched the boy up behind him as Traveller spun on a dime, and the three lunged for the tree line, dirt and grass flying behind them. The roar from the herd was deafening, but McIntyre didn't look back. He could hear shouts and whistles from the cowboys, but no more rifle shots. He held on to Two Spears with one arm and spurred Traveller into an all-out run.

They bounded for the trees and only slowed when there was forest on all sides. Breathing a little easier, McIntyre tugged on the reins and brought his horse down to a jog. They pivoted and helplessly watched the wild-eyed cattle scattered hither and yon, running, turning, charging. Cowboys rode on the fringes, yipping, whistling, slapping whips, waving hats and lariats, all but invisible in the dust cloud.

McIntyre could still smell smoke, but mixed with the dust, it seemed the promise of flames had not materialized.

He rested an elbow on the saddle horn and shook his head.

Smoke? Rifle shots? That was no accident. "Are you all right, Two Spears?"

"Yes."

His voice sounded small and frail. McIntyre noticed then the grip Two Spears had around his waist. The child was clutching him with unmistakable desperation. McIntyre wouldn't make too much out of it, but he was both relieved and gratified he was there for his son. He squeezed Two Spears's hands lightly. "We're all right. All right." He swallowed the fear that had turned his mouth dry as an empty draw. Slowly the thunder ebbed then faded out as the complaining animals bottlenecked at the entrance to the glen. Believing the cowboys had the herd mostly under control, he nudged Traveller with his heels. "Now let's go see what happened and help these boys finish."

It took several hours for them to round up all the wayward animals, and they did it with a wary eye on the forest. McIntyre had told them about the rifle shots, knowing at the same time the bullets had been meant for him . . . or Two Spears.

He felt like the shooter had missed intentionally, so this stampede had been some kind of warning. Could he blame it on a disgruntled, fired cowboy? Or perhaps Delilah had put someone up to the mischief?

Maybe the truth was a combination of the two.

Lane rode up, wiping sweat and dirt from his face. "Well, I reckon we've got 'em all gathered back up." He studied McIntyre for a second, then *tsked*. "You and I know this was no accident. Somebody tried to stampede those beeves. If it hadn't been for the Herefords, these Longhorns would be back in Texas by now."

"Whoever shot at us, I believe missed on purpose."

Lane paused wiping his face with his bandana. "This was just some kind of warnin' then?"

"Perhaps telling us things will escalate."

*M*cIntyre lifted the painting of a tranquil mountain valley off its hook and set it on the floor. His wall safe uncovered, he spun the dial expertly and snatched the door open. As he counted out ten thousand dollars, Ian muttered something in the other room that sounded darn close to a curse word. McIntyre had to chuckle. Putting that old press back together was proving to be a project for an engineer. But they were determined —they *all* were determined not to let Delilah beat them.

Somehow, from this mess and the stampede, during a surprisingly simple prayer for guidance, God had given McIntyre an idea. Perhaps it wouldn't stop Delilah entirely, but it might slow her down. Convince her they would not stop fighting.

He tapped the bills into a tight, crisp pile, then closed his safe.

Behind him, someone knocked softly on his office door.

"Just a moment." He re-hung the portrait and slipped behind his desk. He laid the new money down in front of him as Corky peeked around the door. "You wanted to see me?"

"Yes. Please have a seat."

Corky settled in and leaned forward, rapt with attention. "What can I do for you, Mr. McIntyre?"

McIntyre almost grinned. He slid the stack of cash toward Corky. "There is ten thousand dollars. I want you to take that money, buy a wagon, remove the Chinese girls from The Crystal Chandelier, and deliver them to the mission at Cortes. Give them each $500 and you may keep the rest."

Corky's mouth fell open. McIntyre let the man's silence go on as long as necessary.

Finally, he gulped. "You want me to kidnap 'em?"

"Kidnapping would only apply if they were at The Crystal Chandelier of their own free will. They are slaves. I want them gone before any more of them are auctioned off."

Slack-jawed, Corky fell back in the chair. "I—I—how am I supposed—how much is that exactly?"

"You will give the ladies twenty-five hundred. A wagon, horses, and supplies will cost you less than three hundred. I imagine you'll pocket somewhere around seven thousand dollars."

The round-faced little fellow looked thunderstruck. "Do . . . you . . . want me to come back with the money?"

McIntyre chuckled. "It is yours to keep. And I don't think you'd better ever come back to Defiance if you do this."

"Why me? I ain't never stole no *people* before."

"Corky, I am well aware you supplement your panning income with stealing. You have a quick hand and a sharp mind. Emilio can help you. We three are the only ones to know. You tell anyone else and your life will not be worth a plug nickel."

Corky frowned down at his lap for several minutes, chewing on the offer. Finally, he looked up. "I want to know if I can tell one other person."

"Who?"

"Chang Lee."

It took McIntyre a moment to place the name. "Mrs. Lee's son? The young man who works at the laundry?"

"Yes sir.

"Why him?"

"Sometimes he drives a freight wagon down to Glenwood Springs. He speaks Chinese too. And *you* know that Delilah parades those girls on the street every day at three o'clock."

Interested, McIntyre leaned back in his chair. "And?"

"Well, I was thinkin', if somebody could cause a big enough distraction, I could just herd those girls around to the back of the hardware store, load 'em up into empty whiskey barrels, and Chang Lee and me could ride on out of town, slick as a whistle." He made a slicing gesture with his hand and whistled. "I'd have to pay him somethin', but I think it'd be worth it."

McIntyre agreed. Grinning, he slid the money to Corky. "I knew I had the right man for the job."

CHAPTER 29

"*N*aomi, do you trust me?"

Naomi pulled her attention away from the crowded street, and looked at Charles over Two Spears's head, wondering if she'd heard him correctly. He had asked them to come into town with him today, and he'd had such a jaunty tone in his voice she couldn't refuse. Besides, the last few days his mood had improved considerably. He had been more willing to spend time with Two Spears too, coaxing the boy into shadowing him some around the ranch.

"Do I trust you?" She had to raise her voice. The din on the street from wagons, men, jangling tack, and overloaded packsaddles was intrusive. "Of course I do. If I didn't, well, I wouldn't have married you."

"Don't be flippant, your Ladyship." He steered their wagon around two men arguing in the street. He watched them for a moment, probably to make sure they weren't going to start shooting then returned to the road. "I need you to think about the question, all it entails, and answer it thoughtfully."

She frowned at him. The question annoyed her. "Do I trust you?" She enunciated each word carefully. He loved her. Had her

229

best interests at heart. She ruffled Two Spears's hair and grinned. He would come to love this boy too. "Yes, my beloved, I trust you."

"Something is about to transpire." He brought somber dark eyes back around to her, the Southern lilt in his voice hardened. "It *will* be all right." He raised his brow, as if asking did she believe him? Did she trust him?

"All right."

"Good girl."

He pulled the wagon over and parked in front of the bakery. The scent of warm, fresh bread and cinnamon wafted to them. "Why don't you two get some apple turnovers or some such? I'll be . . . along."

She nodded and waited for him to come around to her side. He offered her his hand and as she stepped down he stopped her at eye level. His face was a mask. She couldn't read him, but she sensed he needed her trust. Slowly he set her down, but a commotion on the other side of the street drew their attention.

Through the traffic, Naomi caught flashes of Delilah prancing down the street, her purple parasol followed by five brightly-colored straw parasols. Beneath them, a gaggle of young Oriental girls trudged forward, heads bowed, eyes averted from the prying, poking, hooting men on the street.

"Will this town ever change?" she wondered aloud in disgust.

"Yes." His firm answer brought her attention back to him. He touched her cheek. "Get inside."

Puzzled, hopeful, Naomi waited for Two Spears to jump down. The boy leaped from the wagon and hurried to the bakery door. She joined him, but turned back quickly for a last glance at Charles. Dodging traffic, he zigzagged his way toward the mercantile. Logan stood under the entryway, and waved when he spotted his friend.

Well, how much trouble can they get into?

A bit more reassured, Naomi stepped into the bakery.

"*N*aomi, what a pleasant surprise." Sara finished sliding a tray of oven-fresh, aromatic peanut butter cookies onto a platter and set the empty pan down. "I've been wondering when I might see you next.

"Sara, good morning. I've missed you." Sara was sole owner of the bakery now. Her husband had been killed a few months back, on Main Street, during a robbery. The couple had supplied the hotel with wonderful baked goods, and Naomi hoped that arrangement would start again as soon as the new hotel was finished. But right now, the most tempting of treats covered the counter and several shelves. A child's idea of heaven. "And this is my son, Two Spears."

"Well, glad to know you." The chubby woman wiped her hands on her apron and offered one to the boy for a shake. A little hesitantly, he accepted. "Ah, there's a good lad. And he has a strong grip. Well," she turned back to Naomi, but slipped Two Spears a fresh cookie at the same time, as if she could hide the generosity, "what can I do for ya?"

The boy turned the cookie over a time or two, took a tiny bite, and then happily took a much larger one.

"I thought we'd each get a cinnamon roll or a turn-over. Do you have a preference, Two Spears? Perhaps you'd like another peanut butter cookie." The boy had all but inhaled half of the gift.

"Perhaps." Mouth full, eyes glowing like a starving man staring at steak, he surveyed all the breads, and pies, and cookies spread out before him. "There is so much." He swallowed the bite. "I have never seen so much food."

The women laughed, and Naomi squeezed his shoulder. "This place is a bakery, honey. Sara makes only sweet treats."

"I am glad," he whispered, struck by the array of tempting pastries.

231

"Well, while he's thinking, Sara, I think I'll have a cinnamon roll."

"All righty." The woman picked up a small piece of wax paper from a stack and reached to the shelf beside her. "Let's get you a nice fat one." She plucked one up with the paper and turned to Naomi. "Here ya—" her gaze shot past Naomi and her face scrunched into a look of disapproval.

Naomi spun, and her heart fell. The traffic on the street had stopped; dozens of men were staring at something, their backs to the bakery. Shoving, jostling, leaning in, standing on toes to get a better view of something, the gawkers pressed in, and more men joined, running from every direction.

Charles.

Two Spears, also staring out the window, froze, the last bite of cookie in his mouth. Naomi laid her hand on his shoulder. "Stay here."

Stomach churning, Naomi marched out the door to find out what exactly was transpiring on Main Street.

---

*N*aomi pushed, shoved, pulled, and shouldered her way through the smelly, sweaty mass of men to emerge on the edge of a circle. Her heart dropped into her stomach at the cause for the commotion.

Charles and Logan circled each other, slowly, carefully, fists up, jaws clenched.

"You've had this coming for a long time, McIntyre."

"Not as long as you."

"I should have killed you that time I drew on ya."

"You may yet have your chance."

Naomi blinked, covered her mouth with her hands. This couldn't be happening. Why would these two fight? "Charles, what are you doing?"

She had distracted him for an instant, long enough for Logan to step in and swing. He caught Charles in the jaw with a sickening thud and Naomi screamed. She attempted to run into the middle of the fight but hands, the hands of complete strangers, held her back. "Let me go!" She squirmed and fumed, but they held her in place.

"You'd best stay outta this, ma'am."

"Can't let you interfere. Men gotta settle this."

She managed one more furious attempt, but stopped suddenly when Delilah emerged across from her. The woman shoved and elbowed her way to the front row, a satisfied smirk growing on her face as she took in the situation.

Naomi settled down, unwilling to look like a . . . a crazed wildcat while Delilah stood over there, all calm and poised in her beautiful lavender dress. Just as carefree as a nymph, she twirled her parasol as punches went back and forth. Behind her, the five Oriental girls tried to hide their faces beneath brightly colored parasols. Watching over all of them, a black man the size of a mountain. His shiny bald head and shoulders towered over the crowd. No matter his size, he moved and swayed with the swell of people jostling one another, trying to get a look at the fight.

In the meantime, Charles kept up this inexplicable battle, trading punches with the preacher. He jabbed Logan in the nose, snapping the preacher's head back. Logan shook his head, wiped away the trickle of blood at his mouth, and took another swing. Charles ducked, and came up with a blow to Logan's midsection.

Logan bent over with a loud "Oooof," but then countered with a punch to Charles's kidney. Tangled, they fell into the crowd, which spit them back out into the clearing, and the punches continued. Men whistled, clapped, and hooted. They surged on Naomi and she was forced forward a few inches, but the hairy, smelly miner beside her spread his arms and pushed back. "Give 'em room," he hollered, sounding cross. "I've been waiting on this fight seven years. Don't crowd 'em."

Charles pushed Logan off him, took a swipe at his jaw, and missed. Sweat poured down their faces, leaving trails in the dirt from their temples to their necks. A red welt rose on Charles's right eye. His left was swelling closed. Logan's mouth still ran a trickle of red which dripped on his shirt.

Oh, God, why are they doing this? Stop them, please.

The crowd had grown to enormous proportions. The cheers were deafening, almost disorienting Naomi. She felt like she was watching a fight in the Coliseum. Still the crowd grew. Men climbed posts for better views, even stood in the saddles of their mounts. Eager spectators leaned from the second-story windows of the assayer's office and leather shop. Somehow, a few determined souls climbed up on the roof of the marshal's office!

Speaking of . . . Naomi scanned the crowd. No marshal. No deputy.

Charles and Logan exchanged blow after blow, some missing, some connecting. The match was almost exactly a tit-for-tat exchange. Both men shared equally of abused and bloodied flesh. Their faces bled. Their shirts hung in shreds. Dirt clung to wounds and sweaty skin. Still, they fought on. The sound of fists on flesh and the stench of the closed-in bodies nauseated Naomi. Several minutes passed and the grueling battle showed no signs of ending.

Winded, moving as if their arms were filled with lead, they continued to circle each other, but they looked more like drunks searching for their beds.

Logan threw a punch, missed Charles by a mile, and spiraled to the ground, landing on his hands and knees. Gasping for air, he stayed put for a moment.

Surely they can't go much longer . . .

But Logan stubbornly clawed his way to his feet again. Charles staggered forward and struck him with a jab to the cheek. Logan went down instantly. Charles collapsed on his back beside him.

Both men could barely talk. Sweat rolled off them. Their chests pumped.

Please, God, this has to be over.

"I can be done . . . if you think we're done," Logan gasped.

Charles, huffing, puffing, surveyed the crowd, paused for a moment on Delilah, then rolled over and climbed to all fours. "We're done."

At that moment, Naomi realized someone was still holding her. She pulled away and ran to her husband. The crowd muttered and booed, unhappy with a tie, and slowly disbanded, but there was quite a bottleneck of people.

Naomi fell to her knees beside her gasping husband. "Are you all right?" She pulled a handkerchief from her hip pocket and dabbed at the numerous cuts on his face. "You scared the life out of me. What was all this about?"

Naomi heard a gasp and the young girl, Mary Jean, broke through the crowd. She pushed past Delilah, who scowled at being swept aside, and dropped down beside Logan. "Oh my gosh, Preacher." She moved to touch his face, then his body, but every inch on the man was black and blue or bleeding. "Here, let me get you back to the church . . ."

Logan raised his hand. "Give me . . . just . . . a minute."

Oh, Naomi did not miss the daggers flying from Delilah's eyes. The queen was clearly contemplating taking off the young girl's head.

Jealousy, thy name be Delilah.

"Here, help me stand, Naomi."

She slipped under Charles's shoulder and rose with him, taking as much of the load as she could. Exhausted, he nearly toppled them. "Come on, you can do this," she said. A determined heave got him to his feet. As they paused to make sure he had his balance, loud muttering and offended grumbling drew their attention to the dissipating crowd.

Delilah and the large black man were pushing people around,

knocking them out of the way, spinning, scanning the crowd as if hunting for a treasure of great value.

"There!" Delilah yelled.

The crowd blocked much of Naomi's view, but it looked like the pair focused in on something pink and raced for it. The color winked between men as they flowed away from the area. Naomi caught a flash of a long golden braid. Then a girl screamed, and her blood ran cold. "Hannah?"

She abandoned Charles and thrashed her way through the men, following the sound. She burst into an opening and found Delilah holding Hannah by the wrist, her other hand reared back with a pink parasol as if she were going to strike her sister.

Naomi's temper exploded. She grabbed Delilah's arm and snatched the woman around. The parasol slipped from her fingers and her eyes widened in astonishment.

"You let my sister go." She clenched her teeth. "Now."

For an instant, Delilah was afraid. Naomi saw it in her eyes, but she quickly regained her confidence and released Hannah. Naomi wasn't quite so fast to gather up her self-control. She wanted to choke this woman. If she had hit Hannah, hurt her in anyway—

"Please release my arm now."

Naomi realized her fingers were cramping from squeezing Delilah's flesh, and let go. She did not, however, take her eyes off the woman. "Hannah, are you all right?"

Her sister scooped up the parasol. "The *owner* gave this to me." Not waiting for conversation, Hannah marched by Delilah with her chin held high.

"Did you see where she went?" Delilah asked quickly, before Hannah was gone.

"No I did not," she tossed back.

Delilah came back to Naomi. The woman's cheeks flushed with color, she held her lips in a tight, thin line, and her nostrils flared. Delighted to add to the woman's frustration, Naomi said, "No she did not."

"Naomi," Charles extended his hand, bloody, and dirty, "let us take our leave."

Naomi couldn't help but evaluate Delilah. As beautiful as a rattlesnake. As deadly too? She had a sudden, puzzling pang of pity for her. Rattlesnakes couldn't change their nature.

"Naomi," Charles prompted more firmly. She took his hand, but didn't miss the ugly glares he and Delilah shared.

As they walked away, the crowd thinned a bit more and they spotted Mollie talking to Emilio and a man wearing checkered pants. Smith, Naomi recalled. Mollie too, held a parasol and Smith looked none too happy about it. He gestured to it repeatedly and with agitation. Emilio positioned himself between Mollie and the man, a grim look on his face.

Charles stopped. He couldn't do anything in his current condition. Should Naomi—?

She was pondering intervening herself when Billy and Hannah walked up. Hannah still held her parasol and now Little Billy. Billy positioned himself alongside Emilio and crossed his arms. Emilio remained calm as the man leaned forward and poked him in the chest. Billy leaned in as well, but Emilio gestured for him to back off. Finally, Smith stormed off in those ridiculous pants.

Charles swayed and Naomi caught him. "Charles!"

"I'm all right. A little lightheaded. Let's get to the Iron Horse and I'll clean up a bit . . ." A weary, but wry grin teased the corner of his mouth, "unless you need to toss me aside again to rescue someone else?"

Naomi gasped. "I had to help Hannah—"

He was chuckling, and flinching before she could finish. "I am only joking," he rubbed a hand across his ribs, "at my own expense." He groaned softly.

"Come on." She tightened her grip on him and pulled him out of the street, where traffic was nearly back to normal. "I suppose you're going to explain this fight to me. Not that I'm suspicious, but it sure looked like you and the preacher didn't exactly have your hearts in it."

Charles paused and Naomi followed his gaze. Fifty yards up, Delilah stood in the middle of the street, yelling and gesturing wildly at Smith. Suddenly, she slapped him, a sting so vicious passersby and horses reacted to the sound.

Charles nodded, looking pleased. "Let's just say it was for a good cause."

CHAPTER 30

ogan did not meet the eyes of the men laughing on the street as he limped home, his arm around Mary Jean.

"Good fight, preacher. Enjoyed it."

"You sure know how to wrangle up a flock."

"Wish you woulda give more notice. I woulda placed a bet."

Logan looked at the ground instead . . . and pondered the few places on his body that didn't hurt. A spot between his shoulder blades and the bottom of his feet.

His face pounded with the beat of his heart. His scalp, temples, even the back of his head had a drumbeat. His knuckles thrummed like a freight wagon had run over them, repeatedly. Even his knees hurt.

"I didn't fight this much when I was drunk, mean, and goin' to hell." He flapped his lips gingerly. They felt twice their normal size and throbbed too.

Mary Jean shifted a little and brought his arm higher up her shoulder. "Heck of a fight. What started it?"

He wished he could tell her the truth, but she worked at The Crystal Chandelier and that made it too risky. One slip and

Delilah might figure something out. "Aw, a couple of sore egos that got out of control. Why'd you dye your hair?"

She flinched a little and tucked a loose, black curl behind her ear. "Delilah thought it made me look more mature."

"More experienced?"

"She never said that."

"She didn't have to. I know what she's doing with you. She's movin' you into the business. Slow. You're pretty. You'll make her a lot of money."

"I'll never do that kind of work. I'll stay behind the bar the rest of my life and hum while I wash dishes. I'll never become a . . . a . . . you know."

"I hope that's true but Delilah's made a livin' outta bein' persuasive."

They clomped up the steps of the church and Mary Jean helped Logan finish the trek to his cot at the back of the building. She eased him down on his bed and wiped her hands. "She can use all the tricks in her bag. I'm no whore. Now, where's your alcohol and rags?"

A few minutes later, Mary Jean sat on the cot with Logan, wiping blood away from the corner of his mouth with half a pair of freshly laundered socks. He knew she was being gentle, but, dang, it hurt. He flinched when she pressed the cloth damp with witch hazel to his cheek. In the past, this clean-up after a fight had occurred while he was still inebriated and, therefore, still numb to the pain.

"You know, I could be a little hurt. Or insulted. You all but said she'd talk me into becoming one of her girls. You think I'm bound for that?"

Logan allowed himself to study Mary Jean's haunting green eyes, flawless, peach-colored skin, coal-black hair twisted up in a bun, and delicate little curls that tickled her cheekbones. And yet he saw Delilah, felt the softness of her shoulders beneath his fingers . . . recalled her pressing against him in the doorway. The thoughts had kept him awake these last several nights, reminding him of his weaknesses.

He shook himself, frustrated by the shallowness. "I'm sorry." For more than he cared to speak, but he'd keep to Mary Jean's concern. "I've kept bad company for too long. My manners are lacking. I did not mean to imply you'll take that path. It'll be your choice, not hers."

"You ever been married?" Mary Jean raised his hand to the cloth on his cheek and pressed it there.

"No."

She picked up the other sock, poured on the witch hazel, then looked up at him with unveiled hope. "You ever wanna be?"

He couldn't stop his eyes drifting down to her lips. Full, soft, pink. He remembered a young girl from what seemed a hundred years ago, overflowing with hope and . . . innocence. She seemed more like a dream now, one he'd let slip through his fingers. "Maybe one day." His guilt over Delilah's choices—choices she'd made out of hate for him—squeezed his heart. "If I can make some other things right."

---

*D*elilah took a long, deep, calming breath and splayed her hands out on the bar. "They have to be here somewhere. Five—no, *six*—girls don't just disappear into thin air." Fury muddled her thinking. She took another deeper breath and closed her eyes. "Mary Jean, give me a drink."

Glass clinked against glass, followed by a scraping sound as the shot slid to her fingers. She waited a moment, searching for some space, some isolated fleck of nothingness that would cancel out all this anger and help her think. The image of Mary Jean gently helping Logan to his feet set off a maelstrom of emotions that Delilah couldn't begin to understand. They swirled in the darkness behind her closed eyes.

She wanted to burn this town and everyone in it to the ground and laugh at the flames. That was no way to do business. Worse, she was thinking with her heart. Revenge and jealousy—a recipe for a disaster.

She tossed the whiskey back and concentrated on the burn, the way it seared her throat, singed her heart . . . cauterized the wound.

The rage started melting. She could feel it flowing out of her.

She had to be smart. She opened her eyes and stared at herself in the large oval mirror behind the bar. Pretty, petite features, skin with a hint of olive in it, auburn hair twisted stylishly atop her head. The lacy violet dress brought out the gold in her eyes, and showed much too much bosom. No wonder they thought they could run roughshod over her. A mere wisp of a girl.

Yet she had more power than they realized. She had the power to stab them in their hearts.

Like she had been stabbed.

She slid her gaze to Mary Jean. "How is our preacher?"

"Oh, beat up. Bloody. He'll be fine, though."

"Cleaned him up well, did you?"

"I tried."

Delilah rotated her head, loosening tense shoulders. "Join me in a drink." She shoved the glass toward Mary Jean.

"I don't like whiskey."

Delilah smiled, sweetly she hoped. "Well, I have some of my special sherry right there," she pointed at a decanter on the shelf. "Pour yourself some. I'd like more whiskey."

"Coming right up."

Delilah made sure Mary Jean took a sip of sherry. "Velvety, isn't it?"

"Yes ma'am."

Delilah downed half her whiskey. "I know you've been practicing. Are you ready to perform in the theater?"

Mary Jean nearly dropped the sherry glass. "The theater?"

"Yes, I think we'll do a show Friday night. A special one, just for you. And we'll let everyone in."

CHAPTER 31

*L*ogan flexed a sore hand slowly, careful not to tear the scabs lose. Four days later and he still ached heartily. Everywhere. He was no slouch when it came to boxing, but McIntyre had a savage punch. Yet he had held himself in check. In the back of his mind, Logan had thought for years he could beat the man. He dropped his hand to the open Bible on his cot. Now he wasn't so sure. He didn't intend to find out, either. Let sleeping dogs lie.

He ran his stiff, swollen finger down the page and stopped at Proverbs 21:15. *It is joy to the just to do judgment: but destruction shall be to the workers of iniquity.*

Judgment . . . justice. There had been justice in freeing those young girls. He did have joy. While the fight had been costly to his body, he would do it again.

But was he prepared for whatever Delilah might unleash in retaliation? He could only imagine her fury at having *all* of her virgins spirited away, so why was she dallying?

He scooped up the box of hymnals, just arrived from his generous church down in Willow, and marched out to the pews. He laid them, one by one, on the seats. As he walked, he prayed—

for people in town, for protection, for freedom, and for redemption.

"Preacher."

Mary Jean's strangled voice brought his head up. She closed the door behind her. Tears spilled down her cheeks as she raised a yellow piece of paper. "I heard from my parents. They don't want me back."

Dropping the box, he rushed to her and let her fall into his arms. She sobbed for a few minutes into his shoulder. He whispered, "Shhh," and let the tears run their course. When they slowed, he led her over to a pew and they sat.

Wiping her eyes with a knuckle, she handed him the paper.

You need not come home. Pa.

Flinching, Logan crunched the note into a tight little ball. He'd given the girl false hope. What kind of parents . . .? "I'm sorry. Perhaps I could write to them—"

"No. It's better this way." She sniffed and squared her shoulders. "Delilah wants me to sing Friday night. In the theater. This is the best course. Maybe my dreams will come true after all."

Friday night in the theater? Anguish slithered into Logan's heart. This was not, he believed, preparation for the dream Mary Jean had in mind. "I thought Friday night was . . ." he trailed off, not eager to speak his thoughts.

"One of the raunchier nights?"

"I know what goes on in there."

Mary Jean picked up a hymnal and flipped through it absently. "She said I didn't have to do anything other than sing."

That answer didn't satisfy Logan. He couldn't bring himself to believe the best of Delilah. She was not the girl he'd known so many years back. His fault. Her fault. Nobody's fault. It didn't matter. She had changed and he couldn't bring himself to trust her. "I'll be there to hear you."

Mary Jean's face lit up. "You will? Thank you. I'm so nervous as it is. To have a friend in the crowd would . . . would mean a lot to me."

He clutched her shoulder for encouragement. "You can count on me."

———

*F*riday night came too soon, but Logan made his way over to The Crystal Chandelier. He stopped at the batwings, surprised by the full house. The shoulder-to-shoulder crowd, full tables, raucous laughter . . . and the heavy, cloying smell of the whiskey brought back all the wrong memories.

Overcome by a sudden unexpected desire for the liquor, he left the entrance and strode to a post in the shadows. He licked his lips, shocked he could almost taste it. The scent. The scent was thick in the air. He leaned on the post and turned his back to a laughing, roughhousing group of cowboys marching past.

He wiped sweat from his upper lip. *Lord, help me with this, please. I thought I was past it . . .*

The Holy Spirit nudged him and Logan spoke aloud, but softly, "In the name of Jesus, get thee behind me, Satan."

He clenched his jaw and prayed for another moment, till the desperate feeling subsided and peace flooded in. He would be all right. He could do this. Mary Jean needed him.

Strengthened, he slipped into The Crystal Chandelier, stayed close to the wall, and worked his way up to the end of the bar. The door to the theater was on his left, the stairs to the second floor on his right. He looked away quickly from two young girls sauntering down the staircase in nothing but the sheerest of covers and black stockings.

Oh, God, how can they live like this? How did I ever live like this? Help me to find a way to put an end to Delilah's business.

"Get you something?" The bartender, a burly, unshaven fellow, pinned Logan with an impatient stare.

"Uh, not just yet. Waitin' for someone." Scowling, the bartender moved to the man parked a few feet down the wood. Logan tugged his hat a little lower and listened to the noise in the saloon. Sounds that seemed as alien to him now as Chinese. Husky voices arguing, laughing. Bottles clinking against glass, the rattle of poker chips, chairs scraping across the floor . . . and underneath it, a piano and a soft, clear voice.

Mary Jean.

Logan lifted his head and looked over at a new pair of French doors that led into the theater. He strained to hear and wondered why her voice sounded different. Less . . . steady? Yes, there was a waver to it, as if she were . . .

Drunk?

His heartbeat picked up. Sai Shang had been drugged. He'd learned that when they'd rescued her from Rizzo's. If Mary Jean was only going to sing, why drug her? His eyes shot to the mirror and he searched the room behind him. He did not see Smith or that black mountain of a man who went everywhere with Delilah.

They were in the theater.

Certain of his next move, he worked his way over to the wall, casual step by casual step. When the doorknob was in easy reach, he turned it and slipped through to the other side.

They did not hear him and he slid a few feet further down the wall into the shadows. Mary Jean stood on the stage, Smith beside her, holding on to her arm. Still, she swayed unsteadily. Dressed up and painted like one of Delilah's gals, she was squeezed into a daringly low-cut dress, and bright rouge dotted her cheeks. Her red lips moved in song, but the words tumbled over each other.

The room was smaller than the saloon, filled with only a dozen or so tables, lanterns glowing in the center of each one. No customers yet. Overhead, chandeliers emitted a weak, somber light. Footlights focused garish attention on the stage, where Smith held onto Mary Jean.

Logan squeezed his hands into tight fists. No matter what it took, he would get her off that stage.

God forgive me . . .

Smith, his face yet showing bruises, scowled down at Delilah who stood just behind the lights. "You gave her too much. She ain't gonna be able to sing a note."

"Like that matters. Just stand there and hold her up. The auction'll go quick." Delilah motioned to the man watching from the corner of the stage. "Otis, get the cashbox. I'll go make the announcement about her."

"No." Logan stepped out of the shadows, his hand drifting down to his gun. Smith and Delilah spun toward the sound of his voice. Otis paused. Mary Jean's eyes flickered with weak recognition.

The fury searing Logan's brain made it hard to speak. "No auction."

"Why you—" Smith shoved Mary Jean to the ground and stomped to the edge of the stage.

Delilah stuck her hand out, stopping him. She flushed beet red. Her lips curled into a sneer. "Can you possibly have any idea how stupid it was to come here tonight?" Her breath coming in short, angry gasps, she took two steps toward him. "Do you have any idea how livid I am?" Her voice rose to an agitated screech. "You've taken *six* of my girls and now you have the *audacity* to think you can stop another auction?"

"Yes." Logan moved toward her, speaking calmly, trying to hold his own anger in check. "Yes. And yes. That girl ain't leavin' here tonight with anybody but me."

A change came over Delilah's face. One moment spittle flew from her mouth, rage evident in her sneer and clenched jaw, replaced suddenly by an eerily calm expression, as if a resolve set with cement had settled somewhere in her dark heart.

"Then you'll pay like everybody else." She picked up a full shot glass sitting on a nearby table and walked it over to him. "One sip. One sip and I'll let you have her." She waved it under his nose.

Logan felt the sweat break out on his upper lip.

"Old Crow. Kentucky Straight. Your favorite, if I recall." She dipped her finger in the whiskey and then dabbed it between her breasts like perfume. "How long since you had . . . a drink?"

*D*elilah didn't push. She knew Logan would take the glass. His gaze darted to Mary Jean once, and then he snatched the whiskey from her hand. Without hesitating, he tossed it back. She heard Mary Jean gasp weakly.

Logan kept his eyes shut for a moment. Savoring or fighting off the whiskey?

Rage writhed in Delilah's brain. He'd never made a sacrifice like that for her. "Otis, get her out of here."

Logan looked at Delilah. His face still showed the bruises of his fight with McIntyre. "I should go too."

She placed her hand lightly on his arm. Her anger drained away. "Could you stay for a minute?"

He regarded her with surprise, perhaps at her tone. It had surprised her as well.

"All right."

Otis escorted the girl out and Delilah poured herself a drink, but held it tauntingly close to Logan. "You said if there was anything you could do to make amends to me, you'd do it."

"I stand by that." He blinked, shook his head.

She moved in close, pressing up against him. He inched back, but didn't leave her. This hadn't been part of her original plan, but she hungered desperately for . . . something real. She cast a sultry glance up at him. The drug was beginning to hit him and she wanted him sober for this choice. Heart racing like a runaway stallion, she licked her lips. "The price to get out of this room is either this shot of whiskey . . . or one kiss."

His brow twitched slightly but he didn't look down at the whiskey.

To Delilah's horror, tears pooled in her eyes. She blinked them away as she tore her gaze from him. She had to look at anything but him. How could she, after all these years, feel like this again? This wasn't supposed to happen.

His hand caught her cheek and turned her face to him. "I never did get to kiss you good-bye." His thumb stroked her jaw and he smiled. "Ah, there you are . . . *Victoria.*"

Logan pressed his lips to hers. Delilah allowed herself to fall into the dream, the memory, of the girl she once was. His warm lips and gentle touch almost moved her to tears. He was tender, but hesitant. Was he afraid of himself or her?

She hooked her arm around his neck and kissed him harder. He fought for a moment . . .then surrendered. He embraced her, drew her against him, and deepened the kiss. A groan escaped him, and Delilah could have fainted. Her heart pounded, she felt lightheaded, on the verge of floating away. No one, no one had ever made her feel like this except Logan. Like she was home.

"Victoria," he whispered against her throat. "Victoria." He kissed her neck. "I can't do this." She heard his anguish, the war in his heart. "You know I can't."

She couldn't let him leave. Loathing her desperation, she brought the drink to his lips.

CHAPTER 32

One of the last things McIntyre ever wanted to hear was 'the preacher has gone crazy.' Yet somehow he was not entirely surprised by the news Emilio delivered.

Now the two of them galloped in the dark, hell-bent-for-leather to The Crystal Chandelier to try to stop whatever self-destructive bent Logan was on. McIntyre suspected the man had received more than a little nudge from Delilah.

He wished they could go faster, but the fight with Logan had taken McIntyre's edge. He wouldn't be his old self for several more days, he feared. Sore muscles and scabs had a way of slowing a man down.

They reined up in front of the saloon. A crowd had gathered outside, looking in through broken windows. McIntyre could hear Logan inside raging and bellowing, and glass shattering. Then gunfire. Someone inside yelped and everyone outside hunkered down in unison. After a moment, well aware the danger had not passed, McIntyre and Emilio shouldered their way into the saloon.

Much of the place was in shambles. Merely cosmetic, McIntyre knew from experience. Righting tables and putting chairs back would go a long way toward restoration. Up near the bar, though, three tables and several chairs were smashed to smithereens. One man lay dead or unconscious on the floor among the shards of wood and poker chips, a revolver in his right hand.

Logan staggered drunkenly back and forth on top of the bar, ranting at something in the corner. Wildly agitated, he waved a bottle of Kentucky Bourbon overhead and held a revolver in his other hand. His red plaid shirt hung open, flapping around his waist as he stomped drunkenly down the wood. McIntyre followed the preacher's gaze to the corner.

Smith was splayed out against the far wall, and bullet holes riddled the wood around him . . . in a clear outline. The man's courage had been shot to pieces along with the paneling. Face white as January snow, he sported a dark stain down his pants leg that ended in a puddle on the floor.

McIntyre took a deep breath and moved within a few feet of the bar. "Logan."

The preacher snapped his head around, then slowly spun his body, but with all the grace of a sick chicken. He grinned, his head bobbing as if it were too much for his shoulders. "McIntyre . . . you're just in time to join me in a little shooting." Logan pointed his gun at Smith and fired, without even looking at the hapless target. The shot went wide, but Smith warbled out a pathetic squeak just the same.

"Logan!" McIntyre hollered in a firmer voice, stepping to the bar, "put that gun down before you kill someone."

"Too late." His eyes darted to the man on the floor. The expression of hapless confusion fled. A thundercloud darkened Logan's face, and he swallowed. "What'd you come here for? To gloat? Get a gander at your preacher fallin'-down drunk?"

"I am not here to gloat, Logan. You are my friend. I have come to help you."

"You can't help me," he spat. He waved the gun around and

yelled at the empty saloon. "Nobody can help me!" He pointed at the man on the floor. "Look what I've done!"

McIntyre peered closer. Shelby lay sprawled among the shattered furniture, dead as a doornail. "This *is* quite the situation and it will have consequences. It is not, however, the end of the world."

"*Situation?*" Logan's voice sounded strangled, on the verge of breaking. "I stuck a stick of dynamite square into the center of my life and lit it."

McIntyre sighed at the mess Logan had created here, a dead man on the floor, a live coward up against the wall. "Smith, why don't you get out? Go clean yourself up."

"No," Logan pointed his gun at his victim as he glared down at McIntyre. "I ain't done with him. He killed Big Jim. He killed your doctor. You know he was about to cut your son into little pieces when I met him? Instead, your son got a piece of him." Laughing, Logan fired and took a chunk of wall out not three inches from Smith's head. The man's chest started pumping as if all the air had gone bad.

"Logan!" McIntyre didn't know if he carried any sway with the preacher, but he could try. "You have humiliated him enough. For God's sake, the man has wet his breeches. Make him walk out the front door, but be done with him." Logan paused and McIntyre prayed he was getting through. "This is no way to serve God."

Logan worked his jaw back and forth, pondering. Calculating? He lowered his gun. Smith didn't hesitate. He dashed for the door, tossing a chair out of his way as he ran. He left the front door open and laughter flowed into the saloon. Emilio quietly closed the door again.

"Now give me your gun." McIntyre extended his hand. "Let's get you out of here."

"What for?"

"We'll get you sobered up, back in your right mind. Get this squared away with the marshal."

"He drew first." Logan stared at Shelby lying on the floor. "Smith faked with his shoulder. Shelby thought he was drawing on me and went for it." He squeezed his eyes shut as if he couldn't stand the memory. "I can't serve God anymore. There's not a sin I haven't put my hand to tonight."

"Whatever has transpired here, the blame is not solely on you."

Logan shook his head, in a wobbly, exaggerated manner, and sat down on the bar, his legs hanging over the edge. "Doesn't matter." He rubbed his eyes—to hide tears? "Gone too far. God won't forgive me."

"No matter what you've done, there is grace. You know that."

Logan erupted. "A preacher, a man of *God* cannot act like this!" He jumped to the floor and pointed the gun at McIntyre. "I turned my back on Him for a shot of whiskey . . ." his voice softened, "and a woman." The tenderness betrayed his heart. "How pitiful is that?"

McIntyre wasn't inclined to discuss it looking down the barrel of a Peacemaker. He knocked the gun out of Logan's hand. For a moment, the two tussled, but McIntyre managed to get hold of the man's lapels and slam him against the bar a few times. "Stop this," he commanded. "Stop it." Some of the fight went out of Logan and the men locked gazes. "You haven't done anything He can't forgive. I would know." Jaw clenched in fury, he slammed him against the wood one last time. "*I* would know." He waited for some light to dawn in Logan's eyes, some hope. Logan merely pushed him away and sank to the floor.

McIntyre let out a breath he didn't know he'd been holding, and pinched the bridge of his nose. *God, help him know You have not abandoned him . . . no matter what he's done.*

Or perhaps I should pray he does not abandon You?

He looked up at the ceiling and motion on the stairs caught his eye. Delilah clutched her evening wrap closed over her bosom as her venomous gaze bore down on him. One bare leg stayed exposed. Had she used every weakness to which Logan was vulnerable?

McIntyre wanted to strangle her. "Satisfied now?"

She looked at Logan. Crumpled on the floor. Broken. Drunk.

Delilah merely turned and disappeared down the dark hallway.

"Will you bring charges?"

Beckwith stepped away from the curtain separating Logan's quarters from the sanctuary. "I don't know." He slipped his hat on. "Witnesses said he didn't start the fight. Smith and Shelby did. He was just protecting himself. If that holds, then it ain't murder. I'll let you know." He stomped down the aisle and out the front door, the thud of his boots almost ominous in the pre-dawn quiet.

McIntyre moved the curtain aside and peered at Mary Jean, sitting on the cot with the preacher, wiping his brow with tenderness. If he woke up and saw her, maybe things wouldn't look so grim.

Logan had done his witness as a preacher great harm. Maybe irreparable harm. Defiance wasn't full of the most forgiving citizens. The town was especially hard on hypocrites. McIntyre didn't want to judge the man—

So he wouldn't. He'd stop right there.

He would pray for his friend. McIntyre had slipped once. Into the arms of another woman. He would remember the pain, the anguish, the shame forever. If Logan felt half that bad, then he at least hadn't abandoned God entirely.

---

*E*ven before he opened his eyes, Logan felt the weight, the warmth on his chest. It constricted his breathing. He raised his hand and touched . . . hair.

Delilah?

His eyes popped open and the morning light exploded in his eyeballs like shards of glass. He groaned and dropped his head back to the cot. Whatever—whoever—was on him, could wait.

Hungover.

His spirits plummeted as it all came back to him. Delilah and the whiskey. He'd had no choice. Run and leave Mary Jean, or take the drink and save her.

But he'd lost his soul in the process. His throat constricted with scorching sorrow. The flashes of Delilah's skin, the sweetness of her, her passion . . . so long since he'd been with a woman . . . a hundred years since he'd been with the one he loved. If only it hadn't happened like that, outside of marriage, himself soused with whiskey. He'd cheapened it. And Delilah.

A frenzy of rabid, wild memories assailed him. Somehow he'd made it downstairs. He recalled Smith and the other man . . . Shelby. Running their mouths.

He dropped his forearm over his eyes, blocking the light, wishing he could hold back the images just as easily. *God, what have I done . . .?*

The body on him stirred, lifted. "She drugged you. That's why you feel so bad."

Mary Jean? He dropped his arm and looked at her. She was still in the gown she'd had on last night, but she'd washed her face. She was tired, but innocence had returned to her eyes. He'd lost so much to save her. Would she be worth it?

"I know you had a choice. And I know what it cost you." She wrung a rag out in the basin beside his bed and laid the damp cloth on his head. "Thank you."

Sunset's lengthening shadows reached across the sparkling Animas River. Behind Logan, the town was settling into the quieter, peaceful sounds of dusk . . . the lull before things picked up again in Tent Town.

Heaving a huge sigh, he stared out at the flowing, swirling water and tried to fight a sense of failure that felt like a kick in the gut. "God, forgive me."

Shame hung over him like a palpable stench. His heart ached from it. He'd come here to share the gospel, save lives, tell people the Good News that Jesus forgives sins. Instead, he had disgraced his Savior. The remorse drove him to his knees. He was no different than the sinners who had smeared the church door with scat. He had treated Christ's sacrifice the same way. As worthless. Meaningless.

One drink. Why couldn't I have stopped with one drink?

The whiskey and Delilah's nearness had driven him past the point of self-control. He flinched at the memory of holding her. He didn't realize the weakness he had for her. But for a few minutes, he had been seventeen again and in the arms of the girl he wanted to spend his life with.

With the sweet memory came another monster wave of guilt. He loved Delilah. He loved God more. Even so, in the darkness last night, he'd lost his way. He couldn't use the drug as an excuse. It wasn't. He'd wanted Delilah and he'd given in.

"Oh, God," he pounded his fist into his forehead, "I've failed You at every turn. On every level. In every way possible. I've shown You nothing but weakness and frailty. I haven't saved anyone. Not one single soul."

The trickle of water and the chatter of birds answered back. And that was no answer at all.

Tears streamed down Logan's face. "I am so worthless."

You are the apple of My eye.

"But I'm a failure."

You are an overcomer.

"I've brought You nothing but shame."

The righteous falls seven times . . . and rises again.

"Then, please, help me find my way back."

Seek Me with all your heart and you will find Me.

Grief and shame strangled Logan, held him back from reaching for that grace. He wanted to scream. Instead, he picked up a rock and, with a wild growl, tossed it into the water.

"*He* said he's not preaching today." Emilio's long face spoke volumes about this disappointment. He ambled down the church steps, hands shoved deep into his pockets.

Disgusted, McIntyre jerked the brake up on the wagon and nodded at Naomi and Two Spears. "Let me go talk to him."

Naomi took the reins from him. "Why don't you meet us at the town hall?"

She glanced over her shoulder at the rest of their clan walking up. Hannah and her son, Billy, Ian, and Rebecca. Mollie and Emilio were already here.

"I'll take them back and we'll get Sunday supper started."

McIntyre kissed her on the cheek, reached to ruffle Two Spears's hair—doubted the wisdom of the move—but followed through. The boy's face didn't change exactly, but neither did he pull away.

Progress? McIntyre hoped so, for them both.

---

*M*cIntyre let himself into the church and listened for a moment. He could hear drawers sliding and slamming shut with too much force . . . and muttering. Or was that praying?

McIntyre had prayed as well. He often didn't get the clarity from God that he wanted—or perhaps he was too impatient to listen—but he knew, at least for this moment, he was where God wanted him. How ironic he was here to remind his preacher of grace when he himself couldn't find it the other day. "Logan."

The drawers stopped. "I'm here."

McIntyre wandered back and pushed the curtain aside. Logan grabbed a pile of clothes from his bed and shoved them with brutality into his saddlebags.

"Going somewhere?"

Logan gave a derisive snort. "Anywhere but here, I guess."

McIntyre picked up a bullet from the counter and fidgeted with it while he thought. "A recent failure on my part, and now your situation, has had me studying."

"*Situation*. You like that word." He raked a handful of socks into the bag.

"I made an interesting discovery. There are no perfect men in the Bible, aside from Christ."

Logan's hands slowed a little.

Encouraged, McIntyre pushed on. "Adam couldn't avoid one simple fruit. Moses had a terrible temper. David thought he could use murder to hide a scandal. Worse, he thought he could hide it from God." He set the bullet down and looked at Logan. "What did all these flawed, foolish men have in common?"

Logan stilled, waiting.

"God used them in spite of their faults. He can still use you, Logan. Nothing you have done is worse than what those Biblical patriarchs did. We have to let go of the condemnation." He made a fist. "Take hold of grace."

Logan stared at McIntyre, the battle to accept forgiveness raging in his eyes. "You know what else those men had in common?"

McIntyre shrugged.

"Their sins had consequences."

CHAPTER 33

"The new girls are here."

Blinking away thoughts of Logan, Delilah lifted her head and followed the sound of Otis's voice. He backed away from the door and three young women strolled into the empty theater. A pretty blond, a brunette, and a redhead stopped and waited for her appraisal. In their early twenties, they were attractive enough, but had that familiar razor's edge to their features. Life had scraped away the innocence and the hope from their faces as neatly as a two-dollar shave.

Restless, bored by this part of her profession, she rose and surveyed the girls top-to-bottom and back again. Better-looking than most, nice measurements, especially up-top. Reportedly very willing girls.

Delilah could not have cared less.

She felt as though a spark had gone out somewhere deep inside her. It troubled her greatly, and made conversation onerous. "Mary Hastings gives you high marks."

"We don't mind the work," the redhead said stepping forward. "Any kind, as long as the pay and the conditions are good. Mary said you were giving us a raise and our own rooms."

Mary had also said the Barbary Coast Kittens, as they were called, were up for anything. Delilah had purchased them planning such lewd entertainment that McIntyre, the fallen preacher, and the rest of the saints of Defiance would simply faint from shock. At the moment, however, the expected conversation was too tiresome, almost repulsive. "Otis, please show them to their rooms. Ladies, join me for dinner later and we'll talk about your act."

After the girls left, she settled into her seat again . . . and for the millionth time relived the few precious moments she'd spent in Logan's arms. Especially that one moment, when she was kissing him, and his resistance had broken . . .

What if she hadn't gone to Stillwater? What if she'd told Logan about the baby?

What if she'd told her mother? Maybe she wouldn't have sent her away.

What if, what if, what if . . .

Delilah growled and slapped the table.

She'd made her choices. She would live with them. And so, by God, would everyone else.

Delilah didn't visit the cribs often. She didn't even like walking around Tent Town. The place was a haphazard assortment of canvas hovels, one-room shacks, and trash—human and otherwise. Folks gawked as she strode by. Her red silk dress and voluminous bustle were as out of place here as a mermaid in the desert.

She lifted her skirt to step over what looked like vomit and walked a few more steps to the first tent on the row. Otis pounded on the door for her then snatched it open.

As he had reported, Mary Jean had indeed come back to her little home here on Crib Row. Delilah thought for sure she'd stay with Logan.

She'll wish she had.

Jealousy. Vengeance. Mere spitefulness. Whatever one wanted

to call it, Delilah was on a tear and Mary Jean was her first target.

"I need your tent. Get out. Oh, and you're fired . . . in case there was any doubt."

Mary Jean dropped the petticoat she'd been folding and stared slack-jawed at Delilah. "What? Why? I don't have any place to go. I need a few days."

"You should have thought of that before you had your preacher ruin another auction."

"I didn't tell him to rescue me, but I'm glad he did. You lied to me. You were gonna turn me into one of your girls without even giving me a choice. I should go to the marshal."

Delilah narrowed her eyes to slits and slapped Mary Jean. The stinging swat left four fingerprints on the girl's cheek and jarred tears from her eyes. "Don't threaten me. I never forced you to do anything—"

"You drugged the sherry . . . and his whiskey."

"Prove it."

Mary Jean blinked. She had no way, of course. Only her word against Delilah's.

"I did try to be gentle with you. A wasted effort, but I'll give you one last chance. Work for me or get out . . . but before you get so high-and-mighty about things, remember you owe me money for rent and food. *That* we can talk to the marshal about."

"I—I . . ."

"Your customers will start showing up around eight."

Done talking, Delilah spun in a red flurry of silk and lace and exited. Out on the weedy path that served for an avenue, she passed a handsome Hispanic boy and a pretty little blonde.

She wouldn't have paid them any attention except they seemed somehow out of place here. And they had stared back at her without fear, perhaps even with a little revulsion. Curious, she turned. The two meandered past Mary Jean's tent.

Otis followed her gaze, but shrugged.

The young man struck her as familiar, but she couldn't place him. From the Chandelier, perhaps? She had never seen the girl before. Delilah drummed her fingers on her skirt, pondering, but decided to let it go. She had better things to do than stand here studying strangers, so she turned up the path to the make her way to the telegraph office.

"*I*s she still looking?"

Emilio sneaked a casual glance over his shoulder. Both Delilah and Otis were on their way in the opposite direction. "No. Let's go."

He took Mollie by the elbow and they backtracked to Mary Jean's tent.

"*I* told you she would only give you two choices." Mollie picked up a hand mirror and sat down on Mary Jean's cot.

"I won't work for her. Not that way. But what am I supposed to do? I need a place to stay and a job."

"I told you there's a room for you at the town hall with us. And if you want to stay in Defiance, you can have a job at the hotel."

Emilio nodded. "*Sí*. You could work there for a while."

"Maybe." Looking a little pale, Mary Jean sat down. "I've been feeling poorly ever since I left the other night. And my hands want to shake." She sounded mystified by her condition.

Mollie put the back of her hand to Mary Jean's forehead. "No fever, but you're clammy. It takes a day or two for the laudanum to leave your system."

Mary Jean hunched her shoulders, rubbed her arms, and looked around the room. She wasn't leaving much, Emilio thought, but he understood the fear of leaving what you knew. He suspected she would overcome it pretty readily. As long as there was hope, he didn't think Mary Jean was the type to give in to Delilah.

"I owe it to Preacher to get out of here. What about the money I owe her?"

Emilio knew a man with money and a heart for these lost girls. "I'd bet Mr. McIntyre can get that taken care of."

"All right." She pulled her shoulders back. "And thank you."

Mollie touched her arm. "You shouldn't be seen with us. Pack and come up to the hotel in about half an hour."

CHAPTER 34

"*I*njuns. Only good one is a dead one. But as my Pappy used to say . . ."

McIntyre stopped inches from the open bunkhouse window. He pulled back to listen, hoping Lane's words were about something else.

Silverware clattered as Lane continued. "My pappy used to say it is what it is. That boy is the boss's son. Don't matter if he's black, white, Injun, or Chinese. You wanna keep your jobs, boys, I reckon you'll suck up what you think." Something sizzling on the stove covered up another man's voice, but Lane replied, "Whether Delilah put him up to it or not, he shoulda been smarter. If you're gonna mess with the kid, make sure ain't nobody else around. Especially McIntyre."

McIntyre curled his fingers into fists. The powerful desire to march into the bunkhouse, grab Lane by the hair, and shove his face into the grease nearly grabbed hold. He took a step back to fight it, and prayed for self-control.

He could at least fire Lane . . .

And, apparently, all his hands.

Disgusted, he ambled over to the other side of the barn

because it afforded the best view of his valley and his cattle. He liked owning cattle. He enjoyed the company of most of the boys, especially Lane. Until now.

How could he look these men in the eye, knowing they would do his son harm? How could he refrain from killing them?

"Charles?"

He smiled, her presence bringing him some peace, and extended his hand, but didn't look at her. Naomi grasped his fingers and slid up close to him. "I saw you walk over here. Or should I say 'slog'? I could tell something was wrong."

He hated to tell her. He knew her heart broke for Two Spears, and for them as a family. "I overheard Lane and some of the boys talking." Shaking his head, he stepped away and gazed out over the view, furling and unfurling his fists. "I cannot force the bigotry out of them, Naomi." He sighed and rested his hands on his hips. "I can't beat it out of them. They'll still hate Indians. What am I supposed to do? How do I protect him?"

"Teach him to be strong, but teach him about love too. Otherwise he'll grow up full of hate, and that would be the real tragedy."

"I know things wouldn't be different anywhere else, but there are days—few and far between, but there nonetheless—when I think about leaving Defiance."

She stepped up beside him, eyes wide as full moons. "Leaving? You've just gotten the ranch started. Would you start all over?"

He brushed a thumb down her jawline. "The idea of a fresh start is appealing at times. If for no other reason than the adventure of it."

Naomi frowned. "My sisters are here."

"I know." Something in his spirit deflated and it surprised him. He'd only toyed with the idea of leaving . . . but a fresh start, new challenges, they held some appeal. He shook off his consternation for her sake. "Just thinking out loud, princess. I take it you don't spark to the idea?"

"I don't know." She unrolled and then rolled her sleeve as she pondered his question. He adored the deep 'v' that etched itself in her forehead when she was troubled. "I guess it might depend on where."

McIntyre slipped his arm around his wife's shoulders. "Don't fret. Merely idle reverie."

"If you say so."

Yet they both knew it wasn't.

---

ave arrived Salt Lake. Arrive Defiance one week. Sit tight. M

Delilah crumpled the telegram and tossed it to the boardwalk. Otis bent down and picked it up. Probably smart. At least he wasn't thinking like an emotional female.

A freight wagon rolled by, kicking up a slow-moving cloud of dust. The stagnant air and dirt from the street annoyed her by turning the hem of her new blue dress a dingy gray. Frankly, everything annoyed her. Nothing made her happy. She was simply . . . angry. She wanted to scream and curse Heaven for the way things in her life were right now . . . or maybe for every single event that had brought her here. Back to Logan.

Refusing to devote another second to thoughts of him, she lifted her skirt higher and marched back toward Tent Town. She winked and smiled at the male citizenry as she went, or at least most of them. She knew the regulars, the big spenders . . . and the skinflints. She glared at Mel Watson as he bent to tip his hat. All show. Argued the price of every single poke. He backed off and cut away from her.

Business. All business. She had to focus. She couldn't have Matthew coming to Defiance with this situation over the Oriental Flowers unresolved. He would try to take over, but the theft of her property could not go unanswered. On the bright side, Phoebe, Melissa, and Bonnie, the Kittens, were adequate replacements for the auctions. Not as profitable, but they were filling the theater every Saturday night.

Sit tight. Easy for him to say.

If Smith still had no word on where those girls went, Delilah didn't think she was going to wait for Matthew. She needed to show him she could handle things here. It was time, *past* time, for McIntyre and Logan to learn a lesson about interfering in her business.

CHAPTER 35

*P*uzzled by the flickering light in the darkness just ahead of him, Emilio pulled Matilda to a halt. *What was that?*

Suddenly the light flared brighter, sizzled to life, and streaked across the open ground of the mine's storage yard like a squirrel running with a firecracker. It raced forward, sparking and smoking, as fast an arrow toward . . .

He looked ahead to where the mysterious light seemed to be heading. A red shack labeled *Explosives*! Not far beyond that, the mine entrance. His heart hammered in his chest as he put two and two together. *No time to snuff it out.*

"Get out!" Emilio jerked his revolver free and fired off all six shots as he and Matilda ran for a lone ore cart sitting on the tracks to the mine. Solid iron. It might save them . . . "Get out!"

The fuse burned toward the shack, like a runaway train. A few men appeared at the mine's entrance.

"Run!" he screamed at the confused miners, "Run—"

The storage shed exploded in a blinding, roaring fireball. The concussion knocked Emilio and Matilda down and they slammed into the ground. Emilio went skidding in the gravel, his forehead ricocheting off the ground as dirt filled his eyes and mouth. A shower of shrapnel rained down on him. He curled up into a ball, protecting his head, and tried yelling for Matilda. He couldn't hear his own voice, only a piercing ringing that threatened to split his skull in two.

Almost immediately, a second explosion lit up the night, rocked the air, and shook the ground, but for Emilio a strange darkness closed in, blurring his vision. The ringing in his head became a deep rumble. It clambered up from the earth below, rolling over him, sweeping him away with the darkness.

*L*ogan raced to the mine, along with scores of other men in town who had heard the explosion. He didn't know where the mine was, and it didn't matter. The blazing sky led the way.

McIntyre stood in the midst of the burning, smoldering landscape, waving, and shouting orders like Hades emerged from the Underworld. Men scrambled to do his bidding.

"Find Danny! Get those shovels! Start digging at the entrance! Let's get a fire brigade going and put these buildings out!"

Apparently the mine entrance had collapsed. Miners were injured, possibly trapped. Men needed to dig and dig *now*. McIntyre spotted Billy and Logan and called them over. "We've got injured men. We need teams of two to take them to Doc's. I need the rest of these men moving debris from the entrance."

As he was talking, the color drained from Billy's face. McIntyre and Logan followed his gaze. At first, Logan didn't see it, then the carnage dawned on him. "That's a dead horse."

Billy swallowed. "It's *Emilio's* horse."

McIntyre slapped Billy on the shoulder, "Let's find him," and called to Logan as they ran, "Get these men digging at the entrance. The mine manager is unlocking the shed to get more shovels and picks."

---

*M*oving the timber beams, twisted iron rails, rocks, and dirt from the entrance was a slow, painful exercise. Logan's hands bled from clawing at the jagged edges of rocks and metal. Debris shifted, pinching fingers, slicing flesh, and drawing blood. Still, he and the other men worked with urgency, even desperation, moving deeper and deeper into the entrance. The pace was agonizingly slow.

Logan prayed hard without ceasing, but not aloud. With his recent downfall, he had no right to let these men working beside him think he considered himself . . . holier than they were. He was no preacher. He was just a man, a fallible, flawed, weak-minded man humbly asking God to show some mercy and grace to the miners buried beneath this rubble. He certainly was not a man worthy of giving spiritual guidance.

The first miner they found was dead. A beam had fallen across his chest, crushing him. The next four men came out in rough shape, but alive, and teams rushed them on makeshift stretchers to the doctor's office.

Two men working to Logan's left lifted a good hundred-pound stone, paused, exchanging troubled glances, then chucked it aside. One knelt down. Logan saw the expression of concern, then pity. The man looked over at Logan. "Preacher?"

He handed off his rock to the man behind him and scrambled over the mounds of rubble. "Yes?"

The man stood. "He said he'd like you to pray with him."

Without waiting for a response, the rescuers moved to a different pile of debris. Logan gritted his teeth. Everything in him wanted to refuse. He was not worthy to pray with anyone, but he stepped around a large rock . . .

The lanterns, faint though they were, clearly showed the man's injuries. Half his skull was badly crushed and blood glittered in his scalp, glistened on his face.

God, I can't do this . . .

Yet even as he prayed that he dropped to his knees beside the man. He took his hand, mingling their blood. "Hey, can you hear me?"

The man's lips moved, but no sound came forth. One eye did manage to open and look toward Logan, but not at him. "Sorry," he barely croaked out.

Sorry? Logan peered closer at the man. "What are you sorry fo —" He pulled back. He knew that crazy eye. He knew this man. "Smith?"

He nodded slightly. "Me . . . I did this . . . Didn't mean for . . . no one to die." He gurgled and foamy blood dribbled out the corner of his mouth.

Logan ran through all the things Smith had done. Attacking Two Spears, vandalizing the church, *murdering* Big Jim Walker . . . and now the mine. This man had a lot to answer for and was moments away from it . . . could Logan watch him die without saying a word? Without giving him hope for redemption? Could he sit back and watch him slip into hell?

The thought terrified him for Smith's soul, and his own.

Desperation seized him. "Smith, I know I fouled up. I reckon I'm about the worst witness for Jesus you've ever seen, but who I am doesn't change who God is." He leaned closer, unable to fight the tears filling his eyes, or slow his pounding heart. "I believe you're gonna see death any second now. Where do you want to spend eternity?" He clutched Smith's hand tighter and tried to get past the knot swelling in his own throat. "Please, let me tell you about the God Who loves you, Who died for you . . . Who wants to forgive—" His voice broke. "Who wants to forgive you, welcome you home. Do you want that peace?"

After only an instant of hesitation, Smith squeezed Logan's hand.

. . . and, once again, a preacher bowed his head to pray.

CHAPTER 36

"Quick, put him in there."

Billy and a man Hannah didn't know hurried to deliver Emilio into examination room one. She gasped as they passed by her. Burn marks singed his clothes, holes burnt all the way through peppered his shirt. A deep cut sliced across the top of his shoulder but more worrisome was the blood trickling from his right ear.

She was no doctor. What if he was seriously injured?

What if he had a skull fracture?

Oh, God, I need Your help now. Please don't let him be hurt badly . . . and please give me the knowledge I need to help him . . . she looked out the window at the glow in the sky . . . *and anyone else who may be hurt.*

Hannah examined Emilio and determined with reasonable comfort that he had a ruptured eardrum, probably a mild concussion. Soon other victims started arriving and filled the entrance. "I'll be right back, Emilio."

He didn't stir and it pained her to walk away from him.

"What can I do first?" Mollie asked as she slipped in the front door.

Hannah rolled up her sleeves and surveyed the new patients covering the floor. She could have fainted with relief at her friend's voice. "Can you clean Emilio up, put some gauze over his ear, and pick the splinters out of his hide?"

Mollie nodded and hurried into the room.

Moving forward with all the confidence she could fake, Hannah checked out the four men brought in on stretchers. Broken bones, deep lacerations, a concussion, but nothing life threatening . . . so far. Unless she couldn't get their bleeding to stop.

"Mollie," she called over her shoulder, "hurry with Emilio if you can. I need eight more hands out here."

*B*efore the night was over, Hannah had stitched wounds, set bones, immobilized limbs, and wiped the brows of eight men. She'd shouted orders to Mollie and Naomi, and put Two Spears to work cutting bandages.

Near dawn, as the sky turned gunmetal gray, Hannah washed her hands at the sink and took a breath. Patients littered the doctor's office, from the examination rooms to pallets on the floor. No deaths. Not in this group, and she praised God for His mercy. Billy said they were digging hard and fast at the mine entrance, because twelve men were unaccounted for.

A sudden desire to weep nearly overcame her. She was tired. She hadn't stopped to think or feel. She had reminded herself over and over to recall everything Doc had taught her. Deal with the serious wounds first. Stop the bleeding. Prevent shock.

Had she done enough? She surveyed the swollen, bruised faces of her patients. Had she done everything right? What if she'd made one mistake? What if infection set in?

"Hannah." Naomi dropped a warm, gentle hand on her shoulder. "You did absolutely wonderful here."

"I'll second that." Billy quietly shut the front door behind him, navigated the handful of men on the floor, and approached her. "I watched you in here through all this. Every time we brought one in. You were," he shrugged, "flawless."

"Well," Naomi backed up a step. "I think I'll go check on Emilio."

Billy gave her a polite smile as she backed away, but he beamed at Hannah. Dirt filled in the fine lines around his eyes, matted his hair. His white shirt was torn in places and turned a filthy brown from dirt. He looked exhausted, yet he glowed.

"Are you proud of me?"

"Ah," he splayed a hand on his chest, "you have no idea how proud. You are something special."

She looked down at the floor. "So, maybe I should keep nursing? You won't drag me into the mercantile or the hotel?"

"What? No." He lifted her face. "Why do you think I've been hiring all this help? Were you worried about that? Is that why you wouldn't let me pin down a wedding date?"

"When we're married, I should go where you want me."

"I want you right here. This town needs you, especially till we have a doctor." Laughing, he hugged her tight. "So that's what this was about. I thought it was Emilio."

"Emilio?"

"I thought you were having second thoughts about me."

Hannah laid her head on his chest. "I love him, but not the way I love you." She felt Billy stiffen. "I love him like, not a brother, exactly, but not a lover, either." She snuggled into him. "You're the only man I'll ever want, Billy Page. Ever."

The light of day revealed the mine explosion's devastation. McIntyre paused from the rescue work to absorb the destruction.

The fireball had obliterated two storage buildings, blown the glass out of the office building, heavily damaged the mill, and littered the ground with rubble for hundreds of square yards. Worst of all, the main entrance to the mine had collapsed. Tons of debris now blocked at least twelve men inside, if it hadn't killed them outright.

Alive or dead, no one knew.

The rescue effort might take days.

Dusty, hands bleeding from digging, clawing, and hacking at the rock with pickaxes, dozens of men continued working with desperation to save their friends. McIntyre prayed they'd make it.

Fighting exhaustion, he trudged back into the mine entrance. He somberly slapped a few men on their backs, and joined them again in wrestling rocks from the tunnel. They tossed them into the mine cart or wheelbarrow, whichever made its way closer to them.

Every now and again, the digging would stop and the men would listen for signs of life. Then Logan, McIntyre, and a few others would pray, and start work again. After each pause, McIntyre sensed their hope dwindling.

Wearily, he wrestled a fifty-pounder up into his arms . . . but stopped when he heard the rumbling. "Get out!" He tossed the rock back and spun toward the entrance. "Get out!"

The ground shook. The mountain roared. Timbers and rocks rained down. Men screamed and scrambled for the light. They burst forth from the entrance, dogged by a crashing cacophony of collapsing earth. Dust belched from the mine. Coughing, wiping debris from his eyes, McIntyre searched for Ian.

He found him, doubled over, coughing.

"It's getting worse," his friend choked out. Ian had warned that if one particular section of metamorphic rock went, the whole mountain might come down on their heads. He straightened, wiped the dust and sweat from his face with a bandana. His expression, downcast, weary, spoke volumes. "She's too unstable, lad. We send any more men in there, I dunna think we'll get them out."

Desperate, McIntyre seized his friend's shirt. "What am I supposed to do? There might be men in there alive!"

Ian clutched McIntyre's hand. "Out here they *are* alive."

CHAPTER 37

$\mathcal{E}$milio opened his eyes. He recognized the plain white walls of the examination room in Doc's office, but the silence struck him as unusually stark.

Puzzled, he twisted his head around. And sound erupted. In the other room, Naomi and Hannah talked in gentle voices. He heard the jangle of a wagon passing by outside.

Mollie shifted in her seat and smiled at him. "Good morning, Sunshine."

He didn't answer as he scoured the room with his gaze.

"Emilio? Is everything all right? Do you feel all right?"

He laid a hand over his right ear. Sound almost totally went away. He removed his hand and sound returned. "I can't hear out of my left ear."

"Oh." Mollie bit her bottom lip. "I'll get Hannah."

Emilio repeated the experiment with his ear until Hannah came in. "Here, let me take another look at that." She gently rolled his head away from her and peered into his left ear with an otoscope. He only knew its name because she had told him once.

"How are you feeling?"

"My head hurts. And my ear."

Hannah sat down on the bed. "I'm no doctor, Emilio. I could be making all kinds of mistakes."

He wrapped his fingers around hers, wishing he could hold her hand forever. "You are all we have. And that will be enough."

She relaxed a little. "You have a slight concussion and a ruptured eardrum. I think your hearing will come back . . . but I'm not sure."

He was glad to be alive. And he still had one good ear. He did not have Hannah. Never would. That hurt worse than his head, but he had determined to deal with it. He pulled his hand away. "It doesn't matter. I think men died in that explosion. I will be all right."

Hannah patted him on the forearm. "I'm glad you're alive too."

Emilio tried not to read too much into that as she rose and left. They were more than friends but not quite anything else. It would take time, but Emilio could heal. He had to.

"Do you think you'll ever get over her?"

Mollie's voice from the corner startled him. "I didn't know you were still here." Pathetic how blinded he was to everything when Hannah was around. He needed to get back to the ranch.

"You don't want to answer the question?"

Emilio pinched his brow, flinching at a spike in his headache. "She is my friend. Billy is my friend. I am already getting over her."

Mollie stepped up and settled gently on the bed. Her long golden braid hanging down called out to Emilio to touch it. On a whim, he did and she leaned closer. Their gazes met, deep and steady.

Her blue eyes sparkled like a mountain lake. "Could you ever . . . care about me? Like you do Hannah?"

He didn't know . . . but he wanted to try. He tugged on the braid, pulling her in for a kiss. She was sweet and warm, and kind. She made him comfortable, and brought him peace. Those were good places to start. "*Si,*" he whispered against her lips. "I would like to find out."

---

*N*aked, curled up on her new divan, Delilah chewed on her thumbnail and stared out the window. Even after a bath, she still felt so dirty. She'd done a lot of bad things in her life, but she'd never committed murder.

She could sugarcoat things all she wanted to, but she'd told Smith to blow up the mine. She had quickly brushed away the possibility someone could die. All she had cared about was getting even for the disappearance of her Orientals. She demanded respect. She would have her revenge.

Now twelve men lay buried beneath tons of rock, dead or dying. And it was her fault.

She scrubbed her face, surprised at the tears that wet her fingers. Delilah Goodnight, alias Victoria Patterson, had done nothing good with her life. Worse, at this moment, she was a blight on the human race—no, a cancer, McIntyre had called her. Running a brothel was one thing, but *killing* a dozen men?

Trying to hold back a tidal wave of depression, Delilah rose and went to her dresser. With all the life of a corpse, she pulled out a chemise and slipped into it, shaking her sleep-tossed hair loose. As the gown flitted down over her head, her eyes fell on her straight razor resting on the marble top.

It glittered and beckoned to her, hypnotizing her. Her fingers meandered toward it.

Two simple cuts . . .

She could curl up again on the divan, stare out over the roofs and tent tops, and drift away with the light.

And all this pain would stop.

She picked it up and examined the blade, running her fingertip over the flat part.

No one will miss me. No one at all.

Instead of that making her sad, acceptance settled in. Choices had consequences. Not cut out to be a saint, she'd become a sinner. A good one. She chuckled at her own pun. But sinners like her didn't leave any broken hearts behind when they departed this world.

She walked over to the divan and sat down. The light in the room darkened, picking up a melancholy hint of orange. Sunset seemed the perfect time for a beautiful suicide. She placed the razor's edge on her wrist. Gripped the bone handle tighter. Her heart beat wildly, her breath came in short, quick gasps. Yet her mind was calm.

Logan's voice came back to her. *I've found a better way to live, Delilah. Peace and joy like I never had. I wish you'd let me tell you about it.*

Peace and joy? She'd taken that from him and now he hated her. How could he help her? She flexed her sweaty fingers. There was peace here. And she wouldn't have to think about Logan, or what-ifs, or mine explosions ever, ever again.

Tears sprang to her eyes, but, determined, she pulled the razor across the perfect, white skin of her wrist—

The door burst open and she squeaked, dropping the tool. Logan stood in the door, dirty, dusty, hands cut and bloodied. He surveyed the room. Delilah rolled her forearm in toward her stomach to hide the cut, but the blood soaked her gown.

"What have you done?" Logan practically flew across the room and grabbed her arm. The wound had left a slick red spot on her chemise and colored his fingers. Pressing his hand to the cut, he snatched a bandana from his pocket, snapped it in the air, and wrapped it around her wrist. "Delilah, what were you thinking?"

She recovered from the shock of his arrival. "What are you doing here?"

He knelt down in front of her and tied off the bandana. "McIn-tyre has called off the diggin' for now. I went back to the church to pray." He held her wrist between his hands and shook his head. "And suddenly, I don't know how to explain it, I just knew . . ." He looked up and the tenderness in his eyes made Delilah pull back. "I just knew I had to come see you."

She didn't know what to say. Had he saved her? Would she try again when he left? *Was* there a God Who for some reason thought today was not the day Delilah should die?

He pulled her hand to his heart. "Delilah, please, if someone has to die to give you peace . . ." He picked up the razor from the floor. "Let it be me." He set her injured arm on her knee, put the razor in her other hand, and wrapped her fingers around the handle. Then presented his wrist. "I *give* you my life. To prove I'm so sorry, to prove that I wish things had turned out different. To prove . . . I love you."

He tugged his sleeve higher. "God's Word says there is no greater love than this: that a man would lay down his life for a friend." He put her hand and the razor to his own flesh. "If you can't forgive me, if you don't believe I'm a different man, know this." He leaned forward. "I love you. He loves you. He gave His life for you. I give my life to you."

Delilah couldn't think. What was he saying? Why would he do this? She looked at the razor in her hand, the blade pressed to his skin. Fear, white-hot, shot through her and she dropped the instrument like it was a burning coal. "Why are you doing this?"

She rose, squirmed past him and rushed to the window. "You don't know what I've done." She stared off in the distance toward the mine. His offer unnerved her. The old Logan would have never . . . "Those people are dying, or dead, in that mine because of me. I ordered him to blow it up because you stole my Orientals."

"I know. Smith told me . . . just before he died."

Smith was dead? And Logan knew the truth. Yet, he was here anyway. She shook her head in agony. "I don't deserve to live, Logan. I've done so many terrible things, but this is the worst."

He hurried over to her and folded her into his arms. "We all deserve a second chance, Delilah. God is eager to give it to us. But it means walking away from our old lives. It means not only being sorry, but also asking for forgiveness. And accepting it."

"That all sounds too hard."

"Sometimes, I guess it can be. Especially that part about *accepting* forgiveness. That's where I struggle. You have no idea how ashamed I am of . . . the other night."

"All of it?" Was he ashamed of having bedded her, sleeping with a prostitute?

He eased back and lifted her chin. "Yes. What we did should never be outside the bonds of marriage. I'm sorry I used you. Back when we were young, and . . . here. You deserve better. To be honored. Respected."

She wanted to be hurt, but he sounded so contrite and . . . loving. "I don't understand . . . you. You've changed so much. Even just from the other night."

He licked his lips. "I think I finally have a handle on . . . grace." He eased her over to her bed and helped her crawl beneath the covers. "Grace is not an excuse to sin, but it is His love in action. He said if we confess our sins, He's faithful and just to forgive them. Then He's done with them. He moves on. I had to watch a man die to understand that. Delilah, who I am doesn't change Who God is. He wants to forgive you and let you start over."

His words, his presence here . . . his *love* terrified her. "Logan, what if I can't forgive myself? What if I just can't live with what I've done?"

He caressed her hand and the tender gesture made more tears flood her eyes.

"I'll help you. If you'll let me. But you have to promise me something."

"What?"

"That you won't ever try to hurt yourself again. Promise me. Please."

The way he looked at her nearly stopped her breathing. Intensity, passion, but not like any she'd ever seen in anyone's eyes before. She nodded.

"Say it."

"I promise."

"All right. I've got to go gather up some candles for a prayer vigil at the church tonight. Will you come?"

She toyed with the bandage on her wrist. "I don't know. Maybe." He'd given her so much to take in, she wasn't sure she could handle any more. "Maybe."

CHAPTER 38

"*H*ere." Ian pointed at a spot on the map. McIntyre leaned in and pulled the lamp closer. The table quivered on the uneven ground as Ian tapped the paper. "If we canna get in from the main entrance, then we might be able to dig in from the side here. The men made it fifty feet into the main entrance before the sides became too unstable. We might," he held up a finger, "*might* be able to dig down and come out the other side of the debris."

McIntyre tapped his fingers on the map. "Risks?"

Ian sighed, deeply. "We're digging blind. We've no idea how much of the mountain collapsed—how much of the tunnel is blocked. We could bring the rest of the mountain down on any survivors in there."

"But they die for sure if we do nothing." McIntyre turned his back on the map and sat on the edge of the table. "I have always known an accident like this could happen. I never once thought how difficult the choices might be to save lives."

"What doesn't kill you makes you stronger." Both men looked up as Logan stepped out of the darkness and shrugged. "So I've heard."

McIntyre flinched. He couldn't even imagine how strong he would be when all this was over.

"You should know too," Logan wandered over to the map, "it was no accident. Smith did it."

"Aye, then, that would be the fuse Emilio saw."

"We're having a candlelight vigil at the church in an hour, if either of you are of a mind to come."

McIntyre folded his arms, hoping his friend could hang his heart on a spiritual breakthrough. "You are back in the pulpit then?"

"At least for tonight. People need comfort and peace. Maybe I can't lead them as a preacher—I don't know—but I can pray with them."

"Amen," Ian added softly.

Logan's humility encouraged McIntyre. Sometimes, the only way a man could truly appreciate the Light was to travel through the darkest night.

"That said, I don't know if anyone will come to church tonight, but you're invited just the same. Hope to see ya there."

*N*aomi squeezed Charles's hand as they sat in the pew. She smiled down at Two Spears, his handsome little face lit by the candle. "Be careful with that now."

He stared into the flame. "Do we do this to honor the dead?"

Charles's breath hitched. "We don't know they are dead for sure," he said, "and men are trying to dig them out. We're here tonight to ask God to bless the rescuers and get the trapped miners out safely."

The boy nodded, as if the event met his approval.

Naomi squeezed his knee in assurance, then she turned her attention to her husband. Charles met her gaze. He too in the candlelight was as handsome as she'd ever seen him, even stubbly, dirty, and a little worse for wear. She had the urge to move an ebony curl off his forehead. Those dark eyes melted her heart every time she fell into them, but tonight, they betrayed his worry.

"I love you. Does that help at all?"

The corner of his mouth turned up. "More than you know."

Aching for him and the families affected by this tragedy, she looked over her shoulder and gasped softly. "Charles."

He turned. Not only were the pews full, but miners, their wives and children, cowboys, even soiled doves, crowded in, lining the walls, gathering in the back of church. And more kept showing up as they watched. The aisle filled, and folks even filtered in along the walls and around the pulpit. Naomi guessed there were folks outside with candles as well, judging by the glow coming from the open door. Motioning for a man standing at the end of their pew to sit, she pulled Two Spears closer, and pushed Charles into Rebecca and Ian.

Mollie and Mary Jean worked their way through the crowd, and grabbed another armload each of mismatched candles from behind the pulpit. Logan had been out all afternoon gathering them up and inviting people to come pray. Scanning the crowd now, Naomi had to fight back tears.

This disaster had brought them together. For the first time, Defiance was a community. The townspeople stood united in prayer.

⁂

*T*he murmur on the other side of the curtain puzzled Logan. At least some folks had shown up for the vigil and he was grateful. Rising from his knees, he pushed the curtain aside and froze. He could only see the backs of people. Puzzled, he gently wove through them, nodding here and there at faces he'd never seen, and emerged at the pulpit. The crowd astounded him.

Oh, God, thank You . . .

Throat constricting, he laid his Bible on the pulpit and took several seconds flipping to his opening scripture. He knew exactly where he wanted to go, but couldn't seem to get his throat, or his heart, under control.

I will never let You down again . . . or them. At least, I'll try harder than I ever have.

He cleared his throat and the soft mutter of the crowd died. Overcome by the compassionate, expectant faces before him, he had to cough again. "Thank you for coming tonight." His voice broke on the last word. He took a deep breath.

God, please help me bring them Your comfort. Give me the words . . .

"Tonight, twelve men lie trapped in the Sunnyside Mine. We don't know if they're alive or dead. At substantial danger to themselves, other men are attempting to reach them.

"We don't know why disasters like this happen . . . or do we?

"Jesus said in John 16:33 that in this world we would have trouble. Of all His promises, I like that one the least." Soft laughter rippled through the congregation. "However, in that same sentence, He encourages us to be of good cheer, for He has overcome the world.

"Trouble comes. It overtakes us. It *tries* to break us. If we have no hope in anything other than in ourselves, it *will* break us. But if we put our hope in Christ, He also promises that we are more than conquerors. We have the victory that nothing in this life can take away. We can survive heartache, failure, death, and disaster . . . because we are loved with an everlasting love. Nothing can separate us from that love. Not our own actions, not the actions of others. But we have to choose to accept that love, to take the hand that is offered to us.

"If we do, then, when trouble comes His love will flow over us. Humble us. Fill us with joy and peace that is beyond words.

"I don't know the men in that mine. I don't know many of the men trying to save them. But I do know that we are all faced with the same choice: to turn our backs on God, or let Him in. I pray those men, all of them, will have time to make the right choice. I pray that for all of you here tonight as well."

"*W*e have to stop."

Ian's words cut through McIntyre like a knife. The dust from the most recent collapse still fogged the air. For the fifth time in two days, the mountain growled and men scrambled from the new shaft like ants from a hill. Now, they lay collapsed on the ground, worn out, exhausted, out of hope.

As was McIntyre. He couldn't risk their lives anymore.

He nodded a move so slight he knew Ian could have missed it. *God forgive me.* "We are done here."

*F*or two days, Delilah contemplated the quiet.

Not silence, but the noises from the saloon were a shadow of their usual selves. The volume of laughing, poker-playing, liquor-swilling patrons was down. Significantly. Even Tony, the piano player, seemed to be striking the keys with more . . . what? Reverence. As if they were all afraid too much noise might cause more cave-ins.

Meandering down the stairs, she stopped halfway and studied the evening's customers. The crowd was less than half. These were the worst of the hard-bitten, selfish, self-absorbed men in town. Men more interested in a drink or a poke than trying to save a man's life by picking up a shovel. None of these leeches had bothered to go to the mine and help. She knew because she'd talked to them.

The dregs of society, and Delilah was swimming with them.

She felt ill. Literally, sick of this whole mess, this whole . . . life.

She didn't want to be surrounded by them anymore. Not the customers. Not the girls.

Cloer shoved through the batwings and marched up to the bar. He turned a few heads with his determined stomping as he went. When he reached the bar, he turned to the meager crowd. "They're gonna quit on 'em."

A soft murmur of confusion rolled through the place and Tony stopped playing. Neils, the new bartender, approached Cloer. "You mean they're giving up on the rescue?"

"They ain't got no choice. Every time they make a little progress with the new shaft, somethin' else collapses. It's leave twelve men buried or lose twenty more."

Neils slid Cloer a drink as shocked silence fell over the Crystal Chandelier like a funeral pall. Delilah's misery deepened.

Leave twelve men buried or lose twenty more.

This is all my fault.

"Get out." She barely spoke loud enough for anyone but a customer at the bottom of the stairs to hear her. He turned at the sound of her voice. A maelstrom of self-loathing erupted in her heart. "Get out!" She marched down the steps and shot straight toward Cloer. "Especially you, you vulture." She knocked the drink from his hand, shattering it on the floor. "Won't pick up a shovel or move a rock, but you'll gawk and spy then come back here with your gossip just so you can get free liquor." She inched forward. "You're a vile, disgusting weasel. Get out!"

The surprise on Cloer's face melted into anger. He pointed a finger at Delilah. "Nobody—"

"I said get out!" She smelled alcohol on him. He'd already been drinking. *The bum.* Fury warped into hysteria and Delilah shoved him back. "Get out! Get out!" She spun on the room. "All of you! Get out!" She picked up glasses, full, empty, and chucked them at the customers. One shattered across Cloer's back as he raced for the door. He and the others ran like scalded dogs from the crazy woman and the flying glass. "We're closing!" She threw one last glass then whirled on Neils. "All of it! Shut it all down! I want everybody out!"

Neils cleared his throat. "Um, yes ma'am." He reached to untie his apron. "But you got folks in the theater . . . a couple of customers upstairs too."

"Out!" she screamed. "I want everyone OUT! On the street. Naked. I don't care, but OUT!"

CHAPTER 39

*L*ogan couldn't walk away . . . not yet. He stared at the gaping black hole of the main entrance. Were any of those men in Hell? Had he talked to any of them on the street? Had he planted seeds that might have comforted them in their last few minutes?

God, forgive me if I failed them . . .

He knew doubts would torment him forever, but for tonight, he was done.

His strength gone, Logan wasn't sure he could make it back to the church, but the idea of sleep in his own cot dragged him forward. Trying to bear up under the grief and self-doubt, he headed to Tent Town.

Shuffling, trudging, he prayed in the quiet night. The whole town felt . . . exhausted. The streets were empty. Only low, muffled conversations went on inside the tents. Even the horses and dogs were quiet. The deaths of these men, or the suffering leading to their deaths, had brought the residents of Defiance around to ponder their own mortality. Or so Logan hoped.

He was at the corner of Bonanza and Water Streets when he

looked around. Something was wrong. Out of place. Then he noticed The Crystal Chandelier. Or, rather, its *silence*.

Lights burned from nearly all the windows, but the place was quiet as a cemetery. He crossed the street and slowly approached the batwings. Hand on his gun, he peered over the door.

Delilah sat at a table near the bar, a bottle of booze in front of her, her fingers caressing a shot glass. He scanned the room, the stairs, as much of the second floor hallway as he could see.

Satisfied that Delilah was, for whatever reason, alone in an empty saloon, he entered, cautiously. "Victoria?"

Her chest rose and fell with a big breath, but she didn't move otherwise. "Come in, Logan."

"Is everything all right?"

"I suppose so."

Still glancing around, he made his way to her table and sat down, but on the opposite side, away from the liquor. "What's happened here?"

The seal was still intact on the whiskey.

"I don't know. I couldn't take it anymore. Knowing those men have been abandoned in that mine, and in here sat the worst of the worst. Not a one lifted a shovel or even said a prayer." She shrugged a shoulder. "All of a sudden, I hated them. All of them. This place. My girls . . . me. I wanted it all to go away."

She reached for the bottle and Logan rose, taking it from her grasp. "I don't have all the answers, but I do know this doesn't help."

He set the whiskey on the bar and returned to the table, sitting next to her this time. "It was an agonizing decision for McIntyre. I reckon it'll haunt him the rest of his life."

"Choices have a way of doing that."

Logan picked up a stray poker chip and tapped it on the table. "Don't I know it."

Delilah dragged her arm away from the shot glass and faced

Logan. "Can people like you and me really live different lives? I mean, can we . . . have futures, forget the past?"

"You don't forget it. With Christ, you make peace with it. You understand . . ." He leaned closer, thought about taking her hands, but didn't. "You understand that who you were then and who you are now, after Christ, that's two different people. Scripture says 'Therefore if any man *be* in Christ, *he is* a new creature: old things are passed away; behold, all things are become new.'"

Her gaze drifted off. "Become new." She closed her eyes. "So many mistakes. So many things I've done wrong."

"He can deal with them all."

Behind them, the batwings creaked and they looked over their shoulders. "Cloer," Delilah sat up, "I told you to get out."

Cloer swayed on the doors, but after a moment sauntered on rubbery legs into the saloon.

Logan eyed the man with caution. Early thirties. A bit gangly. Hat cocked back at an angle. Something about him was keenly familiar. Either way, Logan didn't like Cloer's drunken swagger. The man's hand hovered near his waistband, as if ready to pull that Bowie knife. Narrowed, suspicious eyes avoided looking right at them. He was clearly so sauced he couldn't be much of a threat, but Logan wouldn't take him for granted.

"Who is that?"

"Cloer. He worked for McIntyre till he got fired. He's been knockin' around town, doing odd jobs. Cloer, get out of here before I have Logan throw you out."

Cloer stopped abruptly in his staggering toward the bar. "Logan? You Logan Tillane?"

Logan tensed. "Yes."

Cloer staggered sideways into a table and stopped, rubbing his bleary eyes. He kept his hands over his face and muttered something, but Logan couldn't make it out. He exchanged a puzzled glance with Delilah.

"Couldn't stay away from him, huh?" Cloer's fingers slowly crawled down his cheeks until they curled into fists.

Delilah glared at the man. "What are you talking about?"

Cloer marched to their table and slapped the felt. "You know what I'm talking about. You faithless whor—"

Logan leaped to his feet and pushed Cloer away from Delilah. "You need to go. Right now. Sleep it off somewhere."

Cloer's gaze singed the air between him and Delilah. "Louise, I told you if I caught you with him again, I wouldn't be responsible."

Delilah stood. "What are you blabbering about? Get outta here."

Cloer snatched the knife from his sheath and lunged for Delilah.

In the instant it takes sunlight to glint off the water, Logan knew he had to stop Cloer . . . one way or the other. Drunk or not, the man was fast, or maybe Logan was simply done in from the mine explosion. He stepped in front of Delilah and grabbed for the knife. The blade slipped right between his hands. A sharp, agonizing pain seared its way deep into his gut as his hands clutched Cloer's and the hilt. Logan flinched and hissed, but over so much more than the wound.

Cloer froze. His eyes widened with terror and confusion. Logan tightened his grip and slowly pulled the blade from his stomach.

Cloer jumped back, flinging his hands into the air. The knife fell to the floor, glistening red. "I didn't mean . . . I wasn't . . . Holy God, don't kill me." The man whirled and scrambled from the saloon, tripping over chairs, and lurching out the door like a sick cow.

Logan marveled for a moment over the deep, ruby color of the blood on the Bowie knife. His blood. He looked up. Cloer had meant to stab Delilah. Kill her. He couldn't get away. Logan staggered after the cowboy.

"Logan!" Delilah screamed.

Save her. Save her. Stop Cloer.

Warmth, like bath water, flowed down his stomach, seeped to his pants leg. His vision doubled, but he pushed through the batwing doors and stumbled into the street.

Dark. Empty. Thoughts—crazy, confused, circular—swirled in his head. *Save Delilah. Save Victoria. Save the men in the mine.* His legs buckled and he dropped to his knees. The sudden loss of control puzzled him.

The pain in his gut came back, dull, persistent, not sharp like before. It cleared his head and he sighed.

Not gonna make it, am I, Lord?

"Oh, my God, Logan!" Delilah skidded into the dirt in front of him and fell to her knees. "Logan." She made as if to touch his stomach, but withdrew her hands. "Help. We need help." She scanned the street and started screaming. "Help us! Somebody help us!"

CHAPTER 40

a fog settled over Logan. He touched the area just below his breastbone. Slick, wet, warm. "Victoria." He couldn't say it with any strength. His voice sounded like it belonged to a ghost. He tried again. "Victoria."

Oh, God, I had so much work to do here for You. But her, can You keep her safe? Turn her away from this life . . .

"Please, somebody help us!" she cried again, sounding so desperate. He felt bad for her. Wanted to comfort her.

A flatbed wagon loaded with furniture came around the corner. Delilah rose and raced toward it. "Help us. Please help us, he's been stabbed."

The fog grew thicker, darker. Delilah's arms encircled him, tried to lift him, but Logan was so tired. He wanted to lie down.

"No, Logan, no." He heard the tears in her voice.

"Here, Preacher, let me get a look at that."

Billy? The fog cleared a little. "What are you doing here?"

Billy lifted Logan's shirt, paused, and shook his head. "Come on, Preacher," he moved to slide his arm underneath Logan's, "we've got to get you to Hannah."

"No." Logan pressed his hand to the wound, flinched at the pain, and struggled to lie down.

Billy grabbed him. "Delilah, there's a blanket under the seat. Get it."

His strength all but gone, Logan was grateful for Billy lowering him gently to the ground. The cold sank quickly into his back and shoulders. Yes, he wanted that blanket.

"Preacher, you just can't lay here"

To bleed out into the dirt? Die in the street? "Reckon I can . . . a fittin' end." He managed to clear his vision and look at Billy. The kid's eyes were round as silver conchos. "It's all right. Soon . . . I'll walk the streets of Glory."

"No, no, no." Scowling, Billy jerked out his shirttail and, with violent snatches, ripped a section away. Gritting his teeth, he pressed the cloth on the wound.

New pain hit Logan like a splash of acid in his gut and he cried out. "Let me be, boy, it's all right."

Billy readjusted his hand, as if trying to plug the wound a little better. "I'm not gonna just let you lay here and die."

"Ain't your choice." *Running out of time.* Logan closed his eyes and swallowed. His mouth was drier than desert sand. A great, overwhelming weariness washed up him like a wave. "Where's Victoria?"

"Who?"

"Right here, Logan." Her voice choked with emotion, Delilah dropped the blanket over him. "I'm right here."

---

ictoria?
    And Logan?

The coincidence put the brakes on Billy's mind for a second. No, it couldn't be coincidence. Somehow these two had wound up in Defiance. Did they know the truth about why and how they had separated?

Logan groaned, snapping Billy back to the emergency at hand. Anger sizzled in his brain. Their preacher couldn't die. "We've got to stop the bleeding, Delilah."

"Don't call her that." Logan's voice was weak. "Her name is Victoria."

"Okay. Logan, I need you to hold this right here." Billy pressed the preacher's hand to the gushing wound, a wasted effort. His hand slipped off almost immediately. Billy exchanged a tense glance with Delilah. Not ready to give up, they gently draped the blanket over him and tucked it on the sides. But Billy didn't know what else to do. If only Hannah were here . . .

"No." Logan reached up to touch Delilah's face. "Not gonna make it." His arm fell away as if he simply couldn't bear the weight.

Delilah touched his chest, tears pouring down her cheeks. "Don't say that."

Logan patted her hand, smearing her with blood. "Promise me . . . promise me you'll give God a chance. Get to . . . know . . . Him. Let Him be . . . your friend."

"Logan, I'm so sorry. Cloer should have stabbed me, not you. Please don't die. Please don't die."

He rolled his head side to side. "Told you I would. And I can . . . please . . . make it a good trade."

"No, no, no," Delilah wept on his chest.

"Promise me. Promise me . . . Victoria."

"I promise." A smile touched Logan's lips, his eyes closed, and he seemed to relax. The woman's chest started rising and falling with panic. "Logan, wait. I have to tell you something. Something important."

His eyes fluttered and he came back to her.

"We did one thing right, Logan. We have a daughter." His eyes widened slightly then filled up with tears.

"Momma didn't know when she sent me to the whorehouse," Delilah explained, sounding frantic. "And I never told her. I gave the baby up for adoption to the preacher and his family in Stillwater. Oh, Logan," Delilah fought to speak through the tears. "She's beautiful . . . and decent and sings in the choir. I've kept up with her, but she doesn't know about us."

For Billy, the pieces fell into place. "I don't think she knew it was a whorehouse."

Delilah glared across Logan at Billy. "What do you know about it?"

"I think your mother still lives in Dodge City. She thought she was sending you away to have a chance at a better life. Starting with a decent job. And she wanted to keep you away from . . . him."

Logan clutched Delilah's hand. "She told me leavin' was your choice. That's why . . . I didn't look for you . . . thought you didn't want me to."

Delilah grabbed the man's shirt. "Logan, Logan . . . it all went so wrong. I'm sorry." Sobbing, she laid her head on his chest. "I'm sorry."

Logan managed to drop his hand on her shoulder. "I love you, Victoria." His voice was frail, fading.

She sniffled and wiped her nose. "I love you, Logan." She kissed him. Billy averted his eyes to give them some privacy, and stared up the street. A few men stood outside their tents, watching the drama unfold, but no one moved to help. Truthfully, wasn't much they could do.

Billy's heart hurt for this ill-fated couple. He couldn't help but wonder how their lives might have turned out if they'd stayed together. Apart, they sure had wrecked some lives and lived in a painful amount of darkness.

What if *he* hadn't come back for Hannah? He shuddered at the notion. He was filled with gratitude for the second chance with her and would thank God for it every day for the rest of his life.

The preacher's bloody hand slid lifeless to the ground. Delilah's sobs echoed off the front of The Crystal Chandelier. Tears in his own eyes, Billy clutched Delilah's shoulder and prayed for her peace. At least now, Logan had his.

CHAPTER 41

*M*cIntyre could hardly bear to breathe, neither could he weep. The grief and guilt churning in his soul far surpassed what tears could cleanse. His heart weighed a thousand pounds in his chest at the thought of twelve men buried in the darkness. Buried, but were they dead?

He rode past Lane and Willy, saddling up in the pre-dawn darkness for the morning's work. They regarded him with sympathy and subtle nods. Undoubtedly, McIntyre's posture and countenance told them everything they needed to know. He pulled up to the hitching post in front of the house . . . and sat there.

What have I done? God, what have I done?

Naomi rushed from the house, across the porch, and flew down the steps. Desperate for the comfort of her, McIntyre launched himself from the saddle and caught her in his arms. He squeezed her tightly, burying his face in her hair. The one place, besides in prayer, where he could find some peace.

"Did you . . .?" She seemed to re-think the question. "You called it off, didn't you? The rescue."

He couldn't speak, merely nodded. She held him tighter. "It

was the right thing to do, Charles. You couldn't risk any more men."

"I don't know if I'll ever believe that, Naomi. I do know one thing. I'll never reopen the Sunnyside Mine."

---

*R*ebecca leaned over the blocks of type and used a key to tighten the pieces of wood that framed the letters and snugged them into their layout. Every squeak, every turn of the screw seemed too loud in the tomb-like silence of the town hall.

Her front page.

She had yet to put it in the press to print it. It seemed such a final step and she was in no hurry. She let her fingers drift over the lead letters. Backward, but nonetheless clear. They spelled out glaring news that sent a chill up her spine, and broke her heart at the same time.

Rescue Effort Abandoned

Twelve Men Lost in Murderous Attack

Sunnyside Mine Will Not Re-Open

Those three lines sealed the fate of not only the miners, but possibly Defiance. Would the town survive without the mine?

Charles was adamant the Sunnyside was finished. At least as far as he was concerned. He had admitted to Rebecca perhaps he would sell it, but not anytime soon. When asked what he thought would happen to Defiance, he answered simply, "Change." With that, he had ridden out of town, no doubt headed to the sanctuary of his ranch.

Rebecca rubbed her temples, trying to understand the cruelty behind the explosion. Smith worked for Delilah. Everyone knew she was livid about the Oriental girls disappearing. Was she vindictive enough to order an attack on the mine? Had Smith done this on his own?

Regardless of how the dust settled, twelve men lay entombed beneath the town. Giuseppe Panelli, a stone-carver by trade, a gold-miner by happenstance, was already engraving a stone to sit at the entrance.

Unable to stop her tears, Rebecca picked up the chase holding the front page of *The Defiance Dispatch*, spun carefully, and set it in the press.

---

*B*illy sat on the front porch of the Doc's office, oblivious to the morning sun painting its long shadows down the street. Somewhere a rooster crowed. Logan and Delilah's lost chance haunted him, reminding him of the fleeting existence of life.

Beside him, the door opened and Hannah stepped out, sniffling and wiping her eyes. He reached out to her. Without hesitating, she fell into his arms and curled up in his lap. "She won't leave his side," she managed in a choked voice. "She said Logan was her sweetheart back when they were teenagers."

"I know." Billy stroked her back, hugged her close. "They make me realize how miserable and lonely my life would have been if I hadn't come for you." He held her for a moment, deliriously grateful to have her in his arms, to be able to comfort her. "Hannah, I know a justice of the peace isn't the way you wanted to get hitched, but would you please let the marshal marry us?" He kissed the top of her head to give his voice a chance to steady. "We can have a wedding when the circuit preacher comes through, but I want us to be a family. Now. Today. Before we lose any more time together."

She looked up at him, her big blue eyes magnified by tears. "I love you, Billy Page."

"Is that a yes?"

"Yes."

He kissed her long, deep, and enthusiastically. "I love you, Hannah, more than I'll ever be able to say, but I'll spend my life trying to show it."

"Chick, chick, chick." The hens came running as Naomi stepped out into the yard, a bowl of crumbled stale bread on her hip. Tossing the crumbs to them, she noted the buggy emerging from the trees. Emilio and Mollie. She started to wave, but something was wrong. The lumbering speed of the horse, their posture maybe, sent a chill up her spine.

"Charles, I think you should come out here."

A moment later, he emerged on the porch, a half-eaten apple in his hand. "What is it?"

She pointed with her chin at the buggy coming around the corner of the bunkhouse. Emilio waved half-heartedly as he and Mollie pulled up in front of the cabin.

"Mornin', y'all," Naomi said cautiously.

Charles sauntered down into the yard and joined her. "Mollie. Emilio, good to see you up and about."

"*Si*, I am better. Still no hearing, but I am alive."

Charles tensed at the comment and nodded. "And we are grateful."

"*Si*. Um," he glanced quickly at Mollie and cleared his throat, "but I bring some very bad news."

Naomi clutched Charles's arm. *Please don't let it be anything to do with my sisters, Lord.* But the prayer made her feel guilty almost immediately, and she added, *or any of our loved ones.*

"It is the preacher. Logan is dead."

Naomi gasped and Charles's muscles turned to iron beneath her fingertips.

"Was it Delilah?" he asked.

"No. Cloer tried to kill her. Logan stepped between them and was stabbed."

"Cloer." Charles paled.

"Delilah is . . ." Mollie paused, apparently searching for the words, "I don't know any other way to describe it than to say she's crazy with grief. She's . . . devastated."

Naomi had a hard time believing that, much less picturing it. Charles patted her hand. "They were childhood sweethearts. Logan told me." He took a deep breath and pinched the bridge of his nose. "Some week."

"*Si.* A very bad one." Emilio cleared his throat, breaking an awkward silence. "I would like to escort Mollie back to town, Mr. McIntyre, but Matilda, she was killed in the explosion—"

"Yes, I know. Pick out a new mount. The finest one I have."

A subtle smile on Emilio's face expressed his sincere gratitude. *Gracias.*"

Neither Naomi nor Charles moved as Emilio and Mollie turned the buggy around. After a moment, she untangled herself and commenced tossing out the breadcrumbs again. "You're thinking about leaving again, aren't you?"

He didn't answer right away. "How did you know?"

She paused with her hand in the bowl. "The despair I saw in you when you came home, I suppose. You made the right choice, Charles. Although I guess that doesn't mean it will be any easier to live with."

"That damnable mine. I wish I'd never opened it."

She tossed the last of the bread out and faced him. "A new place might . . . help the healing."

He extended his hand to her. "I love you . . . and I love Two Spears. You are my family. You make my home . . . wherever we are."

She laced her fingers with his and studied his face. Guilt and heartbreak had deepened what she once thought of as intriguing lines, especially around his eyes. His beard, stubbly, not perfectly trimmed now, had sprouted some gray. His black wavy hair also had a few gray strands. Saddest of all, his brow held a melancholy crease.

"I've had a scripture going round and round in my head for days," she said thoughtfully. "Now I know why. 'For whither thou goest, I will go.'" She lifted a hand to his cheek. "'And where thou lodgest, I will lodge . . . Where thou diest, will I die, and there will I be buried.'"

He laid his hand over hers. "I'm going to hold you to that."

"I expect you will."

"I haven't made up my mind yet."

"Maybe not where. Maybe not even when. But you've made up your mind we're leaving Defiance. We'll pray about it. See where the Lord leads."

CHAPTER 42

*D*elilah hated only one thing about leaving Defiance: she would never see Logan's grave again. But then, maybe that's how he would have wanted it.

A summer breeze caressing her face, she knelt down and laid some bluebells on the fresh dirt. Mary Jean and the others had left a variety of wildflowers, but no one else knew Logan had preferred these. She left something else as well. Her desire for revenge and every bit of anger and greed she'd come to this town with was dead now too. She wanted to honor Logan's last request. She would get to know God. If she was fortunate, He would give her the peace Logan had spoken of.

Determined to put one foot in front of the other without weeping, Delilah strode down the hillside back to town. At the stagecoach office, she waited on a bench and studied the ticket that said she was heading to Dodge City. Good idea or not, it was at least a jumping-off point.

Billy had said her mother was still there. The chance to see her again and heal a deep, deep wound gave Delilah a hope she hadn't felt in a long time.

The bench moved and she looked over at Marshal Beckwith

settling in. His eyes glittered at her from beneath his hat. "Goin'
somewhere?"

"Dodge City."

She stared across the street, but the marshal kept his eyes on
her. She didn't ask why. She didn't really care. He'd get around
to it.

After a moment, he stretched his legs out and crossed one
dusty boot over the other, watching the traffic instead. "You order
Smith to blow up the mine?"

"Yes."

He was silent a long time before speaking again. "I figure a
trial will just keep the wound open and those men'll still be just as
dead." He swung his gaze back to her. "A healing needs to start.
And you've got your punishment. Livin' with what you did."

She tried to hold her face still but felt the tick in her brow.
"Yes."

He stood, rested his hands on his cartridge belt. "I don't reckon
I'll ever see or hear from you again."

"No one will."

He nodded curtly and ambled off down the boardwalk.

. . . you've got your punishment. Livin' with what you did . . .

If he only knew.

The thunder of a stagecoach, not hers, rumbled down the
street and came to a stop in front of her. A light rain last night had
settled the dust and cooled the air. She liked summers in these
high mountains.

The door banged open and Matthew of all people squeezed
through the small opening and jumped to the ground. Shaking
golden blond hair out of his eyes, his gaze landed on Delilah. He
grinned broadly and dropped his bowler on his head. "Well, come
to meet me? How'd you know I was on this stage?"

She had hoped to disappear before he arrived. Not because she
was afraid of him. She simply wanted to be done with everything
about her old life, the things she could walk away from, anyhow.

Huffing in disgust, she rose. "I didn't. I'm taking the next stage out."

His brow wrinkled in shock. "What?"

"I'm through. I'm done. I'm leaving."

An angry flush crept into his cheeks. "You can't leave. I sold everything to come here. I'm gonna run the lumber mill, you run the saloon. That was the deal."

"Well, I'm making a new deal." She reached into the reticule hanging from her wrist, pushing aside a substantial amount of cash, and grasped the key. "Here. I was going to mail it from the next town." She shoved it against his chest and he took it, out of shock more than acceptance. "You get to run 'em both. The Crystal Chandelier is all yours now. I don't want any part of it."

"What the . . ." His mouth hanging open, Matthew gawked at the key, then Delilah. "What happened? McIntyre and that preacher running you out? You don't have to leave now that I'm here."

Mercifully, the two o'clock stage from Mineral Springs thundered in from the other end of town. She picked up her lovely violet skirt, eager to shake off this town's dust. "What happened? Delilah Goodnight died in Defiance, that's what happened."

---

*M*cIntyre laid a hand on the batwing and forced himself to refrain from a weary sigh. Rebecca had been right. She'd seen a man disembark from the stage coach who looked like Matthew.

Those mountain-sized shoulders were unmistakable. Carpetbag in one hand, saddlebags slung over a shoulder, he stared down at the bloodstain on the floor. A trail of drops led to the door. He scratched his head then had to rearrange his bowler.

"Hello," he called, and waited.

McIntyre pushed his way in. "They're all gone. Except Otis. He's here somewhere."

Matthew whirled around. A nasty smile of recognition slowly crept across his mouth. "McIntyre. I didn't expect to run into you so soon."

Delilah's mysterious partner. McIntyre would have never guessed it, but why the ruse? "What brings you back? I thought it was abundantly clear you are not welcome here."

Matthew slung his bags atop a nearby table. "I told you I liked Defiance. You said yourself there's plenty of opportunity here. So I'm here to stay. I've bought the lumber mill. I own this place. Probably buy a few more businesses or some claims. I'm ready to make some money. Turn Defiance upside down and shake free some of that gold dust."

"Your timing may prove to be rather poor, especially since I have closed the mine."

"Closed?" The word came out as almost a growl.

Not information he wanted, McIntyre guessed. He twisted the knife a little deeper. "Yes, and miners are leaving by the droves. I've even heard it whispered the creeks are playing out." He pulled a cheroot from his pocket. "But what may interest you more is that in a few days Defiance will be an official, incorporated town.

"As the interim mayor, Ian has said the first things he'd like to see enforced are the Red Light Abatement Act and the public nuisance laws." McIntyre glanced around the empty saloon and smiled. "If I were you, I would familiarize myself with them. The fines can be downright exorbitant. Enough to put a man out of business."

He lit the cheroot, crushed the match under his toe, and sauntered out of The Crystal Chandelier.

*J*f you liked *A Promise in Defiance*, I cannot tell you how much I would **appreciate your review!** Authors on Amazon literally live and die by those things! If you could take a moment, you will have my undying gratitude. Here's the link: https://amzn.to/2wOnqC4

But the story doesn't end here! Don't miss the sneak peek at the novella, Daughter of Defiance. Keep reading!

As always, I would be grateful if you would

Please subscribe to my newsletter
By visiting my website at
authorheatherblanton.com
to receive updates on my new releases and other fun news. You'll
also receive a FREE e-book—
A Lady in Defiance, The Lost Chapters
just for subscribing!

*J*hope that if you're a new follower of Jesus Christ, you'll hang in there with Him even when things don't go your way, even when your past jumps up and bites you. He knows what you've done. He knows what you will do. More importantly, He knows what *He* will do. God has a plan and it is always in your best interest. Believe that! He loves you.

If you don't know Jesus, it's so easy to meet Him! Please follow this link to discover the simple steps to salvation and a relationship with Christ. You'll never regret it. http://peacewithgod.net/

Finally, if you've read a few of my books, you know I have a heart for the American Indian, especially the youth. Their suicide rate is *twice* the national average; domestic violence, unemployment, and alcoholism are common in over 70%e homes. The statistics go on and on. One school is trying to make a difference. I hope you'll check out, pray for, even donate to the American Indian Christian Mission School (http://www.aicm.org/), a wonderful, well-respected organization that is reaching Native Americans one young person at a time.

SNEAK PEEK — A DESTINY IN DEFIANCE

Get your copy of **A Destiny in Defiance** Book 4 today!

Tick. Tick. Tick.

Dr. Hope Clark tried to ignore how loudly the Regulator wall clock resonated in her empty office. She surveyed the tiny waiting room, devoid of patients, and sighed. She couldn't go much longer like this. If just one sick person would walk through that door, she felt certain she could win over many, many of the citizens of Denver.

It could all start with one.

As if in answer to prayer, her doorknob turned and slowly the door began to swing open. Hope jolted to attention, touched the stethoscope hanging at her neck to make sure it was still there, and pasted on a smile.

A cumbersome pink hat buried beneath ostrich feathers appeared in the entrance. It led the way for an older, quite rotund woman in a blue velvet dress who peered with suspicion around the room.

"Good morning," Hope said, crossing the room quickly, before the woman could take in the lack of other patients. "I'm Dr. Clark."

She offered her hand, but the woman's eyes narrowed and she pulled back, as if Hope's greeting was offensive. "Yes. I know who you are."

Spirits sagging, Hope tried not to show her disappointment. Somehow, she knew the woman was not here for a health visit. Floundering, she lowered her hand and smiled. "What can I do for you, Miss...?"

"I'm Mrs. Abbington Chalmers. Perhaps you know my husband? The mayor."

"I am not personally acquainted, but I know of him."

Mrs. Chalmers sniffed, as if the answer didn't surprise her. "I am not here, however, on his behalf. I am here on behalf of the Ladies League of Greater Denver."

Lovely, Hope thought. *Not a patient. Worse. She wants a donation.* "Yes. How can I help you?"

For a moment, Mrs. Chalmers' hauteur wavered. The confidence exuded by her raised chin and squared shoulders faded a bit, or so Hope thought. "Well, it isn't easy to say what I've come here for."

"When I have difficult news for my patients, Mrs. Chalmers, I tell them outright. Beating around the bush can be unnecessarily cruel."

That brought the woman's chin back up. "Right you are. So I shan't beat around the bush, as you say. I've come to tell you, Miss Clark, that you have had no patients and you will not have any."

Hope blinked and wondered if she'd heard correctly. "I'm sorry."

Mr. Chalmers twirled away in a flurry of ostrich feathers and blue velvet, presenting her back. "Women have their place in the world, Miss Clark."

"Doctor," Hope corrected without thinking.

The woman stiffened, slowly turned back to Hope. Her pudgy

face, so round and soft, did not hide the heat in the woman's dull brown eyes, or the disdain in her thinned lips. "I see I need to speak plainly. You upset the balance. Women in Denver and in the rest of the world are happy with their stations in life. We are mothers and caregivers. Helpmeets to our husbands. We run our homes, raise our children, and give our husbands a place to rest from the world. You—'

"Threaten that," Hope interrupted wearily. She had heard all this before but from *men* back in Pennsylvania. The women, for the most part, had been cool and silent regarding her vocation. To hear this nonsense spoken aloud—by a woman—nearly left her speechless. Nearly. "You think I put the idea into your husbands' heads that you're capable of more than birthing babies and hosting cotillions? You prefer the myth that women are the mentally weaker sex. It keeps your credit account at dress shop open."

Mrs. Chalmers gasped. "How dare you—?"

"With grim purpose and determination is how. I harbor the burning desire to help people, Mrs. Chalmers. I know that I am capable of helping them—possibly even saving their lives—and sitting back on my padded bustle simply will not do."

Mrs. Chalmers snapped her mouth shut and her face flushed. "There are men for that vocation, *Miss* Clark. The letters *M-D* do not make you a doctor."

The verbal slap, so wrong, but so vindictive, stung. Hope knew of course, graduating at the top of her class from Pennsylvania Women's College would mean nothing to this grand dame. Worse, Mrs. Chalmers might see it as a threat, to her way of life, her unchallenged, comfortable existence.

Hope did not want to fight this fight against her own sex. She couldn't believe she had to, especially here in the West where women were reportedly so strong and independent. "I'm sorry you feel this way, Mrs. Chalmers. I strongly believe, however, that women are as cap—"

"You've had no patients." The woman leaned forward a little. "As I said, you will have none. The Ladies League will see to it." Her chin rose higher in triumph. "How long can you hold out, Miss Clark?"

Against every woman in Denver? Hope *was* a doctor, a good one, but she was also at her wit's end...not to mention the end of her bank account.

Mrs. Chalmers moistened her lips and softened her stance a hair. "If you truly want to help people, Miss Clark, why don't you go to, oh, I don't know, India or somewhere. Some place they're desperate for medical care."

Any place Mrs. Chalmers didn't have to worry about bumping into a female doctor on the sidewalk? Well, Hope wasn't about to let this woman defeat her. But that didn't mean she had to fight the battle here in Denver where she was so outnumbered. There were other places in this big, wide world to ply her trade. Yes, some place where the people *were* desperate for medical care. India, however, seemed a touch far. "I'll consider your suggestion, Mrs. Chalmers. Thank you for coming by."

The intriguing aroma of human prey mingled pleasantly with the scent of dirt and cedar and the cougar lifted his head. The hope of a meal stirred grumbling in his stomach and he sniffed now with keen interest, whiskers twitching. Led by hunger, he rose from his sun-washed ledge and slipped silently between the rocks, slinking beneath the evergreen branches, staying in the shadows, tracking the peculiar but distinctive odors. Within moments he was hiding atop a boulder, peering down at two humans.

The pair—a woman and a boy—strolled carelessly through the blueberry bushes, plucking the fruit, dropping it in buckets on their arms, eating one now and again. They chattered like magpies and wandered about aimlessly, picking fruit here and there, relaxed, unhurried.

The hunger gnawing at the pit of the cat's stomach grew, but he waited.

And watched.

The boy was similar to the people who had trod these mountains for as long as cats could remember. Dark skinned, his black hair glimmered in the sun like a raven's wings.

The woman was the new breed. She was like the pale-skinned humans who had come here when the cougar had been a cub playing at his mother's feet. She did not wear animal skins or smell of sweat like the Utes and Cheyenne. She smelled of flowers and plants. Her hair was long and light, the color of grass dead from winter cold.

The cat's eyes narrowed. The young one began to wander away from her. Little by little, farther and farther. A step at a time.

The cougar considered his choices, his gaze darting from the child to the woman and back again.

Yes, the boy. Younger. Smaller. Unaware.

Tail twitching, muscles quivering, the cat slithered off the boulder and crept into the base of an evergreen thick with low-lying branches.

Naomi smiled at the sweet taste of the blueberry, pleased this patch was still producing for so late in the season. She could already smell the pie her sister Rebecca would make. One of these days, Naomi would make a serious effort to become as good a cook as her sisters. She stripped off two berries and dropped them in the basket on her arm. Two Spears, the young Indian boy with her, was not her son by blood, but Naomi loved him as if he were. Just as she loved his father, Charles. For them, she would—should—learn to cook better. She tossed a berry up into the air and caught it in her mouth. Yes, these berries would be for her own pie.

Two Spears laughed at her antics and tossed up two berries, easily catching them both in his mouth.

"Show off," Naomi said.

Grinning, the ten-year-old drifted away, his chest puffed out. He was precious and she was so glad they'd finally gotten past his resentment of being dropped on their doorstep. Well, honestly, the resentment had started before that. His mother, Hopping Bird, had been given back by Charles to her father Chief Ouray, for a remuda of horses—the trade a peaceable way to end the marriage. Charles had not known about the child. Later, Hopping Bird had fallen in love with a violent renegade by the name of One-Who-Cries, who hated Charles almost as much as he hated the entire race of white men.

Unfortunately, Charles had been forced to kill One-Who-Cries about the same time Hopping Bird had died on the White Mountain Reservation. Chief Ouray, tired of losing family to the white man, had shown up the day after Charles' and Naomi's wedding with a very special request: for Charles to raise his grandson.

She shook her head and dropped another four or five berries in the basket. Two Spears had run away it seemed about every third day, but finally, just lately, she thought he was settling in. Charles had been taking the boy out with him to check on the herd, making a real effort to—

No conscious thought shot through Naomi's mind when she saw the cougar leap off the rock. She screamed as it raced toward Two Spears, but she was moving too. Her own body felt as if lightning had struck her, and the power of it compelled her forward at an uncanny speed. No earth beneath her feet, only electricity.

The cat lunged as Two Spears turned. A supernatural strength and fury arced through Naomi and, with a primal yell bursting from her lungs, she leaped for the boy, knocking him out of the cat's path. The claws meant for him sank into her back, burned like lava as they gouged into her flesh. She hit the ground hard, air whooshing out of her lungs. She tried to turn but fangs clamped down on her, burrowing into the meat of her shoulder; the claws dug deep and tightened like a vice grip made of needles.

She yowled in agony. Or was it the cat?

Pain, white-hot, vicious, shot down her back, and she could feel her blood soaking her shirt. "Run, Two Spears," she yelled as she tried to fold her arms over her head and neck, to fend off teeth and claws.

Fight or die, something told her. *Oh, God, help me fight.*

Anger and terror mixed in her mind on a primitive level. The need to survive took hold. Naomi had to kill the cat. She jammed her elbow back, connecting with the heavy mass of fur on her back. The cougar shifted. His claws tightened, sunk deeper, but he let go of her shoulder.

Bellowing with rage and terror, she rolled before he could reposition his bite. She hammered the cat's snout as his claws flayed open her back and part of her side. His fangs sunk into her wrist.

Somehow a rock filled her hand and she swung it, connecting with his temple. The cat growled angry over the hit, but only bit down harder.

"I'm not going to die, I'm not doing to die," she screamed as she hit him again and again—

An explosion rocked the air and the cat suddenly leaped skyward, twisting at a grotesque angle, and then disappeared from Naomi's sight. Unsure of where the cat had gone, she kept swinging the rock over and over, pounding the ground, and screaming, "I'm not going to die. I'm not—"

"Naomi!" Running to her, Charles holstered his gun and folded to his knees. "Naomi," he said again, breathless, as he slid his arms beneath her and lifted her off the ground.

She dropped the rock, saw the blood streaming down her arm, felt the slickness of it as Charles held her close. The fury drained away, leaving her weak, confused. She smiled at her handsome husband, those magnificent dark eyes of his and that perfectly trimmed beard. Oh, how she loved him, and it hurt her to see the fear in his face.

"I'm all right," she whispered. "Just a scratch." She suspected maybe it was a touch more, but the weariness that overcame her then stilled her concerns. She would sleep and when she woke up, everything would be fine.

Hannah lunged to her feet as Charles burst through the door of the doctor's office, a bloody and unconscious Naomi in his arms. The sight of her sister in such a state galvanized Hannah; her heart hammered so hard in her chest, she thought it might bruise her ribs.

Oh, God. "Put her on the bed," she ordered as she grabbed a tray already loaded with a few basic medical supplies. "What happened?" *Dear God, please let her be all right*, she prayed as she rushed after Charles.

"A cougar."

Hannah's stomach lurched at the word. Charles had wrapped Naomi in his own shirt and a saddle blanket, both glistening with blood. He laid her on the bed and carefully peeled back the soaked articles. Hannah stepped in close, ready for the examination, and was pleased to see his effort had stopped much of the blood, but Naomi's torso and right arm were bathed in red, .

A quick survey told Hannah they weren't seeing everything. "Here, help me turn her over." Naomi's shirt and camisole hung in bloody shreds. Hannah removed the clothing and flinched at the deep, raw wounds. "Oh," she whispered softly. *Lord, this is work for a surgeon. Help me, oh, please help me.* Tears pooled in her eyes. If only she were a doctor. If only Doc Cook hadn't died. Nevertheless, Naomi was depending on her. Neither of them had a choice. "Look at the depth of those claw marks..."

Charles touched Hannah's shoulder. "We're counting on you, Hannah. You're all she's got right now." His dark eyes pleaded with her to make her whole again. "She's all I've got."

Hannah squared her shoulders, feigning a confidence she didn't feel, and nodded.

To keep reading, get your copy of **A Destiny in Defiance** Book 4 today!

ABOUT THE AUTHOR

"Heather Blanton is blessed with a natural storytelling ability, an 'old soul' wisdom, and wide expansive heart. Her characters are vividly drawn, and in the western settings where life can be hard, over quickly, and seemingly without meaning, she reveals Larger Hands holding everyone and everything together."

MARK RICHARD, *EXECUTIVE PRODUCER, AMC'S HELL ON WHEELS, and PEN/ERNEST HEMINGWAY AWARD WINNER*

A former journalist, I am an avid researcher and endeavor to skillfully weave truth in among fictional storylines. I love exploring the American West, especially ghost towns and museums. I have walked parts of the Oregon Trail, ridden horses through the Rockies, climbed to the top of Independence Rock, and even held an outlaw's note in my hand.

I grew up in the mountains of Western North Carolina on a steady diet of Bonanza, Gunsmoke, and John Wayne Westerns. My most fond childhood memory is of sitting next to my daddy, munching on popcorn, and watching Lucas McCain unload that Winchester! My daddy also taught me to shoot and, trust me, I can sew buttons on with my rifle.

Currently I reside near Raleigh, NC, on my farm with my three boys and lots of dirt, some dogs, and a couple of horses. Oh, and a trio of cats who are above it all. And did I say dirt? #FarmLife

Heather Blanton

Please subscribe to my newsletter by visiting my website at
authorheatherblanton.com
to receive updates on my new releases and other fun news. You'll
also receive a FREE e-book—
A Lady in Defiance, The Lost Chapters
just for subscribing!

ALSO BY HEATHER BLANTON

A Lady in Defiance (Romance in the Rockies Book 1)

Charles McIntyre owns everything and everyone in the lawless, godless mining town of Defiance. When three good, Christian sisters show up, stranded and alone, he decides to let them stay—as long as they serve his purposes...but they may prove more trouble than they're worth.

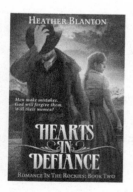

Hearts in Defiance (Romance in the Rockies Book 2)

Notorious gambler and brothel-owner Charles McIntyre finally fell in love. Now he wants to be a better man, he wants to know Christ. But all the devils in Defiance are trying to drag him back to the man he was.

A Promise in Defiance (Romance in the Rockies Book 3)

When scandalous madam Delilah Goodnight flings open the doors to the newest, most decadent saloon in Defiance, two good men will be forced to face their personal demons.

Daughter of Defiance (Thanksgiving Books & Blessings Book 6)

When you hit rock bottom, you have a choice: seek the light or live in the darkness. Victoria chose the darkness. Can someone like her find redemption?

Hang Your Heart on Christmas (Brides of Evergreen Book 1)

A marshal tormented by a thirst for vengeance. A school teacher desperate to trade fear for courage. They have nothing in common except a quiet, little town built on betrayal.

Ask Me to Marry You (Brides of Evergreen Book 2)

Here comes the bride...and he isn't happy. With her father's passing, Audra Drysdale accepts she needs a man to save her ranch. A mail-order groom will keep her prideful men working and a neighboring rancher at bay. What could go wrong?

Mail-Order Deception (Brides of Evergreen Book 3)

Intrepid reporter Ellie Blair gets an undercover assignment as a mail-order bride and heads off to Wyoming where she discovers her potential groom isn't what he appears to be, either.

To Love and to Honor (Brides of Evergreen Book 4)

Wounded cavalry soldier Joel Chapman is struggling to find his place in the world of able-bodied men. A beautiful but unwed woman may be his chance to restore his soul.

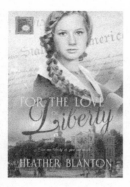

For the Love of Liberty

Novelist Liberty Ridley experiences an ancestor's memory from the Autumn of 1777. Stunned by the detail of it, she is even more amazed to find she's intensely drawn to Martin Hemsworth--a man dead for two centuries.

In Time for Christmas

Is she beyond the reach of a violent husband who hasn't even been born yet? Abandoned by her abusive husband on a dilapidated farm, Charlene wakes up a hundred years in the past. Can love keep her there?

Love, Lies, & Typewriters

A soldier with a purple heart. A reporter with a broken heart. Which one is her Mr. Right? A Christmas wedding could force the choice...

Hell-Bent on Blessings

Left bankrupt and homeless by a worthless husband, Harriet Pullen isn't about to lay down and die.

Grace be a Lady

Banished and separated from her son, city-girl Grace has to survive in a cowboy's world. Maybe it's time to stop thinking like a lady...and act like a man.

Locket Full of Love (Lockets & Lace Book 5)

A mysterious key hidden in a locket leads Juliet Watts and a handsome military intelligence officer on a journey of riddles, revelations, and romance.

A Good Man Comes Around (Sweethearts of Jubilee Springs Book 8)

Since love has let her down, widow Abigail Holt decides to become a mail-order bride, but with a clear set of qualifications to use in choosing her new husband. Oliver Martin certainly doesn't measure up…not by a long shot.

Made in the USA
Coppell, TX
03 August 2024

35557881R00204